Holding Pattern

by

Nesta Tuomey

✳✳✳

Best wishes
Nesta

D1341273

High-flying Irish airline drama and a love affair that refuses to die.

Married on the rebound, air hostess Kay Martin, is shocked to discover her former lover, Captain Graham Pender, believed dead in a Colombo plane crash some years earlier, is alive and a hostage in the Ceylonese jungle. After being rescued, Graham returns to Ireland and flying, and meets up again with Kay. Passions run high in the Miami hotel following a highjack out of JFK to Cuba but their love affair and Graham's career end abruptly when he is forced to return to Colombo to face terrorist charges. Although cleared in Ceylon, Graham's superiors in Ireland are unconvinced of his innocence and Kay, pregnant with Graham's child, loses hope in them sharing a life together.

Years later resuming her flying career Kay finds Celtic Airways is not the airline she once knew. Gone is the camaraderie amongst aircrews and a feud exists between married and unmarried hostesses which can only be resolved in court. When the couple are thrown together once more by the growing friendship between Kay's vivacious nine year old and Captain Pender's family there is another chance of love. But not without further setbacks, even tragedy.

*

Review:

'An adventurous airline drama set in the '70's, *Holding Pattern* is an engaging exploration of high-flying careers and a love affair that survives loss, tragedy and separation.' Laura Elliot, bestselling author of *Guilty* and *The Wife Before Me*.

Biography:

Nesta Tuomey is married and lives in Dublin with her family; educated at the Sacred Heart Convent, Leeson Street and the National College of Art, she worked as an air hostess with Aer Lingus. She started writing for radio, and her plays and short stories have been broadcast by the BBC and RTE . A winner of the John Power Short Story Award at Listowel and the Image/Oil of Ulay Short Story Competition, her short stories have also been published widely in magazines. Nesta Tuomey's one-act play *Whose Baby* won the O. Z. Whitehead Play Competition in 1996, and her first two novels are *Up*, *Up* and *Away*(Emperor Publishing) and *Like One Of The Family (Mount Eagle Publications)*. Her two collections of previously published short stories *The Mask* and *The Straw Hat*.

Website www.nestatuomey.com and www.amazon.com/author/nestatuomey

*

Dedication:

For Larry as always.
In fond memory of beautiful Milly who loved to read,
Nuala, an artist in her own right,
and Anne and Valerie, two great air girls.

*

Quotations:

I will rescue you from that distant land, from the land where you are prisoners.

You will come back home and live in peace. *Jeremiah 46, verse 27.*

*

'If hopes were dupes, fears may be liars; It may be, in yon smoke conceal'd, Your comrades chase e'en now the fliers, And, but for you, possess the field.'
Arthur Hugh Clough.

*

CONTENTS

PROLOGUE

The Tamil boy was a mile from his village when he heard the screaming of the jet engines overhead. Fearfully, he looked upwards, panting in his efforts to outdistance the monstrous thing trailing three long tentacles that came suddenly crashing down on him out of the wet black sky. Deafened by the roar of the engines, his senses blasted by the monster's fiery breath, he fell whimpering to his knees and protectively wrapped his arms about his head. Beneath him, the ground seemed to tremble in a rending explosion. There was a reverberating rumble and then silence.

***

PART ONE
(April 1966)

In the newspapers throughout the world, the Colombo air disaster was on all the front pages and flaring headlines offered little hope of survivors.

In Ireland, Kay Martin, who flew as an air hostess with Celtic Airways, felt a sick twisting in her gut when she read the headlines. 'Colombo Air Crash. Irish Pilot Killed.' She fumbled the paper off the pile on the counter and peered at the print beneath the blurred photograph.

'An Eastline Airways plane, en route from Bombay to Colombo, crashed in a rainstorm and came down in the Ceylonese jungle with187 people on board. The wreckage of the Boeing 707 is still burning and chances of survivors remote.'

The words danced queerly before Kay's eyes and she had a sensation of unreality as though the voices all round her were actually echoing inside her head. It was the first edition so no names were given but she knew, as certainly as if it were printed in capital letters, that the dead pilot was Graham Pender.

Kay had loved Graham almost from the first moment of setting eyes on him, and the big age difference between them might not have existed nor the daunting fact that he was already married and the father of two boys. From the beginning, the attraction between them had been fierce and strong but their love affair had ended just before Graham had flown out to Karachi to do a spell of winter duty for Eastline Airways. Not because he no longer loved her, Captain Pender had been at pains to explain to her that last time they had come together in New York, but because he feared to lose custody of his sons if he left his wife. Listening to him, Kay had come to understand, if not to accept, just how devoted he was to his children and how vital they were to his happiness. At the same time, she had all along been hoping that far away in Karachi he would come to realize just how much he loved her and come back to her. It was the one thing that sustained her through the loneliness of the intervening months.

Standing there, holding the newspaper in hands that trembled, Kay realized how much she had been counting on this as she relived the pain and loneliness of that time, remembering how wounded and confused she had felt, how utterly bereft. But bad as she had felt then it was nothing compared to the agony Kay was experiencing now with the knowledge that there would never be another opportunity for knowing and loving Graham for the grim headlines had brutally stripped her of this hope.

***

Dave Mason was watching television with his family when he learned of the plane crash on the nine o'clock news. Dave had been friends with Kay ever since she was ten years old when, following the tragic death of her parents in a boating accident, she had been adopted by her aunt and come to live in his neighborhood. During their teens they had dated on and off and, indeed, their relationship might have grown more serious if it hadn't been for Kay becoming an air hostess with Celtic Airways and falling in love with a pilot.

Dave got to his feet and hurried over to Kay's house knowing how devastated she would be. Not until recently had he known anything about the circumstances surrounding the ending of her affair with the pilot and then one evening he had taken her for a drive in his new Volkswagen and heard the whole sad story of her breakup with Captain Pender, in her acute distress managing to burrow her way even deeper into his heart. At twenty-seven years of age Dave Mason was an up and coming young accountant working for Maxwell Tailoring, a thriving clothing manufacturer with a number of outlets in Ireland and abroad. An ambitious young man, he had always put his career first, never questioning it was the right thing to do, and when some weeks earlier he had been given the chance of going to Frankfurt to work in a German subsidiary firm he had wholeheartedly welcomed it. Only that day the arrangements had been finalized, his air ticket booked, and in another fortnight he would be finished at Maxwell's and on his way to Frankfurt. But now the news of the plane crash drove all thoughts of Germany away as Dave pushed open the gate to Molly Begley's big old ivy-covered house and walked up the overgrown path. The house was in darkness and getting no answer to his ring, Dave turned away disappointed. Kay must still be in America, he thought, he would call again. Not until that night had Dave believed he might have a chance with Kay but with this latest development he began to think it would be a mistake to go to Frankfurt. Okay, he told himself, maybe he should stick around and help her get over it.

***

In Celtic Airways when the tragic news of Captain Pender's death became known at the airport there was a general feeling of shock and regret on the part of those who had flown with the pilot, and not a little sadness in the hearts of certain air hostesses in whom the feeling ran a lot deeper. Graham had been such an attractive man in looks and manner, always so charming to everyone and his loss would be greatly felt.

Captain Ben Higgins had been in the Irish Air Corps with Captain Pender in the years before joining Celtic Airways, and it was only when he reported for briefing to the flight dispatcher's office that morning on his way out to New York that he learned just who had been in command of the ill-fated Boeing.

'I'm sure you heard about the Colombo crash, Higgins,' his co-pilot hailed him, the third pilot having already gone out to the ramp to join the engineers and complete his pre-departure and safety inspection. 'Who do you think was piloting the Eastline Boeing?' Mossy's bleak grin alerting Ben to the fact the dead pilot was someone they both knew.

'En route from Karachi, wasn't it?' Ben, with typical Irishness, answered one question with another, his mind already leaping ahead. 'Now who went out there recently? Good Christ! Surely not ...'

'Graham Pender,' the other pilot nodded. 'I'm afraid so. Poor devil came down in the Colombo jungle in a heavy rainstorm. All the gory details are in the papers.'

Ben stared at the wall maps and charts without really seeing them. He was reminded of his last conversation with Graham some months previously when his colleague had stopped him in the pilots' lounge and asked him to keep an eye on his family, while he was away in Karachi. 'I'd deem it a great favour, Higgins,' he said, and Ben had readily agreed, never dreaming he would be called upon so soon to keep his promise or in such tragic circumstances.

'If I remember rightly you and Pender were fairly close,' the co-pilot was saying. 'In the Air Corps together, weren't you?'

Ben nodded. It was true that he had been fairly close to Graham, certainly the closest of CA's pilots. As he stood with the co-pilot checking the weather at Dublin and Shannon and examining the routes available to them over the North Atlantic, Ben tried to concentrate on what the dispatcher was telling him but, despite himself, his thoughts kept straying back to the crash and whether he would be called upon to attend the official inquiry. As well as being one of Celtic Airways senior pilots, Captain Higgins was a staunch campaigner for the Irish Air Line Pilots Association and a member of the Airline Safety Committee at Dublin Airport. He also happened to be the chief representative for the Pilots Union and, under section 13 of the ICAO Agreement, was entitled to be present at the Colombo inquiry.

Now Ben was silent as he walked with the co-pilot out to the waiting aircraft. He was aware that the Air Safety Bureau for the official Inquiry normally gave at least four weeks to allow evidence to be gathered and assessed. He only hoped the date set wouldn't clash with his daughter's wedding due to take place around that time. Ben groaned. Not with all the arrangements made and two hundred guests invited to the reception.

***

The day following the Colombo air disaster the accident investigator for Eastline Airways moved slowly, camera angled, taking pictures of what remained of the crashed 707. As Matt Rogan paused for a moment in the brilliant sunshine, the landscape washed clean and smooth in the sparkling aftermath of the Monsoon storm that had brought down the aircraft, he was struck by how quickly the weather could change in the East. He thought of the view from the cabin of the DC-8 two hours earlier as he flew in high above the verdant paddy-fields and banana plantations, the sunny vista beyond the glass one of such idyllic calm it was difficult to imagine the appalling conditions that had prevailed the previous night. And then, looking out to port he had seen the sinister swathe cut by the Boeing through the forest and, with an inevitable dipping of spirit, located the silver heap of wreckage.

In his ten years with the accident bureau Rogan had never ceased to marvel that such a big airship could be reduced to so small a pile of fragments. In this instance the Boeing had broken up on hitting the trees and the wonder of it was anyone had got out alive. Yet despite earlier reports of no survivors, it had transpired that three people sitting behind the wings had been thrown clear - one of the Tamil stewardesses, and an American woman and her child, also sitting nearby. Perhaps there might have been others saved, Rogan thought, if the rescue services had been quicker on the scene. As it was, many of the bodies of the victims had been burned beyond recognition.

Rogan knew that soon there would be other air-crash investigators coming to Colombo - from the aircraft company maybe even the pilots union – but by lucky chance he had been holidaying in Madras when he heard about the crash and so was the first one on the scene. While nearby the Sinhalese police constables got on with their salvage work, methodically searching the undergrowth, Rogan hauled himself up into the aircraft where it was cool and dim. Picking his way carefully to what remained of the cockpit of Victor Echo he studied the instrument panel intently. He saw that the glide path needle on the round face of the ILS was not, as he had expected to find it, in the upward travelling position but rather sitting frozen at the top. So the instrument wasn't functioning, he reckoned. If it had been, it would have indicated that the aircraft was below the beam when it struck. Peering at the altimeter needle, he saw it registered the exact height of the hill at 200 feet and the airspeed indicator was at 140 knots. Well, that was okay, he thought, the correct height and speed. From the position of the throttles fully open and the control column pulled back the crew *knew* they were too low and had made a last frantic effort to climb back into the sky. The fact that the elevators were at full travel upwards corroborated this theory.

Forty minutes later Rogan dropped back down into the grass glad to be out in the air again. It was beginning to look fairly straightforward, he thought, as he hoisted his bag on his shoulder and began to walk down the hill. Despite the rumours of sabotage, sparked by a story that there had been gold aboard the flight, he had found no evidence to support this theory. Clearly the aircraft had not broken up before impacting with the trees and there were no signs of a bomb on board.

Concealed by the trees, the Tamil boy watched the stooped figures of the Sinhalese policemen as they thrashed the undergrowth with their sticks and methodically searched the area about the crashed plane. When he grew tired, Ranjan sat on his hunkers and rocked on his heels to distract himself from the hunger pains in his belly. He had eaten nothing all day but the terrible spectacle of his village on fire the previous night had returned to haunt him, the burning thatch, the savagery of the marauding attackers and the screams of the blood-spattered victims. Hidden in the bushes, he had watched paralyzed with fear as his father and mother were brutally struck down and his sister fled in terror from her attackers into the jungle. He had not waited to see in which direction she had gone but doubled back on his tracks and spent what was left of the night concealed in undergrowth near the Hindu shrine.

Now Ranjan waited for darkness to fall before returning home in search of food. The jungle was alive with night sounds as he chose a different path, one well away from the main track, sensing rather than hearing the far-off tramp of boots as he felt the earth vibrate through the soles of his bare feet. Plunging deeper into the jungle, he became suddenly aware that his way was blocked by a crouching figure. His heart knocked against his ribs and he stopped abruptly. The woman was slumped on her knees with her back to him, her head bent forward as though praying into a pile of rocks. Averting his eyes, he edged past, and was almost clear when he saw the second body wedged in the fork of a tree, about six feet from the ground.

The man lay sprawled on his back, with his left leg stuck out at a strange angle from the knee. Ranjan could see splinters of bone protruding like ivory shoots from the bloodied flesh and although the branches had broken the man's fall he was dead too. Something glinted about his throat. Moving closer, Ranjan saw that it was not gold as he had first thought but a heavy linked silver chain with a medallion attached. Silver was a precious metal, the boy thought, and a worthy offering. He would overcome his fear and take the ornament to offer it in appeasement at the shrine of Shiva the Destroyer. It was his only way of further averting the wrath of the gods.

Ranjan drew in a shaky breath and reached upwards but the chain swung just beyond his straining fingers. He grabbed for it again and this time the chain broke and came away in his hand. At the same moment, the man emitted a loud groan and opened his eyes. Ranjan got such a shock that his grip on the tree loosened and he came tumbling back down again. Scrambling to his feet, he bolted for cover, but he had got no more than a few yards when he ran full tilt into a man coming out of the trees.

He was a black man, over six feet tall dressed in jungle fatigues, with full webbing on, and carrying a rifle. Ranjan felt the cold butt of the weapon against his neck and fell to his knees. Another six or seven dark-skinned men, wearing battle fatigues and with the distinctive striped beret of the rebel Indigiri Lanka Army aslant their shaved heads, came out of the trees. With a shiver of dread the boy recognized the mercenaries who had torched his village and heard one of them call to the leader, 'Hey, what you got there, man?'

In reply, the man jerked the boy up off the ground and held him suspended in the air as though he weighed only a few pounds. He brought the boy's face level with his own and fixed him with the full basilisk-glare of his eyes, then abruptly dropped him back into the grass. Behind them the wounded man in the tree groaned again and the soldiers were momentarily diverted by the sound, turning away to stare up at him. Ranjan took the chance to run. As he ran, he hurled the silver trinket far away from him into the undergrowth, for he knew now it was the crime of robbing the dead that had brought this further misfortune upon him.

***

On stopover in New York, Kay Martin lay on the bed in her darkened hotel bedroom and was unable to focus on anything. She felt dizzy like she was about to get 'flu, and had been that way ever since reading of the Colombo air crash, her mind dominated by thoughts of death and disaster. Her room was on the fifteenth floor of the Sheraton Atlantic Hotel and the endless cacophony of car horns, punctuated by the occasional banshee scream of police sirens, was mercifully muffled by distance and double glazing. Beyond the dusty window New York night life energetically surged and throbbed, while across the street the trains still came into Penn Station and late-night shoppers climbed aboard the subway, all unaware that the world had stopped turning on its axis three days earlier.

Kay was dimly aware that time was passing. Soon she must get herself dressed and go uptown with some of the other hostesses to eat. But still she lay unmoving. Why had she agreed to go, Kay wondered dully, when all she wanted to do was to stay put, even the thought of putting on clothes and applying fresh makeup struck her as too much effort. She sighed and rolled on to her side, knowing anything was better than being stuck with her own dismal company, masochistically regurgitating the events of the past week and hugging her sorrow. It was the reason she had rung rostering the day after the Colombo crash to tell them she would be happy to go out again immediately to America, although entitled to three day stand-down after her Chicago trip. She could still hear the girl's incredulous reaction at this unprecedented waiving of privilege. 'Are you quite sure, Kay? You could be stuck on another Chicago, you know.'

So what? They could send her to Australia twice over and she wouldn't care, not that CA flew long-haul to the other side of the world, more's the pity. Her volunteering to fly so soon again was an act of cowardice. It spared her having to cope with being on her own in the house, having to answer the phone. The phone was the worst. Friends who had heard the news and just made the connection between the crashed Irish pilot and herself, ringing to sympathize and ask questions they would not otherwise have dared. It was all so painful. On the morning after the crash hit the headlines Kay had taken a bus into town after a night when sleep had continued to elude her. In a dazed fashion, she had roamed streets thronging with weekend shoppers. With hardly any memory of doing so, she went in and out of shops, fingering objects and replacing them at random, until strange glances were directed her way and she was in danger of being arrested for shoplifting. What she was doing out of the house in such a state was questionable but she had felt too restless, too driven by sorrow to remain on her own. It had been imperative to get out amongst people and experience bustling life, if only vicariously, and the more bustling the better. Returning home exhausted she had found Florrie Belton on the doorstep, her best and closest friend, come to commiserate. Kay almost wept for the sympathy brimming in Florrie's blue eyes and turned away to hunt blindly for her latch key, desperately trying to keep from breaking down.

'Kay, are you all right? I'm so sorry,' Florrie blurted as she followed her inside. 'I couldn't understand it when I rang so many times last night, and got no answer. I was so worried about you...'

At the kindness in her voice, all restraint was swept away and Kay began to cry, painful releasing sobs. Florrie moved impulsively to put her arms about her, together they stood locked in tearful embrace.

'Oh Florrie!' was all Kay could say through her sobs. 'To think of it...too terrible...the worst that could happen,' and Florrie nodded, stricken by the reality of what they, as flight crew, faced every time they took to the air.

'So lonely...far away with no one who knew him. I mean *really* knew him.'

But Florrie knew that she meant no one who *loved* him. It *was* lonely, she agreed, to be away in a foreign land with a foreign crew. Nothing to alert you to the fact this was your last flight so that you might make your goodbyes, however casual.

The night following the crash - not Disaster Night when Kay had been unable to sleep, the phone ringing incessantly and the cold clutch on her heart as she flicked through TV channels searching desperately for anything new and hopeful on the crash. No, not that night but the one that Florrie had stayed over with her, Kay's mood had been almost euphoric. Like someone punch drunk after so many rounds in the ring, and she was more grateful than she had ever thought possible for her friend's company and the sustaining wine she had brought with her. Kay was reminded of long ago when her aunt had spent all night petting and cosseting her after her parents' death, without comment pouring away the remainder of the hot milk, spiced with what Kay later realized must have been whisky, until finally Molly had brought her into her own room to sleep, the pair of them snugly tucked beneath the eiderdown in the big sagging bed. Holding her in motherly arms as Kay had sobbed through many a night, making up stories to divert her from the tragic reality of her orphaned state and watching over her as tenderly as if she had been the mother the child had lost. Growing up, Kay was conscious of how much she owed Molly and more recently, how much she was missing her aunt since she had gone to live in Kilshaughlin with her daughter, Winifred.

In the same way Kay knew that she would never forget Florrie's goodness to her on that tragic night, letting her weep and bemoan the cruel fate that had robbed her of the only man she would ever love, resolutely keeping her from checking for news bulletins or visual updates on the plane crash. What good to keep the wounds open, Florrie asked reasonably, and visibly bleeding Kay had humoured her.

Now away in New York she could have done with Florrie's discipline, overwhelmed by the extent and breadth of the American television coverage of the Colombo crash. At home or in New York it seemed impossible to escape what she had come all these thousands of miles to avoid, and she soon gave up the attempt.

Watching CBS News, Kay was confronted by horrendous pictures of row upon row of body bags laid out near the shattered aircraft, along with close-ups of the crash site with strewn luggage and intimate possessions belonging to the victims, and more tears came. Then followed what she dreaded most - pictures of the flight crew; inset after inset of pretty stewardesses in gleaming blue saris simpering into the lens of the camera, mainly Eurasians, and smudgy head and shoulders photos of the pilots and the navigator aboard the flight deck.

Until that moment some part of Kay had kept alive a tiny flicker of hope – nourished perhaps by a later report that, contrary to what had been published in the Irish newspapers, there actually had been some survivors of the crash. Even when the American newscaster had declared that all on the actual flight deck had perished, like St Thomas she had hugged her doubt, wanting to believe that somehow an error had been made and in time would eventually be sorted out. But not anymore, not since seeing the visual evidence for herself.

The first time Kay saw Graham Pender's smiling dark-eyed image flash upon the screen it had devastated her. She stiffened in shock, unable to take her eyes away, terrified in case the voice recorder of the last minutes aboard the fatal flight would be played and she would be further spooked by the sound of his voice. But mercifully she was spared. Since then she had watched repeats every chance she got, literally salting her wounds and masochistically wallowing in all that Florrie had wisely advised against. It was a relief in the end to leave the room and join her crew.

Out of habit rather than vanity, Kay had made herself up as carefully as she always did, and from her overnight case she had chosen a two-piece in buttercup yellow she had bought some time earlier, with Easter in mind. The original Easter Bunny, she grimaced, twisting a matching piece of silk about the ends of her dark hair and securing it on her neck. Certainly her appearance was no mirror of her spirit, Kay told herself, as she went down to the lobby, deriving a certain morose satisfaction at so completely fooling the world. Approaching the parked cabs, she found herself next to the First Officer, the same young pilot who had been on her Chicago flight. Kay liked Ned Grehan, he was a really nice guy, known for invariably keeping the party going on stopovers and entertaining them all with lively tunes on his tin whistle.

'We meet again,' he said with a friendly grin, holding the cab door for her. 'Stuck like myself, I suppose. No justice at all in the world.'

Kay smiled, not contradicting him. As he sat into the cab beside her and began talking of the Colombo crash, she wondered if he knew that she and Graham had been lovers. In a way it would be a relief to think he did. Suddenly Kay wanted to say it out loud, tell everyone that without Graham her life was as good as over. Listening to the conversations going on around her, she was shocked to hear Ned admitting how he and his crew had heard of the Colombo crash over the cockpit radio, almost as it was happening. Oh God! Kay shivered. And to think she had been down at the back of the cabin, all unaware. Her heart was stricken once more.

To her embarrassment the crew began discussing Captain Pender and she was forced to listen as hostesses were named who had been crazy about the pilot and apparently shared torrid love affairs with him. Kay squirmed in her seat as there was speculation about his most recent affair with a hostess recently come on the Atlantic. It was a relief when Ned cut in savagely. 'Listen you lot! Captain Pender was a decent chap and merely human like the rest of us. So knock it off, girls. No more bitchy tittle-tattle, if you please. That's an order.'

It was so unlike Ned's usual easygoing style that everyone in the cab was momentarily silenced and an uneasy atmosphere prevailed as the driver, presumably neither deaf nor dumb, weaved his way uptown through the evening traffic.

'Knew *that* would shut them up,' Ned whispered, and Kay was heartened by his compassionate glance. So he did know about herself and Graham, she felt strangely consoled, wondering how it was none of the hostesses present realized she was the hostess in question, she could only presume her comparative newness to the Atlantic route had saved her.

On arriving home a day later Kay found a note in the front door from Dave Mason, expressing his sympathy, 'Sorry to hear the tragic news. Hope you're not too cut up over it.'

Nice of him to call, she thought, dropping it on the hall table and going tiredly upstairs to bed, aware how empty the house felt, her footsteps overloud on the stairs. She wondered if Dave would call again, remembering what a frequent visitor he had been when Molly was there and Florrie still lodging with them. These days Kay missed those friendly visits, the three of them strolling down to the pub for a few beers.

As she stretched out miserably on her bed, Kay found herself wondering why she was bothering to even think about Dave Mason, and was conscious that she had never felt so alone or lonelier in her life. She wished that she could fast forward her life to some happier time, preferably fifty years hence, when presumably she would no longer care about anything, all passion spent.

'Oh darling,' she wept for her dead love. 'What a lonely place the world is without you.' Getting up off the bed, she rummaged in a cupboard until she found Pendy, the fluffy white bear Graham had given her the previous summer. She buried her face in his soft fur and collapsing back into bed, pulled the sheet over her head. The bear smelt faintly of her favourite, long-since evaporated, Diorissimo perfume, another of Graham's gifts. Was there ever going to be a time when something or someone did not remind her of him? Holding Pendy close, Kay slept at last.

***

In Colombo one week later the airport manager packed up for the evening, clearing papers off his desk and locking them into a drawer. It was well after his usual knocking-off time but there was nothing unusual about that, the period since the crash had been a nightmare for Hughes. He had got very little sleep and all his waking hours had been taken up with arranging the burials and insurance and dealing with the legal problems arising out of the disaster. Each hour that passed brought fresh reports of violence between Sinhalese and Tamil workers. The most shocking being the reprisals carried out against the Tamil village near Kasyapamahagiri in retaliation for the deaths of the four Sinhalese stewardesses, victims of the crash. As though, Hughes thought, the surviving Tamil stewardess should be made to bear the guilt. He had felt quite savagely indignant on her behalf and sounded off in no uncertain manner. But when he learned that the warrior-like Indigiri Lanka Force had joined with the Sinhalese in their attack against the Tamils his exasperation gave way to very real anxiety.

Was the violence of eight years ago about to start all over again?

His Tamil secretary, poor thing, undoubtedly terrified of encountering further violence at the airport, had stayed away for most of the week. But Sita Shanti was back now and looking no worse for her fright. Hughes' air of melancholy deepened as he remembered that next day the funerals of the Ceylonese Nationalists would be held. What to do about the pilots and the navigator he did not know. The three men on the flight deck had been accounted for but their bodies had been so badly burned as to be unrecognizable. Fortunately, one of their fellow pilots had flown down from Karachi and identified them from a wallet and a monogrammed cigarette lighter found in the smouldering debris. For the unspeakable hassle the pilot had saved him, Hughes would be forever grateful. Minister Fedneratne had been identified by the gold watch on his wrist but even that portion of his anatomy, when found, had not been fully connected to the rest of his body. There were the usual bloodthirsty spectators and grisly souvenir hunters converging on the scene and only for split second timing, Hughes knew, the watch, if not the wrist itself, would have disappeared along with the less cumbersome pieces of salvage from the B-707.

First thing in the morning, Hughes told himself, he would ring both the British and the Irish Consulates in Karachi to tell them the Death Certificates were signed and ready. They would inform their respective governments when the bodies of the pilots would be released for burial, their coffins given clearance and flown home to Europe.

With a preoccupied expression, Hughes crossed to where his secretary sat slowly typing and placed a pile of letters before her.

'Yes, sah, I'll do that, sah,' her head tilted attentively, Sita listened as he fussily explained what he wished done. But most of what the man said passed over her head and she returned to her leisurely typing as soon as he left the office. Her mind was already fully occupied with her own thoughts and had her boss been privy to them they would have startled him to the core of his placid soul. With her usual reticence Sita had kept silent about the events of the previous week, she was remembering now the rigorous hours she had spent learning how to assemble and fire a Kalashnikov assault rifle, part of the illicit consignment placed aboard the flight in Bombay by Sita's fellow freedom fighters. It was thanks to her tipoff, Sita mused proudly, that this same cargo along with the gold bullion had been speedily harvested from the crashed plane by their leader, Harinath

15

Prasad, who worked the ramp with his fellow loaders, all hand-picked men. Guns for the liberation of their people, Sita knew, and gold to finance the purchase of more arms and ammunition. Four more consignments were scheduled to be flown into Colombo over the following months, with the assistance of certain Eastline Airways pilots, Tamils like themselves and sworn to uphold the cause, even to give their lives, if necessary. Were it not for Sita's worry over the distressing disappearance of her young brother on the night their village had been burned and her parents killed, she would have been fairly content. But now wracked by sorrow and guilt, her greatest regret was having let go of Ranjan's hand, and so failed to keep the promise she had made to her dying parents to always take care of her little brother.

**

On his return from New York, Captain Higgins found two communications awaiting him on the noticeboard in the pilots lounge. One was from the Chief Executive of Celtic Airways informing him that the coffin containing the body of Captain Pender was expected to arrive from Colombo via London on that Friday, the other was from one of the British pilots who had flown with Graham Pender in Eastline Airways and been the one to identify him from his gold cigarette lighter found in the vicinity of his body. He wrote to say that contrary to everyone's expectation the date of the official Inquiry into the Colombo crash had been set for the following week. The Head of the Ceylonese Air Safety Bureau, Roy Sarenesca, had declared it was an open-and-shut case and there was no point in delaying matters any further.

The British pilot went on to say: 'You will be glad to hear - and I have it on good authority - no blame will be attached to the pilots. The Monsoon storm which affected visibility and the faulty ILS were found to be the causes of the crash.'

Ben wondered that the Safety Bureau had rushed ahead and set the date so soon. But on reflection, he decided, it was not so unusual, given the circumstances. He was relieved that pilot error had been ruled out. That was something at least. It would make it a whole

16

lot easier on Pender's wife, Sile, and their young sons. Ben was relieved too, that he did not have to make the trip out East.

On arriving home he tucked the letter behind his pipe rack, pending filing, then stayed chatting with his wife until he yawned so much that Linda shooed him off to take a nap. 'Use the main shower,' she called after him. 'Ours is still blocked. I meant to call a plumber but never got around to it.'

Drying off after his shower, Ben went to sit on his side of their king size bed. Glancing about him, he noticed an addition to the room of a curved seat that fitted so snugly into the bay window it might have always been there. Stroking his hand over the plush upholstery it occurred to him it was the same fetching shade of rose as the velvet drapes that had made *their* appearance while he was away in Algiers, flying charters and bringing pilgrims to Mecca. Just as well he never stayed away too long, he thought, or Linda would have added another wing to their house.

Never a dull moment, Ben yawned in the middle of a reminiscent grin and pulled the continental quilt snugly about him. For a while he lay looking at the ceiling his limbs relaxed after the shower, his mind beginning to unclench, and thought about the forthcoming funeral of the crashed pilot. That would be a grim day for all in Celtic Airways, Ben knew, with its sober reminder of how a routine fight could end so tragically.

***

Some days later, the funeral of Captain Pender took place at the airport. The chapel was full to the doors and beyond. Mourners packed the aisles and those who could not manage to squeeze into the porch, stood about in groups outside. The death of one of their own pilots had cast a gloom on the airport and staff from every department had turned out, without any prompting from management, to pay their last respects.

Judy Matthews, the newly appointed Hostess Superintendent, was more downcast by the pilot's death than she would have thought possible, especially since it was twenty years since she had been young and in love with Graham Pender. As Judy took her place in the front section reserved for the Chairman and the Board of Directors and other high-ranking members of Celtic Airways Executive staff, there was a stir at the back of the church. Turning, she saw the Chairman and Chief Executive escorting the widow and her sons up the church.

Judy felt a lump rising in her throat as she watched each of Graham's sons lay a red rose on the dark wood of the coffin, the youngest boy obviously struggling to control his sobs as he carefully placed his tribute. The older boy wore a grim look too, as though he was exercising a tight grip on his emotions. Not unkindly, Judy gazed upon her former colleague and decided that Sile certainly *looked* the part of the sorrowing widow, all clothed in the height of black fashion. Dubiously, she watched as the widow placed her own long-stemmed rose and then touched black suede fingertips to her lips in a theatrical gesture, before pressing them to the side of the coffin. The effect was somewhat spoiled by the languishing glance she directed at the stout, well-dressed man who moved to allow her back into the pew.

Judy had heard the gossip and did not think Sile would wear her widow's weeds for long. She let the Chief Executive's speech pass over her head. None of it, she felt, bore any relation to the deceased pilot, even the chaplain's few words about Graham Pender did not seem relevant. Not when Judy thought of the vital authoritative person about whom they were speaking. Somehow they had missed the essence of the man, she thought No saint perhaps, Judy permitted a smile to touch her lips, but a very decent guy all the same. She averted her eyes from the coffin, pained to think that so much attractive maleness, such charm and ability should have been extinguished so soon. Glancing about her on the way out of the chapel, she was surprised not to see Kay Martin standing with the other air hostesses. Of all people, she was the one with most reason to be there, Judy knew, the one she had most expected to see. Probably, stuck on reserve, she decided, there could be no other explanation.

As it happened, Kay was not on duty that day. Waking early, she had felt physically unable to attend her dead lover's funeral and wanted only to get as far away from the airport as she could.

Journeying by train to the coast, the scene of so many light-hearted meetings between Graham and herself in the first days of their courtship, she had left the railway station and set off along the familiar narrow track through the barley field to the sea. It was only when in sight and sound of the sea that she had begun to feel some slight apprehension, and wondered if she had been right after all to come. Stepping down on to the hard sand, she was unprepared for the assault upon her emotions as the wind blew her dark hair about her head and the past flashed relentlessly upon her inward eye like a series of cinematographic images, each so vividly evocative, so painfully reminiscent of all that she had lost that she winced at their impact. Lowering her head protectively against the wind, she dug her hands deep into the pockets of her suede jacket and strode down to the water's edge. The tide was out and she had the beach virtually to herself. Overhead the seagulls were swooping and screaming, and the sound they made was terrible and forlorn, tearing at her nerves and deepening the desolation in her heart.

With her back to the wind, Kay stared desolately at the slate grey waves. She was unbearably reminded of the first time Graham had brought her to this spot and how his confession some weeks later that he was married had not ended the affair, but rather marked the beginning of the new, more open relationship between them. It was here that it had all begun, she told herself, remembering how his frankness that night had disarmed her; sweeping away the last of her reservations and compelling her to honestly acknowledge to herself just how much she cared, how deeply she was committed to him. As Judy Mathews had rightly judged Kay had the most reason in Celtic Airways to mourn Graham Pender's death and she was, without a doubt, the one he would have most wanted to be present at his funeral that day. But the sad truth of it was, Graham was now beyond all feeling or expectation and what she most needed was to remember him as she had known him, strong and vibrantly alive. This was only possible, Kay knew, if she did not see his coffin and all the trappings of an emotional airport funeral attended by his family and colleagues, people who had more claim to him and who had known him for so much longer, if not more intimately, than she. Only in this way might she be able to somehow live past the horror and grief she was experiencing. But really there was no escaping any of it, Kay mused, as she walked the length of the beach while all about her the gulls continued their frenzied screaming. Whether here by the sea or back there in the Airport Chapel, it was all the same; pain, regret and overwhelming grief were her portion.

***

In Colombo, one week later, the accident investigator stood in a shuffling line of people waiting to board the London bound jet. It was some hours after the ending of the official inquiry into the Eastline Airways plane crash and Matt Rogan was not sorry to be leaving Ceylon. Once on board he was shown to his seat by a smiling Chinese girl, dressed in a gleaming blue, close-fitting satin dress with high mandarin collar. When the time came for the oxygen, life-jacket demonstration Rogan sat forward and gave it his full attention. No one was more familiar with this safety routine than he was but he always maintained it was a matter of psychological importance to brief yourself at the start of *every* flight. Only then did he feel able to relax back as the smiling stewardesses smoothed their coiffures and stowed the equipment back in the rack.

Rogan felt all played out, as he generally did at the end of an investigation and he looked forward to getting home and sleeping round the clock. The Inquiry had proceeded along much the lines predicted by Sarenesca. Held in the old stately courthouse building, with a Sinhalese judge presiding, the evidence had been presented and a verdict reached, all in a span of two days. Amongst the witnesses were the surviving Tamil stewardess and the American woman passenger. Their testimony had added nothing new to what had already been heard. The American woman was still suffering from shock and grief over the loss of her husband; the Tamil stewardess hampered by her lack of English was bruised and shaken from the recent attack on her person. When it was his turn Rogan had stepped forward and reported his findings; these were confirmed by the read-out readings from the flight recorder on height, airspeed, pitch and acceleration. He also produced evidence of charred particles of tree debris that had gone through the compressors into the turbine. The testimonials of the two pilots were presented and it was established that Captain Pender was on his last flight for Eastline Airways before returning to Ireland. The Irish pilot had a good flying record and had worked several stints in the past with the Pakistani airline. His co-pilot was a lot younger and, up to recently, had flown with the RAF. Although he did not have as much experience on jets as Pender, his flight check records contained good assessments. It was ruled that both were competent pilots. This view was supported by a fellow Eastline Airways pilot who flew in from Karachi to attend the Inquiry and give his evidence. Like Sarenesca had predicted, it was an open-and-shut case.

How tired he was getting of that phrase, Rogan thought. Mainly because he had discovered from experience that if you persisted there was always something more out there, some small thing that threw a different slant on what had already been found. He dug his hand deep in his jacket pocket as all four jet engines roared to full power, and brought out an object which he turned over thoughtfully in his hand. One of the Sinhalese constables had brought him back to the spot in the jungle where he said he had come upon it, low down near the ground, entangled in a begonia bush.

Matt cupped his hand about the bunched silver and gently bounced it in his hand. The severed chain was made from heavy link silver such as a man would wear, he reckoned. The medal although slightly warped was otherwise unmarked, and still retained its sheen. Clearly it had not been in the fire. Rogan gazed at the image and recognized the engraving of a man with a staff in his hand and the Christ child on his arm. St Christopher was the patron saint of travellers, he told himself. Any amount of people aboard the flight could have been wearing it but he would give ten to one it had belonged to one of the European flight crew. Rogan's tired mind from force of habit began at once carrying the supposition further. Supposing the chain had snapped from about the pilot's neck in the minutes before the crash and maybe fallen out through an opening as the aircraft ripped through the trees?

But if this had happened, Rogan reckoned, the medal would surely have separated from the chain mid-air. Unlikely the two would still be linked when discovered nearly a mile away. Another even crazier explanation. That one of the pilots had fallen from the plane and the chain had broken away in the fall? Might be possible, Rogan thought, if he *had* fallen out but according to the evidence at the Inquiry, backed by the crew manifest, the bodies of all three crew on the flight deck were accounted for and their remains identified. Captain, co-pilot and navigator.

With a last look at the medal and chain, Rogan slipped them back into his pocket. Wearily, he closed his eyes thinking it was unlikely they would ever find out what had really happened.

Further north, Ranjan Shanti huddled in the corner of a tiny stone cell, with only a narrow gap high up in the blocks to allow in light. Even at the brightest time of day no more than a glimmer filtered through. Nevertheless, he was made to keep his blindfold down over his eyes. Whenever he judged it safe he lifted the corner of the threadbare cloth and peered under it at his companion sprawled on the wooden pallet. The man had been in a fever since taken into captivity and the rough bandage about his wounded leg was stained and matted with blood. He was raving and calling out in his pain, and Ranjan did not think he would live long.

The boy shifted position on the floor and, with a shiver of fear, remembered his futile dash to escape his captors, hearing again the charges of shot slashing into the foliage about him, feeling rough hands hauling him back. He remembered watching the soldiers pull the wounded man out of the tree and hearing his agonized grunts. They had lashed mopane poles together to make a litter and laid him roughly on it. At a word of command from the leader, one of the soldiers had caught hold of the loosely waggling limb and jerked it straight, and Ranjan heard the man's high scream of pain and saw the way his head lolled to one side as he lost consciousness. The soldier had taken a sweat rag from about his own neck and roughly bound the injured limb to the pole, and the party had moved steadily forward. They had travelled all night, making only two brief halts on the way, and darkness was giving way to light as they reached the camp deep in the jungle. Wearying days and nights had passed since then in the airless cell. The boy had lost count of just how many.

In the moments before the pale sky showing through the gap in the blocks deepened to navy, there was a sound outside the cell, and the Indigiri guard cautiously pushed open the door and slid a tin inside. It was half-filled with rice, and lumps of goat meat which Ranjan's Hindu religion prevented him from eating, and the boy's mood sank even lower. When the door closed he took up the bottle of water he had filled at the pump when allowed outside, and drank a small amount, before administering to the wounded man. The water spilled back out of his slack mouth and, mindful of the night ahead, Ranjan put the remainder of the water carefully to one side, and squatted in his corner. The hours passed slowly and the incessant babbling of the raving man only served to increase the boy's sense of aloneness. For the injured man hanging by a frail thread to life, the days and nights swung past in a blur. At times he raved in delirium, imagining he was back high above the impenetrable cloud, struggling at the controls of the storm-tossed B-707 and desperately trying to land the aircraft in the blinding rain. Living again the horror of their first heavy impact with the trees, the branches slicing like knives into the skin of the fuselage; it had been like going through a shredder as the aircraft hacked its way through the forest. Sometimes the man peered at the Tamil boy imagining he saw instead his son's downcast face, the way it had been on the January day he had said goodbye to him and his elder brother, before flying to the East.

'It won't be so bad,' he whispered. 'The time will pass quickly enough, and I promise we'll do things together in June when you get your holidays.' At other times he was high above the cloud being buffeted by the storm as the crew prepared to make another attempt at landing, having earlier overshot the runway. 'What's the visibility?' The fever gave strength to his voice.' I need to know it *now*.' Almost shouting out the words, his voice tense with suppressed anger, and the Tamil boy could not hold him on the bed. 'This is no picnic up here, you know. It's coming down like the hammers. For God's sake! Why don't you answer?' And another abrupt mood change. 'It will be all right, just sit tight,' he told the crew. 'We'll make it in next time, you'll see.'

For hours he dozed fitfully, oblivious of everything, even the nagging pain in his leg and when he awoke he felt less ill, his temperature lower. He looked about him and saw that the walls of the tiny cell were made of stone blocks, the unpainted surface glistening with damp. He had no recollection of being brought to this place, just fragmented memories of the last few minutes on board the aircraft when he had found himself flung towards the roof of the cockpit as the jet bounced free of the trees, before making its final plunge earthwards. Fleetingly, he recalled the other pilot and men on the flight deck, of the subtle blackmail exerted by the airport manager in Bombay threatening to further delay the flight unless they agreed to breach security and admit some Australian buddy of his as a jump seat passenger on the final leg to Colombo.

And then as the fever took hold of him once again he began to shiver, and hearing someone with a raging thirst calling out for water, he realized it was himself. As though he had spoken his need aloud – perhaps he had - he felt something pressed against his lips and taking the warm liquid into his mouth, he gulped it painfully down. But when he eagerly reached for more the bottle was gently removed from his grasp.

'More later, Sah.'

By his gentle act of rationing the boy showed unusual wisdom in one so young. 'Wise head on young shoulders,' he approved. Once he opened his eyes to see the young woman bending over him, her silky dark hair brushing his face and he stared at her in wonder.

'How did you know where to find me?' he asked her.

She did not reply but placed a heavy hand on his forehead. The weight surprised him, her touch had always been so light, her fingers soft and caressing. He shrank from it then relaxed. 'You're probably tired,' he said. 'And no wonder! You have come a long way.'

She stayed with him on and off that night. He talked to her without ceasing but she rarely replied. 'Darling, I'm sorry,' he told her, remembering how they had parted, overcome by shame and regret for the past. 'Won't you say you forgive me?'

His voice was full of yearning for the way things used to be between them. His confused mind was filled with bittersweet memories like it had so often been in the long wearisome months away from home. He drank the water when it was put to his lips, but without interest, his throat was harsh and dry from so much talking but her presence and his need for reconciliation made him indifferent to everything else.

When just before the dawn the Indian woman left the cell and he was on his own again with the wounded man, the boy inclined his ear to the babbling mouth but could make no sense of what he heard. He thought it might be the name of a woman the man kept repeating but he couldn't be sure. And now he was speaking in the breathless intimate tones of a lover, tender and joyously confiding, sounding so utterly content that the boy felt lonelier than ever.

***

In the weeks after the funeral Kay experienced bouts of depression during which she bitterly regretted ever having met and loved Graham Pender, days when she did not want to get out of bed and nights when she never went to bed at all, restlessly seeking some anodyne for the agonizing pain of a wound that refused to heal. At such times she found herself vividly recalling everything about her dead lover, the way he had looked and moved, every tender word he had ever spoken or written to her, and she felt him all about her so intensely it was impossible to believe that he was not still alive.

But despite everything she lived through it, did not die of heartbreak as she once believed, even when something catastrophic happened just as time was beginning to blunt the edge of her anguish and brought back all her sorrowing emotion in full force. It was the shocking sight of the envelope addressed to her in Graham's distinctive handwriting that initially jolted her heart. But on opening it, she knew he must have written it before embarking upon that last flight and whoever found it amongst his effects had posted it on to her. It was full of love and reassurance and the mention of another letter he had sent her from Karachi some months before but she had never received. Why, he plaintively asked, hadn't she replied to it?

With a kind of dread, Kay read on, her head whirling at his confession that he loved her too much ever to give her up and how he was cutting short his time in Karachi, to return to Ireland.

'When I come,' he wrote, 'let's make up for lost time, my darling. We could go down to Portugal. It's magical at this time of year. Or Paris, if you would prefer.'

Regret! Kay had felt her heart swamped by it. To think that there had been a letter she had never received and here now, too late, she was being offered everything to which she had ever aspired. Oh, God! How wonderful it would have been.

With the arrival of this letter, all the sorrow Kay had felt at the time of Graham's death returned. It was many months before she was at the stage where she was ready to accept that no matter how much she still loved and willed him back to life, it was time to put aside useless longings and accept that the great love they had once shared was over. Time too, to give her relationship with Dave Mason a chance to develop for he had been an unfailing support in these lonely months and she was coming more and more to find consolation and pleasure in his company. Nothing stronger than that, certainly not love, but affection and trust, and they counted for a lot. So she was able to tell him two years later that she would wear his ring. She was relieved when he seemed content with that and did not at once press her to name the day. Grateful too, telling herself, she was getting there in her own time. Had he rushed her he would have lost her but once Kay accepted that she was never again going to be swept away by the grand passion she had known with Graham, she hesitated no longer. She might as well settle for one man as the next, she decided, particularly a good man like Dave Mason and he was certainly that.

For her engagement ring she chose a ruby flanked by two sparkling diamonds believing Dave when he assured her humorously, 'Go ahead, Katie, be as extravagant as you like. I'm prepared not to eat for another year or two! There!' he told her, examining it with approval. 'See how well it goes with your other ring.'

The other ring, he referred to, was the ruby and gold ring Kay wore on her right hand. It had belonged to her dead mother, the only memento of Evelyn Martin she possessed and infinitely precious to her. That evening the couple drove up country to Kilshaughlin to share their good news with her aunt. As Kay expected, Molly was delighted, having always shown her fondness for Dave.

'Oh, my dear, what wonderful news. Like my own son,' Molly gasped, hugging Kay to her frail chest. 'Did I ever think I'd live to see the day? I couldn't be happier for you both,' and Dave, beaming all over his face, had leaned close to get a hug too.

Winifred did not say much beyond congratulating Dave. No doubt imagining it was his duty as Kay's nearest male relative, Cahal, spent some time quizzing Dave as to his job prospects and his ability to support a wife. All of which the newly engaged man suffered with his usual composure.

It was a short visit; before they left Molly had insisted on marking the occasion with a 'tiny' gift dispatching Winifred to fetch her jewel case.

'There!' said Molly, lifting out the diamond necklace and earring set she had inherited from her grandmother. 'The diamonds are good and you can always have them reset.' A tiny gift! Kay gasped with pleasure. When she stammered that it was too generous and she really couldn't accept them, Molly brushed aside her protests.

'Nonsense. You always looked best in them, alannah,' she said fondly, seeming unaware of her daughter's outraged expression.

It was late by the time they got back to the apartment and. despite a heavy duty continental flight that day, Florrie had waited up for her.

'What! You didn't think I'd be able to sleep, did you?' she protested, admiring the ring and exclaiming over Molly's generosity before hugging Dave. 'Oh, Kay, it's fabulous and so are your aunt's diamonds. You must be terribly excited?'

Kay admitted that she supposed she was and Florrie sighed romantically.

'Over the moon. Go on! Admit it. I'd be on cloud nine!'

But Kay just grinned having heard too often Florrie's droll, 'Marriage is greatly overrated. Just give me the runaround any day without the ring!'

'We must celebrate,' Florrie cried, running off to get the wine she had cooling in the fridge. 'This isn't too bad. Should be champers but that went out the window when I got stuck on Frankfurt. What a day?' She pulled a face and splashed the wine into tumblers as she chatted away.

Kay sipped her wine watching her friend with a half smile as Dave keeping her hand firmly tucked in his chuckled at Florrie's jokes; she could always make him laugh, Kay thought, tiredness beginning to hit her. It was all very merry but she was not sorry when Dave got up to go, excusing himself saying he had an early start in the morning.

When Kay came back from seeing him out, she slipped into a fleecy robe and joined Florrie on the bed for a chat, tucking her feet cosily under the covers. But it had been a long day and Florrie's blonde head soon drooped apologetically against the headboard and she fell asleep. Smiling, Kay pulled up the covers over her and tiptoed out of the room. She was soon in bed herself, with the pillow tucked behind her head.

Letting her mind roam back over the day she was disturbed to find herself wondering if Graham Pender had been the one to put his diamond on her finger and had come with her to Kilshaughlin to announce their engagement that day would her aunt have been as thrilled as she was at the prospect of having Dave in the family. Or would she have been disapproving that he was a married man with two teenage sons? Almost defensively, Kay told herself that all Molly had ever desired was her happiness and she would surely have shown the pilot a similar display of warmth and affection as she had shown Dave. Unaccountably, the thought of Graham after all this time brought a sudden rush of tears to Kay's eyes and she choked back an unhappy sob, startled and upset at herself for such weakness on this day of days. Assailed by a terrible sense of betrayal, she fiercely rejected the notion that she was giving up on Graham, for you couldn't give up on a dead man, could you? Not in that way at least. She was tired, that's all, Kay excused herself, muffling her sobs in the pillow, fearing that Florrie might hear her and come in. It had been such a long emotional day, she sighed shakily, nothing more than that!

Even so, another twelve months had passed before Kay could finally bring herself to set the wedding date and then, like a lot of her fellow air hostesses, she planned to marry early in April and beat the tax deadline.

***

Sitting in her spacious new office overlooking the pilots' car park, the Hostess Superintendent was also focusing on weddings. Or rather the exact date when the present crop of betrothals would end in matrimony, and how many of her air hostesses were actually planning to tie the knot *before* the summer. Vital information, if she was to effectively plan her autumn training program.

It troubled Judy that those summer brides were required by the airline to tender their resignations on marriage and having done so, would cease to be employed by Celtic Airways at the end of March. Of course, this marriage ban was not merely confined to CA but rigidly enforced by all other semi-state bodies. Judy considered the regulation was unfair and outmoded and absolutely crying out for reform. She was not alone in this opinion. Every career-conscious woman in the country felt the same. If only Ireland could have been more enlightened, Judy mourned, but in this respect they might have still been in the dark ages. That she would lose some of her best hostesses to this archaic system troubled her. True, a proportion of the newly married girls would return to take up temporary employment during the hectic summer months. Not the same thing at all, she told herself. They would be regarded as merely summer temps by management, given the worst rosters and, at the end of the season, callously laid off. Two flight tickets enabling them to travel with their spouses to anywhere in the world was the miserly pay-off, with the limiting injunction they travel *only* at off-peak times.

Judy's lip curled in scorn, convinced by the law of averages the day *must* come when the marriage bar would be lifted, but just when that would be was anybody's guess. Probably, not before the next millennium, she mused cynically. Well, no one could say *she* wasn't doing everything in her power to hurry things along.

Judy sighed when she thought of all those frustrating meetings that she and her colleagues had shared with the Chief Executive, Oliver McGrattan, and the number of times he had assured them something would be done to improve working conditions for the married girls, only to disappoint them yet again. No wonder Oliver had been nicknamed Fabius Cunctator, she thought, after another infamous delayer. Judy was convinced his appointment as Chief Executive to the airline had effectively slowed progress by five years. Another brake on progress had been the former Hostess Superintendent's somewhat Spartan outlook dating back to the early pioneering days of Celtic Airways when an advantageous marriage was the height of Amy Curtis's ambition for *her* air hostesses. Judy's dearest wish was not only to improve the working lot of air hostesses, but to give them the option to marry *and* have a working career too.

Hearing a knock on her door, Judy temporarily shelved thoughts of future glory to call, 'Come!'

The cleaner's plastic-rollered head appeared into the room. 'Okay to do your windows now, Miz Mathews?'

'Go ahead, Sadie,' Judy waved her in graciously. No matter what other areas the cleaners might neglect she insisted on them keeping *her* windows sparkling.

Watching Sadie's muscular arms efficiently tackling the dust and grime, Judy was struck by the fact that the only women so far in Celtic Airways to enjoy recognition of their right to work after marriage were the airport cleaners. Now that's a really strong body of women, Judy told herself approvingly. If only the hostess group could take on some of their strength they would swiftly improve their own conditions. Another tap at her door, and her secretary entered waving a sheet of paper.

'More cannon fodder,' Colette grinned, handing it over with a flourish.

Judy ran her eye down the list. Seeing Kay Martin's name amongst those soon to be wed she murmured, 'Well, well, so Kay has finally buried the dead,' and made a note on her pad to invite her back to work during the summer months. The pity of it, she couldn't offer Kay and her soon-to-be married colleagues a better deal.

***

There was frost on the ground and overhead the sky was bright and cloudless on the day Kay Martin married Dave Mason. On that day Kay sat at her dressing-table and viewed her image with a sense of wonder. It might have been some dazzling stranger gazing back at her. Behind her, Florrie picked up the snowy wedding veil from off the bed with both hands and, advancing with a solemn expression, she placed it carefully on Kay's dark head. Lifting the filmy panel of lace obscuring the bride's face, she gently drew it back over the delicate headdress of seed pearls and remained poised in admiration. She thought that she had never seen her friend look more beautiful. Kay's creamy skin was radiant with health and excitement and her eyes sparkled under shapely black brows. Her aunt's diamonds glittered in her ears and about her throat, and the thick tresses of her gleaming jet black hair were piled on top of her head, the one dusky coil that escaped only emphasizing the elegant line of her neck. Beneath the ethereal cloud of lace that adorned her proud head Florrie fancifully imagined her friend had an almost Spanish aristocratic look, and she stared at her so long that the deep-lashed, verdant-green eyes she had always admired became tinged with doubt as Kay enquired in concern.

'Am I okay, Florrie? *Say* something for goodness sake!'

But Florrie only nodded her head, too moved to speak. 'What's it feel like?' she found her tongue at last. 'I mean… you're quite sure and all that,' uneasily remembering the aftermath of the bridal shower when all the hostesses had departed and she and Kay had sat down together to finish the wine. Then she had been given a glimpse of Kay's soul as she had talked brokenly of an old love, one whom she vowed she would never forget nor would ever be replaced in her heart. Waiting anxiously now, she saw Kay nod.

'Yes, Florrie,' she said staunchly. Well, as sure as she would ever be, Kay thought, after all, she had had a whole year of her engagement to examine her feelings and all she wanted to do now was to tie the irrevocable knot and get it over with. Maybe even at that very moment Dave was reviewing his own past, she thought, much as she

31

had been doing ever since waking that morning. It was only natural, after all. From below came the toot of a car horn.

Kay sighed. That would be Cahal in his battered old Hillman, she thought. For want of a closer relative Winifred's husband had been prevailed upon to give her away.

Shoving up the window, Florrie leaned perilously far out. 'We'll be right down,' she shouted, then ducking back into the room said with a grin. 'Your escort is here, milady Complete with pumpkin!'

Florrie smoothed Kay's dress and stroked her veil into place, before laying the fragrant bouquet of freesias and lilies in her arms. Stepping back, she viewed the effect.

'Will I do?' Kay asked her affectionately.

'Will you do, girl?' Florrie's Cork accent became even more pronounced with emotion. 'Listen! You put JackieKennedy in the shade, Kay. You're a knockout! Believe me, Dave will die on the spot, you look so brilliant.'

'Thanks, Flo,' Kay smiled mistily back. 'You look gorgeous yourself.' She did too, in a gown of delphinium blue, the delicate floral helmet emphasizing her elfin features and just showing the feathery tips of blond hair.

As Florrie glanced down at herself pleased, Kay thought on a sudden rush of emotion: Where, Oh where, would I be without you, dear loyal Florrie? All the time doing her very best to make it up to her for having no mother to support her at this time; mutely sympathizing with her for having to depend on the awful Cahal to reluctantly do what every father considered an honour, and give the bride away.

Blinking back tears, Kay picked up her train and led the way down the steep stairs to the front entrance. Looking unusually solemn, Florrie followed on her heels holding up her train to keep it clear of the dusty stair.

Kay was not far off the mark for if Florrie could only have produced a full blown family for Kay, doting parents and fond brothers and sisters to give her all the love and reassurance she deserved on this special day, she would have done it, no matter what it cost her. As it was, she was near to tears herself, mourning the fact that poor Kay was a real Cinderella where family was concerned. Ah, but wouldn't Dave make up for it all, Florrie thought in sudden relief. With him to care for her, Kay would never know loneliness again.

Three hours later the wedding reception was almost over. All that remained was for the cake to be cut, the telegrams read. Then they could change into their going-away clothes, Kay thought, and head for the airport. She glanced about her, glad to see that everyone was having a good time. As Dave chatted to someone across the table, he squeezed her fingers to show that he was thinking of her and Kay let her hand lie in his. Almost in surprise, she thought how smoothly it had all gone; nothing awful had happened and she was well and truly married.

She had imagined that she would feel different but she didn't.

Returning her husband's gentle pressure, she was remembering how he had turned to look at her as she reached the altar. His grey eyes had held a slightly stunned expression and giving a shaky grin, he'd said 'Wow!' under his breath, before taking her hand and drawing her nearer to him. When later they had all assembled outside the church to pose for photographs Kay had been amazed at the amount of women who had hugged and kissed her. Even her cousin Winifred had approached to touch cheeks. Kay had never been the kissing type herself, feeling it smacked a bit of insincerity but in the circumstances, she decided, there had been something rather nice and warm about it. Like being admitted to a confraternity of wives. She had been moved to see the sparkle of tears in the eyes of the older, more mature spouses and wondered if at every wedding you attended over the years you found yourself reliving your own special day. With the telegrams read there was an unexpected treat when Dave's sister, Breda, stood up to sing '*The Joys Of Love*'.

Kay listened as entranced as everyone else, never having suspected that Breda possessed such a fabulous voice. In a low husky contralto, her sister-in-law sang poignantly about the joys of love lasting but a moment, the pain of love enduring the whole of life long. Kay was visited by a memory of Graham, so vivid and disturbing that she was hard put not to burst into tears, and felt the hairs standing on her neck. To hide her confusion, she pretended to be searching the floor for her fallen napkin, her emotions torn by the plaintive words. *'Your eyes kissed mine, I saw the love in them shine. My love loves me, and all the wonders I see.'* At last, the song came to an end to enthusiastic applause.

'Time to get changed,' Dave murmured. 'Want to go on up?'

Kay nodded but she didn't. There was a curious reluctance in her to move as if by doing so she would be inviting disaster of some kind. Only by keeping everyone around her could she stave it off. She shivered, her nerves strung out by the song, wishing she could hold the moment and yet somehow let it run on, and wondering why she was feeling this way. It had to be the song, she thought troubled. It was one that had always saddened Kay reminding her of her parents and the tragic shortness of their lives. Thoughts of Graham Pender came disturbingly into her mind again and she felt sudden sad shock as she thought of all the loving passionate feeling she had once felt for him now dissipated and gone. How could it have happened, she wondered bleakly, remembering how after his death she had not wanted to go on living, feeling in her acute misery that without him in her life she had wanted to die herself. Lost in unhappy thought, she found herself comparing the brief joys of love that she and Graham had shared to those momentary ones in the song. Certainly when taken in the context of a lifetime that short span could be similarly compared. At the morbidity of her thoughts her face clouded.

'What's the matter?' Dave asked gently.

Kay felt sudden tears sting her eyes and was unable to answer him. She honestly did not know what was making her so melancholy. Unless it was the inevitability of suffering once you deeply loved someone or the vulnerability of humanity when stalked by tragedy. Either was enough to give one pause. But it was none of that; in her heart she knew it was the finality of the wedding vows she had taken that day, the enormity of turning her back on her dead love and giving herself to another. It was the same devastated feeling she had experienced at the time of her engagement of having somehow betrayed Graham. It was with her again, she recognized, and saddening her more than she could bear. All that day it continued to nag at her and she couldn't shake it off, no matter what. Only when hours later she slept the sleep of exhaustion in a hotel bed in Rome did blessed oblivion come at last.

***

Another wedding took place later in April, this particular bride having no need to avail of the tax exemption for Sile Pender, Graham Pender's widow, was marrying a very wealthy man and was, besides, very well off in her own right. As was to be expected, it was a very glamorous affair, the wedding of the year the magazines later dubbed it. Captain Ben Higgins resplendent in morning suit and with a white carnation set jauntily in his buttonhole was there with his wife Linda having witnessed the somewhat upsetting scene at the moment the bride said, 'I do,' for at that moment her youngest son jumped up with an inarticulate cry and, careless of whose fashionable toes he stepped on, ran from the church. It was all caught on camera, his desolate expression, the bride's outraged glance and Tom Conway's children gleefully watching his exit.

Ben wondered if he should go after Nicholas but Linda laid a restraining hand on his arm, so he remained seated. He was not the only one gazing compassionately at the older Pender boy, who was rigid with embarrassment over the spectacle his young brother was making of himself. Stoically, Jeremy stared ahead, determined not to give the gossips anything more to gloat over. He told himself that he should have been prepared for something of the kind. All week Nicholas had been acting strangely and only that morning he had expressed his intention of staying at home, rather than attend their mother's wedding.

'She's letting Dad down before everyone,' Nicholas had declared despairingly, going about with a stony expression and refusing to eat his breakfast.

'For God's sake lighten up,' Jeremy beseeched him, not at all happy about the situation himself but prepared to make the best of it. But when Auntie Moya came down from their mother's room, she took the situation in hand telling Nicholas he was the one letting down his mother by behaving in such a selfish way. Only then had Nicholas sullenly changed into the suit that was laid out for him.

Poor lad, Ben thought, knowing how much Nicholas had adored his father. Of late the brothers had become fairly frequent visitors to his house, sometimes staying overnight. Ben decided that he would invite them to stay the coming weekend He was well pleased with his decision on arriving at the reception taking place in the bridegroom's palatial property and observed the small solitary figure sitting some distance away from the marquee on an upturned flower pot.

Heading over, Ben went down on his hunkers. 'How's it going, Nicky?'

The boy looked up startled. 'Hello Captain Higgins.'

'Jeremy not with you?

'He's over there… with them,' Nicholas told him, looking betrayed.

'Oh well, I expect he's just trying to be friendly,' Ben said. 'Look, I hope you and your brother will come over to the house this weekend, what do you say? Martin is always talking about how famously the pair of you get on together. He tells me you are aiming to be a pilot too, eh?'

Nicholas nodded. 'Yeah, same as my Dad.'

'Did you know that your Dad and I flew in the Air Corps together before joining Celtic Airways?'

Nicholas regarded him with interest. 'You and he were friends?'

'You could say that. He was a fine pilot but I expect you know that.'

Nicholas's dark eyes shone. 'Yes, the very best,' he said proudly. Then his expression clouded, he looked bewildered and very vulnerable. 'But…what I don't understand is how he could have crashed his plane. My Dad *never* made mistakes. *Never*!'

Ben was silent for a moment. 'Nicky,' he said gently. 'At times even the best pilot finds himself in a bad situation. No matter how good he is at flying a plane he can be outmatched by circumstances. Bad weather maybe… or mechanical failure. He has to rely on his own good judgment and training to get himself and his crew out of such situations. But luck isn't always with him. That's what happened in your father's case. Not only was there a bad tropical storm that evening but the instrument landing system was defective. Believe me, all of that spells trouble.' Ben sighed, sobered by this irrefutable truth. The boy was watching him with painful attention and Ben was unaccountably disturbed by the miserable uncertainty he saw in his eyes.

'You mean no matter how brilliant a pilot he was,' Nicholas said slowly, 'He couldn't have saved the plane and all the people in it?'

'I'm afraid not. There were too many things stacked against him.'

Nicholas heaved a sigh, so deep it seemed to start way down inside him. Ben had a sudden insight into the boy's mind and began to understand something of the doubts and fears plaguing him since his father's death. He stayed with him for a bit longer, chatting about flying and airplanes, deliberately bolstering the image of his father as a great pilot and a great friend. Then he turned away promising to have another chat before long, and was rewarded by a sudden sweet uplifting of the boy's countenance as Nicholas shyly smiled back.

Good God! Ben felt shaken at his uncanny resemblance to his dead father.

As the day progressed and the meal was followed by dancing, Ben found himself becoming nostalgic. Perhaps it was because of all he had had to drink or maybe it stemmed from his poignant conversation with Nicholas Pender. Whichever it was, he couldn't help observing how the sons of his dead colleague were outsiders at this lavish wedding feast, and more than ever he felt the burden of responsibility weighting on him to help them in any way he could.

***

Only to herself did Kay ever admit to disappointment in her marriage, deciding early on it was a lottery and some people just had better luck than others. She sometimes felt as though having wooed and won her Dave considered himself free now to give all his passion and attention to his career. The term workaholic was an accurate description of her husband, she considered, and with him out at work all day and sometimes half the night, she couldn't help feeling cheated, having believed that marriage would provide a bulwark against her sorrow and inner loneliness. Too late she realized her mistake. Desperately she missed her old life and the cheery atmosphere aboard flights, more than ever she regretted turning down the Hostess Superintendent's offer to come back and work the summer months. Kay had not been the only one who had declined to take Judy up on her offer and for the simple reason it was well known the summer temps, as the married hostesses were known, were given the worst rosters and literally run off their feet. But, at least, she would have had some money of her own, Kay told herself, even if it was a lot less than she had earned before marriage, enough at least to get her hair and nails done, she calculated, and buy some badly needed things for the house. It had soon become apparent that their honeymoon had put them in the red and there were things they would have to do without until Dave had paid it off. So he admitted with a rather shamed expression. Kay told herself that she would have been just as happy to have booked into a less luxurious hotel if it meant they could have a television set now and maybe a comfy couch on which to watch it. But that too would have to wait. It would be time enough to rent a set in the autumn, Dave had insisted, pointing out that in the meantime they would be out and about in the summer months soaking up sunshine or going on healthy hikes up the Dublin mountains.

Kay looked at him in disbelief. Sunshine she would believe when she saw it and hikes were not on her agenda. With an effort, she swallowed her disappointment telling herself it was not the end of the world, she could live without television for a bit. The trouble was they were doing without too many things already, what she considered the bare necessities for every day. Surely they could afford a small fridge to keep food fresh, she fretted, and what about a washing machine? She felt like she had taken a step back in centuries, slopping undergarments around in the sink and pegging them sodden on the washing line to dry.

'How did our mothers manage?' Dave's comment did not help. Kay wanted no reminders of Eileen who hid her dislike of her daughter-in-law with an assumption of vagueness and had the temerity to criticize Molly.

In her frustration, Kay reminded Dave every chance she got of her dissatisfaction, spouting to-do and to-have lists at him, until in self preservation he stopped listening and heard her no more. At times it was the absence of a spare bed that would have made it possible for her to have a friend to stay the night that set her off, at others a dining-table to entertain would-be guests. In truth, she grew weary, just visualizing their needs. Forced to live in her new Spartan surroundings it became increasingly important to Kay to try and salvage some remnants of her former glamour. Defiantly, she painted her toenails red and continued to wear high-heeled, slingback sandals, despite mud and potholes all over the estate. When Dave chuckled and shook his head over the vanity of women, she ignored him. Let him, if it made him feel superior, she told herself haughtily, he didn't have a lot to be superior about. But it was only a token defiance. She never ceased to mourn the old life, which in retrospect, had become the perfect life. She sighed remembering how she had always been going somewhere exciting, was never on the ground for long. She gazed wistfully skywards on the lookout for a glimpse of jet stream, envying her hostess friends walking the aisle bound for New York, and would have given any money to be back there with them. Sometimes she thought of going out to the airport and seeing if it wasn't too late to get herself back on to the roster for the summer months, but something always held her back. Maybe it was the admission of defeat that daunted her, the humiliation of acknowledging that married life was not all it was cracked up to be. So instead she kept telling herself to 'give it a chance,' grimly trying to make the best of her marriage

Dave had his agenda too, saying it was essential to first tackle the rocky patch of ground behind the house. He got help from his cousin Ruari who came to the house after work a few evenings a week, an attractive man in his mid-thirties, optimistic and outgoing. Kay felt immediately cheered at the sight of him coming through the side gate. As he and Dave strenuously dug into the cast-iron earth she busied herself rolling pastry for the apple pie with which to reward them when the light faded and they came in to slump down tired and sweaty at the kitchen table. One of the advantages of buying a corner house was the fact the garden was slightly bigger than the other houses, but it soon became apparent it had served as the builders' dumping ground. That first evening Dave and Ruari had dug out a load of rubbish, flinging it at the end of the so-called garden until soon there was a steadily growing mound of broken bricks, empty milk cartons and crushed cardboard containers bearing the brand of a popular fast food chain. Once the worst of the excavation was behind them, the grass seed planted and string carefully criss-crossed over it to discourage the scavenging birds, this pressure was replaced by another as Dave insisted they must invite his family over for a meal in their new house. Kay had been expecting and dreading this but there was no way out it seemed, she would just have to grin and bear it and get busy with her menus.

'Don't go to any trouble now, Katie,' Dave advised as he headed for the telephone to ring and invite them before she could protest.' Just keep it simple," as if this was the blueprint for success.

Kay sighed, convinced the only simple thing about any of it was herself in believing him. There was no way you could have three people to an evening meal without going to any trouble, not if you were as inexperienced at entertaining as she was. When the day came she had done her best but philosophically accepted that the meal was a disaster, impossible not to notice the way her mother-in-law attempted to conceal half-chewed lumps of meat under lumpy grave. Breda, valiantly making conversation, had stoically munched away but Reggie gave up early on and concentrated on the wine. Kay knew from what Dave had told her that his father had a drink problem. Under duress, she ended up drinking too much herself, regardless of Eileen's scandalized gaze and paid for it next day with a bad hangover, only too glad to 'lie on' as Dave advised before he vanished to the office, despite it being Saturday. She had lain there all day feeling unwell and for once, she was not sorry when he didn't return until evening. Her failure to make a good showing at entertaining her in-laws convinced Kay that she should give up playing at house and return to work, even if it were only on a temporary basis with all its drawbacks. But when her tummy upset persisted and she was so overcome by nausea couldn't hold anything down for days, she realized with mixed emotions, this was no longer an option, she was pregnant.

***

January, 1970

Colombo was hot. A humid heat, with no cooling breeze from the Indian Ocean to bring relief to the captives confined to their narrow cell. Every so often the pilot turned restlessly on the narrow wooden pallet, almost overbalancing on to the stone floor as insects buzzed in the darkness. He felt one zoom close and land smack on his sweating face. Fretfully, he brushed it away finding it hard to breathe in the stifling blackness.

Across the room from him the boy shifted in his sleep, and he repressed the sigh that was working its way up from the depths of his being, agonizingly conscious of time passing, days and nights blending with each other. After so many months imprisoned in the tiny cell, with only a peephole on the sky, the pilot thought he knew how it must feel to be incarcerated. The absence of the sun was the greatest deprivation of all, even worse than his loss of liberty, and on the infrequent occasions he was allowed outside in the air he looked forward to the feel of it on his skin with the same passion that he felt about one day being reunited with his family. Sometimes he thought it was the presence of the Indian boy that kept him from going insane. Without the consolation of Ranjan's gentle companionship he would have found these four years since his capture by the ILA intolerable. In the beginning the pilot had not made any attempt to keep note of the days. Only when the first year had passed did he begin to keep a reckoning, judging the time of year by the Hindu festival of lights known as *Deepvali* which took place late October. At this time the boy was permitted to keep a night vigil in the cell, sitting hunched within the half circle of flickering lamps and, despite himself, the pilot gained a measure of peace from the ritual.

Some time earlier with a sense of shock, he had witnessed the celebration of the fourth festival of lights since his capture. But back

41

in those early days, the pilot had believed it was only a short time before he would be rescued, that once the search was made and his body not found in the wreckage, they would come looking for him. It was not until much later that it was gradually borne in on him that more than likely the aircraft had disintegrated on impact, and been consumed by fire. Dwelling on those last minutes before the crash as he had wrestled with the controls of the jet in the monsoon storm, he remembered that his migraine had been triggered by the lightning flashes. He had fumbled awkwardly in his pocket for his pills, but with full emergency harness strapped on they were not easy to get at. Finally, by releasing the catches and struggling clear of the harness, he had been able to get a tablet into his mouth. Subsequently, with the breakup on impact with the trees he had found himself thrown free of the aircraft. He remembered reading of a wartime pilot who had not been wearing his regulation flying boots when his Spitfire was shot down and had managed to escape by untying the laces and leaving his shoes behind in the cockpit. To a similar lucky fluke he realized he owed his own life. As always, when unable to sleep in the sweltering heat, the pilot found himself going back over his first months in captivity when subjected to endless interrogations and torture by his captors. They appeared to be convinced that he had been part of some conspiracy to smuggle guns and ammunition into Colombo, they had even spoken of a consignment of gold bullion aboard his flight demanding to know the names of those involved. 'Where is the gold now? Which country sold you the guns and ammunition? When is the next consignment due?'

These and many other questions were repeatedly fired at him by the GOC of the camp, the huge black man he had come to know as Colonel Mauser, one moment savagely threatening, softly bargaining the next, 'Tell us what you know, give us the names of the Tamil dissidents you conspired with and we will set you free.'

The pilot had repeatedly denied all knowledge of the guns or the gold and, indeed, of being part of any conspiracy with the freedom fighters. And then the brutality had begun, the savage beatings, the long periods of starvation always ending in the resumption of the relentless inquisition. Again and again, he vehemently denied all knowledge of what they were accusing him, genuinely at a loss, until at last he had stubbornly adopted the wartime practice of speaking only his name and rank, nothing more. All through the worst of these times the Tamil boy had ministered to him, patiently feeding him sips of water, wiping his bruised and bleeding face, respectfully addressing him as 'Captain Tuan' for it seemed that his mother had been a Malay and always addressed his father thus, convincing the pilot of something that he had always believed but never personally experienced until then; in time of trouble God sent angels. Lying there, recovering from the beatings, he often wondered if there could be any truth in the accusations made by Mauser that his fellow pilot had been in collusion with the Tamil freedom fighters to smuggle arms into Colombo. No doubt whoever had helped them would have been well paid. But almost at once he rejected the notion. No, he was a decent sort of chap, out east like himself doing a spell of winter duty with Eastline Airways. No way would he have engaged in anything criminal. It had been a relief when the interrogations abruptly ceased and he was allowed back to the cell.

Unlike the pilot, the boy was given a measure of freedom by the guards. They put him to use around the camp doing menial tasks, helping the women to gather charcoal for the cooking fires. Sometimes they sent Ranjan shinning up the tall palms to gather coconuts, it was the only time he was allowed out through the stockade gate into the jungle. Within the confines of the camp the boy was fairly free to come and go during daylight hours but the pilot was guarded at all times. There came a time when he was allowed in the open at last and he had felt almost dizzy with joy at feeling the sun on his skin once more. Painfully, hobbling up and down on his injured leg, he noted the stockade fence about the camp, beyond which the jungle sheered up on all sides, and he began to think more constructively of escape. But even if he somehow managed to get beyond the gate and into the jungle, the pilot was aware that he wouldn't get very far on his gammy leg. It was imperative, therefore, to build himself up. And so he had begun the most rudimentary of his Air Force exercises, doggedly keeping to a program aimed at strengthening his leg muscles and improving his breathing, watching in some amusement, and then with respect, when the Tamil boy began exercising alongside of him, for the boy was just as determined as

43

he was to strengthen his own body. Next time he was allowed into the open the pilot had looked about him with fresh eyes. Catching sight of cigarillo packet under a bush, he had got a sudden idea for its use. He had already gathered sticks of charcoal from the cooking area and now, keeping an eye out to see if he were being watched, he discreetly slipped the packet into his pants pocket; Once back in the privacy of the cell he printed his name and rank and the date of the air crash on the flap of the carton with a stick of charcoal, before concealing it under the wooden slats of his bed. As he did, he felt his spirits lifting.

Further support came when amongst the paperback books the guards brought to the cell, he discovered a tattered copy of the psalms. He had never been an overly religious man but he found himself experiencing new solace in the spiritual, and took comfort in learning the verses by heart, strongly identifying with the militant lines, 'Though an army encamp against me my heart would not fear. Though war break out against me even then would I trust.'

It was so redolent of his own captive state, the pilot thought, imprisoned and surrounded by the rebel army, deprived of his liberty, his very life in the hands of ruthless savages. But undoubtedly the psalm that most helped him to maintain hope in his ultimate rescue was the 139th psalm giving him to believe that even here, far away in an alien land, the Lord had not forsaken him. 'If I should take the wings of the dawn and dwell at the sea's furthermost shore even there would you lead me,' he read often, 'Even there would your right hand hold me fast.'

The pilot had been tested often in the early years since his capture but never given up his steadfast belief in being rescued, not until the freedom fighters' plan to rescue the boy and his abducted sister had failed. Some time earlier Ranjan had been out filling the water bottle when he had heard his name softly called, and going closer to the fence he had found to his joy that his sister, Sita, was at the other side. There had followed a whispered conversation between them, brief because of the fear of discovery, but enough to reassure him of how diligently she had sought him all this time. On learning of her promise to return with the freedom fighters and rescue them from the camp, the pilot had been filled with a similar elation, and then to the boy's dismay a week later, one evenings at dusk, the stockade gates had opened and a woman, bound and hooded, was dragged into the camp between two guards. When the hood was removed Ranjan was devastated to see that the weeping woman was his sister and followed fearfully as she was thrown into a hut by the exultant soldiers and the door banged in his face. Following in hot pursuit next day at dawn, the Freedom Fighters raided the camp rescuing Sita and Ranjan and reluctantly taking the pilot along with them too. But only because the boy had refused to leave without the Captain Tuan. During the escape Sita had been injured in the cross fire. Hampered by their wounded comrade and the injured pilot the company had not got very far when the pilot's leg collapsed beneath him and he could not make it any further. Urging the boy to go ahead without him, he had crawled off the path into the bushes but Ranjan had stubbornly refused to leave him. Much to Sita's distress the Freedom Fighters were forced to continue on without them or risk being captured. Before they went, however. the pilot gave Sita the message on the cigarillo packet and she promised to pass it on to the authorities. Before long, he and the boy were discovered by the rebels and dragged back to the camp where the pilot was subjected to beatings and prolonged spells of solitary confinement. Buried for long periods in a sweltering hole in the ground something broke in the pilot's spirit. He still hung on to his hope that the message entrusted to Sita would be delivered but when first one year passed and then another, without intervention of any kind, that hope withered. With the capture of a Tamil scout, brought into the camp late one night, what the man had revealed under torture brought desolation to the boy and despair to the pilot as they learned that on the night of the raid Sita had died from her wounds in the jungle. And to think all this time she had been dead. Sick to his heart, the pilot turned his face to the wall, all hope gone.

Harinath Prasad, the Tamil leader, had spent those same two years in sorrowing remembrance of Sita whom he had loved and lost that same night, forced to leave her body lying unburied in the jungle. With an effort, he had put aside his sorrow and continued on fighting for the Tamil cause without her. In the following months,

Prasad had seldom thought about her young brother or the wounded pilot still held captive by the ILA but, whenever he did so, he was vaguely troubled by his failure to carry out Sita's dying request. Towards her brother, he had felt a certain responsibility but he could not bring himself to help the pilot whom he believed had betrayed Sita to the ILA. Hatred for the man had entered Prasad's soul and his thoughts were vengeful. Until by chance, he learned the truth about a Sinhalese office worker at the airport, who had been bitterly jealous of a Tamil holding a position superior to her own as the official secretary to the airport manager, and informed the ILA of Sita's connection with the Freedom Fighters. With this knowledge that she and not the pilot had betrayed Sita, Prasad was only now two years later carrying out Sita's dying wish, telling himself he was doing it for her brother's sake. Accordingly, the Tamil leader dispatched a courier to the airport with strict instructions, 'Give this package into the hands of the airport manager. None other.'

With this duty finally discharged, there remained only one more debt to Sita's memory. Prasad vowed that he would not rest until he had found and killed the woman who had betrayed her.

The airport manager accepted the envelope from the courier and dismissed the man, whom he did not recognize. It was Monsoon time once more, the air conditioning in the airport manager's office had broken down and the temperature was 32°. Hughes mopped his forehead with his handkerchief and carefully wiped the palms of his hands, what it would be like in another twenty-four hours he dreaded to think. He had been surprised when Daya, his new secretary, had sullenly entered his office and told him there was a messenger at the door refusing to speak to anyone but himself. He was uneasily reminded of the day that Sita Shanti had been kidnapped right before his eyes by two men in the battle fatigues of the rebel ILA, so he was careful this time to contact security before cautiously emerging. Glancing at the envelope the courier had given him, he was relieved to see that it wasn't big enough to contain an incendiary device. In the troubled times they were living that was the way the airport manager's thoughts continually ran. Conscious of Daya's eyes upon him, he went back into his office and firmly closed the door. The woman was a real disappointment, he thought, she lacked ability to take the initiative and was a disastrous typist. He would have got rid of her if he could but she was the sort to make trouble, and he would have to put up with her. Ah, he thought regretfully, if only Sita had not - Hughes was about to say 'been killed' but his thoughts broke off at that point. He really meant if only she had not betrayed his trust or even that she had not been found out. Either way, he would not be stuck now with Daya, desperately trying to manage.

On opening the envelope, he found another unpleasant surprise awaiting him. Drawing out a sheet of paper he read in bewilderment the cryptic line printed in capitals. 'Go search in the camp of the Indigiri Lankas.' There was also contained in the envelope what looked like an empty cigarillo packet, and when he turned it over he saw some words dustily marked on it. After a moment he deciphered the word 'Captain' and what looked like a date in April some four years previously. All too swiftly Hughes made the connection. Never while he lived would he forget the date of the Eastline Airways plane crash, it was forever burned on his brain.

***

One week later Matt Rogan paused on his way out the door of his apartment in Porchester Square and cast a swift eye over the letters just delivered by the postmam. He selected several from the pile and shoved them into the pocket of his trench coat, the others, mostly bills, he threw back on the hall table and pulled the door after him.

Once outside, the accident investigator walked briskly to the corner of the square and hailed a taxi aware that in less than thirty minutes he was due in court to give evidence at an Inquiry into a recent crash of a DC9. As the taxi moved smoothly through the streets of London, he tore open his letters and read the contents. His mother had written from the Lake District, which she described as 'a foretaste of heaven' and was obviously enjoying her holiday in that idyllic setting. Matt smiled to himself before turning his attention to the long white envelope bearing a foreign stamp.

Gazing at it, he wondered who was writing to him from Ceylon. He had not had dealings with anyone there in several years. But as soon as he read the enclosed letter his expression lost its puzzled look and became intent again. Of course, he remembered the Colombo crash. The plane had come down in the jungle in the middle of a Monsoon storm killing nearly everyone on board. It was rumoured there was gold on board. At the time he had felt there was more to that particular crash than the evidence presented at the Inquiry and now this letter from the airport manager confirmed his hunch. On drawing out the enclosed sheets the investigator read the cryptic lines printed in charcoal on what looked like an empty cigarillo packet and a date in April some four years previously. Swiftly, Rogan made the connection vividly reminded of the silver St Christopher medal that had been found in the jungle some distance from the site of the crash. He still had it stashed away in his desk, along with all the other loose ends salvaged in plane crashes. Just as well he had held on to it, Matt thought. It might yet be required.

His eyes returning to the letter, he read the station manager's comments which seemed to suggest that one of the pilots had survived the crash and was being held prisoner in the jungle by the ILA. The Airport Manager went on to say how all along he had had his suspicions about his Tamil secretary who turned out to be a member of the dissident Freedom Fighters and was later abducted and killed by the rebel ILA. Rogan wondered why Hughes had been so slow off the mark in exposing the mole in the airport, especially if, as he had suggested, he had already had his suspicions about her. The accident investigator had the uneasy feeling that the ball was being passed into his court long after its force was spent.

Captain Higgins came in from the airport that same week where he had been on standby all afternoon, and found a pile of letters awaiting him on the hall table. Seeing the London postmark, he opened it first.

'Darling, I've poured you a drink?' Linda stuck her head into his study. 'I'm doing Beef Wellington and it doesn't improve with hanging about.'

'Sounds good! I'll be right in,' Ben murmured, deep in the accident investigator's letter, hardly able to credit what he was reading. Good God! he thought astounded, the more he read the more bizarre it seemed.

Ben made himself go back to the beginning and start all over again. But it was as he thought and Rogan concluded, 'I've written to the head of the Ceylonese Safety Board with the suggestion that he should inform the National Transport Safety Board of the situation. Following upon that we will in conjunction with them approach his government with the request for the release of the pilot....'

Ben lowered the letter and stared in a daze across the room at the model of a Boeing 707 gracefully poised for flight on the mahogany bookcase. The possibility that Graham Pender might still be alive seemed too fantastic to be true and his mind was filled with all the implications of such a miracle. Ben was visited by a vision of Sile Pender elegantly clad in an ivory brocade gown and wide picture hat, as she swept down the church on the arm of her new husband. Almost at once this was replaced by another image, this time of the lonely figure of Sile's small son sitting on an upturned flower pot, his dark expressive eyes so like Graham's fixed trustingly on him. Captain Higgins was struck by the damage that could be done if the news leaked out too soon or turned out to be false. There was nothing after all to identify the pilot as Pender, he thought, it could equally have been the other Captain on the flight deck. There and then, Ben decided he must be very sure to have all his facts correct before taking it further. Accordingly, first thing next morning Ben called on the Chief Pilot.

Andy Hegarty took the news in his usual calm way and agreed that the Chief Executive must be informed at once, if only for the sake of protocol. Neither had a high opinion of Oliver McGrattan and he was not generally liked. When Ben was finally admitted to McGrattan's office having been made to cool his heels in the outer office for ten minutes, he was under no illusion that the man would be overjoyed at the revelation that one of his pilots might have miraculously survived the Colombo crash, but he had expected that Oliver would at least *appear* to be glad, if only for the look of it. Not moaning on about the huge cost to their airline of freeing an imprisoned pilot from the clutches of rebels, if indeed the man did turn out to be Captain Pender. McGrattan even spoke of the expense already incurred of flying the pilot's body back four years earlier and of giving him a first class funeral.

'I would have thought that would be the end of the matter,' McGrattan said. 'Now I suppose we are looking at more expense.'

Unbelievable! Ben felt his temper rising. 'Well, let's just be very clear about this, McGrattan,' he growled. 'There's a man's life at stake here, perhaps one of our own pilots, so to hell with the expense. We have a duty to do everything in our power to get him released and brought home. If necessary, we'll apply to the UN for help.'

'Very well but I will have to consult with my Board of Directors first. In the meantime, we'll just have to wait and see.'

'Well, you may wait,' Ben snapped. 'But as president of the Pilots Association I do *not* intend hanging about wasting precious time while you and other petty civil servants haggle over money, not when the life of a pilot is in jeopardy.'

'Now see here just one minute,' McGrattan blustered, but Captain Higgins had already banged out the door.

In the days that followed Ben congratulated himself on his good judgment in paying no heed to McGrattan and immediately engaging the support of the Chief Pilot and the committee of the Pilots Association. The meeting they called was attended by Pete Kenny, secretary of the Pilots Association and Captain John Brennan, another senior pilot and a man Captain Higgins both liked and respected; it would be time enough later to call a general meeting of pilots. In the meantime, the committee of four were briefed on the situation and sworn to secrecy. It was decided that one of them should accompany Ben to London, just as soon as a meeting with the President of the British Airline Pilots Association could be arranged. Captain Brennan then proposed Captain Kenny, all in agreement, the motion was passed.

One week later, Ben and Pete were on their way to London having set up a meeting with BALPA, and been assured that a representative of the International Federation of Airline Pilots Association would also be attending, as well as Matt Rogan, the accident investigator for Eastline Airways.

'So what's the procedure, Ben?' Pete asked as they were landing.

Ben took his time replying, remembering his discussion with Andy that morning and the Chief Pilot's emphasis on the importance of how they presented their case, not as a matter concerning an Irish pilot or a British pilot but a pilot full stop. Like Ben, Andy had started his flying career in the Irish Air Corps and with typical military decisiveness, he advised, 'Go through the obvious channels, Ben, and if you find you're not getting anywhere then summon the big guns. But the way I read it, they'll be only too happy to co-operate. For all they know the captured pilot could turn out to be one of theirs.' It made sense to Ben; the mood he found himself in he would have happily gone to Downing Street and put the case to Harold Wilson. Admittedly strong measures but not, as it turned out, necessary for the Irish pilots found their British colleagues only too willing to co-operate, and they spent two productive hours in conference with the President and committee, all of them only too anxious to help once they realized that Pender's co-pilot had formerly been one of their own Royal Air Force officers. Everything had proceeded smoothly, and when Rogan had produced the evidence that the pilot was being kept hostage it was passed around for inspection. But the clincher had come when the investigator had produced further evidence and, opening his fist, he had dropped a silver medal and chain on the table before them.

At the sight, Ben had been seized with sudden excitement. Good Lord! He *knew* that medal, he thought, picking it up and rubbing an explorative thumb along the bent edge. 'I can identify this,' he told them positively. 'It belongs to Captain Graham Pender. I can even tell you how it became dented like this,' going on to speak of a day long ago in the Air Corps when the cadets were returning from a cross country run, with their shirt tails out flapping in the summer breeze, about a mile from the barracks one of the group had produced a beer bottle concealed in his backpack.

'Here, give us a lend of your dog tags, Pender,' he'd said flippantly, grabbing hold of Pender's St Christopher medal and using it to prise off the cap. Graham had been furious and gone for him bald-headed, calling him a cretin and a Philistine; and in the end they had had to haul him off the other cadet.

51

By the time Ben had concluded his story the atmosphere fairly bristled and now all about the table were sure they were on the right track. He and Pete had come away from the meeting with the assurance of the IFALPA agent that pressure would continue to be put on the Ceylonese government to carry out an investigation into the matter of the captured pilot and, at the same time, a resolution would be tabled before the General Assembly of the United Nations in New York, requesting their cooperation in obtaining his release.

'So not a bad day's work, eh?' said Pete, his mood and thoughts in accord with Ben's as they sat enjoying well-earned gin tonics in the bar at Heathrow. 'This rightly hits the spot, eh?'

Ben just grinned wearily. Hours of talking had given them both a thirst and this was their first opportunity to quench it in the dash to make their flight on time.

'That was quite a story you told back there,' Pete said thoughtfully. 'You know, about Pender and the medal. You really grabbed their attention.'

'Listen Pete,' Ben interrupted him. 'Not a word to anyone, not until we get a chance to notify the family. Understood?''

'Sure, Mum's the word!' Pete said, meaning it.

But Pete had not reckoned on meeting up with Judy Mathews as they were disembarking at Dublin. In the past he and Judy had been very close and although Captain Kenny was married now he was still carrying a torch for Judy, and not proof against her when she agreed to have a drink with him at The Hollow, a popular pub with aircrew.

'Just a quick one and then I really have to get on home.' Judy sank down with him on the sagging velour seat in one of the heavily curtained booths.

'Fine by me,' agreed Pete, forgetting his wife patiently awaiting tea at home and falling under Judy's spell, even to the point of indiscretion.

'What did you say?' Judy turned her violet eyes upon him in shock. 'Would you mind repeating what you just said,' hearing again words like incredible, unbelievable. 'Is this one of your jokes, Pete?' she said faintly, knowing Kenny's reputation as a practical joker.

Pete shook his head solemnly. 'Believe me, Judy, this is far too serious a matter for jokes. I'm sure I don't need to remind you what I'm telling you is strictly confidential. Not a word to anyone, you understand?'

'Yes, I understand,' Judy assured him. She laid a manicured hand on his arm and he shuddered at her touch. 'Pete, you will let me know the minute you have anything definite. Can I rely on that?'

'Of course,' he said, not proof against those eyes. 'You *know* you can, Judy.'

On returning from New York a few days later Captain Higgins intended paying Sile Conway a visit and breaking the news to her that there was the strong likelihood that her first husband might be alive and being held hostage in the Ceylonese jungle, only to find somehow in his absence the news had already got out. Ben's mood was in no way improved on being summoned to the Chief Executive's office where he had to stand and take all the abuse hurled at him by McGrattan, the Chief Executive still smarting over Sile Conway's aggrieved telephone attack that morning. Who the blazes could have leaked the information, Ben wondered, coming away in a rage. 'By God', he swore savagely, 'I'll not stop till I find out, and may God help them when I do.' It did not take him long to trace the leak to Pete Kenny, this when Judy had vehemently denied being the one to repeat what the pilot had told her. She was not, however, backward in voicing her opinion that if Graham was ever to be rescued then the more people who were apprised of the situation the better, not keeping it concealed from the pilot's own family. She had never heard of anything so ridiculous in her life.

Ben lost no time in tracking down the shamefaced Pete and found that not only had the weak, besotted fool succumbed to Judy's charm but he had also been guilty of blabbing to a fellow pilot. Having given the hapless Pete short shrift, Ben now wanted only to get home and make his peace with his wife for Sile Conway had been badgering Linda too. 'I've been ringing your house all morning and getting no co-operation from your wife,' Sile had said aggrieved.

'She couldn't or wouldn't tell me your whereabouts,' as if Linda was an inefficient secretary falling down on her duties. 'This is a matter of extreme delicacy, Ben, the boys must be told about their father. What if they should hear of it from someone else?'

'Of course, they must be told at once,' Ben growled into the phone. He supposed the woman had a legitimate grievance but to complain him to the Chief Executive, really there was no standing her. 'Look, Sile, I'd be happy to drive down to the college and break it to them myself. Do you want me to do that?'

'Not if the whole thing is going to take as long as it took *you* to tell *me*!'

'No question of that,' Ben said crisply. 'I'll go first thing tomorrow.'

***

Once Captain Higgins had been to Mellwood and broken the astounding news of their father's survival to Jeremy and Nicholas, he then had a word with the headmaster and leaving the boys an opportunity to talk it over between themselves, he returned home.

The following day the headmaster called both Pender boys into his study and suggested in the circumstances they might like to go home for the weekend to discuss things with their mother. He appointed one of the masters to drive them to the city. The boys arrived home to find their mother in a state of shock and disinclined to discuss the situation, they were still stunned themselves, still trying to come to terms with it. The most revealing comments came from their stepfather who was overheard saying, 'It's ruddy time that loafer Pender came back and assumed responsibility for his sons.'

Tom meant it as a joke but it worried Jeremy who had become accustomed to the luxurious life-style of his stepfather's mansion and his stepfather's promise to give him a sports car on his eighteenth birthday. Secretly, Jeremy feared if he were to withdraw his support he would no longer be able to continue his education at Mellwood, and the prospect of changing schools for somewhere far less prestigious so near his final year filled him with dismay.

Nicholas had his own fears plaguing him. They had nothing to do with money, but rather to the disturbing conversation he had overheard between Conway and his mother as he passed their bedroom door, with Tom loudly sounding off,

'Those savages keeping your ex captive, Sile, they aren't going to give him up easily, you know. Wouldn't give much for his chances of making it out of there alive. Ruddy so-and-sos will probably end up killing the poor bastard,' casting a chill upon Nicholas who was already terrified for his father's safety.

By the time Jeremy and Nicholas returned to Mellwood they were silent and withdrawn, each taken up with gloomy thoughts, not surprisingly their schoolwork began to suffer. Before long, their teachers brought the matter to the attention of the headmaster and sought his advice on how best to deal with it.

'Well, it's to be expected in the circumstances,' Fr Coyle frowned. 'Still, it's a pity to see two such promising lads going downhill. Better send them to see me. I'll have a chat with them before they fall any further behind with their studies.'

Ten minutes with Jeremy soon sorted out the older boy's problems and the priest was able to reassure him there was no reason to fear he wouldn't be able to continue his education at Mellwood.

'We have a special fund for the sons of past pupils and when your father was believed dead your case was discussed and provision made. So you'll get down to work, eh? Make up for all the time you've been wasting?' and Jeremy nodded in relief, yes, he certainly would.

When questioned about his younger brother he was noncommittal. 'Nicky takes everything very hard,' was all he said, before leaving the room with a lighter step.

Fr Coyle did not imagine he would get to the root of Nicholas's trouble so quickly. He had never found it easy to communicate with the younger lad and suspected few could penetrate the barrier he instinctively erected.

As it turned out, it took a couple of sessions in his study before he was able to win Nicholas's confidence and the boy relaxed enough to tell him of the fears crippling him since learning of his father's capture by the ILA. The priest was moved as the boy poured it all out, his night-time terrors and his extreme unhappiness at living in his stepfather's house, his great love for his father and his fear that he would die before he could be rescued. The priest wished it was in his power to lighten some of the load Nicholas was carrying but the situation regarding Captain Pender's release was still unknown. Thinking it might be good for Nicholas to have something positive to do, he suggested that he write a letter to his father.

'I will personally see to it that Captain Higgins receives it,' he told the boy. 'And no doubt, he'll know the next step to ensure its safe delivery.'

'Oh, could I really write to my Dad?' Nicholas was bowled over.

'Why not?' Fr Coyle said genially. 'Hostages have been known to receive word from their families before, you know… and the other way round too.' He patted Nicholas on the shoulder. 'Can't do any harm and could do a lot of good,' and Nicholas sped away, thinking how wonderful if his Dad received his letter, even more wonderful if he could send one back.

***

At Dublin airport the amazing story of Captain Pender's survival was all anyone could speak about. Judy Mathews had set up the support group - FOGP - Friends of Graham Pender - and she was already deep into her petition-signing campaign designed to arouse public support for the hostage. Posters of the uniformed pilot soon appeared in the hostess corridor captioned, 'Out of sight but *not* out of mind'. Word had it there was to be a demo in front of the arrivals building with uniformed aircrew carrying placards; all were encouraged to attend. Florrie Belton would have been happy to take part only she had requested leave and was going home to Cork.

With so much coverage given to the story she was convinced that Kay must know about Captain Pender's amazing survival but incredibly Kay did not. Since her advancing pregnancy had taken over her life Kay could not work up much interest in anything other than her own body and what was going on inside it. That first winter

Kay had spent most nights sitting in the house on her own except for the very occasional time Dave came home early and they went to the cinema together. But work came first and he was happiest at the office or on the phone talking business with his boss, regardless of the hour. On reflection, Kay was just as glad to be having a child so quick, telling herself that at least she would have someone to talk to, even if it was only baby talk. Florrie's visits were her only consolation and she always made sure to get in chocolate cake when her friend came over for an evening, familiar with her friend's sweet tooth. She had sworn off all such temptation herself, at least until her baby was born. Even at Christmas she had exercised great willpower and heroically confined herself to one fat finger of fruit cake, admittedly along with two helpings of almond icing, but then marzipan had always been her undoing. How she had managed to keep so strictly to her diet Kay would never know, maybe it was her longing to put aside maternity wear and get back into her normal clothes once the baby was born.

Sitting by the fire waiting for Florrie to arrive, Kay sipped weak tea in deference to her heartburn and mused nostalgically on the happy past. She found herself doing that a lot lately, only now realizing how carefree those adolescent years had been living with her aunt and how much she missed Molly these days. She stared into the leaping flames reminded of Dave's phone call earlier. It appeared something had come up at work and he wouldn't be able to join Florrie and herself for supper after all. Nothing new about that, Kay thought, just as glad not to have him there, knowing that she and Florrie could speak a lot more freely on their own and looking forward to catching up on the airport gossip.

Not that she had a lot in the way of news to contribute herself, the highlight of her week had to be her anti-natal class run by their elderly, but amazingly agile, instructor. Pouring herself more weak tea she was remembering how the previous week how Connie had bidden them to choose a special tune to sing in their heads as a distraction from discomfort during labour (pain was not in Connie's vocabulary), but when later Dave had wanted to know which tune she had chosen Kay couldn't bring herself to tell him. Only to Florrie could she admit the truth.

Comfortably ensconced with a glass of wine in her hand, Florrie's ribald reaction was every bit as Kay had expected.

'You chose what, Kay? You're joking…I don't believe it!'

'I know, I know! But Connie didn't give us time to think,' Kay defended her action. 'I was playing *My Fair Lady* all week and the tune somehow stuck in my head.'

Even yet Kay was wondering if it wasn't too late to change her mind, aware that 'I'm getting married in the morning' was not the thing to be roaring out in the delivery room. Still, as she said to Florrie, it was undeniably catchy and after only one session (as Connie had predicted) it was firmly lodged in her head, and had to be worth anything if it actually succeeded in easing, what she privately dubbed, B-day agony.

Florrie gave a dubious grin, more interested in hearing about the double-jointed Connie and Kay's fellow sufferers-to-be. She chuckled as Kay described the session, making it all sound a lot funnier than it actually was, describing the glamorous but fickle Cassie, who formerly flew with Pan Am and only stayed pally with Kay long enough to extract info about applying to CA for a job once her baby was born.

'Typical!' Florrie exclaimed, sticking out her glass for a top up. 'Don't I just *know* the type. Users! Hope you didn't tell her,' she added, but Kay had, of course.

'So what about Brian?' adroitly Kay changed the subject, aware Florrie was furious her boyfriend had gone on holidays without her, not seeming to see anything illogical about giving him a hard time and then expecting him to dance attendance.

'Oh well, you know me, 'Florrie gave her limpid grin and began waxing lyrical about the importance of double standards for women, ending with her own version of, 'What's sauce for the gander is saucier for the goose.'

Kay chuckled, not taking any of it seriously, knowing how hard Florrie found it to commit to a relationship. She had never really got over her beloved father's death and no man had ever measured up to him since. Soon it was time for her to go.

Walking unsteadily back to her flat Florrie was conscious how more than once during the evening she had been on the point of revealing the incredible news about Captain Pender to Kay but observing her friend's contentment, her absorption in homemaking, she had kept it to herself. After all Kay was married now and soon to have a baby, Florrie reminded herself, the last thing she needed to hear was anything so bizarre. Yeah, more than likely if she *had* come trotting out with it Kay wouldn't have batted an eyelid. That grand passion was in the past and that's where it should stay.

When a day later Dave saw the newspaper headline 'Husband Returns from the Grave' his first impulse was to turn to the financial page, it being rather more to his taste than what he imagined was cheap sensationalism. But on seeing the reference to Celtic Airways he continued on reading and suffered a jolt when he realized that the husband in question was an airline pilot believed to have died in a plane crash some years earlier, and what's more the same pilot that Kay had once been in love with. By some miracle it seemed the man had survived the crash and was alive after all. Deeply discomfited, Dave lowered the newspaper and thought long and hard. Then he deliberately dropped the newspaper into the waste basket. It would only upset Kay, he decided, no point in taking that chance.

Once or twice in the next couple of weeks Kay came close to learning the truth but was so relaxed and uncomprehending each time it somehow passed her by. Hearing her neighbor talking about delays at the airport due to staff pickets in support of some colleague who were 'out foreign' she assumed it had to do with Chicago or New York where CA ground staff were always in the middle of some dispute. Had she been able to stay awake long enough to watch the evening news on television she might have wondered at the reason for the long lines of air hostesses and pilots walking up and down holding placards. But these chilly nights Kay wanted only to get into bed once tea was over, her eyes closing on leaden lids. Downstairs, Dave got in the habit of watching television on his own and knew the uniformed lines could only be to do with the captured pilot. With a sigh, he wondered just how much longer Kay could remain in total ignorance of what was going on.

***

In Colombo better food rations and a slight relaxation of the security surrounding him had been Captain Pender's first indication of some alteration in his situation. He began to entertain the hope by some miracle he might be released after all this time and then just when the edge of his expectation had begun to dull there was a stir in the camp. One night that week when the moon was at its fullest the soldiers came through the gates of the Indigiri camp intent on bringing the boy and himself to a city back street in Colombo. It had been at the time of the *Thai Pongal* harvest festival described by Ranjan as, 'Really big, man, in honour of the Sun God. Parades and dancing. You like it, Captain Tuan. Everyone have pretty good time.' The pilot had pretended an interest, knowing the boy was merely trying to lighten their spirits for he was still deeply grieving over his sister's death. When Ranjan had continued for his sake to be cheerful he had been touched by his consideration and made a special effort to go along with him. On the night in question Ranjan was not in the cell when the guards had awakened Captain Pender as he lay dozing fitfully.

'Put this on,' they told him. 'You go now.'

Graham had shivered with nerves as he accepted the cotton sweater and trousers they gave him and struggled into them, afraid to hope he was being freed at last. He had given one last look around the tiny cell that had been his home for so long but there was nothing to take with him, nothing but memories.

'What about the boy?' he put the question urgently.

'He go too.'

Outside in the compound, Pender looked swiftly about him and was relieved to see Ranjan standing some distance away, the soldiers nearby with their rifles slung on their shoulders. At a word of command, they opened the gates of the stockade. So it was really happening, they were out of here at last, Graham hardly dared to believe it.

'Goodbye, Captain. You walk now - not far.'

60

It was the first time they had given him his title and he nodded stiffly in acknowledgement. With their hands bound in front of them, he and the boy had gone stumbling into the jungle, an armed guard at either side of them; moving some miles along the rutted track to where a van was waiting. Into this, they were bundled, made to lie down and sacks piled on top of them. Some hours later when the van came to a halt, they were blindfolded and taken into a building.

That it was in the city Captain Pender reckoned from the street sounds, and this was later confirmed from what he could glimpse through the partially boarded window, six or seven storeys up from the ground. Each morning the call to prayer booming out from a nearby mosque awoke him and he was brought to fresh awareness of his captive state, shackled by a length of chain to the radiator. That first week in the new place a man in a suit had come and spoken to him, expressing a wish to make a video of him to show on television. With him there had been a man with a camera, he had been completely enveloped in a burka with only his eyes showing, but even so it was apparent from his trembling hands and hoarse voice that he was nervous.

Captain Pender was reluctant to do anything that might compromise his principles, but the thought that his picture might be seen on television and spur the government to obtain his release had decided him. So he spoke the words given to him by the man, merely his name, stating that he was being treated well and strongly advising that the demands of the kidnappers should be met. He was not sure what these might be, and imagined it was money. Following this incident there had been one bright spot, with the miraculous arrival of a letter from his youngest son. When the guard handed him the heavily marked envelope, with the original address of the British embassy struck out and 'By hand' written across it, Graham would never forget his joy and disbelief on discovering it was from Nicky. Reading the boy's emotional outpourings, he was conscious of the wonderful affirmation that somehow it had become known back home that he was alive after all.

Some miles from where Captain Pender and the Tamil boy were being held prisoners, Harinath Prasad listened in concern to his in-

61

formant's report that Sita's brother and the pilot had been moved from the jungle camp to the city, and were now undergoing interrogation at the hands of the terrorists. If only he had got word earlier, he might have intercepted their vehicle on a lonely stretch of road and managed to rescue them before they reached the city. Still, there had to be another way, he mused, aware that before long Sita's brother would be of an age to join forces with them, and how important it was for every able bodied man and woman to support them in their fight for an independent Tamil state. In the few years that the UNP, supported by the Federal Party, had swept to power the situation in his country had fast deteriorated. With each new piece of legislation causing further grievance to his people, the Tamils were steadily losing the battle of human rights and becoming alienated and dispirited. Any protest against the prejudiced government rule was followed by violence and death, from the enforcement of the Sinhala-only law with its choice of Sinhalese as the official language of the country to the rapidly growing emphasis on the all importance of the Buddhist religion, already protected and fostered by the state. There was even talk of the adoption of a new Sinhalese name for the country and Tamils might not have existed for all the notice paid to *their* issues and beliefs. At least now when the time came, Prasad told himself, they would be well armed and equipped to fight, for North Korea had been generous in their provision of guns and ammunition, stoutly pledging their support in the struggle. As for Ranjan Shanti, Prasad was counting on the boy joining the Freedom Fighters like his sister had done before him, aware that the youth would be eager and willing to avenge her death and the deaths of his parents, all of them victims of the ILA. Of this, Harinath Prasad had no doubts for had he not suffered at their hands himself and bore the scars on his body? But the ones branded on his soul, the leader knew, went deeper still, never to be erased. Hatred surging in his veins for that savage lawless group, he got restlessly to his feet and went to stare morosely through the dusty window of the shack.

Time was passing, he thought, soon it would be Tamil New Year.

***

The man in the suit was back, this time Captain Pender saw that he was on his own. His manner was pleasant, almost ingratiating as he offered the pilot coffee and cigarettes, enquiring if Captain Pender had everything he needed.

Graham declined to answer him, he wanted only one thing – his freedom.

It seemed that the video was not clear, the man feared the message would not get across. 'You help me and perhaps I can help you,' he said, handing Graham paper and a pen. 'You will write letter to your government. You will say my name is Graham Pender. I am well but living in very bad and dangerous conditions. Understand that I will not be allowed to go free unless the two prisoners being held in British gaol on the charge of hijacking are released. You must do as they say or my life will be in danger.'

Graham's spirits sank as he wrote down the words, aware how poor his chances were of being released under such conditions. Up until that moment, he had believed he was caught in the crossfire of a racial conflict, with no particular gain for his captors, and now it was all he could do to hold fast to his joy in his son's letter. As an airline pilot, Graham was aware just how severely hijacking was regarded by all on the flight deck. Knowing at last where he stood came as a cruel blow for the British government would be equally impervious to the threats of terrorists. Near to despair, he recalled their proud boast when another country had given into terrorist demands. 'Unlike them we do not crawl at the foot of scum'.

***

Captain Higgins was well pleased with the way the Free Pender campaign was proceeding. With the intervention by the UN much red tape had been cut through, and with their might solidly behind them considerable progress had been made. But that was prior to receiving a copy of the Sinhalese chargé's report forwarded on to him from London. On reading it, Ben realized the situation was not looking good for his imprisoned colleague, the gist of the report being if Britain wanted Ceylon to help in the case of its hostage in Colombo, then Britain would have to release two Moslem terrorists they were holding, pending trial, on the charge of the attempted hijacking of a BEA Rome bound B707 some time previously. From various other sources came the advice that strong pressure would need to be brought to bear on the Ceylonese government in order to speed up Captain Pender's release, for a suspicion was being rumored that the pilot had been involved in gun running and charges could be brought against him, not to mention the suggestion that with Pender's survival the Inquiry into the crash might be reopened. This last convinced Ben of the need to approach the Board of Directors with his proposal to fly out to Colombo and personally negotiate for Pender's release. When he did, the Chief Executive predictably vetoed the expedition and tried to influence the Board to do the same. But Ben took heart from Andy's advice, 'Stand no nonsense from them, Higgins. If they want us to keep their planes in the skies they had better support our pilots.'

Ignoring McGrattan, Ben forged ahead, quoting Amnesty International and the other peace groups who stated that hijacking was too serious a crime for barter, and pointing out that some other method must be found to free Captain Pender.

'Gentlemen,' Ben concluded, 'It is my opinion and the opinion of our own pilots - and in this we are backed by BALPA – we are running out of time.'

For a moment he debated whether or not to pass on some of BALPA's rescue plans structured on the lines of the Trojan Horse, advising them to infiltrate some of their own military pilots under the guise of Pakistani aircrew, but on studying the group's closed expressions he decided to save his breath.

'Should you go to Colombo what do you hope to achieve there, Captain Higgins?' the chairman suddenly shot the question. Eyes down, he waited for a reply.

Ben took a deep breath wishing he knew which argument would carry most weight with the board, then said, 'I feel it's imperative to try and make personal contact with the terrorists via television or the Colombo newspapers, anything to get negotiations underway. It's important that we get a message through to Captain Pender informing him that we are not far away and doing everything in our power to bring about his release.' Seeing no change in the faces about the table Ben's control snapped,

'For God's sake, men!' he desperately appealed to them, 'Whatever about Graham Pender's physical condition, the poor chap's morale must be in sore need of a boost. Why don't we stop asking ourselves *if* we can afford this humanitarian gesture and instead tell ourselves it is our duty to do everything in our power to save him.'

All of a sudden the atmosphere in the room significantly altered and those nearest the chairman put their heads together for a quick confab.

'We are agreed, gentlemen.' The chairman leaned forward to address the pilot. 'Go pack your bag and be on your way, Captain Higgins. Whatever funds you need are at your disposal. And speaking for myself, as well as the Board, may I wish you God speed,' out shot his hand. 'Every success with your mission.'

Ben's face broke into a relieved smile and he reached forward to shake the proffered hand. Not a bad old skin, he thought, and inclined his head towards the others. And not a bad valedictory toast either! He was damn well going to need it!

***

Ben was two days in Colombo before he made contact with an intermediary introduced to him by BALPA's British contact who agreed to set up a meeting with the ILA. The previous day Ben had met the Sinhalese chargé, one of the people on his contact list, and given him to believe that the Irish government was fully backing the exchange of prisoners, feeling it was important for Pender's sake that the message being passed on to the kidnappers was one they wanted to hear. The following evening the intermediary came to collect Ben at his hotel and bring him to his own apartment; from there Ben would be brought to another spot to meet the spokesman for the kidnappers. But although the first half of the plan proceeded smoothly enough Ben was then left waiting at the man's apartment until it grew so late it became unlikely anyone would show. Deeply disappointed, he returned to his hotel. By the evening of the third day the telephone still had not rung nor contact made. Deeply dispirited, Ben wondered if this whole trip to Colombo would turn out to be merely a waste of time, and debated whether or not to ring the airport and book his return flight. Only the thought of the Pender boys eagerly awaiting word of their father and counting on *him* to bring about his rescue, held Ben from making that call.

Restlessly, he paced his hotel bedroom, glancing out every so often, aware of the festive air on the streets. Below his window the crowds dressed in traditional costume and wearing exotic masks shifted and swayed to the by-la music and the banging of drums. Vaguely, Ben remembered reading something about it being the Tamil New Year and was conscious of the sounds of revelry growing louder; obviously some procession was drawing near and must soon pass under his hotel window.

He crossed the room to take a closer look, when all at once the merry sounds died away and the singing and happy laughter changed to cries of terror as the air was filled with the rattle of gunfire and the crump of exploding shells. Startled, he froze. Then, taking the precaution of first turning off the light, he cautiously eased open the slatted blinds and peered down into the street. Outside panic prevailed. Everywhere people were running and screaming. Shaken, Ben let the slats drop shut. Could this be factional warfare and the reason why the ILA had not shown up? He sank down, his brain teeming with questions, and then there was another tremendous explosion, and the chair on which he sat shook violently and the room reverberated with the impact.

Several streets away the explosion was much closer to where Captain Pender was being held, it was followed moments later by the sound of the outer door of the apartment crashing open. Men in battle dress and carrying AK-47's swarmed into the room. One man stepped lithely over Graham and gunned down the guard, and then more armed men entered and he and the boy were released from their chains.

Now that the moment had arrived Graham was possessed by a strange hesitancy, fear almost, and only for the responsibility he felt towards the boy he could not have maintained his outer calm as they were hustled down the back stairs.

'Who are these men, Ranjan,?' he asked urgently, stunned by the speed of what was happening. 'Where are they taking us?'

'Captain Tuan, don't you see?' Ranjan turned a joyful countenance on him. 'My friend Hari has come to help us. We are free at last.'

Slumped in the back of the speeding car, the jeep following close behind carrying the jubilant members of the assault team, Graham's thoughts and emotions were in turmoil. He was only dimly aware of the whispered conversation taking place between the Tamil leader and the boy, but he could well understand the leader's triumph and that of his men in the success of the attack. Eventually, Graham became aware of the man speaking to him and it took him a moment to understand what Prasad was saying, and he realized they were on their way to a place where eventually he would be handed over to his own people.

'But first understand we must get far away from the city.'

Vaguely, Graham remembered this man from the night of the raid on the Indigiri camp, when the leader had shown him little friendship or sympathy. The pilot had better understood his attitude when Ranjan had later told him of Harinath's great love for his dead sister and she for him, and how the leader believed it was the Captain Tuan who had betrayed her to the ILA. Well, whatever had caused Prasad's change of heart, Captain Pender knew that he was deeply in this man's debt. Yet despite his obligation to him, Graham instinctively mistrusted Prasad, some gut feeling telling him he was a ruthless and dangerous man. It was only afterwards he recalled Ranjan having once told him that the warlike man he called his friend went by the alias of Aziza Khan and few knew his true identity. With a shudder, the pilot acknowledged that he would not feel safe until he was boarding a plane for his own country, only then could he look forward to the reunion with his family and the woman he loved.

In the darkened hotel bedroom Captain Higgins was jerked awake by the shrill ringing of the telephone. Struggling up, he fumbled about for the receiver and put it to his ear. The voice he heard was faintly accented and only a few words were spoken.

'Pender has been freed,' the voice said. 'Do not try and make contact again.'

'Who is this?' Ben demanded, but the phone went dead. He dropped the receiver back on the cradle and light blinded him as he hit the ceiling switch by mistake. Shielding his eyes, he found the bedside switch and cancelled the other.

Incredibly Graham Pender was free, actually free! Ben felt unable to take it in. Could the ILA have let him go? It was the last thing he would have expected.

Seeing from his watch it was after twelve, Ben was reminded of the all-night Embassy help line, and dialled the special number given to him by his British contact.

'Something has come up,' Captain Higgins told the impersonal voice at the other end, and exercising caution he merely requested that the ambassador's secretary get in touch with him first thing in the morning.

***

Leaning on the Tamil boy's arm, Captain Pender slowly climbed the steps to the RAF VC-10 and was greeted by a rousing cheer as he stepped aboard the aircraft. He felt a rush of emotion as he raised his hand in acknowledgement, before sinking down and turning to help the boy with his seatbelt. Ranjan submitted to Captain Pender's ministrations looking about him with wide-eyed amazement, he had never been aboard a plane before. Indeed until recently, he had never travelled more than a few miles beyond his village. Graham was very conscious of this as he pointed out the safety exits and tried to prepare the boy for the noise of take-off, when the roar of the jet's engines would sound like thunder in his ears. There seemed to be a lot of people travelling with them, between two full flight crews and medical personnel and various members of the diplomatic corps. Before boarding, Graham had granted his first press conference to an excited press corps in a foreign capital, speaking about his role as plane crash survivor and hostage of the ILA. They had taken pictures and put questions to him, making him glad he had asked Ben Higgins to keep the boy out of sight until they were about to board the plane. It would be impossible to keep Ranjan's presence secret for long, Graham knew, but he hoped to shield him from the press as long as he could.

On looking back, Graham could not get over how quickly it had all gone in the end, the manner in which he and the boy had been so dramatically rescued by the Tamil Freedom Fighters. There had been a car, a change of car and one night in the suburbs of Colombo, before being driven to the British Embassy early next morning. Having complied with Prasad's terse instruction to get out of the car, Graham stood with the boy waiting to be admitted to the embassy and watched the vehicle drive rapidly away. Once admitted, they followed the uniformed attendant and waited in a room off the hallway while the ambassador was summoned

'How do you do, Captain Pender.' The smiling blue-eyed man had come forward and warmly shaken the pilot's hand, before saying, 'Someone to see you,' and there at his shoulder stood Captain Higgins.

Ben smiled and shook hands with Graham saying, 'Good to see you alive and well, Pender,' before introducing him to another pilot, Lieut. Colonel Williamson who had flown out from RAF Lyneham, and then to some other RAF officers standing along with members of the medical team and the Red Cross.

Graham had returned their greetings, conscious of his disheveled appearance, his unkempt beard and the loose fitting sweatshirt and baggy trousers that Prasad had given him to replace the singlet and shorts he had been wearing when rescued. Going with them into another room he had sat down at a table with the Foreign Minister and the Sinhalese chargé. Pleasantries were exchanged and during the translation of these Graham had taken the opportunity to turn to Ben Higgins and say, 'I know from Nicky's letter that Sile has married again but tell me how are my sons?'

'They are fine, and very excited about coming to meet you at Lyneham. You'll be able to spend a few days with them once you get to Dublin. Arrangements have been made.' Ben smiled. 'Believe me, they can't wait to be with you.'

Graham nodded, before saying diffidently, 'If I might have a shave and a trim beforehand. Don't want to shock 'em any more than I have to,' and Ben had laughed understandingly. 'Of course, just as soon as we finish here. They have set a room aside for you to freshen up before we go to the airport.'

Gazing out the window at the clouds massed in snowy peaks below the aircraft, Captain Pender tried to imagine how it would be when he saw his sons again, and how they would feel about Ranjan. He leaned back against the headrest and, closing his eyes, thought back to the moment when it had occurred to him the boy might return with him to Ireland. They had been sitting in the stone dwelling Prasad had brought them to and the man was asking him questions about the Indigiri camp and, with regard to his more recent detention in the city, the number and strength of the guards. Graham had answered to the best of his ability and then Prasad had turned to the boy and spoken to him in Tamil for some time. At one stage the discussion had become heated and Ranjan had got up and walked across the room, turning his back upon the leader. It was only then that Graham had got some indication that he might be the cause of their disagreement, for it seemed the boy was refusing to be parted from him, the Captain Tuan.

Graham was startled at first but he began to understand the situation better when he thought back over their four years of captivity and their growing dependence upon on each other for survival. With his sister's death the last link with Ranjan's family had been severed and, not surprisingly, the boy looked now upon him as his closest relative. The pilot felt deeply moved, responsible too for the lad, and in that moment knew he must bring him back with him to Ireland. It seemed the very natural outcome of all that had gone before. It was evident this came as a blow to the Tamil leader, but no matter how many times Captain Pender weighted it all up in his mind it always came down to the same thing, his duty to the boy took precedence over all other considerations. And so it was finally agreed that he would make application for a temporary visa in order to bring Ranjan back with him, and he had stood silently by that morning as the leader and the boy made their farewells.

'Do not forget me,' he heard the leader telling him. 'Nor the plight of our people. Give me your promise you will return to your homeland when you come of age.'

'I will not forget,' Ranjan assured him. 'And do not fear for I will return.' At which, Harinath had pressed his shoulder hard saying, '*Namasta!*' and Ranjan replied in a choked voice, '*Bhi visitu,*' placing the leader also in the protection of the gods.

This much of the Tamil language Graham knew from his time in captivity, and despite his mistrust of the leader, he acknowledged that Prasad was deeply attached to the boy and appeared genuinely grieved over parting from him. Well, he would keep his part of the bargain, he told himself, and in the meantime if he were granted custody of the boy he would raise Ranjan like one of his own family. With that decision, he dropped into a doze, exhausted by the events of the past twenty-four hours.

Frowning, Captain Higgins glanced across the aisle to where Graham sat slumped in sleep, with the boy sitting upright and wide-eyed in the seat beside him. Ben was struck by how pitifully frail Pender looked, he couldn't have lasted much longer in captivity. What he found hardest to accept was the white hair; he had been prepared for a certain amount of physical deterioration but undeniably the hair had been a shock. He told himself that this hollow-eyed, prematurely-aged man bore no relation to the vigorous pilot he had known, remembering Pender's dark arresting good looks and no trace of silver in his hair. Only when he lifted his head and spoke in his cultured voice was it possible to get a glimpse of the charm and charisma of the man he had been.

Ben sighed and turned away, his pity tinged with frustration. Why in God's name was he compounding the situation by bringing this Indian boy back home with him? he asked himself. It defied all reason and was bound to cause talk!

***

At RAF Lyneham Captains Pete Kenny and Andy Hegarty strolled around the airbase with the station commander, Group Captain Tony Shelley. The CO was describing the day-to-day flying duties at the base and Andy, with his empty pipe clenched between his teeth, shooting pertinent questions. Although earlier Pete had exhibited a show of interest himself he was no longer listening. Instead, he was wondering if he had been right not to inform Judy Mathews that Graham was actually on his way home from Colombo at last. While very much taken with the notion of Judy accompanying them to Lyneham that day, Pete had in the interests of preserving his marriage summoned up strength from somewhere to deny himself the pleasure. At the same time he entertained a certain anxiety at the thought of her wrath when she discovered that she had been excluded from the welcome party. Sile Conway, on the other hand, had been invited to join them but firmly declined the opportunity

'My boys are flying out to meet their father,' she'd said haughtily. 'Surely that's enough?'

For some people it might be, Pete conceded, but to his mind any kind of woman would surely have made the journey that day, if only for old times' sake.

Across the ramp Nicholas Pender was also watching the sky, convinced he would pass away from sheer excitement if his father's plane did not soon appear. Screwing up his eyes, he peered steadily upwards, anxious to catch the first glimpse of the VC-10 as it broke cloud with its precious cargo on board.

Nearby, Jeremy was going through his own brand of nervous excitement but he was better at concealing his feelings than his younger brother, and affected nonchalance as he walked about the air base with the young Second Lieutenant, detailed to take the Penders under his wing, and putting fairly intelligent questions (or so he hoped) about the performance and capabilities of the different types of aircraft. But for all his outward show Jeremy's mind was restlessly wandering back over the weeks leading up to this auspicious day, and especially his involvement in the Save Pender campaign. He had got a real kick out of being able to do something practical to help his father. Along with his schoolmates, he had raised quite a respectable amount of money and had a lot of fun besides, pushing the mockup of an aircraft all the way to Cork. They had been interviewed for the newspapers and the journalist had asked him, 'Do you think you'll be going out to Colombo to meet your Dad when he's a free man?'

Jeremy had no notion of it but he nodded and said, 'Sure, I might do that,' delighted when the newsman had snapped him holding his father's picture.

Now the young RAF officer was observing how temperamentally different the two brothers were. 'Want to see the inside of the cockpit then, Jeremy?' he asked with a grin, and saw the indecision in the lad's eyes. Afraid he'll miss the first sight of his Dad's plane coming through the clouds, he correctly guessed. 'Flight's not due for another few minutes,' he reassured him, and Jeremy gladly climbed aboard.

'Wow!' Easing back the stick and imagining he was about to take off, Jeremy suddenly caught sight of his brother pointing madly at the sky.

'Dad's here!' Nicholas shrieked, and Jeremy scrambled down again and ran to join him. With the embarrassed young airman following the boys tore across the ramp.

By the time the VC-10 had touched down and raced forward engines screaming, both brothers were standing eagerly to attention with the rest of the welcome committee. They watched as the steps were pushed against the side of the aircraft and the engineer ran up them and unlocked the forward door. Almost immediately some figures appeared and hovered in the doorway, and the CO stepped forward to shake their hands, while beside the brothers the camera men began taking pictures.

With fast beating heart, Nicholas kept his eyes trained on the aircraft door, eager for his first sight of his father. He experienced painful feelings of letdown as the first passenger to disembark, an elderly white-haired man, moved slowly down the steps leaning on a walking stick. After him came a brown-skinned boy, whom Nicholas judged to be about his own age, and then Captain Higgins appeared and Nicholas's heart lifted knowing that Ben would not have lied about anything of such importance.

But where was his father? Nicholas wondered anxiously. Surely he should have been the first one off the plane? Even as he was thinking this, he felt a gentle thump between his shoulder blades and turning, he saw the way his brother was staring at the white-haired man. And then Jeremy ran towards him and the man embraced him, before looking across at himself and calling hoarsely, 'Nicky... Nicky, my boy.'

At the sound of his father's beloved voice Nicholas felt a catch in his throat and his eyes filled with tears, and then he was running forward too, and his joy knew no bounds when his father's arms closed strongly about him.

***

Dave shoved a pile of papers into the top drawer of his desk and turned the key. Nothing that couldn't wait until tomorrow, he decided, relieved everything had gone so well, the baby's birth and Sinead's baptism which had taken place that morning from the hospital. He had been anxious to get it over with before Kay went home, knowing how busy she would be with looking after the new baby. Well, to be honest he didn't know a lot about it, Dave admitted, but so everyone had advised him; saying not to expect too much sleep in the first weeks, how he and Kay would be up nights with the new baby. So far she had been really good, he thought, feeding well and as far as he knew sleeping well too. Oh well, it was all before them.

Shrugging on his jacket, Dave murmured the names they had chosen for their little daughter. Sinead Margaret Anne. A lot of names for such a small scrap, he mused, but he had taken into consideration Kay's preference as well as family obligations. Of course, the baby's first name had no connection with either family, he reminded himself, but he and Kay had both liked it. Margaret for Kay's aunt, not that Molly cared about such things, he thought, seeing the way she had pulled a face at the thought of her grandniece being saddled with the nicknames of her youth - Mad Moll and Hairy Molly - and he had chuckled at her lugubrious expression. Thankfully, his sister Breda hadn't expected her godchild to be named after herself, though Dave wasn't so sure about his mother; Eileen had been dropping heavy hints for weeks. Oh well, that was another thing they could expect, doting grandparents although Dave couldn't see Reggie being all that interested. Thinking of his father, he frowned. Reggie was getting worse, two benders already that month. His mother refused to talk about it but then she was always in denial. To painful to face up to, Dave supposed, and tried to recapture his earlier joy.

He was on the point of leaving when his boss stuck his head into the room. 'Heading off? Good man!' Tony said jovially. 'Give Kay my regards.'

'Will do,' Dave told him. 'By the way she sends her thanks for the flowers,' adding with a rueful grin. 'They put mine in the shade.'

'Nothing but the best,' Tony swaggered, he had a weakness for air hostesses.

'Better not have you over too often then,' Dave joked, aware of his boss's reputation with women. Not that he felt any real concern knowing that Tony didn't appeal to Kay. Too obvious, she had written him off.

Recalling how in Celtic Airways Kay had been exposed all the time to charming, handsome men, whether passengers or pilots, Dave was in danger of denial himself as he turned his mind away from the past with its unsettling connotations. It was another subject he didn't wish to dwell on, certainly not on this special day when he had held his child in his arms and seen how well Sinead had endured the ritual of baptism. Not even a whimper, he thought, well pleased. In his euphoria he could almost have credited it to the excellence of her Mason genes. Seeing the pitfall, he laughed. He had never been interested in children and here he was, only days into parenthood, becoming maudlin.

With both families long gone from her hospital room and the place restored to order, Kay relaxed on the banked-up pillows glad to have some time to herself before the baby's next feed, still on a high after the birth and all the emotion of the Christening. What a relief it had been to see her aunt fully recovered from bronchitis and so merry and fond, Kay mused, the only living relative who had ever meant anything to her.

'D'ye know, Kay, that doty baby of yours is the image of your poor dear mother,' Molly had said fondly. 'She has the same high brow and determined chin. Oh, it's Evelyn to the life. You'd swear you were looking at her. Ah, but you can take it from me that little one is going to be another beauty just like yourself. She'll have the lads around her in droves, you wait and see.'

Kay had laughed and hugged her aunt, pleased to think Sinead resembled her maternal grandmother and not that other awkward lady, bossily taking over and acting as though she were the child's godmother and not Breda, who hardly got a look in.

Still, the whole thing had passed off well enough, even her cousin Winifred behaved herself. And then, Kay fell to thinking back over her contentment in the months leading up to the birth. And still further back to the tragic circumstances that decided her to marry Dave Mason, as some of her less charitable colleagues had suggested, on the rebound. That they might have been right was not something Kay had ever admitted, not even in her thoughts. But now in the highly charged atmosphere following the ordeal of giving birth and becoming a mother for the first time, she honestly acknowledged to herself that the marriage would not otherwise have taken place. Oh, but just look at us now, she quickly amended, who would have ever believed it could have all turned out so well.

By the third evening back home with the baby Kay couldn't have said she was getting used to round-the-clock feeding and nappy-changing, but at least she had become organized enough to mix two bottles of formula at a time, and so keep ahead of the posse. She would never forget that first evening as she rushed about trying to get everything done, nervously tackling the baby's bath, terrified she would drop her. It had been nine o'clock by the time they had sat down to eat, and what seemed only like minutes Kay had found herself having to feed Sinead again. When her head had finally hit the pillow she was deep in sleep when she heard that thin, newborn mewling cry once more and, struggling up to heat the bottle, told herself she would never take nights of uninterrupted sleep for granted again.

At least this evening, Kay congratulated herself, the meal was already in the oven – chicken casserole and roast potatoes – and so she felt under no pressure as she finished bathing Sinead and carried her snug and fresh in her pink baby-grow into the sitting room. Sinking down on to the couch, Kay prepared to relax and watch the evening news while she fed her. Turning on the television, she wondered if Florrie might drop in later for a chat remembering how she had been unable to hide her amusement when Kay spoke in awe of the wonder of being a mother.

'Okay, 'Flo, 'Kay cut her raptures short, 'I suppose you think I'm crazy?'

'No, just half gone in the head,' Florrie had grinned tolerantly. 'I must say you look terrific and you don't seem to have put on any extra weight. You'll be able to get straight back into your own clothes again.'

Shifting the baby into a more comfortable position, Kay angled the bottle and began watching the screen while Sinead sucked steadily away. Beaches and palm trees and then a band of foreign soldiers appeared on screen, arrayed in full battle dress, rifles held high. They looked a brutal lot, Kay thought with a shudder. Most of them were black or very dark-skinned and the voice-over described them as a group of mercenaries who, earlier in the week, had bombed a bus in Colombo.

Absently, she jogged the dozing baby thinking Colombo had a familiar sound to it, but not at first making the link with the plane crash in which her former lover had died. Not straightaway. And then she caught her breath in sheer disbelief as the photograph of a dark-haired smiling man filled the screen, and her heart almost stopped as she realized that she had not only known this man, she had once *loved* this man.

Kay gripped her baby so tightly in the shock of the moment that Sinead awoke in fright and began to cry. Frantically, she tried to hush her, leaning forward in her seat, desperate to hear what was being said but only managing to catch the last few words and unable to make sense of any of it. In effect, it seemed, the pilot until recently had been believed dead. Amazingly, it had turned out he was being held hostage by terrorists all this time and finally been released that week as a result of the tireless efforts on his behalf by some group calling itself the FOGP. More pictures followed and to Kay's bewilderment the Hostess Superintendent appeared on the screen, it seemed Judy Mathews had in some way been involved, and this was followed by a boy standing on a float holding a picture of the pilot, whom the voice-over identified as a son of the rescued pilot. Kay felt as though she had been sandbagged. Fragments of conversation overheard over the months came together like pieces of a puzzle, the women on the bus, the man at the Christmas party, even the babbling of her neighbour about 'some man out foreign' making sense to her now.

She wondered at her ignorance and began to cry. Tears poured down her face and fell on the baby's blanket. She thought her heart would break all over again and in her present highly sensitive emotional state following the baby's birth, she was devastated by the knowledge that Captain Graham Pender was actually alive and how much he must have suffered; it was too horrendous to contemplate.

'I'm home,' Dave called. She heard him through a fog of distress as if from a long way off. 'How are my girls?' His bantering tone died in his throat. 'Hey, what's up?' he asked in consternation. 'Is it the baby?' only partly reassured on seeing her safe in Kay's arms. As he soothed the whimpering child, Kay continued to cry brokenly.

'What is it?' Dave kept asking, 'Tell me, Katie.'

He began to be alarmed and then downright frightened at the depth and hopelessness of his wife's distress. He was just about to ring their doctor for advice when suddenly he sighed and relaxed. Of course! It was what his secretary had only that day referred to as the dreaded 'baby blues' and from all she had said it afflicted quite a lot of new mothers. Dave felt almost cheerful as he brought a still weeping Kay up the stairs and helped her slip off her shoes and lie on the bed.

'Don't worry,' he murmured, drawing up the quilt. 'Yes, I'll give Sinead the rest of her bottle and change her nappy. You lie there. You don't have anything to worry about. I'll see to it all.'

With a last murmured word of comfort, he left her in the darkened room and Kay turned her face desolately into the pillow, her mind full of heartbreaking images, most of all the memory of Graham's last letter to her before boarding the fateful flight.

'My dearest, I think I loved you from the first moment of setting eyes on you, only in my blindness I refused to see it. Whatever the future holds, I will gladly face it so long as you are with me.'

Kay realized how all along she had been living a lie and the bitterest of betrayals was her marriage to Dave. She could only mourn how ready she had been to forget Graham, how quick to settle for less, and was stricken to the heart by the vision of what she might have had if only she had waited.

Burdened by regret, Kay lived through her days in a blur of misery and depression. If the fates had conspired to ensure she would miss all the earlier publicity surrounding Captain Pender's amazing survival, they now saw to it she was privy to every dramatic moment of his triumphant return. There was not a newsflash she missed of the white-haired man slowly descending the aircraft steps at RAF Lyneham or visual replay of his touching reunion with his family and former colleagues. Nor did she miss the aerial view of the RAF VC-10 being escorted into England by fighter jets or later the Celtic Airways Boeing with Captain Pender on board entering Irish airspace at which time four Irish Air Corps Fouga jets took over from the British jet fighters and escorted the pilot the rest of the way home. Several times each day some aspect of the pilot's return was relayed on the screen and lively discussions took place between the hosts of various chat shows, all agreeing his survival was nothing short of miraculous.

For the second time in four years, Kay relived intense feelings of sorrow and regret, bitterly she mourned those lost years and was consumed with longing to see him again. Existing on scraps of information fed to the public via the media and television, she learned the Irish nation had been so moved by his story that an incredible amount of new friends and well-wishers had sprung up all over the country strongly petitioning the government for his release. She was awed at the huge numbers involved, and to think she had not even been aware of his plight, she felt cut to the heart. So often during their relationship she had hungered for the personal details of his life, the names and ages of his children, what their interests might be, and if not wholly desirous of hearing overmuch about the pilot's glamorous wife she had at least craved the reassurance that Sile Pender was no longer her rival to Graham's affections. About the pilot himself Kay had early on accepted she could never know enough. In this regard she no longer had cause for complaint for Captain Pender was not only discussed in depth at every opportunity on television and radio but his family and close friends interviewed, photographed and generally asked to bare their souls before the cameras.

'What did you feel when you learned that he wasn't dead after all?' was the most commonly asked question.

During such sessions Kay came to know more about the emotional and mental workings of Sile Conway's mind than seemed decent for it appeared the woman had married again and her only emotion when learning of her former husband's return was her oft repeated concern that she might find herself charged with bigamy. Studying the various emotions passing over Sile's delicate features Kay found herself caught up in the drama, determined not to miss any of it. Indeed, the whole thing was taking on an air of unreality. She spent so much time in front of the television that she was in danger of neglecting Sinead. Sometimes Kay imagined that she was the one being interviewed and found herself mouthing replies, pleading ignorance of the tragic situation. She became so confused that she thought she must be guilty of bigamy too, before realizing that unlike Sile she had not actually been married to Graham. It became increasingly difficult to differentiate between dreams and reality and Kay grew nervy and tearful, angry too, if her husband tried to insist that she had watched long enough. Until unable to reason with her anymore, he ripped the television plug right out of the socket causing a short circuit. Chaos ensued, sobbing wife, screaming baby and the evening ended once more with him leading her upstairs to bed – not knowing what else to do with her and came away from the darkened bedroom resigned to yet another evening looking after the baby.

Dave tried not to show his anxiety but he was convinced that Kay was heading for a nervous breakdown. He took to regarding her with a slightly apprehensive air, constantly beginning sentences and never finishing them, afraid the wrong words would set her off again. On retiring each night it was like sleeping with a stranger, the affronted look Kay turned upon him when he caressed her or indicated they might make love made him feel like he had somehow stumbled into the wrong bed. He never ceased to regret not telling her about the pilot when she might have been better able to cope with it, but coming in her emotional postnatal state it had totally unhinged her.

At work Dave and his boss were in the midst of merging with another clothing manufacturer and Dave could not afford to take off time from work. He considered asking his mother for help but soon realized she would first need to set aside her prejudices before agreeing to come to the aid of her daughter-in-law. Eileen did make the offer, however, to mind her granddaughter in her own house a few days each week, and this he gladly accepted. In the office, once the situation was known, there was a general air of sympathy and interest. Dave's secretary, having been through it all with her own sister, was very understanding and one of the marketing managers from the new firm approached him one morning to say, 'So sorry to hear about your wife, Dave. If I can help at all in any way please let me know.'

Dave was struck both by the offer and how pretty she was. 'Thanks, Anne. That's really kind of you,' he told her, glad she had not attempted to trivialize the problem.

Of course, they had no idea that Kay's breakdown was mainly due to the shock of her dead lover's return and Dave saw no reason to enlighten them. There was enough gossip circulating as it was.

***

For the returned hostage his first few months back home were not easy either. Home, Captain Pender often thought with weary cynicism, if only it really were! Oh, not that he wasn't grateful for a place to stay and for his former mother-in-law's generosity in providing it. But in no way was Nonie's house like the home Graham had known for years, the spacious property in Blackrock to which he had been so attached, and the thought of which had helped to sustain him in captivity. To lose that house had been a real blow. What made it even more difficult to accept was the fact that Sile had only very recently put it up for sale. If only she could have hung on a bit longer, he thought regretfully, what a difference it would have made, when all else was lost to him.

His sons were the one bright spot in his life and the few days they shared following his return to Ireland were the lifeline he needed. They were at first shy of him but rapidly gained confidence as he sought to get to know them again and fill in the gaps when believing him dead. The four of them were accommodated in the private suite attached to the tropical medicines wing of the hospital and given every chance to be alone without interruptions from the staff. Only when it was absolutely necessary or Graham needed his medication did they ever intrude upon their privacy. Graham and Ranjan shared one twin-bedded room and Jeremy and Nicholas occupied the other, and they all ate together in the staff dining-room. Although aware of a certain amount of puzzlement and jealousy on the part of his sons at this arrangement Graham felt it was imperative that he keep the Hindu boy close to him during this time, aware how lost and confused Ranjan was feeling while struggling to understand the language and customs in a strange country far away from his homeland. It helped that in their suite there was a comfortable sitting-room with twin couches and a television set which they watched together in the evening after a day spent walking and talking. Graham did his best to answer all their questions making light of his own sufferings, feeling there was no need for them to know about any of that. Instead he focused on the positive, assuring them that his love for them had never wavered or his belief in his rescue, even at the worst period of his isolation and loneliness.

Graham was conscious of great joy to be reunited with his boys again after years of deprivation. He had not been too bothered by his wife's marriage, philosophically accepting that period of his life was ended. What concerned him most was the present whereabouts of the young woman he had loved all this time, she had been his chief reason to go on living during the darkest hours of his imprisonment.

Constantly, he wondered where she could be, if she was even aware that he was alive? He put these questions to himself in a fever of impatience, every nerve straining towards the moment they could be together again. In the meantime, he rejoiced in the company of his sons; putting aside all thoughts of her while with them and entering fully into the joy of their reunion. In turn, they told him of their own sadness in believing him dead, the subsequent disruption to their young lives when their mother married Tom Conway and sold their family home. Graham could well picture Conway's irritability when foisted with another man's children and the resulting turmoil in his household, with his own brood already suffering from parental break up. On hearing of Captain Higgins's many kindnesses to his sons and perceiving the esteem in which Nicholas held the pilot, Graham's gratitude was mixed with pain, and even a kind of jealousy that Ben had been the one to take his place during their formative years. On observing their animosity towards Ranjan, their deep-rooted aversion to the thought of the Hindu boy joining their family, he quite understood their reluctance to share him with anyone, and in particular a foreign boy who didn't speak their language. At the same time, he felt sure once they got to know him better they would happily accept him as their brother. In this Captain Pender was guilty of wishful thinking and it accounted for much of his optimism. Not something Nicholas shared; he could not even begin to understand why his father would *want* to foist the Indian boy on them and was horribly jealous of the fact that Ranjan was allowed to share his father's room. When the pair of them spoke together in the strange language called Tamil, he felt totally shut out.

His father's wish that he and his brother make friends with Ranjan filled Jeremy with angry dismay. He told himself there was no way would he ever accept Ranjan as part of their family and knew Nicholas felt the same. Even when Captain Pender took them aside and tried to change their thinking, the brothers clung to their aversion.

For the Indian boy his life since arriving in the Captain Tuan's country had been a bewildering jumble of new and sometimes frightening impressions. Coming as he did from a very different background and culture, he needed more than merely time to make the necessary adjustments. Compared to the Captain Tuan's sons, he felt clumsy and stupid and was convinced he must be trying the patience of everyone around him. Although the two boys were not actively unkind to him he could sense their perplexity and, at times, hostility, when it became a question of who would sit closest to their father or be the one to help him over uneven ground during their walks in the open. Because of the injury to his leg that had never healed the pilot found it hard going and was often in a lot of pain. The last thing Ranjan wanted was to further aggravate the situation and so each evening after the meal, he got in the habit of sitting a little way off, knowing it would not be long before they sons returned to their own room to sleep. But even then the Captain Tuan would insist he draw closer, and when he did the brothers would get that brooding look again and all his earlier efforts went in vain. It was only when they all left the hospital, the boys to return to their stepfather's house and he and the Captain Tuan to take up the old auntie's generous offer and move into her house that Ranjan felt the strain easing.

Nonie was invariably kind to him and very fond of the pilot so Ranjan settled down happily enough in her house near the mountains. Indeed, the more Nonie thought about her former son-in-law's situation the greater her sympathy and compassion for him grew. If what the TV presenter had said on his chat show was to be believed, she told herself, then all Captain Pender's worldly goods were now the property of her avaricious daughter, and it was more than likely the poor man would find himself embracing an existence even more austere than the one he had so recently escaped. It was what had encouraged the tender-hearted Nonie to offer her home to Graham for as long as he wished to stay including, of course, the charming little Indian boy whom he appeared to have adopted.

In those early months Graham had other issues troubling him apart from his poor state of health and the rivalry between his sons and the Hindu boy. The phantoms that had once haunted him in solitary confinement returned in force to plague him. Tormented by his inability to sleep for longer than an hour or two at any time, Graham often thought he would give any amount of money for an unbroken night's rest. And yet, even if he were to sleep for weeks he knew that he would never be anything but bone-weary, never ever succeed in catching up on all the life and love he had missed out on during his captive years.

'Such feelings are not unusual,' the doctor told him. 'You must give yourself more time. I'll prescribe something to help you relax. Try not to worry.'

But Graham had a lot of things to worry about, his penniless state, the fact his former wife had never been to see him once since his return and the way she was withholding his sons from him, after the initial period she would not allow them near him in weeks. Only for his awareness of the dangers of slipping into trance-like states he might have taken the pills and let go of reality. He wished that he was well enough to go back to work in any capacity, but most of all he yearned to fly again.

'I'm afraid you have a long way to go before you'll be fit to take up flying again, Captain Pender,' the medics told him. 'First we'll need to operate on that leg of yours and get it right.' The RAF surgeon had already intimated as much to Graham, and so he resigned himself to surgery followed by a fairly lengthy convalescence, otherwise he could not hope to walk normally again.

It seemed there was a succession of tests to be carried out first. Because of the high incidence of arsenic found in hostages held for any length of time, the doctors had taken nail-clippings and some samples of Graham's hair for testing. As they suspected, the results showed that his arsenic levels were ten times higher than normal and they put it down to empty paint tins, the contaminated containers used to hold the prisoners' food. And when they took X-rays of his leg it showed fragments of metal imbedded in his flesh, no doubt the result of injuries sustained in the plane crash, the primitive and inadequate application of splints resulting in the bones knitting crookedly.

Following tests his surgeon told him, 'I'm afraid we may have to break the bone and reset it.'

'Just get on with it, please,' Graham told him tersely. 'I need to get home to my family,' concerned as to how Nonie was coping with Ranjan in his absence.

Graham did not look forward to the surgery on his leg knowing it would be extremely painful and slow to mend but he wished to get it over him. But to his dismay there was another delay before he could go under the knife, it had, something, the doctor told him, to do with his blood levels. He was relieved when Ben Higgins offered to take Ranjan to stay in his house while he was in hospital which promised to be a lengthy stay. He knew that Ben and Linda would look after the Hindu boy like he was one of their own, and their sons would keep Ranjan company and help him learn English.

It was much later, while Graham was in the post-operative stage recovering from the trauma and pain of surgery, that Judy Mathews paid him a visit and gave him the information he sought about Kay, but it was not at all what he had hoped to hear.

Stooping to kiss him Judy murmured, 'Dear Graham, how good it is to see you free at last,' and Graham was reminded of all Ben and Pete had told him of her tireless efforts on his behalf. 'If you only knew how many times I envisaged this day, my dear, how many times I wondered if I would ever see you again,' her voice unsteady, her violet eyes misting with tears.

Graham's own voice shook as he told her, 'Ah Judy, what a friend you have proved yourself to be. Ben told me how you never gave up belief in my rescue.'

All the time they talked the question he burned to ask was at the forefront of his mind, and yet he experienced a certain courteous reluctance in the presence of one woman to rush too soon into queries about another. Until at last he got an opening.

'These days I'm working overtime to get a better deal for my air hostesses, 'Judy was telling him, 'But typical of McGrattan he keeps shooting me down.'

Graham nodded, thinking how passionate Judy was about her job. 'Well, if I know you, Judy, you'll get around him,' he told her, and she flashed a smile.

'I'd like to think so!'

'Talking of your air hostesses whatever happened to Kitty Martin. I often wondered?' he tried hard to keep his voice casual but, despite himself, it shook.

Judy glanced at him. 'Well, you couldn't know, of course. She's married now …very happily so I'm told. She had a baby daughter recently.'

'Married?' Graham's thoughts blurred and his breathing became stressed. Dear God! Oh dear God! She was lost to him.

It was the one thing he had not prepared himself to hear. His heart plummeted and his face drained of colour, so that Judy leaned forward in alarm.

'Graham! Are you all right? Would you like me to call the nurse?'

'No, no. I'm fine…just a bit tired.' Desolately, he turned his face away, his heart still thudding from shock. After a moment he told her in a tone devoid of all emotion. 'Thank you for coming, Judy, I'd like to sleep now.'

At once she got up. 'I've stayed too long,' she said contritely, gazing helplessly at his drawn face beneath the snow white hair, something she knew she would never get used to. 'Try and get some rest. I'll come another time. Goodbye, my dear,' and dropping a kiss on his brow, she left.

Graham waited until he heard the door click shut behind her, only then did he draw in a deep quivering breath and gradually the tumult in his chest eased. Married, he thought in despair. Married! He was aware how naive it was but somehow he had never envisaged that. In his thoughts he had preserved her exactly as she had been, and he had clung to the image during the difficult times and been sustained by it. Only now the terrible grief he was experiencing threatened to destroy him.

Three weeks later he was discharged from hospital. Back in Nonie's house convalescing, it was another fortnight before his former wife contacted him. She told him she would bring the boys to visit him at the weekend. Ben called over early that same Sunday afternoon. He knew the score. How for weeks Sile had ignored all urgent communications from Graham's solicitor expressing the need to discuss his client's finances, or rather the lack of them.

Nonie showed her daughter into the room where the men were sitting and Sile briefly touched cheeks with Graham, her smile fading at the sight of his white hair.

'How are you, Graham?' she asked doubtfully, and sat down.

That was a good question, Graham mused, as his sons came to hug him. Well, all things considering he was not too bad, he supposed. The operation had been successful and there was no reason why with the help of a good physiotherapist he shouldn't be walking without a stick before long. This hopeful prognosis, more than anything else, had helped to restore Graham's mental balance, and although sorrow continued to gnaw at his heart over the loss of Kay, he knew for the sake of his family, as well as himself, the sensible thing to do would be to set aside all thoughts of her and get on with his life. But whether or not he could bring himself to do so was another matter. As regards this afternoon's meeting for all that Sile pretended otherwise this was no social get-together. It was crucial they reached some kind of financial settlement, he could not live forever on Nonie's bounty.

Waiting only long enough for the introductory chit-chat to cease, Graham reached determinedly for his stick and struggled to his feet, thinking it was time for the parleying to begin. 'Will you excuse us please, Nonie...Ben! We'll make up for lost time later, lads,' he told his sons. 'Just a few things your mother and I need to discuss first. After you, Sile,' and she had no course but to get up and go with him.

'Now I *know* what you are going to say,' she forestalled him as soon as they were seated in the privacy of Nonie's front sitting-room. 'But I would really rather you didn't ask, Graham That cheque Tom wrote some weeks ago is all we can give you.'

Graham recognized it was going to be a battle all the way. Keeping hold on his temper he said, 'Look Sile, I'm not asking for charity, merely my rights. The house, for instance, was in my name and as my wife you are entitled, of course, to half share of it but no more than that. And please don't insult my intelligence by expecting me to believe you have already spent the money. I know for a fact it hasn't been three months since you sold the house.'

Sile fidgeted with the clasp on her bag and avoided looking at him. 'I'm sure you don't mean to be offensive, Graham, but I really don't like your tone. You were declared dead and everyone attended your funeral. That was the position. I had to make the best of things and bring up the boys without you. There wasn't a lot of money and I had debts to pay when I sold the house. There was also my wedding expenses, and the cheque from the insurance was spoken for before ever it was paid out.' She frowned. 'I don't know what I shall do if they insist on me returning it.'

'Very well,' Graham said as patiently as he could, prepared to go along for the moment with the image of the impoverished bride. 'I understand you have been through a rough time and you have had a lot of expenses, but it isn't as though you are married to a poor man. All I'm asking for is half the proceeds of the house as well as the return of my Celtic Airways shares and any other stocks and shares not in our joint names. I'm prepared to meet you, Sile, but I must have enough to support myself. And there is the matter of the custody of the boys. Maybe not an issue at the moment,' he told her hurriedly. 'As yet I have no place to bring them. But at some stage this will have to be discussed and decided upon.'

But it was soon clear to Graham that even if he were prepared to meet her halfway, Sile was not willing to meet him. No compromise was the signal she was sending, as she got up and abruptly left the room. Hobbling after her, he was further distressed to hear her rounding up the boys and insisting they leave at once.

'But Sile, can't you come back for them later?' Nonie protested. 'We haven't had our tea yet and I made their favourite cakes.'

'I'm sorry, Mummy but we need to leave *now*. Come along, boys!' Ignoring Nicholas's emotional outburst and Jeremy's anger, she bundled them into the car.

Graham balanced awkwardly on the front step, hungry for his last glimpse of them, as faces pressed to the glass they forlornly waved goodbye. Feeling unaccountably weary and depressed he pleaded a headache and went upstairs, unable to face Nonie's well-meaning attempts to cheer him or Ben's unspoken sympathy. Stretched on his bed, he came to the conclusion that his solicitor was right, he would have to take a tougher line with Sile if he hoped to move things forward. Increasingly, it was borne in on him in order to regain restoration of his property rights he must take her to court, and the sooner the better.

***

Kay had her own issues to cope with too, as she retreated into a world of her own and virtually stopped caring or communicating.

When Dave suggested tentatively. "Why don't you take up your walks again? It would do you good to get out and the air will be good for Sinead too,' she showed no sign of hearing him, merely positioned the pram in the back garden, where she believed the baby would get all the sun and air she needed.

Even when Florrie came to see her she refused to open up and discuss the taboo subject, beyond saying, 'I can't understand why you never told me he was alive,' resisting all her friend's efforts to draw her out.

'Please don't, Florrie,' she said at last, 'It's far too distressing to talk or think about, and it's too late now anyway,' and Florrie had seen it was useless. Like Dave, she wished she had not tried to protect Kay from the truth but been more open with her.

Sadly, she kissed her friend goodbye and drove away, feeling so sorry for the pair of them she could have cried.

One afternoon when Dave was at work his cousin Ruairi turned up on the doorstep, and Kay invited him in. She had always liked him, and so made an effort to be hospitable, offering him tea and biscuits, telling him how grateful she was for all he had done to help them in the garden during their first months in the house.

'Oh, now, Kay, I wasn't the only one hefting a spade,' Ruari chuckled.

'Maybe not, but only for you it would still be a mess,' she insisted. 'You more than earned those apple pies I used make,' feeling a pang for those early uncomplicated days when she had happily fed the men after their labors.

'And very welcome they were too, Kay,' Ruari admitted. 'But it wasn't all down to myself, you know, Dave did his fair share too. I suppose you're a dab hand now at the baking... not that I ever had any complaints on that score, let me tell you.'

'To be honest, I haven't done much baking since the baby arrived although you probably wouldn't think it to look at me,' painfully conscious of her increased weight.

'You've filled out a bit but it suits you,' he told her tactfully, and Kay shrugged knowing he was merely being polite. He did not stay long and beyond suggesting it would do Dave and herself the power of good to get away on their own for a few days, seemed unaware of her lack of vivacity. 'Maybe Eileen would take the baby and give you a break. From all accounts she's the doting grandmother. And sure doesn't everything look better with a change of scene,' he suggested, watching Kay with kind eyes. 'I know I'd try it if I were you.'

Kay nodded but felt the old helpless feeling coming back down over her again. How could a few days away in a hotel take away the terrible guilt she felt at having put Graham out of her heart and settled for someone else? She would never forgive herself, no matter how irrational it might seem for no one else could ever take his place. It would have been better to have lived out her life on her own for the rest of her days.

It was many months before Kay felt any different, months sunk in depression and useless regret, until the onset of spring somehow managed to lift her heart and spirits, if only marginally. In the meantime, she had to live with her heartbreak and the disgust she came to feel whenever she caught sight of herself in the mirror. For so long she had studiously avoided her reflection that it came as a shock now to see the deterioration in her appearance. She even took a bitter satisfaction in seeing how low she had sunk, was almost glad of this confirmation to what depths heartbreak had brought her. She who had always taken pride in her looks and slim figure, it was difficult not to feel revulsion. And yet, it was not enough to make her do something about the excess flesh, her pale pudgy face devoid of makeup and her hair in dire need of styling, hanging long and lank past her shoulders, without lustre, where once it had gleamed with the assiduous application of expensive shampoos and conditioners. When she thought of how disciplined she had been in the months before the baby's birth and the importance she had placed on diet and exercise, it was like she was a totally different person, and in a way she supposed she was. In the light of all that happened none of it, of course, mattered anymore, she continued to tell herself, condemning it for the false, shallow way of life it was, with too much emphasis placed on trivia and too little on more important issues. She told herself she had been right to systematically root out all such tendencies, just as it had once been her duty at one time to nourish them. But over the months with the gradual improvement in her outlook and a healthier frame of mind she came to realise if she were ever to get better she needed to first do something about her appearance and the first consideration was to lose weight. She owed it to Sinead, if nothing else. Poor baby, she thought pityingly, she doesn't deserve a frump for her mother, how will she ever grow up normally if her role model is what I have become?

With that, Kay found the motivation she needed to *want* to make the change. There was something else she needed to do and that was make things right between herself and Florrie. It was time she stopped blaming her. Poor Florrie had only done what she thought was best in the circumstances.

Florrie felt relieved when Kay asked her to call over to the house for coffee, it was too long since they had met, she said, and she wanted to make up for lost time. It sounded promising and Florrie nervously took hope that her friend was gradually coming out of her depression. If she felt shocked at her friend's appearance she hid it well but from the warm hug Kay gave her and the first eager words of welcome out of her mouth Florrie knew that all her earlier hostility towards her was gone and Kay was genuinely sorry for their falling out. Best of all, Florrie thought, her friend no longer blamed her for keeping quiet about Graham's miraculous survival and subsequent return; and what was just as important, she no longer blamed herself.

With hindsight, Florrie recognized that none of it had been anyone's fault, few could have withstood the emotional shock of a dead lover's return to life.

Indeed, now that spring had officially kicked in Kay found it hard to remain indoors with the sun shining and the crocuses and daffodils filling the flowerbeds, if not in their own garden, at least in those all around them. It reminded her of the time Sinead was born when she had been so proud and hopeful. While Kay firmly set about putting the past few months out of her mind she knew that nothing had radically changed, it was just that now she was making an effort to regain her health and looks, and determinedly switching channels whenever thoughts of Graham took over instead of wallowing in regret. She still longed to see him, still felt a terrible aching regret at the whole tragic mess up of his life and hers. But it wasn't as if she would be bumping into him in her social circles, she told herself sadly, and the publicity having died away there was nothing in the newspapers or on television to remind her of him. From Florrie, she knew of the court case involving Captain Pender and his former wife, how he had sued her and won the case. The insurance company had sued her too, for failing to return the insurance money paid out on his death, and only on the steps of the court had it been finally settled.

But Kay was more interested in Graham's action against his wife.

'Was it in the papers, Florrie?' she asked, wishing she might have seen it.

'No, the whole thing was conducted in a private sitting of the High Court. Even so it still leaked out. One of the European hostesses is going with a barrister on the case and she gabbed about it on reserve.'

Kay was shocked. 'You mean he actually discussed it with her?'

'Yeah. But then nothing remains hidden for long in CA, Kay, you know that.'

How true, Kay thought, only glad that Graham had come out of it so well. Florrie did not know how much he had been awarded but believed it was sizeable.

'And the judge...he made Captain Pender's wife give him back all his stocks and shares. Can you imagine! Kay?' her tone was awed. 'She was trying to hang on to his CA shares.'

Kay was amazed at the woman's greed and she married to a millionaire. Well, good for the judge, she thought. No prizes for guessing on whose side *he* was on. She felt like a load of worry and guilt had rolled off her heart and on looking back, Kay saw it was at this point that she had begun to get better. When the Hostess Super's group letter arrived, urging the married girls to come back flying for the summer and promising them a better deal all round, Kay made up her mind to accept. With the decision made, her spirits lifted further and she set to with a will to get back her figure as speedily as possible. Even though it meant starving herself to achieve her goal.

It soon became clear that Dave did not approve of her leaving the baby to return to work although the thought of a second salary coming into the house must have pleased him. 'What!' his face fell. 'You're going back flying.'

'It's only for a few months, Dave,' Kay coaxed. 'Hey, don't look like that. I'm not signing up for the seven year work contract or anything like that.' Even though she was secretly considering it.

'I should hope not!' Dave blanched. 'But what about Sinead, you'll be away a lot. Won't you miss her?'

Kay's bright expression faded. Of course she would. But then a lot of the hostesses had young families and went back to work. 'You did say anything I wanted,' she reminded him of his promise during her depression, and at that he hesitantly agreed. It was only when Dave remembered the pilots she would encounter and the opportunities in New York for forgetting him on overnights, he began to wonder if he had been out of his mind. By then it was too late, she had already sent off her letter of acceptance to the airline.

***

With all Judy Mathew's efforts on behalf of Graham Pender the Hostess Super had neglected another project close to her heart, aware with the growing number of married air hostesses already signed up to return to the airline for the summer months, it was high time to have that long overdue meeting with the Chief Executive on the important subject of better salaries for the married hosties. There was besides, the vital issue so far evaded by McGrattan whether the married hosties intending to merely work the summer months would be paid the same salary as those prepared to sign the new seven year work contract?

Judy believed they should, but so far Oliver had not given her a satisfactory reply. Hence the delegation to his office that morning. Sitting opposite the Chief Executive, Judy was confident he couldn't hope to hold out against them much longer Not that she was expecting much help from the Chief Hostess Europe, Ciara's fatal flaw being her over eagerness to please her superiors. Any real support, Judy decided, would come from Elinor, the Hostess Administrator.

Dragging her attention back to what Oliver was saying, Judy wished that Ciara would stop her sycophantic nodding. Really though, there was no agreeing with the man, what they needed to do was stand firm and take no nonsense. The married girls were entitled to a decent salary and should not be offered anything less than the figure they were earning at the time of their resignation. After all, they were filling in at the busiest time of the year and right now was the time to make this clear to McGrattan, not nodding away like Mandarins.

'Might I make a suggestion, Oliver,' Judy broke through his boring, repetitive drivel about the airline's failing economy, their long-standing policy of paying minimal salaries to temps and married women. 'Could we regard this year as a trial run and embark on it as optimistically and generously as we know how? Perhaps we should bear in mind if we don't make the deal attractive enough we may not get anyone prepared to fly for us, whatever about signing up for the summer slog.'

'Balderdash!' spluttered Oliver, with unlovely mirth at the preposterous idea of Celtic Airways being left high and dry. 'We'll *always* have girls flocking to us in droves. We have only to advertise and they come running.'

It was annoying but true. Judy repressed a desire to put the waste basket over Ciara's head, and said forcefully, 'Yes, of course, we draw hundreds of applications every year. I don't deny that. But how many of these girls turn out to be suitable? I mean how many do we actually engage? That's an area we can't afford to make too many mistakes in, you know, Oliver. Training and uniforms, the whole thing is far too costly, even if we do take it out of their salaries during training and pay it back on their being made permanent. Apart from anything else, we have standards to keep up.'

'Yes, yes,' Oliver nodded in an impatient 'I've heard it all before' fashion, picking up his showy gold Rolex from the desk. *Could it be true he was calling it his Golex!* 'Time is running out, ladies'.

But Judy had one last little trick up the sleeve of her Yves St. Laurent suit in the shape of their rival airline MacDoolAer. Crossing her shapely legs in the sheerest of stockings, she said, 'Of course, Oliver, I suppose you do realise that we can no longer afford to ignore the competition we're up against since MacDoolAer's turnover last year reached four million? I believe they have recently increased their fleet by five new Boeings and are recruiting more pilots. Won't be long now until they start snapping up all the prettiest hostesses too,' adding archly. 'I believe their latest slogan runs, *'Howdie, MacDool. So long Celtic!'*

'Not, of course, that we have anything to *really* worry about,' Elinor murmured on cue. 'Not yet anyway.'

Oliver scowled, touched on the raw. He had never taken the new low cost airline seriously. When they had set up at the airport at such close proximity to CA he had predicted their sure and certain collapse within a year. Now it was a sore point that in a relatively short space of time the airline had actually grown to the stature when it might be considered a threat. Not only were they *not* collapsing but actually doing very well. And their provocative slogans were a continual irritant. Celtic Airways had such a proud tradition, galling to think of that little upstart actually pitting itself against *them*.

'Very well, Judy,' Oliver sighed, knowing he was licked. 'Give me those figures again.' And when she obeyed, 'Very well. But we'll need to review it in twelve months and let me tell you right now your scheme for maternity leave is *not* feasible whatever you may say about other airlines – none of them Irish, by the way.'

But Judy was not bothered. She had got what she came for, and thankfully been spared the usual hassle over the new miniskirts, Oliver still strongly resisting the shorter length, despite Air France and Pan Am having led the way.

Captain Higgins was also using MacDoolAer to his advantage in his negotiations with the Chief Executive. Since Graham had made such an excellent recovery the question of his reemployment with Celtic Airways needed to be discussed. As Ben had pointed out to Oliver in the presence of the Chief Pilot, a pilot of Pender's seniority and caliber would be quickly snapped up by the rival airline currently on the lookout for more pilots. Perhaps, Oliver was not actually aware that MacDoolAer had already sent out feelers to the pilots' lounge, clearly determined on poaching from under their noses some of their best flyers.

'What if, in the absence of a clearly delineated proposal from Celtic Airways, Captain Pender was seduced by their offer,' Ben posed the question, and Andy murmured, 'Damn shame!'

Oliver took his point. It was the same argument so recently posed by Judy and he was in no need of further reminders of the long and pillaging arm of MacDoolAer.

'Very well,' he found himself wearily agreeing. 'First thing tomorrow the letter will go out. Just as soon as Pender is fit to resume duty, he will be welcome back.'

Ben's eyes twinkled as they met Andy's, and the pair of them rose, well satisfied. Strolling back to the pilots' lounge, they agreed it might be a good idea to line up some refresher courses for Graham, now that his convalescence was at an end.

'Gameball! Thanks, Andy. I'll let him know straightaway.'

Ben found Graham taking the sun on Nonie's little red-bricked patio. He was looking very well, at least five years younger as a result of care and good food, thought Ben, glad to see the dreadful pallor replaced by a light tan although the white hair continued to shock. 'Thought you might like something to read,' he tossed him a copy of Time magazine. 'So how's it going?'

'Not bad,' Graham smiled. 'Every day in every way getting better and better.'

Ben chuckled, familiar with Couē. 'Glad to read the court case worked out well. We were all jolly pleased - the only fair outcome.'

'Thanks.' Graham grimaced. 'Pity it had to go to court at all. I suppose you know Sile got custody of the boys but it was what I expected. I'm only hoping she'll let me have 'em once I find a house and get back working again.'

'Well, I have good news for you on that score,' Ben told him cheerfully. 'Andy said to tell you … as of now you are back on CA's payroll.'

Graham's face lit up and he shot out a hand to grasp Ben's. 'Most grateful to you and Andy …and for a lot more besides. I've never really thanked you for the way you kept in touch with my lads over the years and helped them through the bad times. Means a lot to me.' He met Ben's eyes. 'More than I can ever say.'

'For nothing,' Ben made little of it. 'Nice lads! It was a pleasure.'

'Heard anything more about the crash?'

'Nothing definite at the moment.' Ben knew how difficult this must be for him. 'It turns out there was a considerable amount of gold bullion aboard and it was never found. There was talk of collusion between the Eastline Airways pilots and the Tamil separatists but no evidence was ever produced.' Ben shrugged. 'Just have to sit tight and wait.'

Graham nodded. 'I thought it had to be something of the kind… all those interrogations the ILA put me through, battering away all the time. Maybe the other pilot on board was involved but I doubt it. John was a decent chap …not at all the sort to get mixed up in anything criminal.' Graham's expression grew wretched. 'You know, his wife and family were on to me since. The hardest thing was having to tell them he had died after all…made me feel guilty to be alive.'

Ben seeing his anguish got up to go. 'Look, take it easy,' he gripped his shoulder in sympathy. 'I just wanted to give you the good news. If there's anything you need be sure and let me know,' and with a brief salute he strode away.

***

By the beginning of May Graham had completed his conversion training on the Jumbo and was back on the pilot roster. He was delighted to be working again although his leg was giving him a bit of bother when over tired and he was inclined to limp. But that had eased when he took up swimming twice weekly, rejoicing in all the improvements to the airline in the years since the crash. Thanks to Judy's lobbying on behalf of aircrews a 50 metre swimming pool and sauna was now a part of the airline and a fully equipped gym with all the latest equipment for keeping fit.

Graham had already made his supernumerary trip plus two more flights to New York. Only for the stalemate situation between Sile and himself regarding custody of their sons, he would have been fairly content. The trouble was Sile had always been a poor loser and on their infrequent phone calls Graham invariably ground his teeth and banged down the phone in frustration. Bitterly, he told himself, he was foolish to expect any kind of normal decent behavior from his ex-wife, reminded of how she had deliberately prejudiced his case that day in court when she had told the judge his job as an airline pilot made him an unfit person to have custody of their sons. As if, Graham thought incensed, he would fly away leaving them unattended, and undoubtedly it had influenced the judge in his ruling.

On the advice of his solicitor, Graham had appealed the decision and was now waiting to hear the outcome. And yet despite Sile's unyielding attitude, he was still hoping against hope to have his boys with him when they got their school holidays for the summer, he had even promised to buy them a full-sized table tennis table Nicholas and Ranjan having finally bonded and eager to keep up their skills in the holidays.

On the morning Graham was due to fly out again to New York the long-awaited communication from the solicitor arrived, but it was disappointingly clear there had been no change of heart on Sile's part. In dismay, Graham read the few concise sentences informing him of 'my client's absolute refusal' to allow him custody of his sons for the school holiday period. Ironic that he received word at the same time that his new house was ready for occupation; instead of the delight it had promised to be it now seemed like an albatross about his neck, a cruel reminder of all he would not now have. Utterly cast down, Graham drove to the airport thinking that Sile had deprived him of the only thing in his life, apart from his lost love, that meant anything to him.

Kay was back on the roster too. On the morning of her first flight out to New York she was ready and waiting for the crew car when it drew up outside the house. Climbing in, she was cheerily greeted by members of her cabin crew and felt time melting away as if by magic. It might have been merely a week or two since her last flight, not two years, with a wealth of living and suffering endured in between. On hugging her husband and baby goodbye and mentally switching off any emotional part of herself that she had not already closed down earlier, she listened with interest to the other air hostesses chatting. Predictably enough, it was all about the latest bargain buys in Macy's basement and what the fashion conscious were wearing on the streets of New York that summer. It was just what she needed, Kay thought, already looking forward to doing a bit of shopping while away, even if it was only window shopping.

Despite Dave's somewhat jaundiced comment that she was viewing her return to work in too frivolous a fashion, she was not totally possessed by the selfish and extravagant desire to shop till she dropped. Rather she was anticipating a pleasant day or two in adult company after so many months confined to the house with a young baby. Another thing she looked forward to was her first flight on the Jumbo, everyone said it was a beautiful aircraft and the take-off almost vertical compared to the B-707 which she had flown on before marriage. She smiled when she remembered her training instructor referring to it as 'the city in the sky' joking with so much food and drink on board you could stay aloft for weeks. Kay had spent four weeks in the classroom, renewing acquaintance with former friends, many of them married like herself. One face had stuck out, it took her a moment before she recognized Cassie, the former Pan Am stewardess from her prenatal class.

'Hi Katherine,' Cassie had greeted her. 'I contacted the Chief Stew like you told me. Reckon that Judith is one classy dame. Amazing she never married.' Kay smiled, everyone in CA knew the Super was married to the job. 'Oh well, what the hell!' Cassie grinned, 'She's making out okay, isn't she? Sure is Captain material, if you get my drift.'

Praise indeed coming from a former employee of one of the world's leading airlines, Kay thought amused. As for herself, it would seem she was destined to be known as Katherine but to quote Cassie, or was it Cassandra, what's in a name?

On arriving at the airport, Kay was pleased to run into Florrie. On her way out to Paris, she had delayed going on board so that they might meet.

'Wanted to wish you luck on your first flight back,' Florrie hugged her hard, then held her off to look at her. 'Gosh Kay, you look terrific. Oh, wouldn't I just love to be going with you. We'd have a fab time.'

Kay had to agree, she often thought it was a pity Florrie had been assigned to Europe instead of the Atlantic. With an eye on the clock, her friend quickly filled her in on her new boyfriend, clearly having an enjoyable fling with this Danny. It was all so lighthearted and reminiscent of so many chats in the past that Kay could have almost imagined it was her turn now to confide the highpoints of her own latest romance, and smiled at the notion.

'Have a great trip and don't go wild in America,' Florrie cried, already on her way to the door. 'Oh, you lucky thing,' she called back with a doleful grin, 'Gay Paree! Here I come,' making Kay chuckle.

Graham was still mulling over the disappointing news from the solicitor, as he went on board his flight to New York that morning, all unaware that Kay was in his crew, or even that she was back working with the airline. Casting his eye over the crew list no name stood out as familiar and he was struck anew by the amount of crew carried by the Jumbo compared with that of the smaller B707. Today's crew was twenty-one, made up of seventeen hostesses including the supernumerary, and four pilots including the supernumerary Third Officer. The Captain was one of the more senior pilots, John Brennan, and Graham was his co-pilot. By a coincidence Pete Kenny was also on board. Normally, the Jumbo carried three pilots, including the third officer, and a flight engineer but, perhaps, because of Graham's newness to the Jumbo the Chief Pilot was making sure there were three fully qualified captains on board, or maybe with all of them fairly new to the aircraft he was taking no chances.

Shortly before take-off Captain Brennan pressed the hostess bell, and when the senior hostess stepped into the cockpit he lifted his headphone and turned to say in his genial fashion, 'Ah Marion, how are you doing? Any new hostesses on board who might like to come up for take-off?' And Marion replied, 'Yes, Captain, we have one supernumerary. I'll pass on your message.'

'Right-oh, and as soon as we're up I could do with a cup of coffee like only your delicate hands can make it,' raising a smile from all present knowing only catering's usual tarry brew would be forthcoming.

Soon the Jumbo was taxing along the inner taxiway and Graham was kept busy calling out the before take-off check to the Captain. He was aware in the background of the cockpit door opening and shutting as the hostess Captain Brennan had invited up for take-off came in and took up position. By this Graham's whole attention and that of the other pilots was on the combined task of getting the Jumbo off the ground as the aircraft sped down the runway. Forty seconds later it lifted off and they were airborne. It was only when they had passed 5,000ft that Graham glanced behind and saw the face of the dark-haired young woman balancing against the back of Pete's seat. Good God! Surely not, he thought, his heart suddenly beginning to pound with shock and excitement, hearing from a long way off Captain Brennan calling for the after take-off check and Pete responding.

As Kay shyly thanked the captain before returning to the cabin, Graham's mind was filled with the image he had received of her in the shadowy cockpit and he tried to match it with his memories of her, and was only sure of one thing, that she was as lovely as she had ever been. And then he was forced to concentrate on his flight duties, as over the radio he heard Area Control instructing them to change to Shannon area and requesting that they report flight level at 31,00ft.

Kay too, had been startled by that fleeting glimpse of Graham in the cockpit. Naturally, it had already occurred to her she might bump into him one day, and might even share flights. But not so soon, she thought, not on her very first flight back!

Next morning lingering in her hotel room, Kay was expecting the phone to ring and the caller to be Captain Pender. The previous evening the pilot had stopped by the crew check-in desk, exciting and confusing her by the way he had looked at her, as well as by his suggestion they might share a coffee together. She had been in a slight panic as to how she should reply, wondering if he thought she was still single, when he had added with the hint of a smile, 'I'll ring you…not too early, of course,' she realized that he meant next morning. Even then she had been too weary to do more than just stare at him, for she had forgotten how tiring it was to be on her feet all the hours it took to cross the Atlantic. Her jaw had begun to wobble and a mortifying fit of yawning overtook her. Tiredly excusing herself, she had seen humour rising in those dark eyes, making something in her ache unbearably for the past

'Never mind. Go to bed!' he told her gently, and it was with reluctance that she had obediently turned away from him and followed the bellboy to the elevator.

Now the sudden shrill sound of the telephone in the quiet room interrupted her thoughts and when she picked up he was on the other end. 'My dear Kitty,' he said. 'I hope I'm not ringing too early. I've been awake for hours. I couldn't wait any longer.'

'N…not at all,' Kay stammered suddenly shy, no one but Graham had ever called her by that name. 'I awoke some time ago myself.'

'No hurry but would you like to meet me for breakfast?' and when she did not immediately reply he said, 'It would be a chance to talk. I do so need to see you.'

Kay felt suffused by sudden heat. 'Yes, yes I would like that.'

'Take all the time in the world,' he told her, then admitted honestly, 'My dear, I don't think I can wait *that* long. Would you…could you meet me down in the lobby in half an hour, less if you can make it?'

'Yes I can,' Kay's heart leaped. 'I'll see you there.'

***

On that first evening that Kay was away Dave was surprised at how long Sinead took to settle down. It was as though the baby somehow sensed that her mother had gone and was fretting for her. At first he had put it down to teething but when the little girl continued to cry he went upstairs and brought her downstairs. Balancing her on his knee, one hand holding her firmly against his chest, he tackled his frugal dish of macaroni and cheese. It might have been morning she was so alert, not after nine o'clock and way past her bedtime, chuckling when he played hide and seek with her behind a napkin and gleefully tearing it off his face.

'Now young lady, time for bed,' Dave said at last, carrying her back to her cot. This time she settled down at once and was asleep before he had left the room, convincing him that all she had needed was reassurance.

For the first time in his married life Dave felt exasperation with Kay and if he could have spoken to her at that moment it would have been in strong language. Then he sighed and tried to be more understanding, telling himself that she had been through a lot and needed this break away from home. But it didn't make any of it any easier. He was conscious of missing her like mad and she only gone since morning. It was just so flat coming into the house when she wasn't there, he thought. Even Sinead, much as he loved her, appeared more of a burden, obliging him to remain in the house when what he really wanted was to head out somewhere cheerful for his tea.

Dave went to the press and poured himself a whisky. Usually he didn't drink during the week but tonight he felt the need of it. Glass in hand, he stood gazing out at the summer garden, still visible in the fading light, feeling lonely and a bit down. Manfully, he tried to look on the bright side. It was only for a few months, he told himself, but somehow he was unable to snap out of his dark mood. Okay, he admitted at last, he was jealous and a bit worried too, that she might get a fresh taste for the career she had always been crazy about. Dispiritedly, he wondered what he would do if she never wanted to come back to being just a wife and mother again.

***

The Manhattan shoreline receded and the brown river water billowed and foamed in the wake of the Staten Island Ferry. Coming up soon on their right was the Statue of Liberty rising up out of the waves with torch held proudly aloft, and Kay gazed about her entranced by it all. She had never gone on the ferry-boat in her brief time on the Atlantic and she had never expected to make the trip with Graham at her side. But now it all seemed so right and when he suggested taking a round trip she had been thrilled and, at the same time, conscious of a feeling of unreality again, as though living out one of her dreams.

From the moment she had emerged from the elevator and seen him waiting for her in the lobby there had been a wondrous quality to it all, and they had immediately gone out together into the Manhattan sunlight. Over coffees and bagels in a nearby café they had sat and talked, or Graham had done the talking and Kay the listening, until the years in between might never have been. It was still too early for her to take in the full horror of his story or the depth of his suffering. For the moment her mind was bemused by his declaration that ever since reaching the moment of decision to cut short his time in Karachi and return home to be with her, he had never stopped thinking of her.

'Only it wasn't to be,' Graham concluded with a shrug. 'Believe me, during those years of my imprisonment I never regretted anything so much as the opportunities I'd wasted, and most of all not having posted the letter telling you of my return. If only I had,' he sighed.

'Oh, but I did get that letter,' Kay told him. 'Someone posted it on to me.'

'Aah, thank God!' he sighed, reaching for her hand. 'So you *did* know'

'In it you mentioned some other letter you had written before going out to Karachi,' Kay said, acutely conscious of his hand holding hers.

'I always wondered why you had never replied.'

'And I always wondered how it was you went off without a word of goodbye.'

Graham winced. 'How callous you must have thought me,' he sighed again, and she made no attempt to deny it, merely nodded, remembering how rejected she had felt at the time. 'Darling, I'm so very sorry.' There was a wealth of regret in his tone and at the endearment Kay's breath caught in her throat and heard him say with a sigh.

'I wish to God I had done things differently.'

As the ferry drew closer to the Brooklyn dock Kay sat silently mourning the white hair and the depth of sadness in his dark eyes. It was the eyes that betrayed his suffering, she thought, and yet at times when he looked at her they were no longer melancholy but dark caressing pools, stirring her every bit as much as they ever had in the past. She was remembering what he had told her regarding his years in captivity, awed by his single-minded determination to survive and moved by his tender avowal that it was thoughts of her that inspired him to keep on hoping when no hope existed. Listening, she had more than once brushed away tears, wishing she could somehow make it up to him for all he had gone through. He had spoken of the months since his return and of an Indian boy he had shared captivity with, admitting he had come to look upon him like one of his own sons. She was so close to him she could smell his shaving lotion mingling with whatever soap he used, and when she looked up at him she could see the new lines about his mouth and creasing his brow.

For the first time she noticed the seam of a scar puckering the flesh behind his ear and extending below his collar, almost certainly it was a legacy of his hostage years. What other scars did he bear, she wondered. Giving in to an impulse, she laid her hand flat against his neck, tracing the injury with gentle fingers.

'Kitty, my dear Kitty,' he said unsteadily, turning his head to look at her. Overcome by sudden shyness at her boldness Kay removed her hand and stared down at her lap, overwhelmed by the explosive feelings the touch of his skin aroused in her.

'Please believe me when I say that I renounced all the hopes and expectations I had been entertaining when I learned that you had married. It was only when I saw you and all the old feelings came back in force that I knew I had to speak to you. But I see now it was wrong of me.'

'Wrong?' Kay seized on the word. 'But we have the right to talk at least.'

'No, I don't have any rights,' Graham said roughly. 'None at all. I have no right to interfere in your life and maybe take away your peace of mind. If I thought any harm would come to you from meeting like this I would make sure we would never meet again.'

Kay felt her throat go dry and her chest constrict with panic at the thought of losing him just when it seemed she had found him again, and seeing her expression he slipped his arm about her saying contritely, 'No, no, I wouldn't... couldn't...not if the decision were left entirely to me,' fearing by his too hasty words he might have already forfeited the choice.

Kay remained motionless with her eyes fixed on a seagull swooping down to pluck a crust from the water, only slightly comforted by his assurances, and then raising her eyes to his she said, 'What if I don't want you to stop?'

She felt his arm tighten convulsively about her and saw on his face a mixture of hope and reckless joy and something else she could not explain just then, but which she would later identify as trepidation. But whether this was for her or for himself she did not know, only that she was feeling the first true peace and sense of belonging since learning of his death.

***

Dave was relieved to have Kay back but surprised that after all her talk she had bought nothing in New York except a fluffy toy dog for Sinead, admitting she had picked it up at Kennedy before returning.

'Hey,' he teased, 'What about all those great bargains in Macy's waiting to be snapped up.'

'Didn't get around to it,' she said vaguely. 'Maybe next time.'

Puzzled, Dave put it down to extreme fatigue. Indeed, he thought she looked desperately pale when he had come home to find her still in her housecoat, valiantly trying to deal with the dirty laundry that had piled up in her absence. When he had given Sinead to her she had hugged the baby with more fervor than he had seen of late but, contrary to his expectation, she did not appear to be at all elated by her trip. For a wild, hopeful moment he thought that maybe the stark reality of her return to work had shown up the so-called glamorous life for the tough slog it really was. Yet in his heart he knew this was too much to hope for. That night, when she clung to him and caressed and loved him as though she had been away for a month and not merely three days, he felt only disquiet. Even while reaching heights of passion with her unknown to him before it seemed to Dave as though he were peripheral to her needs and she was acting out her desires in the grip of some unhappy, demanding fantasy.

At first Kay found it tiring being away from home for three whole days and having so much to catch up on her return, but she soon got the hang of it and began finding the new regime a lot easier. But while she was balancing her life quite well at work and at home, she was handling her emotions not well at all. She found herself constantly thinking of Graham, hoping they would share another flight. She took to packing something glamorous in her overnight case, adding heels and an evening bag, never knowing when, or indeed, if they might be needed. Conscious of a dull ache of longing that never grew less, she wondered if he ever thought of her and found herself recalling those few precious hours they had shared on the Staten Island Ferry, and going back over everything he had told her, analyzing every word he had said. She knew that such thoughts were disloyal to Dave and for a time guilt sent her touring the stores on stopovers in search of gifts for Dave and Sinead. On 42nd Street she had picked up a soft leather briefcase in a sale - his was worn with the lock broken - and with the purchase felt a lot easier in her conscience. The model airport she chose for Sinead completed her buying. Toys, like most things in America, were half the price you would pay at home. By buying nothing for herself, she felt somehow purged.

On her return, Kay's well-chosen gifts were received with pleasure although Dave was afraid that she had paid far too much for the brief case. Sinead had spent an enjoyable half hour playing with the tiny planes and doll figures, pushing them contentedly about the floor. To all appearances, she was coping well in Kay's absence. With the adaptability of children she had become used to waving her mother off one day and welcoming her back another. Of course, it was difficult to know what was really going on in the baby's mind and the first indication of her confusion only became apparent when she began imitating Dave and calling Kay by her Christian name.

Kay was amused at first and then she tried correcting the child, pointing at herself and saying, 'Mama' but the little girl became frustrated and upset and insisted 'No, no, my Mama' clinging to her grandmother, until it no longer seemed funny, and Kay grew angry with Eileen for allowing the ambiguity to exist.

'It will sort itself out,' Dave insisted, unable to refrain from adding, 'Of course, it would never have happened if you had stayed home and looked after her yourself.'

'Oh, I see,' Kay said bitterly. 'So it serves me right!'

'Hey, don't get it out of proportion. The baby is confused, that's all.'

'I'm not getting anything out of proportion,' Kay was close to tears. 'It seems I can't go away for a few days without my child being completely taken over by your mother. Did you see her face?' she demanded. 'She was positively enjoying it.'

'Not at all, Kay, I'm sure my mother never meant to put between you and the baby,' Dave was upset. 'It's just a natural mix-up, that's all.'

When she persisted, Dave grew angry himself.

'Don't be ridiculous, Kay,' he said coldly. 'Get a grip. Only for Ma helping out like she does you couldn't have gone back to work. You might show some appreciation.'

Kay stared, completely taken aback by his criticism. Never before had he sided with his mother against her and she found she didn't like it one bit. She felt hurt and aggrieved, and only she was relying on Eileen so much she would have immediately removed Sinead from her care. Instead she buried her pride and put up with it. But only for the moment, Kay vowed, just until she could make other arrangements.

***

On his return from New York Graham had made an effort to furnish his new house, buying divan beds and bedside lockers for the boys' rooms, determined to be ready if by some miracle Sile had a change of heart and allowed them to stay with him that summer after all. Attending to such matters was not as painful as he had imagined it would be. Since meeting Kay and experiencing the joy of finding that she still cared for him, his anguish and frustration over his ex-wife's attitude had abated somewhat.

Now thoughts of Kay filled his mind to the exclusion of everything else and he almost succeeded in convincing himself it was enough that she still cared and, secure in this knowledge, he could get on with his life and leave her to get on with hers. But it was not long before he realized this was very far from the truth for he wanted her more than ever and justified himself with the thought if anyone had prior claim to her it was him. After all he had known her first. Initially, Graham had felt loth to cause pain to Kay's husband and child but now his own needs were gradually sweeping away all other considerations. Without being arrogant, he knew there was no way that Kay would ever have married this man if she had not believed that he had died in the plane crash. His one objective before leaving

Karachi had been to put behind them all past misunderstandings and to woo Kay and win her back. It was what he had written to tell her in the all important letter and he was confident he would have successfully carried out his intention, if only he had got the opportunity. Maybe he was just fooling himself into believing she cared enough to turn her life around for him, but he knew that he must give himself the chance of finding out or he would deeply regret it. Right or wrong, he told himself, it was *owed* him.

Graham co-piloted his next three flights to America and then he was passed by his check captain as fit to take full command on the Jumbo. Given his history it was an incredible achievement. Congratulations were in order, drinks laid on and Ben and Andy passed on the good news of their protégé to the Chief Executive. Judy Mathews expressed her delight by kissing Graham rather too passionately which gave him to think that she might be reading rather too much into the occasional dinner dates they shared. At the same time he was fond of her and knew that he would miss her company if they ceased. In the meantime, there was the frustration of checking his crew list before flights only to find that Kay's name was never on it. Longing for a glimpse of her and beginning to despair of their ever being rostered to fly together again, he went out to the airport in his standoff period at an hour when the Atlantic crews gathered in the canteen for their pre-flight meal. Again he was disappointed for she was not amongst them. And then he realized that he was going about it the wrong way. All he needed to do was pick up a copy of the current hostess roster, that would give him the knowledge he sought.

Visiting the roster office on the pretext of checking his own flight schedules, he picked up a copy of the hostess roster along with his own, and once outside began checking it. He saw that Pete Kenny was captaining Kay's flight to New York the following week and, by a great luck, he ran into him in the pilots' lounge shortly afterwards.

'Pete,' he approached him. 'I was wondering if you might do me a favour.'

'Sure. Be glad to if I can.' Pete tossed his empty coffee carton into the refuse bin and leaned up against the wall to hear how he could oblige a fellow pilot.

'Any chance at all you might let me have your New York on Tuesday and you take my Boston? I need to be back in time for the furniture guys on Friday.'

An excuse admittedly, he could have left the key with his next door neighbor who would have been more than happy to oblige. But he was conscious of the need to be discreet.

'Sure,' Pete checked it out and nodded. 'Okay by me.'

'Great! Be glad to return the favour any time.'

Graham delayed a few more moments in polite chat then headed for his car, whistling as he went. His heart lifted at the thought that very soon he and Kay would be sharing a stopover in New York, his life was picking up at last.

Captain Higgins was pleased to see how well Graham was settling back into CA and glad of the support he was getting from his fellow pilots. Much of it was due to the pep-talk Ben had given them at the last pilots' meeting when, amongst other things, he had urged them to give Pender every assistance on his return to work, pointing out how crucial it was that he pick up his old skills as quickly as possible.

'Don't think he won't be critically watched from all sides and the least little fault noted down on his reports,' he told them. 'Just imagine yourself in his position and you'll know what I'm talking about.'

This had got right to them, as Ben had known it would. Several of the pilots present, particularly Christy Kane, nodded vigorously, for he knew better than most that it only took a couple of poor assessment checks to find yourself on the black list, continually scheduled for further and more severe training checks. All those listening, especially the younger pilots, were aware just how cold and ruthless check captains could be. They had only to put down on your report something damning like 'Indecisive' or 'Doesn't have quite what it takes to make the grade' and your career was down the Swannee, along with your hopes of gaining those coveted gold stripes.

Ben was satisfied he had done all he could to ease Graham's way back into the airline, and he was prepared to help him further in any way he could. Having some knowledge of his past from the time they had been in the Air Corps together, he could empathize with the shock and trauma Graham had suffered in his teens on the death of his twin brother, and in more recent years his unhappy marriage. What a pity he had married Sile, Ben thought regretfully, as he had so many times before. She had always been wrong for him but he had been too dazzled to see it. Pender's devotion to his sons too, had always struck Ben as being rather too intense, and now he considered his colleague's affection for the Indian boy contained much of that same obsessive quality. No doubt much of it was due to the absence of the right woman in his life. Ben was conscious of how lucky he was, if only Pender could have met a woman like Linda it would have been the making of him.

One afternoon as Ben was about to leave his office and head home he received a disturbing call from the secretary of BALPA who notified him of the Ceylonese government's intention of indicting Captain Pender, along with three other Eastline Airways pilots, on charges of terrorist conspiracy, drugs and arms smuggling.

'They now have the evidence they have been seeking. You might be good enough to inform Captain Pender of this. We will contact him directly as soon as we have a date for the hearing.'

Anxiety creased Ben's brow as he replaced the receiver. From all accounts it would seem as though Pender would be required to go to Colombo to answer the charges in a Colombo court. He did not underestimate what a blow this would be to Graham having to return to the country of his imprisonment.

This same court issue was also troubling Harinath Prasad but the Tamil Leader was more concerned with the fate of the three Eastline Airways pilots, Tamils like himself, who had helped the Freedom Fighters to smuggle all five consignments of guns and ammunition into the country. These pilots had cooperated mainly for the money paid them, nevertheless, he felt a certain responsibility towards them. Another cause for anxiety was the fact that his own name was on the government's black list since a link had been traced between Sita Shanti and himself. What disturbed Prasad most was the betrayal had come from within his own ranks, the informant was one of his own men. Much became clear when Harinath realized that the man in question had been secretly consorting with Daya Begum, the Sinhalese woman, whom he had since discovered to have been the one to betray Sita which led to her abduction by the ILA. This latest treachery of Begum's cut deeply for the Tamil leader would have staked his life on the loyalty of his men. Consumed by rage and anguish, his face became a stony mask as he vowed to revenge himself on this woman who had robbed him not only of the love of his life but the respect and integrity of his followers. So far she had managed to evade him but now he swore that he would not rest until he had destroyed her. As to the informer he had yet to decide what action to take, but first he needed to be sure there were no other traitors in the company. Prasad had little time to do more than wonder how Ranjan was adapting to his new life, he had received only one brief letter from the boy since he had left Ceylon, but he was keeping faith with the pilot's promise to bring the boy back to his homeland one day. Prasad reflected in the light of these new developments, this might come about a lot sooner than either had envisaged.

***

By the time Kay flew out again to America the tension between herself and Dave was still unresolved. In the meantime some subtle change had taken place in her own attitude and she realized that she no longer felt guilty about the intensity of her feelings for Graham, nor did she make any effort to repress them. The night before she left Sinead had refused to allow Kay to put her to bed, holding up her arms pitifully to Dave, big tears rolling down her flushed cheeks. When Kay had insisted on carrying her upstairs to her cot, she had cried so hard they both feared she would go into convulsions, and Dave had taken the baby forcibly from her. Then it was Kay who wept, affronted at her own child making strange with her, and the evening ended with everyone miserable. This time Kay did not make the mistake of blaming Dave's mother, but the inference was there and the atmosphere grew more strained.

It was their first real row.

Next day walking across the ramp deep in gloomy thought and with none of her usual anticipation at the prospect of spending time in New York, Kay was almost at the top of the aircraft steps when she collided with one of the pilots on his way down.

'Sorry!' she muttered automatically, and glancing up was startled to recognize Captain Pender. She had just enough presence of mind to step on into the aircraft, hearing his polite murmur, 'My fault entirely,' before he went on down the steps.

Shaken, Kay stared after him and was struck by how little surprise he had displayed on seeing her. Almost, as though he *knew* she was part of the crew. There was not a lot of time to dwell on this for the flight had been chartered by a football club and every seat was taken. They were all heavy drinkers and kept the hostesses busy. By the time they were landing in New York and exiting unsteadily from the aircraft the bar was empty and everyone was glad to see the back of them.

Queuing tiredly behind the other hostesses at immigration, Kay watched the pilots walking on ahead towards customs, her eyes on the captain especially. She hoped no one was observing her but she was unable to take her eyes off him, becoming aware for the first time how he walked with a slight limp. Vaguely, she remembered something about him undergoing surgery, but then he had told her so much in that all too short time on the Staten Island Ferry that she had not been able to take it in.

'Some hold up in customs,' one of the hostesses remarked, and those ahead slowed down as the word traveled back that the co-pilot, Joe McLoughlin, had been caught trying to smuggle in four bottles of Scotch. He stood unrepentant with folded arms, staring defiantly at the customs officers..

'Why don't you bastards just hold on to them,' McLoughlin suggested with a scowl.

'Gee thanks, sir,' the official exclaimed in mock gratitude but Joe was made to pay the fine nevertheless.

Everyone stood about feeling embarrassed. Crew regulations were rigidly strict. When eventually the crew moved out to the waiting taxis no one had any sympathy for Joe, all of them anxious to get to the hotel on that sweltering night.

Kay settled back in her seat and slipped off her high heels, knowing she would probably regret it later when she couldn't get her feet back into them. As usual some of the livelier hostesses were discussing the possibility of going out on the town and others, with less energy or dollars to spare, were compromising with plans to meet up for a snack in the café across the street from the hotel. Whether or not Kay went with them to Ruddley's depended on Graham, and she experienced slight panic at the thought that he might have other plans. But as it turned out she need not have worried. Having signed her name in the crew register, she turned around to find him behind her.

'Kitty!' On his tongue, her name was an endearment, and for the second time in so many hours, she felt a blush mantling her cheeks, 'My dear, how good it is to see you again.'

'You too,' she told him, and his face lit with pleasure.

'I hope you're not too tired but I thought…well, I hoped you might come out and have a meal with me. Or just a snack,' he added quickly, as if unwilling to be denied her company on that count. 'There's a very nice little restaurant I think you'll like,' he went on, as they picked up their room keys. 'Not far off…about ten minutes by taxi,' and Kay just smiled and let him take her over.

Entering the restaurant a short while later Kay was wearing the elegant black dress, the one she had so hopefully packed on her last three stopovers in New York, and knew she looked well. She found confirmation of this in Graham's glance and no sooner were they were seated when he began reminiscing about the first meal they had ever shared in another Italian restaurant, some years before in London.

Kay felt her face growing warm and then hotter still as Graham's eyes lingered on her neckline. 'You are more beautiful than ever,' he told her softly. 'Maybe because you have had a child.'

Kay glanced away embarrassed. She hoped he wouldn't say anything more and yet, at the same time, found herself longing for greater intimacy. Nearby the waiter hovered ready to take their order and when Graham suggested fettuccine with wild mushroom to start, followed by *piccata limone*. Kay nodded, only too happy to let him choose for them both.

'Well, that's done.' He reached again for her hand, and Kay relinquished it without a struggle. 'At times it astonishes me to be here in America eating such good food and in such company,' he was saying. 'When I think of my situation not so long ago, the whole thing seems truly miraculous. And you,' his voice thickened with emotion. 'Are the greatest miracle of all.'

Kay's eyes misted and she stroked the hand that held hers, any words that came to her seeming inadequate. With a flourish, the waiter set the plates in front of them and, lifting the bottle of Chianti, playfully pretended to take it away.

'No?' he asked in mock surprise. 'You want more?' and chuckling filled their glasses. 'The wine is good, eh?'

They nodded and smiled, as yet unable to bring themselves to speak. But the somber mood was broken, and when the waiter had gone Graham did not refer again to his hostage years but rather to mutually happier times in the past.

Two hours later they stood side by side in the elevator as it rushed them upwards to the hotel's fifteenth floor. It had been a wonderful evening, and as the doors slid back Kay was wondering if Graham would see her to her room, and if he did what she would do. But as she was thinking this he merely leant down and kissed her cheek.

'Sleep well,' he murmured.

Stumbling towards her room, she was feeling the effects of wine on top of her tiredness, and mulled over the disappointingly flat ending to an evening that had started with such promise. So what on earth had she expected, she asked herself, as she let herself into the room, that he would make passionate love to her? Well, hardly! But that he would *want* to do so, she told herself, unzipping the dress that earlier had drawn such compliments and letting it fall unheeded to the floor. Slipping into bed, she switched off the light, too tired to watch television as she usually did or to continue puzzling things out. Despite herself, she slept at once, worn out by long hours on her feet and all the emotion of the evening.

Graham stayed awake desperately needing time to think. If he and Kay were to experience any more such enchanted evenings, he told himself, they would almost certainly be courting disaster and end up one of the statistics they had been discussing earlier when the conversation had turned to the airline's strict policy forbidding romantic relationships between aircrews. He felt like someone considering the consequences about to press the time switch on a bomb. If he had only himself to consider Graham would gladly have pressed any switch guaranteed to deliver Kay into his arms, but he genuinely desired only her good. His original intention had been to woo, win and marry her, but in the circumstances he had found himself cast in the role of the philanderer or the 'other' man, neither of which was to his liking. Loving her as he did, he knew that any man of honor would now retire from the arena, loth to break up a marriage still so young and tender, and with a child's welfare at stake. But theory was one thing, he knew, practice quite another. In truth, Graham had been through more than his quota of suffering and rejection to feel able now to adhere to the required gentlemanly code of honor and restraint. He was painfully reminded of the all too short weekend he had recently spent with his sons, their delight mingling in equal proportions with their resentment on hearing that they would not after all be spending the summer with him but would be forced to remain in the hated Conway household.

It had pained Graham to have to tell them. 'Look, it's just for the present, lads. It won't be for long I promise. In another while Jeremy will be old enough to decide where he wants to live and by then, who knows, but you will have a say too, Nicky.'

Nicholas's look of disillusion had cut him to the heart. At that moment, Graham had honestly felt like throwing Sile to the wolves but something had held him back. Let *her* explain it to them, he thought, striving to be fair. Nothing would be gained by stirring up hatred. At the same time it was impossible not to feel aggrieved. And yet despite it all, he and his sons had shared a wonderful two days, he remembered, and one of the evenings Ben and Linda had come

118

over with their boys and they had all enjoyed a barbecue in the new house or rather outside in the balmy summer air. After the Higginses had gone home he had sat out late beneath the stars, sipping beer and remembering how pleasant it had been, how well Ranjan had got on with his sons and their friends. Until beset by a sudden crippling loneliness, Graham had got up and gone into the house Going into the room Nicky shared with Ranjan, he sat down quietly in the shadows watching his youngest son as he lay sleeping, his heart once more filled with regret for those lost years. Nicholas had stirred, perhaps sensing his presence, and opening his eyes he had seen his father sitting by the bed and given him a smile of such sweetness and trust that Graham's heart had turned right over; he had been hard put not to gather him up and hold him close. Going back at last to his own room, he had lain awake until the first birds were chirping in the trees. Only then had he slept. And now here he was lying wakeful once more in his hotel bedroom in New York, remembering those two days and how bereft he had felt on leaving his sons back to their mother next day, all the more painful because of Sile's lack of courtesy in practically banging shut the front door in his face. When Graham eventually drifted off to sleep it was the early hours in the Big Apple. On waking, his immediate dilemma was whether or not to give into his overwhelming desire to ring Kay, and for a time he fought the impulse. In the end he could hold out no longer and rang her room, only to find he had left it too late, she had already gone out.

***

Wandering the New York streets aimlessly in the oppressive heat next morning Kay finally retreated into Macy's blessedly air conditioned store to sit and brood over a Cappuccino, feeling unhappy and frustrated by the uncertain way Graham had left things between them the night before. She had been so sure that he would ring her room first thing and arrange to meet, but when he had not, she was disappointed all over again. These few hours on stopover were all they would have and she bitterly mourned the waste. Returning at last to the hotel, she was collecting her room key when she became aware of Graham awaiting her in the lobby, and she was at first joyful, then shocked, as she took in his gaunt appearance.

'Kay, I must speak to you,' he said in a strangled voice, and she allowed herself to be guided into the coffee bar. There with the coffee cooling in her cup, she had listened in a bemused fashion to the words pouring from him, not making much sense of what he said, beyond the fact he had not been able to sleep for thinking of her and how he had regretfully come to the conclusion it would not be fair to endanger her reputation any more than he had already.

'Believe me it's the very last thing I want,' he told her unhappily, 'But I think it might be best if we didn't meet again like this.'

At his words, Kay's spirits sank even lower. This time around she had honestly believed the fates were on their side, and now she saw how wrong she had been. For crying out loud, was she *never* to have any say in what happened between them? Since she had first met him there had always been something keeping them apart, she mused sorrowfully, if it wasn't his wife then it was her reputation or his fear of losing his sons. No matter what, she saw it all too clearly now, she would always be the loser. Getting hurriedly to her feet, Kay ignored his anguished plea that she sit down again, desiring only to get away before she broke down in front of him.

She spent the few hours before pick up lying on her bed, unable to rest, turning restlessly, her thoughts miserable and unhappy. At pickup time she saw that he was late coming down to the lobby and, with the eyes of love, she noticed the improvement in his colour since afternoon, but he still looked desperately tired, almost ill. For the first time it had struck her what an immense responsibility it was being in command of the Jumbo, especially for someone in poor health until comparatively recently. When she moved outside with the rest of her crew she didn't miss the glance he shot in her direction when she chose not to ride in his taxi, but his eyes were hidden by his uniform cap and it was impossible to decide whether he was pained or relieved.

In Kay's taxi, the other hostesses soon relaxed their guard in the absence of the captain and began openly discussing him. It seemed that everyone thought Pender was sexy as hell and the white hair very distinguished, like an American senator or some film star. No one was surprised that he was having an affair. Hearing this, Kay was shocked, she had no idea who or what could have started such a rumour. But maybe it wasn't a rumour, she thought, but an actual fact. Dinner dates were mentioned, some hostesses had seen them together. The more Kay heard the more shocked and desperately jealous she felt, angry too, and received another jolt when the woman in question turned out to be Judy Mathews. How could he have concealed it from her was Kay's next anguished thought, after all his protestations of never forgetting her in captivity? Lies, lies, she thought despairingly, but oh, how eagerly she had wanted to believe him. With plunging spirits, she acknowledged the fact the couple had once been involved. She knew this because he had told her so himself saying it had all been a very long time ago, when Judy was young and before he had married Sile.

They must have drawn close together again, Kay told herself with heavy heart, her disillusion complete. There could be no other explanation.

Graham's own spirits were equally low as he stood in the briefing room at Kennedy one hour before the scheduled time of departure, studying the weather conditions at New York and Shannon, while awaiting the computer print-out of the flight plan. He was acting like a fool, he told himself wretchedly, going to the trouble of swapping flights and then perversely screwing the whole thing up. No wonder Kay had opted to sit into a different taxi, he couldn't blame her.

Beside him the co-pilot's continuous griping about all things American was not only foolish in their present surroundings, Graham considered, but hugely irritating. The man had not stopped bitching since stepping out of the crew taxi. Graham sighed, and felt like offering to pay the duty on the bottles of Scotch.

'Be a good chap and go carry out the safety inspection,' he bid Joe pleasantly enough. 'You might check the fuel while you're about it. I'll stick around here for the flight plan and follow you on out.'

There was no real need for the co-pilot to do any of this for the third pilot had already gone out to meet the engineers but in Joe's present mood he was no asset in the briefing room, and quite frankly Graham had had his bellyful of him. He accepted the flight plan the Flight Dispatcher handed him and studied it intently. Their trip time was to be 5 hours, 55 minutes, with a calculated fuel consumption of 70 tonnes.

Graham's thoughts were still preoccupied by his crumbling love life as he bid the dispatcher 'So long' and went to join his flight.

Kay saw him come on board and instinctively moved back, wishing she could fade even more into the background. She was conscious of his deep voice uttering some pleasantry to the senior and Marion's laughing reply,

'You can say that again, Captain.'

To her shame, Kay could not help craning her neck to get a glimpse of him as he passed all too quickly in and out of her line of vision, and then in a flash of gold braid he was gone up the spiral staircase to the cockpit. While waiting to go on board Marion had selected Kay to work with her in the First Class cabin on the flight home, telling her it would be good experience for her. Although Kay preferred working with the other hostesses in tourist she was glad now of the diversion from her thoughts as with a smiling word of welcome, she showed the passengers to their seats.

In the cockpit, Graham finished calling the pre-take off checks and relaxed back in his seat. They were fifteenth in line for take-off and as the jet in front began rolling, he released the brakes and came up close behind. It was a very hot night and the temperature even hotter in the enclosed cabin and there would be no relief until they took off and the air conditioning switched on.

Graham felt the sweat running down his face and loosened his tie. In the passenger cabin he had no doubt the temperature was even higher. Beside him his co-pilot pressed a handkerchief to his glistening forehead but was mercifully silent. One by one the heavy jets ahead of them reached the runway and the mounting roar of their engines was audible as the pilots held the brakes and allowed the power to build, and then they were off and pushing slowly up into the sky their lights fading and their exhaust smoke dispersing over Jamaica Bay.

More time passed before the controller called on the radio. 'Okay, you're cleared for take-off Irish.' And they lined up and thankfully followed the Lufthansa jet up into the darkness.

Kay did not have time to dwell on her problems as she competently, if a little unevenly, assisted Marion in making sure those passengers who had paid so heavily for the pleasure of the singular service offered by CA actually received it. Marion was an agreeable working companion, if a demanding one, and Kay quickly got to know her likes and dislikes, learning to anticipate rather than wait to be told, and after the first fraught ten minutes was not caught napping again. They soon began setting up the hors d'oeuvres trolley, with its delicious selection of smoked fish and caviar and laying out the bone china and cut glass. While Marion went out to the cabin to take drink orders Kay began measuring the first lot of gins and selecting the mixers until the senior returned to the galley and took over from her.

'Good girl,' she said, when she saw all that Kay had done. 'Oh listen, before you help me serve the drinks you might slip down to the back with the drink doilies. The loaders left the lot up here and they'll be needed in tourist.'

Kay nodded, and picking up the sizeable packet set off pleased to have the opportunity of a chat with the girls at the back. Stopping at each station off-loading doilies, she was vaguely aware over the muted roar of the Jumbo's engines of a rumpus going on somewhere. Somebody celebrating a birthday, she thought tolerantly, but as she worked her way further aft the sound struck her as more of a rallying cry.

Suddenly, she found her way blocked in the aisle by a bearded man standing and shouting what sounded like 'Viva! Viva! and all at once she felt herself violently seized about the waist and pushed headlong back up the cabin. Even then she hardly protested, memories of the Third Officer's practical joking on the outward journey still in her mind. It was only when she found herself rammed hard against the bulkhead and heard the man mutter, 'Take me to the flight deck,' the full horror broke on her. They were being hijacked.

**

In the cockpit, Graham relaxed back from the controls and glanced out of the window. It was a clear night with a star-studded sky and a full moon lying down below on the clouds. In the right-hand seat the co-pilot munched on a tuna fish 'special' and despite his earlier grumping, appeared to be enjoying it.

Graham found himself looking forward to his own meal and realised that he was starving. Remembering how little he had eaten since dinner the previous night, just coffee and bagels, he was not surprised. Before he could pursue that thought, the door of the cockpit abruptly opened and, glancing around, his heart jolted at the sight of Kay. He had just time to register her distraught expression when he saw that the bearded man following immediately after her was holding a gun to her back.

Thrusting her to one side and rapidly approaching the captain's seat, the man pressed the gun against Graham's ribs, saying in a thickly accented voice,

'Do as I say, Captain, or you will all die.'

Graham felt the sweat breaking out all over his body and with an effort he remained still and listened to what else the man had to say.

'My name is Paulo,' the bearded man went on. 'Fidel has summoned me back to Cuba. I have three more undisclosed backups in the cabin and provided you do as I say you will come to no harm.'

'Very well,' Graham said as evenly as he could. He was determined not to be dominated by the man, memories of his hostage years strongly flooding back, and he tensed with hate and determination. Conscious of Kay, he resolved that no harm would come to her. Turning to the other pilots he said coolly,

'Gentlemen, we are being hijacked by this man and his friends, but the safety of our passengers comes first so we will do precisely what he says so long as I give the orders.' He looked at Paolo for confirmation, 'OK Paulo?'

The hijacker nodded. 'OK man.'

'So Mr Paolo what do you want me to do?' Graham asked pleasantly.

'You tell ATC you're hijacked and we will make our needs clear in due course.'

Graham put his hand down and turned the transponder to another code. Within minutes the reply came through.

'Tango 904, this is New York Radar. I am receiving your transponder code.'

Graham picked up the mike and said, 'New York Radar our flight has been commandeered and we have agreed to cooperate with our hijacker who assures us we will come to no harm.'

Later, having gone down the cabin to reassure the passengers and to declare that the bar was open 'all drinks on Celtic Airways,' Graham returned to the cockpit where Paolo had his gun aimed at the co-pilot's head. That should take Joe's mind of his ruddy Scotch, Graham found himself thinking, and then Sandy handed him a slip of paper on which he had written the details from ATC giving them onwards clearance to Havana Cuba, and asking them to maintain present transponder code.

Graham sat back into his seat and before long he became aware of the first of the F-16's coming alongside of the Jumbo. They came in close and stayed in tight formation. Looking out the cockpit window, Graham made eyeball contact with the Lt. Colonel whose wing tip was barely thirty feet from him. Then he noticed that on the space under the fighter's canopy was painted the colonel's name. Lt. Colonel Harvey R. Blagmar, and he made a transmission on 121.5.

'Glad to see you, Colonel. Graham Pender here, captain of Tango 904. Situation not to my liking but making the best of it.'

The colonel responded saying he understood and giving his call sign Air Force Seven, his assurance that they would remain with them in United States airspace and no one would fire at them or endanger them by unsafe maneuvers.

'Roger Air Force Seven,' Graham signaled back. 'Your support much appreciated.' He found he was tensing at the controls and made a determined effort to relax his shoulders. He'd been in tougher situations than this, he reminded himself grimly, and he had managed to get through them.

With that, the memory of Ranjan's anxious face as he had bid him goodbye thirty-six hours earlier returned to trouble Graham.

But what if this time he didn't make it back, he asked himself, what would become of the boy?

***

Ranjan was relieved when Captain Higgins had offered to take him to his house for a couple of nights while the Captain Tuan was away in America. Since Mellwood College had broken up for the summer he was at a loose end, and missing Nicholas badly. At least now he would have Martin to knock about with, Ranjan told himself, already looking forward to his friend's company as he sat into the pilot's car.

On arrival, he was given the usual warm welcome by the Captain Sahib's wife who told him with a smile. 'I've put you in with Martin. Off you go and unpack your things.'

'Come on, Ranji,' Martin grabbed his hold-all and began lugging it upstairs. 'If we hurry we'll have time to fence before tea.'

'Sure thing, man,' Ranjan loped after him, hoping to be in the top bunk.

'Nicky is a real cool chess player,' Martin was saying. 'Wait till you have a game with him, you'll see for yourself. Of course, he's bound to beat you every time.'

Ranjan scowled but refused to be daunted. Soon he would be just as good as Nicky, he told himself, and then it struck him it would be cool if Nicky were to join them for the night. Better still, if Nicky's mother would agree to let him and his brother stay with the Captain Tuan and himself for the summer.

'Yeah,' Martin agreed. 'Why don't we get up a petition and all of us sign it and stick it in his mother's letterbox. Then she'd *have* to give in.'

Ranjan grinned. 'Say what about getting *your* mother to invite Nicky over here right now to join us?'

'Okay, let's go ask her.'

When apprised of the situation Linda needed no urging, as she had often told Graham his sons were no trouble, neither was Ranjan for that matter. To their delight, Nicholas arrived over within the hour with permission to stay two nights. They all of them had high jinks, cooking burgers at two in the morning and running outside, with Martin's young brother tagging after them, to kick football in the intermittent glare of the sensor lights. Linda kept a discreet eye on the nocturnal festivities but otherwise gave them *carte blanche* to enjoy themselves and, in turn, she enjoyed the extra liveliness about the place with the 'three musketeers' as she had got in the habit of calling them, banding together.

Nicholas soon made it clear to his friends that he had no intention of accepting his mother's ruling and, following the council of war in Martin's bedroom, he suddenly cried, 'Eureka' and leapt up on to the bed intoning dramatically, 'Let my people go,' before squatting down again and Martin said, 'Okay, so what have you found, Nicky?'

'Nonie!' Nicholas announced portentously, 'My gran!' and Ranjan's face immediately brightened at the name of the beloved elderly auntie.

'If we can get Nonie to agree to come and live with us in Dad's house for the summer then Mum can't possibly object.' And the others nodded. Grandmothers had inviolable rights.

That evening he rang his grandmother and took heart remembering his mother was always saying that Nonie was tougher than she looked.

'Now Nicky, does your father know about this?' Nonie demanded

'Not exactly,' Nicholas admitted. 'We thought he might feel it would be too much for you. But it isn't, is it?' he appealed. 'Honestly, we wouldn't give you any bother, Gran. We'd even weed the garden,' he offered recklessly, knowing she prized neat flowerbeds. 'Anything …just say you'll come.'

***

In the first class cabin of the Jumbo Kay was outwardly calm as she assisted Marion in serving drinks to passengers. Beyond the cabin window the sight of the American fighter jets was reassuring, if slightly disturbing, a constant reminder of the acuteness of their situation. She found it difficult to keep focused with the other hostesses continually slipping into the first class galley to commiserate with her. 'You poor thing! I would have died if it happened to me,' was the most often repeated phrase. Indeed, when the hijacker had pressed the .38 pistol into her side and forced her up the staircase to the cockpit, Kay had been convinced her end had come. She knew it was .38 because he had told her so, adding that it was a special pistol adapted to fire at short range aboard an aircraft and was both deadly and efficient. 'So just do what I tell you and you won't get hurt.'

In the terror of that moment Kay's first thought had been for her baby left motherless at so young an age, illogically, mourning the fact that Dave's mother had come to mean so much to the child and feeling only desolation that her baby knew her so little and might not even miss her.

On the flight deck the tension eased somewhat once the hijacker left the cockpit and took up position in the first class lounge where he ordered food and wine to be brought to him. In his absence the crew took the opportunity to exchange views on the situation and various suggestions were made. Graham let them talk for a bit before rejecting out of hand any plan to try and overpower the hijacker.

'The man is no fool,' he told them tersely. 'From the beginning he has shown himself to be intelligent and orderly,' pointing out this had been confirmed by Paolo's insistence on opening the half-bottle of Medoc himself, clearly he was taking no chances of being drugged or incapacitated in any way.

'No gentlemen,' Graham ruled decisively. 'There will be no sudden moves. We have the safety of our passengers and crew to think of and please remember that I will be making the decisions when the time comes.'

He resolved to bide his time and await his opportunity. Earlier he had conceived a plan. For everyone's sake, he told himself, it had to work!

'You can tell the escort *now* that we are leaving United States jurisdiction,' Paolo ordered, more to show his knowledge and authority, Graham felt, for undoubtedly Colonel Blagmar was already aware they were reaching the limit of USA controlled airspace.

Graham made the transmission on 121.5 and the F-16's immediately broke away and were gone within seconds, leaving only dissipating circles of jet stream to mark their passage. He was aware of conflicting emotions, both relief and regret at their departure. Military trained himself, he was aware of the potentially explosive situation should any of the US pilots jump the gun and commit an act of aggression, but there had been comfort also in their presence.

Once Paolo had returned to the first class lounge Graham outlined his plan to the rest of his crew, and Sandy nodded enthusiastically, he was to reenact the gory prank he had played on the outward journey with tomato ketchup and the fire axe

'Make it realistic, Sandy, but don't over do it,' Graham urged. 'Remember the element of surprise is what we're after here.'

'Aye, aye, Skipper, you can count on me.'

'I know I can!' Graham gave him one of his rare smiles, so charming the Third Officer that he was filled with new fervor not to let his captain down.

Before long the hijacker returned to the cockpit, and when they were 200 miles from Havana he took the mike from Graham and spoke in Spanish to the controller. The discussion became heated and Graham received the impression that Cuba did not want Paolo to land, but after a bit they acknowledged he had something to sell that might be of interest to them. The controller told Paolo to stand-by and he would check out the position. Within minutes he called back to say permission had been granted for him to land by parachute. Paolo was triumphant.

'Now Captain when we reach our destination I want you to descend to 1500 feet. We will be exiting through the number five left door and taking one of your flight attendants with us. When the door 'open' light shows on your panel, maintain a steady heading across the airfield and after one minute commence depressurization.'

'Out of the question,' Graham said shortly. 'I cannot allow you to take one of my crew.' Chances were Kay, in his range of vision, would be the one he would hit upon.

'You do not have any choice, man,' Paolo pointed out. 'We are merely safeguarding our own safety and if you try any tricks I will come back up and blow your head off.'

For a moment, Graham experienced a surge of blind uncalculating rage for the brutal words recalled the identical threats made while imprisoned by the ILA. Then with an effort he gained mastery of himself and nodded, 'Very well,' while inwardly more determined than ever that the hijacker would not be allowed to go free if he had to overpower him with nothing but his own two hands.

'That's good, man.' Paolo approved. 'She free when we reach the ground'

Graham nodded, his nerves tense, his thoughts racing, aware that Paolo had not mentioned the other hijackers to the controller, and now Captain Pender was more than ever counting on their non-existence. As soon as the hijacker had left the cockpit for the cabin Graham told the Third Officer, 'Get going Sandy,' adding grimly, 'Only this time you can leave the fire axe to me!'

As the Jumbo descended lower and lower, all the passengers strained to look out of the windows, and began chattering nervously amongst themselves. Although partially reassured by the captain's frequent announcements they were, nevertheless, aware the dangerous moment was approaching. Everyone longed for the hijackers to be gone from the aircraft, and at that stage every moment seemed an eternity.

In the meantime, Paolo came down the stairs and beckoned imperiously to Kay, 'You come with me,' he said, and her heart beating faster in terror she was reluctantly stepping forward, when Marion barred her way having already got her instructions from Captain Pender.

'No Kay,' she said firmly. 'You are to stay here.' Turning to the hijacker she said quietly, 'I'll go with you,' and courageously followed him down the cabin.

From under his seat, Paolo drew a bulky package and, opening it, he took out the parachutes and handed one to Marion, telling her to put it on. She was genuinely at a loss having no experience of such things, but used her ignorance to advantage, pretending to be even more helpless than she actually was so that he had to practically put it on her himself. As he picked up the other parachute she gave the arranged signal to the hostess anxiously watching from the galley, and at once she disappeared through the curtain and dialed the cockpit.

On the flight deck Graham was becoming uneasy when the door 'unsafe' light suddenly came on and the cockpit telephone chimed. At last! He unbuckled and stood up. 'Take over, Joe,' he said tersely, and the co-pilot nodded.

By this, they were lined up at Jose Marti International and at 1500 feet O'Loughlin held the Jumbo steady on course for the runway. Graham swiftly left the cockpit and descended the stairs, and making his way behind the galley he collected the fire axe from the point where Sandy had left it in readiness.

Cautiously, Graham peered across to the port side, past the seats already cleared of passengers according to his instructions, and sighting the hijacker bending over to don his parachute with the pistol momentarily unattended on the seat in front of him, he took a deep breath, and tensed himself for action. 'Now Sandy, now!' he breathed.

Right on cue, Sandy came hollering from the direction of the first class cabin, his shirt ripped exposing his blood-stained chest and the ragged blood-stained edges of the empty cut off shirt sleeve horrifyingly realistic. The diversion was all that Graham needed to make the last few yards without being observed by the hijacker and he brought the blunt end of the fire axe down hard on the back of the man's neck, almost but not quite felling him.

The gun went off but thankfully the shot went wide, hitting the bulkhead behind Sandy's shoulder, and in that moment Captain Pender raised the axe again and with his next blow managed to lay the man out. The adrenaline still pumping and breathing hard, he picked up the gun and handed it to the Third Officer.

'Good work, Sandy!' he told him. 'Go at once and put this in the dip-locker for safety.' As the gratified young pilot hurried to do his bidding, Captain Pender then turned to two of the male passengers standing by, 'Tie him up,' he said curtly, before going over to close and secure the cabin door.

'You betcha! Rightaway, Captain!' Jubilantly, they took up position at either side of Paolo, using a leather belt offered by another passenger to tightly bind his hands behind him, as he came to groaning noisily.

'Well done, Captain,' Marion babbled in relief, and began struggling out of the bulky parachute. Kay approached with a white face, her own relief visibly showing, and shakily echoed the senior's heartfelt congratulations and thanks.

Graham smiled at the pair of them then turning to face the cabin, he announced almost cheerfully, 'Emergency over!' and raised a hand in laughing acknowledgment of the cheers sounding throughout the cabin.

Graham set the jet down in Miami and within minutes of landing it was impounded by the military, and Paolo was handcuffed and led from the aircraft under heavy escort. Once the passengers and crew had disembarked the Jumbo was moved to a less public parking area away from the camera-popping paparazzi, the passengers were screened for onward release to Europe and the crew given an eight hour turnaround and placed in hotels adjacent to the airport to allow them to rest before taking the Jumbo on next day to Shannon.

There was an air of exhilaration amongst the crew as they sat drinking together in the hotel bar; if Captain Pender was the hero of Tango 904, Marion and Kay were considered by all to be the heroines. Even Sandy, despite his earlier unpopularity, came in for lavish praise and now everyone wanted to sit near him, eagerly plying him with questions as to how he had managed to achieve such realism and whether he had been at all afraid when the hijacker fired at him. But Sandy considered he had got off lightly and was not tempted to claim any more credit than was his due, and so he just grinned and said, 'Scared shitless,' which made everyone laugh and to like him far more than any show of bravado.

Kay thought she would remember for the rest of her life the terror she had experienced when the hijacker had seized her. Glancing across to where Captain Pender sat talking with the co-pilot and an airline representative, she was reminded yet again of how courageously he had acted. All the hostesses were talking about him and how Marion had been prepared to go out the door with the hijacker and it struck Kay how very lucky she was to be part of such a great crew. Feeling a lump in her throat, she surreptitiously brushed away a tear.

Seeing it, Graham guessed she had been worrying about her child and now the reaction was hitting her. Speedily, he wound up his conversation with the airline representative and went to join the hostesses and commend them on keeping their heads in the crisis. But to his dismay, Kay slipped away to the washrooms on his approach. Keeping an eye out for her return, he lingered chatting to the crew.

'I'm off to bed in a few minutes,' he told them. 'Enjoy the evening but don't stay up too late. We have an early start.' Then seeing their faces he relented, 'Not too late anyway,' and they chorused, 'Yes, Captain, and thanks again for everything. You were brilliant.'

One bolder than the rest said suggestively, 'What do you know, Captain - we might even be in bed before you,' and there was a burst of slightly hysterical laughter, and someone told her to shut up.

Graham neatly turned it back, saying with a grin, 'Steady on, girls – one at a time, *please!'*

This time the laughter was genuine and he raised his hand in friendly salute and turned away, for out of the corner of his eye he had glimpsed Kay emerging from the washroom and heading out of the bar. Moving just as quickly, he was in time to make the elevator before the doors closed.

Kay looked up startled as Graham stepped inside. On an emotional high following the events of the past few hours, she had delayed in the washroom remembering Graham's concern and tenderness towards her at the height of the danger. She felt stirred and vulnerable, adrift on the sea of her emotions, with no course to steer except towards him. The unguarded besotted talk of the other hostesses had served only to deepen her own desire, exciting her to the point when she could not trust herself to be near him. Even his reported love affair with Judy Mathews had ceased to have any meaning for his courage and his authority in handling the crisis had conspired to leave her with no armor against him.

'Why are you avoiding me?' he said roughly.

'I wasn't avoiding you.' She glanced up at him with an anguished expression. 'Why do you say that... how can you say that?'

But he ignored the question and drew her towards him, and she shivered at his touch. Looking up into his face she saw the intense longing in his eyes and something dissolved within her. With a long sigh, she offered her mouth to him and his lips came down hard on hers, not giving her the peace she craved but inducing an urgent new longing so that she instinctively pressed even closer. At once his arms tightened about her, and she felt the heavy beat of his heart against her.

As the elevator doors slid back they stood for a moment breathing hard, barely conscious they were stopped at her floor. Without a word, she put the room key into his hand, and he hurried her down the corridor. The moment seemed endless as he bent and inserted the key in the lock and she felt she could not endure another second without feeling his mouth on hers and his hands touching her body again, and she shivered convulsively against him as though plagued by fever.

Once inside the room, with the door closed behind them, they came almost violently into each other's arms. 'My darling, my lost love,' he was murmuring and she pressed her hips forward, frantically welding herself to his, and felt his flesh harden against her. His lips were hot and urgent against her own, his kisses sweet and prolonged and she trembled under the insistence of his hands as he undressed her, and knew that his need was as great as her own.

And then unable to contain herself a moment longer, she flung herself against him and there was the sound like the roaring of the sea in her ears and her head became light and dizzy with the force of her desire. All caution and restraint were washed away on a great tide of feeling as he lifted her in his arms and carried her to the bed.

When later, Graham rose and dressed himself, the light was beginning to filter through the slatted blinds. He leant over and watched Kay sleeping for a few moments longer, and then he made a conscious effort and turned away. With one last look at her sleeping form, he softly let himself out into the corridor and with the exquisite memory of the past few hours like a seal upon his heart, he rode the elevator down four floors to his own room.

***

The airport buzzed with the story of the hijacking of the CA Jumbo jet, but long before it became public rostering had already contacted the families of the flight crew. Dave was shaving when the telephone rang and he was at first alarmed on hearing who the caller was and then reassured to learn that his wife was safe and due to land mid-afternoon from Miami. He immediately switched on the radio to get the news but the incident was not mentioned.

The one o'clock news had the full story and there was a spate of phone calls to the airport from journalists wanting to know when they could interview the captain and crew, and most of the city news editors were keeping space on the front page of the final edition of the evening papers. For a time a certain amount of confusion existed as to who had actually piloted the hijacked Jumbo. Captain Kenny's name was on the roster and it was at first thought that Pete had been the one to overpower the hijacker.

Judy Mathews only learned her mistake when she bumped into Pete on his way up to flight operations and he explained how he had swapped flights.

'Sorry I missed the fun,' Pete grinned. 'Although I believe Pender handled the whole thing very well and the Cuban guy didn't get away with it.' The rest of the conversation was on a rather more personal note for the besotted Pete was intent on making the most of their chance meeting. But Judy was too distracted to listen and hurried back to her office, anxious to check the hostess roster and see who had crewed with Graham. On discovering Kay was aboard Judy's concern gave way to unease, and with regard to the duty swap she would have given a lot to know which pilot had obliged the other. She stared at the blotter feeling horribly insecure and vulnerable. Perhaps better than most the Hostess Super knew the intense feeling generating between crews on stopovers and when a hijacking was added to an already charged situation, there was no knowing how high passions might run. Sharing regular dinner dates with Graham since his return to the airline she had hoped they were getting back on the old affectionate footing, and now she didn't know what to think.

Dave, had no way of knowing who else had been on the hijacked flight apart from Kay, until he saw the early edition of the Evening Herald, and when he did he immediately recognized the Captain's name, so familiar to him it might have been engraved upon his heart. Florrie felt a similar disquiet on learning who had been in command. She felt incensed on hearing some of the hostess reserves criticizing Kay for having brought the hijacker to the cockpit, even quoting the case of an airline stewardess who had swallowed the cockpit key rather than hand it over.

'Would you mind telling me just *where* the key to the cockpit is kept on CA flights?' Florrie demanded in so threatening a tone the girl looked around startled.

It seemed no one had actually heard of the existence of such a key but then someone volunteered the information that in future locks would be put on the cockpits of all aircraft or, at least, those flying Atlantic routes, and the spare key would be given into the care of the senior hostess. In fact, there was to be a whole new system aboard flights, the same knowledgeable hostess informed them, and at the first sign of trouble cabin crew were supposed to dial the cockpit and address the captain by his Christian name. Florrie was amused. And what, she thought cynically, of all the hostesses who were already taking the liberty of addressing captains by their Christian names as well as sharing their beds on stopovers. It was all a bit of a joke, she surmised, and wondered what other crack-brained scheme would be suggested.

In the pilot's lounge an equally critical atmosphere prevailed but it was not directed towards any member of the crew of the hijacked Jumbo – on the contrary they were one hundred percent behind their fellow pilots – they were just angry at the slack attitude to air piracy worldwide. When Ben Higgins called an impromptu meeting of pilots pointing out it was time they all took a stand to halt the senseless terror afflicting the skies since the late fifties, there was a good turnout and the response was strong. Captain Higgins intended sending the result of the vote to IFALPA, and was confident they would see a radical change of attitude before long. Unfortunately, the effect of it all was rather destroyed when some days later Captain Dan Tully, in one of his ill-timed practical jokes, carried a toy handgun in his uniform pocket into Kennedy Airport and waved it about the customs hall, whereupon he was immediately seized by security police and the Shannon-bound Jumbo delayed four hours, while he underwent intensive grilling by the CIA. He was eventually released through the intervention of the airline's lawyer, and then only on bail of one thousand dollars. For those who had been victims of a genuine hijacking his action seemed not only irresponsible but foolhardy, and everyone agreed it could have triggered dire repercussions. Captain Tully's only comment: 'Those effing Yanks have *no* sense of humor whatever!'

The same might have been said of CA's Chief Executive when the lawyer's astronomical bill landed on his desk but for once Oliver McGrattan was speechless.

***

On Kay's return home, Dave was surprised by how little she spoke of the hijack, saying she just wanted to forget the whole thing as fast as she could. He respected this, but wondered why she never even mentioned Captain Pender. Surely it would have been the most natural thing in the world, after all she had once been in love with the guy? But the truth of it was Kay was afraid to speak of Graham for fear she might reveal too much, not realizing her very reticence was far more suspicious than if she had got it off her chest at once. She would have liked to have told Florrie what had happened in Miami. Instead, she put off the moment, wondering a little wistfully when she and Graham might get another opportunity of being together, not something they had had a chance to discuss as they deadheaded back from Miami. On disembarking, she had merely glimpsed Captain Pender's back as he walked away from the Jumbo with the other pilots, the security police keeping the press from surging towards them. Those first few days home Kay's spirits were buoyed by her memories but inevitably reaction set in. Chances were she and Graham might not share another flight for months, she thought dispiritedly, not seeing it was unlikely having loved her so intimately that Graham would be content to allow such an unsatisfactory situation to continue for long. But in those lonely, introspective moments there seemed no certainty of anything anymore. She would have been consoled had she known that Graham went through similar highs and lows, his thoughts dwelling continually on her and their glorious coming together. He was briefly diverted on discovering that in his absence Sile had been prevailed upon to allow Jeremy and Nicholas to spend the summer with him after all. While not fully comprehending the intricate ins-and-outs, as excitedly relayed by Nicholas and Ranjan, each of them taking turns to bring the story forward to the moment that Nonie had agreed to come live with them in the holidays, he was pleased at the outcome.

Not wishing to put too much of a burden on the old lady he cast his eye around the kitchen to see if there was any way he could lighten the domestic load.

'What about a dishwasher, Dad?' Jeremy suggested, up to his elbows in suds, knowing it would almost certainly be one of his duties. 'Mum has one and it's fantastic. Everything comes out shining clean and only has to be put away,' firing a tea towel at his brother, with the curt order to begin drying pronto. 'What do you say, Dad? Nonie would love it. I *know* she would.'

Feeling the soft-hearted Nonie would more than likely let the boys off and do the dishes herself, Graham nodded. 'First thing tomorrow,' he promised.

None was delighted with the house and went about exclaiming over everything. 'Ah Graham, my dear,' she said taken by a fit of nostalgia as they sipped their sherry. 'It's so good to see you in your own house once more and you deserve it all. The only pity,' she went on reflectively, 'You have no one to share it with although I'm sure that won't be for long. I'm only sorry my daughter didn't bring you more happiness.'

It was the nearest Nonie had ever come to openly acknowledging Sile's shortcomings. Graham squeezed her hand gratefully. 'But I do have someone,' he responded gallantly. 'Sitting right next to me and how fortunate I am.'

Next morning, Graham looked in to the boys 'room to say goodbye. 'See you on Friday,' he called, and was touched when Nicholas jumped out of bed and came running after him. Ranjan stood in the doorway, shyly watching.

'Bye, Dad,' Nicholas threw his arms about him. 'Be sure and mind yourself,' and Graham guessed the hijacking was still on his mind.

'Will do,' he smiled. 'Bye, Ranji,' hearing his gentle, *Namasta, Captain Tuan.*'

In the kitchen, he was pleased to see Rita, his new housekeeper, chatting to Nonie, the pair of them getting on famously. The old lady was still in her dressing-gown and slippers, sipping tea and clearly enjoying the attentions of the younger woman. Graham felt further reassured when Rita said cheerily, 'You can safely leave your Ma to me. I've told her if she so much as picks up a sweeping brush I'll report her to the captain,' winking over Nonie's head.

Graham smiled back, not bothering to correct her mistake. Nonie was as close as a mother to him, he sometimes thought. He patted her frail shoulder and told her not to get up, but she insisted on accompanying him to the front door.

'Have a safe trip, Graham dear, and don't let those nasty hijackers on board your flight.' And he grinned and said he would try not to.

As he drove away, Graham's thoughts switched to his work and he found himself wishing there were some strong measures they could take to protect themselves against the rash of Cuban Paolos menacing their skies. Ben had rung to fill him in on the pilots meeting and to discuss future strategies regarding air piracy, and of course, to congratulate him on his own masterly handling of the Cuban hijack.

'You know, Pender,' Ben had opined, 'Ultimately, it will be up to us to protect our passengers and ourselves by flatly refusing to fly into any country that does not fully honour its anti-hijacking obligations.'

Graham fully agreed, adding his own belief that sanctions should be imposed against any country or airline that continued to serve offenders. But they both knew they were still a long way off from the worldwide adoption of such strict measures.

Yet on that sunny morning, despite the dangers so recently experienced by himself and his crew and the very real threat of further encounters in the unforeseeable future, the only real cloud on Graham's horizon was his inability to know when he would see Kay again. It nagged away at him until he determined not to leave it to chance but take matters into his own hands. Only that way could he be sure of them flying together again. But then a chance joking remark made by one of the pilots about him 'having the pick of the rosters *and* the women from now on' made him realise he had reckoned without rostering's view of the situation. He smiled wryly at the notion of himself now as their white-headed boy who could do no wrong and decided to wait until he got his advance copy of the hostess's fortnightly roster. And when he did what he saw did not disappoint him. On the contrary.

***

Flying out to New York for the first time following the hijacking Kay was aware of a different atmosphere amongst the crew. It took her a while to identify it. Everyone was apprehensive that the whole horror might begin again, only this time they might not be so fortunate as to come out of it unharmed. Of late, the talk in the restroom had been full of violence and some Atlantic hostesses had refused pointblank to fly. It seemed a number of other airlines had also been hijacked to Cuba and disturbing stories abounded of crews being roughed up on the ground at Havana by Cuban authorities. While not immune to fear herself, Kay had to admit it was really only her first flight after the hijack that was scary. All through it she had kept reminding herself that lightning seldom strikes in the same place twice, but it was about as little consolation as the same thought in the midst of a bad thunderstorm. She had found herself warily eyeing passengers, never knowing when one might pounce on her with some nefarious plan in mind. She was not the only one with such thoughts and it made for an uneasy atmosphere amongst the crew. It might have helped if they could have discussed it between them but those with service had been called into the Super's office before the flight and Judy had given them strict instructions,

'Keep up morale on board and no scaremongering.'

However, with the advent of the new roster Kay quickly regained her confidence for thankfully Captain Pender was once more in command on the flight deck, and crewing with him were the same tried and true mix of pilots and hostesses that had shared the Miami experience with him. The atmosphere immediately lightened and the passengers, on learning that their captain was the hero of the Cuban hijack, sent so many congratulatory messages to the cockpit that Kay had the pleasure of hearing Graham's resonant tones over the PA as he acknowledged their tributes and, with a slight humorous inflection, told them much as he would like to order a free bar sadly such gestures were not permitted *except* in the event of a hijacking. Whereupon the cabin had broken into delighted laughter and clapped so hard that the girls were convinced the passengers must have misunderstood, and believed drinks actually *were* on the house!

'What ever will we do?' one girl asked Kay worriedly, and she had felt like saying, 'Give it to them. Let's celebrate *not* being hijacked.'

But that had all been some weeks ago and now as Graham and Kay embarked upon their last scheduled flight together for some time they were nostalgically planning to make the most of their precious stopover in New York. Too much to expect rostering would continue to favour them for another month.

With the dinner service over and the lights dimmed in the cabin, Kay went into the galley to take her meal only to find one of the pilots already there before her, drinking coffee and chatting up the hostesses. When he turned his head she recognised the vulpine features of Captain Tully and almost turned again on her heel.

'You're looking fantastic, Kay, marriage suits you,' he told her. 'What do you say we do the town tonight in Noo York and have ourselves a ball?'

Kay laughed and, seizing a tray for the look of it, murmured, 'Work now, I'm afraid, pleasure later. Mustn't forget our passengers, must we?' escaping in to the cabin until it was safe to return to the galley and have her supper.

Captain Pender was anything but pleased that Dan Tully was travelling jump seat to New York on a three-day vacation. Had he been given prior warning Graham would have refused permission on any grounds to prevent Dan from entering the cockpit. All in the pilots lounge were familiar with Tully's infuriating behavior on the flight deck when other pilots were in command. 'Rotate,' he would call out at the exact instant when the jet was due to lift off the runway and mega seconds before the co-pilot got around to uttering it himself. He would then proceed to carry out all the after checks from the landing gear up to the ignition and engine anti-icing on, to flaps checked in, and all lights out; and even calling the altimeter check as they passed 10,000 ft and at the same time reminding the, by now, furious captain and co-pilot, to switch off the outboard landing lights.

Irritating and obnoxious were some of the milder epithets hurled at Dan.

Today throughout it all, despite the annoying and often confusing duplication of cross checks, Graham had managed to keep his temper and his wits about him, and was vastly relieved when Dan went aft, as Tully said himself, 'To take a pee' but not so glad when he came back raving about one of the hostesses he had bumped into.

'Oh my God! Looking sens-sational!' Dan groaned. 'Unbelievable what marriage does for those dollies. Ooh, la-la but this baby is hot!'

Graham ground his teeth when it was revealed that the 'hot' little number was none other than Kay Martin Mason and he growled at his co-pilot who was logging down the terminal forecasts for New York.

'So what's the temperature there, Joe?'

'Hold on, Skipper,' O'Loughlin removed his earphones and, with unusual good humour, grinned across at him. 'Would you believe 32 degrees? Whew! we'll be as limp as marshmallows.'

From behind came Dan's irritating chortle. 'Nothing like heat to raise the blood and get rid of inhibitions. Add ice cold martinis for two and it's open sesame.'

Graham frowned at his vulgarity, only regretting Sandy and his gory fire axe were not available on this trip to lay out Dan for the duration.

Within minutes Gander had cleared them to Kennedy Airport on North American routes 57 and given instructions for them to climb to and maintain Flight Level 3500. Dan and the Third Officer simultaneously reached forward to adjust the throttles to give climb power and the latter, viciously elbowing Tully aside, got there first. Graham noticed the scuffle and decided to ignore what he heard.

'Keep your effing hands off the throttles, Tully,' and wondered if he would be within his rights to banish Dan from the flight deck.

The situation was saved by the entrance of the senior hostess carrying food trays for the crew and a congratulatory message from a passenger who realized that Pender was the pilot who had successfully foiled the Cuban hijack attempt weeks previously.

'You don't say, Marion,' Graham was pleased. 'You might convey my thanks,' and at once Dan said with a sneer, 'If I'd been in your shoes, Pender, I would'a laid the bastard out permanently, only way to treat scum like that.'

'Oh, is that the reason why you brought a gun into New York last week?' Graham inquired pleasantly, but with a slight edge to his voice. 'Well, I just hope you didn't bring it aboard my flight today, Tully, or I'm afraid I shall have no course but to hand you over to the security police when we land.'

All on the flight deck hid grins as Dan subsided furious and red-faced in the jump seat, and was mercifully quiet for the rest of the trip. Graham pushed back his own seat from the controls and placing his meal tray on his lap, tucked into his chicken with relish. Thank God for a bit of peace, he thought, and fell to visualizing the stopover in New York. Maybe tonight they might have dinner somewhere special.

Whether or not it was the result of the oysters they had been served at 'Sparks' or the knowledge they might not be able to meet again for quite some time, their lovemaking that night exceeded all Kay's expectation. When she spoke about it, Graham muttered something about all men should undergo a spell in a prison camp, nothing like it for improving performance. But Kay did not really believe this and in the confident knowledge that she and only *she* inspired such reciprocal emotion in the depths of Graham's being, she reached even greater heights than before.

Captain Tully did not have a good night despite his high expectations, starting with the cocktail to end all cocktails, but which turned out to be quite beyond the ability of the unfriendly Irish barman who had not been long enough in New York to learn the art nor the humility to recognize it. In disgust, Dan returned to the hotel hoping to meet up with any aircrew still lingering about and bribed the desk clerk to show him the crew register.

'There was a great party hours ago, Dan sweetie,' one hostess mumbled sleepily. 'You should'a been there.' And another not so friendly hostess, whose voice sounded strangely familiar for the good reason he had already woken her ten minutes earlier, reminded him with a touch of asperity that no, she had *not* attended the party and did *not* want to share a nightcap with him, and that he now had the distinction of having *twice* ruined her night's sleep.

'Curse the wench,' he muttered, peering blearily at his list until seeing one name he should have rung long ago. The gorgeous Kay who had earlier played hard to get, bless her heart. Generously, Dan decided to give her second chance but was so taken back on hearing a sleepy male voice grunt, 'Wrong room,' that he replaced the receiver without another word.

'Who was that?' Kay murmured, not really caring.

'Some nut,' her lover answered, having straightaway recognised Tully's drunken voice. Bloody nerve, Graham thought, no longer sleepy and filled with unreasoning anger that so many pilots thought married hostesses were fair game, and then, with despair, acknowledged he was acting no differently himself.

He sighed and drew Kay closer, willing her to go back to sleep and yet knowing he wanted to make love to her again. No other woman had ever had such an effect on him. She was so passionate and yet strangely shy, he mused, further aroused by the thought.

'Oh darling,' he whispered, 'I wish we had somewhere special we could be together,' for while appreciating the convenience of crew stopovers he was aware the humdrum location fell far short of what their meetings should and could be. 'If we were only free to go to Italy or Spain,' he told her. 'Even for a few days, how wonderful it would be,' but an idea was already forming.

Kay felt only alarm at the suggestion. To her nothing could be better than their present whereabouts, thousands of miles from home and with the valid excuse of working for the airline to protect them. 'I suppose so,' she said cautiously. 'But these past few weeks have been marvellous.' Wide-awake, she pleaded his understanding. 'You must see how lucky we've been.'

Of course he did, but he had never liked subterfuge or tatty situations, and Dan Tully's phone call had made him see just how little claim he had to Kay. His frustration grew with the realization he could not even ward off the kind of sexual propositions that Tully, and other pilots like him, might make her. Most frustrating of all, he could not openly declare his love for her as he so desperately wanted.

'Go to sleep and we'll talk of it again,' he told her gently, the last thing he wanted was to pressurize her in any way. 'I just wanted to see you in a bikini, that's all,' and she giggled and relaxed against him.

Graham stared over her head into the darkness. There was always the apartment in Fuengirola, he mused, and once he first okayed his dates with Sile he could make use of it. They shared ownership and it was just the place to bring Kay, safer and more intimate than hotels. They would have their time together, he swore to himself, just as soon as he could arrange it.

***

Their time in Spain passed all too quickly. At first it had looked as though Kay would not be able to get away for Dave 's business conference in London, the first of three to be held that summer, overlapped her own absence by a week.

'How will we manage Sinead with both of us away at the same time,' her husband fretted, not wanting to use a child-minding agency which had been Kay's only suggestion. He was still upset, she knew, since calling into Kilshaughlin to visit her aunt on his way back from doing business in the north, shocked at the frail state of the old woman, even more to learn that Winifred was putting her mother into a home. Dave had always been fond of Molly Begley and often felt concerned as to how she was adjusting to country life, she had so loved her house and her life in Dublin. At first, Kay had been anguished at the news - poor Molly, she thought - surely Winifred and Cahal could have paid for someone, a retired nurse perhaps, to help them out with her aunt. But after her initial outburst, Kay quickly forgot, too distracted by the forthcoming trip to Spain with Graham and all the planning she must do in order to get away without arousing suspicion. In the end, Dave had prevailed upon his family to help out while they were both away. Eileen agreed to move into the house in their absence and mind the little girl; she would have to make sure that Breda helped out with Reggie, she said, but didn't see any problem. Kay had expected Graham to express relief and a similar delight to her own when she joyfully told him that she could get away after all, but he merely smiled and nodded as though never at any stage had he entertained any doubts. Men, Kay sighed to herself, but like always accepted that it was different for him.

On the fourth day of their precious six day holiday break Kay wished that she could put back the clock and begin it all over again; she felt like a bride on honeymoon with a passionate older man who could not bear to let her out of his sight. Even when she tentatively mentioned her air hostess friend, Sally, who had married a Spaniard and lived in Malaga with their two little sons, she saw how quickly he brushed aside the notion of visiting. She was the only one he wanted to be with, he told her, and she let it go like everything else. He was her whole world and nothing had ever quite filled the void left when she had thought him lost to her forever, not even the love Dave had offered her. But now, it was being filled to capacity by the one and only person capable of filling it and her life seemed to have a completeness missing before.

Of course, Kay knew the reentry would have to be faced soon, but not just yet. She relaxed under the beach canopy, crumbling bread for the sparrows hopping fearlessly about their table. Who knows, she thought, it may never happen. Which was taking the whole ostrich thing a bit far, even she had to agree, but so nice to dream on a bit longer. Drowsily, she returned Graham's smile and seeing something caressing and knowing in his glance, she was not surprised when he soon began gathering up their beach things with the suggestion they return to the apartment for a nap. Not that either had sleep on their minds as, arms entwined, they strolled back up the sandy track to the road. With another whole day and night before them Kay willed the hours to move slowly, wishing they might never end.

Later, lying behind drawn shades in the aftermath of lovemaking, there was more occasion for in-depth introspection as they spoke of a possible future together, ending wistfully with, 'Ah, if only's and maybe's' before Graham bunched his pillow beneath his head and slept. Kay slept too, but never so easily or trustfully, unable to rid herself of the fear that Captain Pender's former wife would come bursting in on top of them. Even when he assured her that Sile was away in the West Indies, she still felt nervous. Maybe it was not so much the thought of Sile, as anyone at all discovering them together that was causing Kay's unease, for her conscience was troubling her. She was unable to forget how affectionate Dave had been before he had left for London, expressing concern as to how she would manage in his absence and he away a whole fortnight. He was so conscientious and decent, she mused wretchedly, aware that by any standards she was treating him rottenly. And yet she had still set off for the airport next day by taxi, having explained away the unavailability of crew cars to the gullible Eileen as a one-day-lightning strike by crew drivers. She and Graham had flown down to Malaga on the same flight, although prudently seated apart, both relieved that none of the crew of the BAC1-11 was personally known to either of them. On arriving at the apartment Kay had thought how good it was being back in Spain, and then all too quickly the days had passed, and now regretfully time was flying even faster.

Our last night, she was thinking, as she and Graham sat watching a spectacular floor show, her senses stirred by the tempestuous music of the flamenco which to her mind epitomized all the passion and grandeur of Spain. The night was made memorable by the opportunity afforded them to dance once the floor show was over. The perfect ending to a perfect few days, Kay thought, as they went smoothly through the movements of the tango as though dancing it every day of their lives. She felt bemused by the surety of her own steps as she moved her hips and let herself be carried by the passionate beat, attributing this instinctive ease of movement to the fact that this was the dance of love and the seductive rhythm of lovers. In that enchanted moment Kay would have sacrificed everything, even her precious babe to be with Graham for all time, and in her momentary madness considered it would all be well lost for love.

In London Dave was also having an enjoyable time, he had always liked the city and considered the conference was a great opportunity to become familiar with it again. Since the merger, Maxwell Tailoring had been turning itself upside down in an effort to find new ways of improving their business. Of late, everything was being put under the microscope and their production, advertising and working methods closely scrutinized.

These two weeks in London would be spent in discussion with other clothing manufacturers and there was the possibility of opening a branch of Maxwell's in Kensington. What they needed was a more youthful, sporty image, Dave knew, for according to market studies young men were not going for tweed these days but turning to continental style jackets in mohair and other lightweight fabrics.

Perhaps they should be rethinking on similar lines. In this, Dave was somewhat influenced by the fact that his assistant, Anne Stack, had already enthusiastically supported this viewpoint, making it clear that, like himself, she was all for creating a trendier style. At the same time, he was pleased that she had some good ideas about retaining the traditional tweed, knowing this could only find approval amongst senior members, tweed sports jackets being one of the company's most popular lines.

'Well, let me tell you my tweedy plans have mainly women in mind,' Anne warned, pausing to gauge Dave's reaction. 'How about introducing a new line particularly aimed at the tourist market? You know the sort of thing. Designer suits, capes and jackets in heather tweed mixtures. I believe they could really go down well with Americans and in time we might carry it over to accessories.'

They were sitting in the hotel bar at the end of a day of continual meetings, enjoying a welcome drink. 'Well, I don't see why it wouldn't catch on, I think it's a good idea,' Dave pronounced, and Anne looked pleased

When he went back to Tony with her suggestion, his boss was plainly impressed. 'Good thinking,' he approved. 'Definitely worth pursuing. Put it forward at the next meeting, Dave, and you can count on my backing.'

'Sure,' Dave agreed, thinking the more dealings he had with Anne, the more he admired her work. At the same time, he was becoming increasingly aware that Anne, the woman, was producing in him emotions of a far warmer kind.

***

That same week Captain Higgins did his best to get a good severance packet for the undeserving Captain Christy Kane, whose over-fondness for alcohol had finally ended his rocky career with CA when the morning after a stopover in Barcelona, the pilot had been too hung over to get the flight off the ground. Neither Ben nor Andy were sorry see the back of him. It was not as if it were Christy's first offence, far from it. He was on his last warning. They prided themselves on CA's excellent safety record and in it, they agreed, there was no place for negligent pilots. Christy didn't take it well, threatened and blustered, determined not to go without a struggle. In the circumstances they did very well for him, Ben thought, not that Christy was grateful. Still, as Andy put it, there was a certain loyalty owing to a brother officer, and undeniably they had gone out of their way to give him every chance.

Now Captain Higgins had another pressing matter on his mind, this time to do with his friend and colleague, Graham Pender, who was at present away in Spain on leave. That morning Ben had received the expected notification from BALPA regarding the preliminary court hearing of the legal action being taken by Eastline Airways that was now scheduled to be held in Colombo in one week's time.

'We can arrange for a barrister to represent Captain Pender at the initial session,' the officer advised Ben, 'But Pender will have to personally attend the court hearing to be held later in the month. He will receive a summons shortly.'

Ben scribbled a note to Graham apprising him of the situation and placed it prominently on the noticeboard where he would see it on his return. Not the nicest of homecomings, Ben sighed, and went across the corridor to update Andy on the matter.

On arriving back from Spain, Graham was deeply disquieted to find the summons awaiting him and his heart sank at the thought of returning to Colombo, and the inevitable publicity it would bring. He consoled himself with the thought that at least he would be spared the preliminary court session, but knew it was only a postponement of the fraught moment. He felt a further sense of letdown on finding the house empty and a note from Nonie on the kitchen table. Linda Higgins had kindly invited them to a barbecue at her house and she urged him to join them there.

Graham crumpled it up and went upstairs to unpack. He was conscious of missing Kay already, indeed from the moment they had walked away from each other at the airport he had felt immediately bereft. With a pang, he recalled her acute disappointment at not sitting together on the flight home. Although greatly tempted to give in to her plea, he had deemed it wiser not to. It had been so damnably hard, forced to coldly part from each other without even a handshake, when his every instinct had been to sweep her into his arms and to hell with the consequences.

Selecting a fresh shirt from his wardrobe, Graham slipped it on and began doing up the buttons. As he did, his fingers touched the medal hanging about his neck, and his tense expression softened, remembering how Kay had come in from shopping one morning with the silver St Christopher medal on a heavy link chain, saying, 'It saved you once before, darling. Won't you please wear it always?'

In return, he had given Kay a gold antique ring with a solitaire diamond sunk in its centre. He knew it would not be easy for her to find opportunities to wear it but she had been thrilled with the gift and told him she would keep it for those times when they were together. In retrospect, Graham wondered if he should have put such a burden on her but he had been unable to resist the impulse, even though it fell far short of the wedding ring he most wanted to give her.

Walking in the side gate of Ben's house the appetizing smell of barbecued meat reached him, and Graham realized just how hungry he was.

'Dad!' Nicholas was the first to spot his father and came eagerly running. 'Gosh! Dad, you really got the sun.' Gripping his father's arm possessively, he marched him back to the others.

'Graham, so glad you could come,' Linda touched cheeks with him and Nonie smiled at him from her comfortable basket chair

Ben raised a lazy hand. 'Come and sit down, Pender.'

Graham sat into an adjacent chair and, accepting a beer from Linda, he smiled absently down at Ranjan, sitting cross-legged on the grass beside him. The summons was still very much on Graham's mind and he resolved to have a word with Ben as soon as he got a chance, knowing his opinion would be valuable. In the meantime, for politeness sake, he kept to general topics, enjoying the beer as he caught up on the airport doings and Captain Kane's ignominious departure.

It was nearing ten o'clock when the lads came down from the loft where they had been fencing, and ignoring Graham's reminder of how late it was getting, they ran off into the gathering dusk, intent on prolonging the fun.

'You might as well have another beer, Pender,' Ben chuckled. 'That lot don't sound like they are ready to go yet.'

Graham accepted defeat and the drink gracefully. 'Thanks, but then we really must be off and let you all get to bed.'

'No rush.' Ben offered him a cigar, and for a time they talked of flying matters until Graham got restlessly to his feet.

'I'd better go round them up,' he said, and Ben walked with him to the end of the tennis court, every so often stopping and hollering for his sons to show themselves. As they drew nearer there was the sound of scuffling and muffled laughter in the shadows, and then all was quiet again.

'Little blighters,' Ben said tolerantly. 'Time to exert some parental control, I suppose,' but saying it with such a lack of interest that Graham philosophically decided to let him handle it in his own way. Both men relaxed against the bole of a mature oak tree bordering the court and Graham took a last pull at his diminished cigar, before stamping it into the ground.

'By the way thanks for your note. No further word from BALPA I suppose?'

'Just the phone call from London,' Ben admitted. 'They have engaged a barrister to represent you and he seems to think the actual hearing will be sooner than expected. Bit of an ordeal I imagine going back to Ceylon again,' casting Graham a sympathetic glance. 'It's not looking too good there at present with activists bombing buses and the usual repercussions from the military.'

Graham nodded, but declined to pursue the topic. 'So you think the actual hearing will be fairly soon then?'

'By the end of the month possibly. Of course, it depends on certain factors, the availability of witnesses, evidence and so on.'

'What worries me is their claim to have two strong witnesses,' Graham's voice was strained. 'I can't think who they might be or how they came to be called, and should the case go against me how I am ever going to prove my innocence.'

"Don't think too much about it,' Ben advised. 'It won't come to that. We'll have the best lawyers preparing your defense and don't forget our counsel will be calling their own witnesses too, and doing everything to support you.'

'Thanks, Higgins. I appreciate that.' Both men fell silent for a time until suddenly rousing himself, Ben let out a ferocious roar for his sons to appear. 'Right now! On the double!' At once, three figures materialized out of the gloom and Jeremy hurriedly joined his father.

'What the hell do you mean keeping Captain Pender waiting about like this?' Ben growled, and the lads chorused sheepishly, 'Sorry, sir.'

Ben sighed. 'Okay, where are the other two?'

'We'll go get them,' Conor offered, and Martin eagerly turned to go with him but Ben, with his hands on their necks, firmly pushed them towards the house.

'Oh no, you don't. I'll find them myself.'

Unseen, high in the branches of the oak tree, Ranjan and Nicholas stared at each other in consternation, and the latter began trembling violently. 'Did Dad really say he's going back to Colombo?' Nicholas asked in a shocked whisper.

'Yeah,' Ranjan nodded. 'Sounds like he's in real trouble, man.'

As he swung himself down to the lower branches, Nicholas's thoughts were at once fearful and hopeless. Surely Dad couldn't be going back amongst those savages again, he thought in horror. This time they'll kill him for sure.

Ranjan's thoughts were fearful too and he remained awake for a long time that night, staring beyond the window at the moon. If the Captain Tuan was forced to return to Colombo, Ranjan decided, then he must go with him and protect him. The boy was filled with longing to be back amongst his own people again, wistfully envisioning the blue skies and flaming sunsets, the vivid flowers and vegetation.

Over the years he had deliberately suppressed his memories, refusing to allow himself to dwell on all he had left behind him. But once the self-appointed lock on the past was removed he was overwhelmed by images, both sad and bittersweet, as he recalled his childhood years growing up in the presence of his parents and his beloved sister, Sita; and then he found himself dwelling on Harinath Prasad whom he admired and longed to see again. Perhaps there was some way his friend could help the Captain Tuan, the boy thought, and resolved to write at once to the Tamil leader. His decision made, sleep came to him at last.

***

Kay arrived home that Sunday afternoon feeling acutely lonely following her parting from Graham, striving to keep in mind that she was supposed to be returning from a week in Chicago when answering Eileen's questions.

'Got in very late today, didn't you?' her mother-in-law asked. 'I thought you would be home at your usual time. Chicago, wasn't it?'

'To begin with yes,' Kay cautiously agreed, desperately wondering what she had said on leaving for Spain, then mercifully remembering. 'But then we were diverted and had to pick up an out-of-hours crew from Boston,' although it was extremely unlikely any such thing would have happened so far off course but Eileen was unlikely to know that. It was her next remark that struck panic in Kay.

'It wasn't all work I see…you got a bit of the sun. That's nice, dear.'

To Kay's relief that was the end of it but she would not have been quite so happy if she had seen Eileen's puzzled expression when coming across sand in the laundry basket. When later Kay was on her own again and the telephone rang, her heart leapt in the hope it was Graham breaking their agreed rule, and she almost gave herself away when it turned out to be Dave.

'Good timing!' she forced congratulation into her tone. 'Baby bedded and your mother returned to base. How's it going?'

'Great! Really great,' Dave said cheerfully. 'Great ideas generating and altogether a most satisfactory first meeting.' There was a plummy resonance to his tone, making her to wonder if he had been drinking.

And why not, she thought, remembering all the wine that she and Graham had drunk in Spain, not to mention their lovemaking.

'And yourself...how are you?'

'Great!' Kay echoed parrot-like. 'Sinead sunny as ever, she and Eileen closer than twins,' adding hastily. 'Your mother was really terrific. I don't know how I would have managed without her.'

'Good old Ma,' said Dave, with unusual affection. Definitely, he'd been drinking. Kay was amused. 'So the conference is all you hoped?' she enquired.

'And more,' Dave agreed enthusiastically. 'Tell you all about it when I see you. Less than a week to go now and I'm really looking forward to being home again.'

'Me too.' Kay was surprised to find she meant it, nothing else could bring her back to earth, she thought. The past weeks free of all restraint had been heady and unsettling but dangerous too, she saw that now. Any more freedom and she would become utterly relaxed and uninhibited, intimate visions of herself and Graham flooding her mind, making it impossible to concentrate.

'So when are you flying again?'

'Tomorrow,' she spoke without thinking, and heard the surprise in his voice. 'Isn't that a bit soon?'

Kay could have bitten off her tongue. 'What am I saying?' She forced a laugh. 'But I just may have to fly a day earlier, we deadheaded part of the way this last trip.'

'So Ma said. She seemed more than a bit confused as to which part of America you were. I thought she even mentioned Boston at one stage.'

'Well, it started out that way and then we had delays and an extra overnight and I don't know what else,' she lied drearily, wishing they could get off the subject.

'Poor Katie,' Dave said with such sympathy that Kay felt even worse. 'You sound like you've had an exhausting trip.' His voice became concerned. 'I hope I won't find you pale and wasted by the time I get back. Listen, I've got to go. Mind yourself!'

'You too.' She replaced the receiver, only glad he was unable to see how wrong he was, and she positively blooming from an excess of sun and sex.

Next day Kay flew out to New York. On her return Eileen informed her that some young woman 'refusing to identify herself' had rung twice. Guessing Florrie to be the anonymous caller, Kay invited her over for a chat. She had just put Sinead to bed when her friend arrived, and straightaway asked, 'What's all this about being in America when the roster says you're on holidays?'

Kay sighed and wondered whether to tell her the truth. 'I got the chance of a few days away in the sun,' she said vaguely, but Florrie was not to be fobbed off, immediately putting so many pertinent questions that Kay cried, 'Oh, for God's sake, Florrie, don't put me on the rack. You *know* I was away with Graham.'

'Yes, I did think you might.' Florrie fell silent, an unusual occurrence for her, so that Kay felt required to justify herself.

'I know what you're thinking but in the present circumstances it's almost impossible to meet and he wanted it so much…well, I did too,' she admitted. 'It was a fantastic few days…like nothing you could imagine.'

Seeing Florrie's skeptical expression, Kay cut short her raptures, 'I never asked to be involved like this. I hate what I'm doing to Dave. Look, I know you find it hard to understand but I'm awfully fond of him. I always have been but Graham… he is my whole life.' There, she had said it at last.

'Take care of yourself, Kay,' was Florrie's only comment as she hugged her goodbye in the old affectionate manner. As if, Kay thought bewildered, none of what she said had got through to her.

But it had got through all right. Florrie saw more clearly than Kay imagined just how deeply her friend was enamored of Graham Pender. In that moment, Florrie was filled with great pity and compassion for Dave, knowing he was going to be very badly hurt and there was nothing she could do to prevent it.

***

With only days to go before his departure to Colombo Graham managed to arrange a swap with the pilot of Kay's flight, as a result they had a two-day stopover in New York to look forward to. Kay's delight at this unexpected bonus was somewhat shadowed by the prospect of the impending separation and she found it impossible to put aside all thoughts of the dangers Graham could be facing and the uncertainty of the judicial outcome. Graham was troubled too, but he did his best to hide it and went all out to spoil her with a delicious pre-opera supper of oysters, fillet steaks and glasses of Merlot, before they attended a magical production of *La Bohème* at the Metropolitan Opera House. It was the last night of the opera and they had been lucky to get tickets. But inevitably, their weariness, the food and wine consumed before the opera, was their undoing and Kay found herself dropping off to sleep during the performance. Once on waking snow was falling on the stage, another time there was a real live donkey and cart before her lids came wearily down once more. Graham began nodding off too. In the end, he suggested with a sleepy chuckle, that they end the agony and go back to the hotel and sleep. It was rather an expensive waste but neither had wanted to miss the chance of seeing the production of their favourite opera and from the glimpses they got from behind drooping lids they agreed with the reviews that it really was spectacular. It was a good start and they continued to make the most of their time together, aware it was their last opportunity for some time. Maybe they overdid it, but Kay felt unwell next day, wryly putting it down to the oysters and fearing she might get sick.

'As a rule the standard is very good at that restaurant,' Graham frowned. But even in the best of restaurants, they both knew, you could be unlucky with shellfish.

But maybe it wasn't the oysters, Kay thought, maybe she was just upset because Graham was going far away and she had no idea when they would meet again. It might have helped if they had been able to talk about it but each time she tried to bring it up, he immediately changed the subject. All he would say was that he was bringing the Indian boy and his youngest son along with him on the trip for company. True, they would miss the beginning of the school term, he shrugged, but it wasn't as if they were in exam classes, they would quickly catch up on their return.

Not until Kay awoke during the night from a nightmare in which she was being tortured to the point of screaming, did she realise just how much Graham was dreading reentering the country in which he had been held hostage. Her heart thumping in fright she became aware of the violent thrashing movements in the dark beside her, but before she could press the light switch she heard Graham scream again and her blood ran cold.

'Graham, darling, what is it?' Distraught, she scrabbled for the switch then peered into his face, feeling terribly frightened.

All at once he was awake, looking at her in a daze, recognition gradually dawning. 'Oh God! I'm sorry!' he groaned, throwing an arm across his face while she tried to calm herself, the dreadful sound still trapped in her head.

At last, he took down his arm and turned to look at her. 'Are you all right? I hope I didn't hurt you.' He looked so unhappy, so remorseful.

Kay shook her head, hugging her arms to her chest, still not over her fright, but wanting to reassure him. 'I'm all right...so long as you are.' He kissed her and held her close, and then by his even breathing she knew he had fallen asleep again. For a long time she hovered on the edge, before finally losing consciousness herself.

On arriving home from what had been an idyllic two days apart from the frightening nightmare, Kay tried to come to terms with the prospect of being without Graham for God knows how long. Soon Dave would be attending the second business conference in London and she would be reliant once more on Eileen for help in managing

Sinead in his absence. But none of it seemed to matter, only the terrible waste with both men away at the same time and no chance of Graham and herself making use of their precious weeks of freedom. Her only consolation was the memory of those wonderful two days in New York and the conversation they had shared in the hour before crew pickup, when Graham had suddenly turned to her saying,

'Dearest Kitty, if only you would come and live with me I would gladly take care of you and your little girl.' For a crazy moment she had considered just upping and taking off, until reality reasserting she knew that Dave would do everything in his power to prevent her. Besides, whatever he felt about losing her, he would never give up his beloved daughter, madness to even think it!

And then Graham had said in a low voice, 'Would you leave all and come live with me?' Looking into his face, she saw that he meant it but still she said, 'Are you actually asking me or is it a hypothetical question?'

'It's not a hypothetical question.' His dark eyes were serious.

'Darling,' she stroked his hand. 'If I were free and hadn't Sinead to think of I would not hesitate to say yes.'

'That's not what I asked you.'

It was unfair, Kay thought, wishing she knew what to say, wishing most of all he had not put the question. And then she saw he was frowning and looking away from her and terrified of losing him, she blurted, 'Yes, yes, of course I would.'

'And will you?' He could not have put it more bluntly.

'Yes, if you really mean it.' She waited and then chose her words carefully, 'But I can't give up my child and Dave will never let her go, you must understand that.'

'Believe me, I do understand. But that's something we'll face when the time comes. The main thing is that you are prepared to share my life,' and all constraint gone from his manner he had taken her in his arms and made love to her with tenderness and passion. Every waking moment since then Kay was torn apart at the thought of losing Sinead, for she knew that she was only fooling herself to think that she would not give up everything, even her precious child, to be with him.

Within hours of Graham's departure Kay dropped Dave to the airport. With the car engine idling in the parking lot, she heard him say, 'Don't bother to come in with me, Katie. It's too awkward with Sinead. We'll say goodbye here and you can head off.'

Kay was about to protest then changed her mind. 'Okay, whatever you like,' she agreed. It was probably more sensible than dragging the baby all the way inside for the few minutes that were in it, she told herself, but she felt a bit disappointed.

The previous night Dave had not availed of the opportunity of making love to her, his last chance for some time, and she had attributed his failure to his preoccupation with getting ready for his trip. It was neither natural nor flattering – it was all of four weeks since they had last lain together - and she was at a loss to understand it. As it was, there were too many evenings when he fell asleep in front of the television or else went up to bed ahead of her. Still, she had not believed he would go away without making some effort to love her. As she waved goodbye to him, Kay thought it was ironic how Graham was unable to sleep for wanting to make love to her and Dave could not remain awake long enough to get up any interest.

Almost clinically, she wondered how her husband would react if she were to blurt out the plans that she and Graham had made to spend the rest of their lives together. 'We'll discuss it as soon as I come back from Colombo, darling,' he had said, before parting from her. 'We can't go on as we are.'

Driving back to the empty house Kay's heart was rent with a new kind of sadness at hearing Sinead plaintively calling, 'Bye-bye, Dada,' from the back seat. Oh, if only she weren't caught up in this awful emotional tangle, she thought, feeling overwhelmed. One good thing was the improvement in her skin, she cheered herself, remembering how the unsightly rash on her forehead and cheeks had sent her hurrying to the doctor before the Super noticed and grounded her. The doctor had sent her to a skin specialist and he had prescribed tablets which had thankfully cleared it up. But even this undoubted relief was tempered by the fact that Kay still felt unwell, no doubt from the bug picked up in New York. But maybe it wasn't a bug after all, she thought for the second time, maybe it was just that the skin tablets was not agreeing with her. But whatever the reason they were doing their job, she thought, loth to give them up.

***

In the seven days since Graham arrived in Colombo the prosecution had relentlessly questioned each of the Eastline Airways pilots, hammering away at them until they became sullen and uncooperative. It had not been easy forced to sit each day listening to the evidence piling up against them, the way counsel for the prosecution, a Sinhalese barrister with hooded lids and full sneering lips, managed to keep twisting the facts and present the Tamils in a criminal light. From their beaten expressions, Graham saw that they had given themselves up for lost. From the first morning heavy security was in place. Armed members of the Colombo security forces with riot shields and tear gas were lined up in front of the courthouse, and demonstrators displayed anti-terrorist banners and chanted slogans. Graham was body-searched before being permitted to enter the building, and his briefcase examined. Nicholas and Ranjan were required to produce identification and to empty their pockets. Graham was relieved when his turn came at last to take the stand, anxious to clear his name and get the whole thing over him. But it soon became clear that from very little the prosecution had built a damning case against him, and by the time he had been subjected to his own share of rigorous cross-examination he felt his confidence draining away. Their first witness was an elderly Australian who told the court how his son had left home to seek work in Colombo six years earlier. When he had not heard from his son again he had believed that the young man had done well for himself and, in his newfound prosperity, forgotten his family. Some time afterwards the elderly man's neighbour, who had been away for some years, recently returned to live in Bombay. In passing, he had happened to mention seeing the old man's son at the airport waiting to board the Eastline Airways flight on the day of the crash. Breaking down, the old man said it was this that convinced him his son must have perished along with all the others who lost their lives in the raging Monsoon storm that brought the plane down that day. Eventually, stepping down from the witness stand, he was led weeping from the court.

Listening to his testimony, Graham was stunned, wondering how he could have forgotten the incident, it was like a thick fold of memory in his brain had suddenly opened out. All too vividly he recalled the Bombay airport manager's insistence that he agree to allow the Aussie entrance to the flight deck, threatening to further delay the flight if Graham did not comply. Prosecution then accused Captain Pender of being in collusion with the young Australian, insisting that he had given him access to the cockpit in order to gain his help in absconding with the gold on board. It was even suggested that Graham had not, as he claimed, been imprisoned by the ILA for four years. Instead, he had been working all that time alongside the terrorists, training new recruits in warfare and the use of military explosives.

'Is it not very strange,' the prosecution sneered, 'that the leader of the freedom fighters, Harinath Prasad, twice risked his life and that of his men in an effort to rescue Captain Pender and yet he has all along repeatedly denied any association with them?'

Counsel for Defense sprang to his feet, 'Objection, my client speaks the truth. It was merely coincidental that he was rescued by Prasad at the same time as Sita Shanti's brother.'

'Overruled,' the judge snapped. 'Please continue.'

Prosecution beamed. 'Thank you, my lord. And was it merely a coincidence that afterwards Captain Pender brought this boy back to his own country to live with him, paying for his expensive schooling and even seeking to legally adopt the boy? Or is it a coincidence that this same Tamil youth is here in Colombo today - in this very courtroom - having accompanied Captain Pender and his son all this way?'

The barrister opened the folder he was carrying and drawing out two envelopes and a brightly-colored postcard, he held them triumphantly aloft. 'The fact that Ranjan Shanti has all along kept up correspondence with Harinath Prasad is no coincidence I assure you. What I have here in my hand is concrete evidence that Shanti communicated with Prasad as recently as one month ago,' and dispensing with the usher the barrister for the Prosecution went right up to the bench and placed the letters before the judge.

At once there was an uproar in the court and two reporters jumped up and left the room. The judge rapped his gavel sharply to restore order, and as the prosecution's damning implication burned into Graham's brain a wave of hopelessness washed over him and he had to stop himself from burying his face in his hands. They had already found him guilty, he thought bitterly, and to think only that morning he had told Nicholas and Ranjan in another couple of days they would be winging their way home.

***

Daily, Kay searched the newspapers for mention of the Colombo trial, but could find nothing. She was glad for Graham's sake knowing how much he dreaded the unwelcome publicity, but for her own peace of mind she would have welcomed some indication of how the hearing was proceeding. Without him, her days seemed endless and she was missing him terribly. Stopovers in New York were dull and boring and only deepened her sense of loss, for she was constantly reliving their times together.

At home, without Dave, she was similarly conscious of the space beside her at night, but was untroubled by the kind of hunger for his touch that tormented her in Graham's absence. The hope of sharing a few days with her lover on his return was the only thing sustaining Kay; more and more she was coming to accept that Graham Pender was vital to her happiness, regardless of whom she must hurt or sacrifice. She did not have a choice anymore. It was that simple. And then one afternoon having wheeled Sinead to the shops to pick up the evening paper, she was taken aback to see the damning headlines, 'Latest Evidence in Colombo Trial Links Irish Pilot with Tamil Separatists.'

Kay's thoughts whirled in dismay as she released the brake on the stroller and pushed it vigorously along the pavement, almost running in her haste to get home.

'Not saying hello to anyone today,' the woman from three doors down called, briskly pushing her own children past in a double baby buggy. But Kay did not slow down intent on gaining privacy behind her front door.

Once inside, she left Sinead sitting in the buggy surrounded by shopping bags, and scanned the newspaper in horror and disbelief. Oh God, she thought. Graham had been so sure he would prove his innocence and be on his way back home within a week or so. What could have happened to change all that?

Gripping the paper tightly, Kay read with dread that Captain Pender could be facing up to twenty years in prison, if found guilty. If that were to happen, she thought, he would be as dead to her as he had been following the Colombo air crash. Only this time she would not get over her loss, she knew, this time she would be losing not only her lover but the father of the child she was carrying. Her heart twisting at the thought, she remembered how the persistent bouts of nausea had driven her to seek an appointment with her skin specialist, convinced the tablets he prescribed were not agreeing with her.

'I never feel well these days,' she confessed. 'Isn't there something else you could give me?'

And he had shot back, 'Tell me, Mrs Mason, are you by any chance taking the contraceptive pill?'

'Why, y..yes,' Kay stammered, thinking what that had to do with anything? 'I've been on the pill since Sinead was a few months old but it never made me feel sick before.'

'Don't you see it's not the pill or the skin tablets that's causing your nausea, Mrs Mason. Antibiotics *have* been known to suppress the pill, you know. You had better have a pregnancy test.'

'But you never told me,' she protested, feeling betrayed.

'Nor did you tell me that you were taking the pill,' he replied smoothly, and she felt suddenly outraged. Surely it was his job to ask such questions and to warn his patients? She wasn't a doctor, was she? She felt a wave of despair. How could she possibly have known that one tablet could wipe out another?

Now her situation, devoid of any redeeming feature, struck her and she felt panic rising. It should have afforded her some measure of relief, even joy, to be so sure it was Graham's baby - in very different circumstances it surely would have - but just then Kay would have welcomed a measure of doubt, if only to save her from exposure. Supposing Graham did not return, what then? How could she ever tell Dave for he would know at once the baby was not his, they hadn't made love in weeks. But maybe it would be all right, she told herself, needing something to hold on to, Graham loved her. He had said it and, indeed, proved it many times.

Yes, Yes but what if he doesn't come back?

The question plagued her like a relentless creditor refusing to be dismissed, and she was overwhelmed by the vulnerability of her position. Pregnant and alone, all her career plans fast dissolving, facing the very real possibility of being cast off by her husband, and maybe her lover too. It was just as well that she didn't live in some Eastern country, she thought bitterly, or she could have been stoned for adultery,

A pathetic wailing cry recalled Kay to her surroundings, and she turned blindly to where she had left Sinead. The child was watching her collapsed parent with flushed face and frightened questioning eyes, and now she broke into heartrending sobs. Controlling her own grief with an effort, Kay hurried to pick her up.

'Hush, baby, hush, it's all right,' she told her thickly. 'Mommy hurt her finger. See it's better now,' and the little girl checked her sobs and inspected it gravely.

'Mama saw finger?'

'That's right,' Kay hugged her close and Sinead gradually calmed, for she had recently caught her own finger in a door and well understood the pain.

'Kiss better.' That had been the ritual and Kay's heart swelled with love and contrition as the tender little mouth pursed up and pressed gently against her skin.

'Let's go lie down,' she suggested, carrying the child upstairs to her cot. Arriving breathless on the landing, she suddenly changed her mind and put Sinead into her own bed, then slipping out of her jeans she got under the coverlet with her.

It felt good to stretch out. Everything seemed better from the horizontal. Giving herself up to the warm comfort of the bed Kay welcomed the weight of the child lying against her. It was a painful reminder of how little bodily contact she had had lately, how much she missed being held and caressed since Graham had gone away. Her eyes filled with sudden tears and she was assailed by wave upon wave of loneliness, aching for his touch and her shivering need of him.

***

In Colombo, the prosecution produced another witness in court, the usher handing the Sinhalese woman into the witness stand and swearing her in. Every man in the room avidly watched Daya Begum, all except Captain Pender. This woman was about to perjure herself and destroy them all, he thought in despair. He shifted in his seat and deliberately refrained from glancing up at the boys in the gallery, remembering their anxious questions during the brief lunch period, when he had been unable to eat anything but a piece of chapata bread and swallow a few sips of water. Instinctively realizing things were not going well, they had shown little appetite either.

The prosecutor took his time as he approached the stand seeming to invite the packed court to admire the witness, his full lips curved in a lascivious smile. Dressed in a close-fitting scarlet sari tailor-made by her verandah *darzi* to fit every curve and indentation of her voluptuous figure, Daya had chosen high-heeled strap sandals and dangling ruby ear rings to complete the effect. Her jet black hair was twisted in a coil, loose strands falling enticingly upon her neck.

What followed passed in a blur for Graham as the prosecutor put questions to the witness and she answered readily, admitting that she had all along had her suspicions about the traitor, Sita Shanti, who was the airport manager's secretary.

'But he refused to believe me,' Daya frowned. 'He could see no wrong in this woman for she had bewitched him.'

'And when he did not heed your warning you took the matter further?'

'Yes. I informed the ILA of this woman's involvement with the freedom fighters and *they* took immediate action as I knew they would.'

'They kidnapped her and subsequently killed her. Is that correct?'

Daya pouted. 'She got only what she deserved.'

'Undoubtedly!'

And then had come the question Graham was dreading.

'In the matter of the pilots who were in league with the freedom fighters you have given us certain names. Can you tell point out to us if any of these persons is at present in the courtroom?'

Daya's heavily kohled eyes swept the dock and the benches, and then she nodded. 'Yes,' extending a pointing finger at the Tamil pilots, and Graham's heart sank as her gesture included him. 'There they are, those are the men.'

Involuntarily, Captain Pender raised his eyes to the far corner of the high gallery, fearing the adverse effect of Begum's testimony on Nicholas and Ranjan. In a panic, he searched the wooden benches and his heart thudded in shock for there was no sign of them. They had already left their seats, were no longer in the courtroom.

Ranjan ran down the stairs to the entrance of the courthouse unable to sit and listen any longer to what his sister's betrayer was saying about her. Lies, lies, all lies. Anxiously, Nicholas hurried after him.

'Wait, Ranji, wait,' he called. 'I'm coming with you.'

But the Indian boy gave no sign of having heard him nor did he slacken his pace, his brain teeming with the witness's callous admission that she had sent Sita to her death. And now she was brazenly intent on destroying the Captain Tuan, Ranjan thought, in his sorrow and rage feeling new determination.

'But I will not let her do that,' he swore. 'I am a man now and I will not stand by and see it happen. If you are watching over me,

Sita, you need have no fear for I will avenge your death,' he promised, and through a blur of tears, became aware of the security man blocking his exit.

Mindful of the Captain Tuan's strict instructions, Ranjan automatically slowed but the man waved him on without comment, the day was almost over and only those entering the courthouse concerned him now.

Once outside, Ranjan walked away rapidly, barely conscious of the direction he took, anxious to put distance between himself and the courthouse. On colliding with a burly bearded man, he was startled to hear his name softly called.

'Say nothing, Ranjan,' the man told him in Tamil. 'Just follow after me, my brother,' and with a thrill of shock Ranjan recognized Harinath Prasad.

Despite the instruction to remain silent, he blurted, 'Hari, is it really you?' the Tamil words coming slowly to his tongue after so long.

Harinath did not reply but walked on quickly and Ranjan swiftly followed. Some distance behind, Nicholas broke into a run in an effort to catch up.

'Ranji, where are you going?' he shouted, but Ranjan had rounded the corner and disappeared from sight. Moments later, Nicholas was in time to see him getting into a black sedan car, and making a tremendous effort he raced forward managing to reach it before the rear door closed.

'Ranji!' he shouted in to him. 'What am I to tell Dad?'

At once, the bearded man turned his head and spoke rapidly, and one of the men in the back seat got out again. Grabbing up Nicholas, he bundled him roughly into the back of the car and jumped in after him. Engine roaring, the car took off at speed.

***

The boys were gone two days and there was still no word of them. Graham felt torn by worry and the Chief Pilot's words kept returning to haunt him. 'I suppose you know what you're about, Pender,' Andy had said dourly, 'But believe me I would hesitate before bringing my sons into that hellhole.'

Andy Hegarty could not have been blunter nor given better advice but Graham had not heeded his words, too busy insulating himself against his return to enemy country to be able to think rationally. He realised this now when it was too late.

On the advice of his lawyer Graham had not contacted the police, instead he had put a call through to the British ambassador who told him, 'Of course, it's early days yet, Pender. The Indian boy may be merely seeking to find his relatives and your son went along with him. You know how adventurous young boys can be. It's probably nothing more than that, you'll see.'

But Graham did not believe that Ranjan would disobey his express instructions not to leave the court room or go sightseeing on their own without good reason. He had been quite clear about that under penalty of punishment. But what about Nicholas, Graham wondered uneasily, remembering how disappointed his son had been when told they would not have time to visit Adam's Peak. From the beginning, he had talked about climbing all 5,500 steps to the summit and seeing for himself '*Sri Pada*,' the sacred footprint carved in stone he had read so much about. 'If we do the climb at night, Dad,' he had said excitedly, 'The sunrise and the view are supposed to be spectacular.'

When Graham mentioned this to the ambassador he chuckled, 'Well, we won't rule it out. All of us have played truant at that age, Pender. I'll do what I can my end and, in the meantime, try not to worry.'

Feeling somewhat reassured Graham had replaced the receiver.

It was a relief when Captain Higgins arrived in Colombo, coming straight from the airport to attend the court and give evidence on his behalf. Graham had spent a sleepless night consumed by worry about the boys, but his heart lifted at the sight of that familiar stalwart figure and hurried forward to greet him.

'Good of you to come, Higgins,' he told him and Ben's handshake was firm and his tone encouraging as he replied, 'Only too glad, Pender, you'll beat this you'll see.'

The defense were intent on making up for any gains made by the prosecution the previous day, and Graham felt more cheerful by the time the judge declared a recess for lunch. By this several witnesses had taken the stand, the first being Hughes, the airport manager, then Matt Rogan and finally Captain Higgins, the latter telling the court how he had known Captain Pender for over twenty years having flown with him both as a military and commercial pilot, and he could vouch for his impeccable character. He had gone on to speak of Graham's impressive flying record and his shockingly frail health at the time of his rescue concluding, 'Even his own sons failed to recognize their father in the frail white-haired man who had to be helped from the aircraft when we landed at RAF Lynam,' and Graham felt a lump of sorrow in his throat for the truth of this.

Others took the stand to vouch for him too, and Graham listened in weary gratitude as representatives of BALPA echoed Ben's good opinion of him, and vouched for his integrity and excellent war record, when like other members of the Irish Air Corps in the forties Graham had courageously united with pilots of the Royal Air Force in the defence of Britain then under attack from the Lufftwaffe. These were followed by an independent witness from Ireland in the person of a senator who had travelled along with Ben and she described the activities and findings of the FOGP at the time it was campaigning to have Captain Pender freed, vigorously repudiating the suggestion that his captivity had been merely a sham and he all along engaged in terrorist activity. Such an allegation was outrageous, she maintained, and totally unacceptable.

So many good things were being said about him that Graham began to take heart. But all the fine sentiments went for nothing when the court reconvened after lunch and Daya Begum was recalled to the stand, and once again repeated her damning evidence. Asked when she had realized that Harinath Prasad, a loader on the airport ramp and the notorious terrorist leader, Aziza Khan, were one and the same person, she had replied, 'When he threatened to kill me and my fellow worker, Benjamin Sakalana, if we gave evidence against the Eastline pilots.'

At that Graham's spirits plunged. So the connection had been made at last.

**

That evening at dusk Harinath Prasad sat in the darkened cab of a freight truck, smoking a cheroot and reviewing his plan carefully. Normally he would have sent someone else to do this type of job but he had to make sure it was done right. The car would be a Range Rover, he knew, and there would be three of them, Daya and her bodyguard, and the usual driver designated by the Defence force.

Harinath had picked the interception point with care, and had chosen the truck for its weight and anonymity. It was the kind used for transferring plantains and would not arouse suspicion. Coming up to the bend the Range Rover would have to slow down, and the occupants would be at a disadvantage for those few vital moments. And then there was the boy's involvement, it too was vital. He must ensure that Ranjan fired the killing shot, Prasad thought, only then would he truly be one of them. The driver and the bodyguard he would take care of himself.

Beside him Ranjan sat motionless, his eyes fixed on the empty road ahead, unable to forget Nicholas's anguished questions and the lies he had been forced to tell him. How he was helping Hari to deliver a consignment of bananas in the truck and would not be back until dark.

'Why can't I come with you?' Nicholas had called plaintively after him, clearly not relishing the thought of being left behind with the warrior-like men, and Ranjan had pretended not to hear and forced himself to keep on going.

Now Harinath addressed him encouragingly. 'Do not worry. When this is over you will be at one with us in our search for justice.' He laid a comradely hand on his shoulder and the boy shivered. The first time was always the most difficult, Harinath thought. After that it grew easier, and then you no longer counted.

'Have you got the weapon?' he asked, and Ranjan reached down between his knees and lifted up the Colt 45. All morning he had aimed and fired at tin cans imbedded in the mossy bank. 'She will be sitting in the back, aim for her head and leave the others to me.'

Ranjan nodded and swallowed with difficulty.

'Do you understand?'

'Yes.'

'Don't think about it – just aim and squeeze the trigger like I showed you.' Away in the distance a glow of light flared and faded then swelled again as the Rover rounded bends and drew nearer. The Tamil leader felt the familiar clenching spasm in his stomach followed by the sudden rush of adrenalin.

'Here they come,' he said, and started the engine of the truck.

Back in the hut where he and Ranjan had spent the previous night, Nicholas was dozing on the straw pallet when the sound of the truck outside woke him and he sat bolt up, his heart thumping. When he went to the window he saw Ranjan and the bearded man in the light from the moon coming down the track towards the hut. As they drew nearer, Nicholas could see that Ranjan was carrying a fearsome-looking pistol with the same alarming ease as his older companion, and his Tee shirt was splashed with dark stains that looked like blood.

At the sight, Nicholas was filled with alarm and threw himself back down to await the moment when Ranjan came to bed. It seemed an age before he came softly into the partitioned-off section and stretched himself out beside Nicholas, and the smell of recent carnage on his clothing and hair was so overpowering in the small airless enclosure that Nicholas gagged in terror, and kept his eyes tight shut.

'You awake, Nicky?' Ranjan whispered, leaning over him, and it took Nicholas all his strength not to scream. He lay there, his heart thumping, struggling to keep his breathing even so as not to alert Ranjan to the fact he was awake, and when the Indian boy's own breathing signified that he slept, Nicholas acknowledged the awful admission that he was afraid of Ranjan and no longer trusted him.

Graham and Ben had just arrived at the courthouse next morning when they heard the shocking news of the death of Daya Begum whose body, along with that of her driver and bodyguard, had been found on a back road to the airport in the early hours. For a time it distracted Graham from his overwhelming worry about the boys as he discussed with the defense team the implication of the murder of the prosecution's chief witness.

The lawyers' comments had been frank and straightforward, if not downright disturbing, for they considered the brutal killing had in no way helped their case. Clearly, they saw it as a major setback.

'If only we'd had a chance to question Begum we might have broken down the edifice of lies she erected. As it is, prosecution are managing to use their slain witness against us, and there is always the possibility they are holding a few other tricks up their sleeves.'

Graham cursed the nemesis dogging his footsteps for so long, and wondered who had killed the woman. But then there was no real mystery about it. More than likely Harinath Prasad had had some part in it for the man had sworn to avenge Sita's death and, indeed, everything seemed to point to him now. What Graham had found most disturbing was the lawyers' suggestion that they immediately find and put Ranjan on the stand.

'If we could find him in time we could maybe turn things around.'

But Graham would not hear of it. 'Under no circumstances,' he ruled, having seen how the prosecution had managed to fabricate a case against himself, with practically no evidence. No way would he risk the same thing happening to Ranjan.

Another long day in court and that evening the lawyers having said goodnight and gone, Graham and Ben sat on for a while talking, but for the most part Graham was lost in unhappy thought and Ben soon got to his feet.

'I think I'll turn in. I rang Linda earlier to tell her I'll be on the plane home tomorrow,' he laid a hand on Graham's shoulder. 'Try and get some rest, old man. Keep up the heart, you'll soon have news of your boys.'

Back in his own room, Graham was unbuttoning his shirt when the telephone rang. Nerves on edge, he snatched up the receiver and heard a man's voice with an Asian inflection saying, 'I have a message from Ranjan Shanti. Listen carefully. You must leave now at once and take a taxi to the courthouse. Walk to the street behind the fruit market and someone will contact you there with the name Shiva. Follow these instructions,' the caller told him. 'And do not tell anyone where you are going.'

'Where is Ranjan …and my son?' Graham burst out but the connection was broken and the line went dead.

Graham debated whether to go along to Ben's room and enlist his help, but after some deliberation he decided it was too risky and went alone. Some fifty minutes later the car he was travelling in turned off the jungle road and came to a halt some twenty yards or so along a rutted track. The driver flashed his lights on and off twice, and higher up the headlamps of another vehicle flashed in response.

'Wait, please,' the man got out and disappeared into the darkness. Graham felt his muscles tensing, and was conscious of the driver lighting up a cheroot and puffing pungent smoke through the open window.

Figures appeared out of the gloom. In the blur of faces, Graham recognised Nicholas and Ranjan, and behind them the taller, bearded figure with an AK 47 slung on his shoulder. At once Graham reached for the door handle before the driver realized his intention. 'Stay where you are,' he growled, but Graham paid no heed and shooting forward grasped hold of his son.

'Nicky! Are you all right?'

'Dad!' Nicholas gasped. 'Oh Dad!'

Graham held him close, recognizing the fear quivering in his son's voice. 'Okay, it's okay, Nicky,' he reassured him, and felt a light touch on his arm, heard the murmured, 'Captain Tuan!'

Immediately Graham embraced him. 'Ranji,' he said in concern. 'Are you all right?' and saw the boy nod.

'No harm has come to either of them,' the bearded man said, and Graham felt immediately apprehensive as he recognized Prasad, or Khan as he was coming more and more to think of him. As he struggled between the need for caution and an explosive anger building up in him, he heard the man saying, 'I meant only to take Ranjan but your son followed us, Captain Pender. We had no choice but to bring him too. It was not possible to contact you.'

When Graham thought of his three dreadful days in court harassed by the prosecution, and nearly out of his mind with worry about the boys, he could have struck the man. 'I don't accept that,' he snapped. 'You should have contacted me.'

Prasad shrugged. 'Any contact from me could have proved dangerous for you. Your position is precarious, your movements watched at all times.'

'Isn't it a bit late to think of that?' Graham told him, all his previous sense of obligation to the man who had once risked his own life to rescue him washed away in a flood of righteous anger. Let there be no mistake, he reminded himself grimly, this man was a killer, the author of all his misfortunes.

'I regret that you have become linked with our movement, Captain Pender,' Prasad was saying. 'But we are fighting a bloody and bitter war here for our lives and liberty.' He spoke curtly in Tamil to the man standing a few feet away, then turned again to Graham. 'You will be brought back now to your hotel.'

Turning to Ranjan, the leader solemnly gave the handshake of the freedom fighters and embraced the boy. 'Remember what we spoke of, Shanti. We will meet again before long.'

With a sense of dread, Graham registered the use of the formal title and the special handshake. Something had clearly happened here. He could not help noticing that even Ranjan's stance was different. Gone was the easy-limbed graceful slouch, the conciliatory dip of the head. Now he was carrying himself erectly, his carriage was almost military, and even in the poor light Graham could not but be struck by his mature and resolute expression. He is no longer a child, he thought with a sense of shock, and his mistrust of the rebel leader changed into a sudden frightening hatred for the man who had brought about this disturbing change.

Harinath lowered the AK 47 and stood looking after the car's disappearing tail lights. It was not part of his plan that Captain Pender should be convicted and sent to languish in a Ceylonese gaol. He would pay a visit to Benjamin Sakalana, he decided and find out how effective was one thousand rupees and a pistol held to his head. The man would be a useful informant to have at the airport, fearful and grateful, Prasad thought contemptuously, two invaluable commodities.

By the following day all the headlines on the Colombo trial ran, 'Prosecution Witness Turns Evidence For The Defense. Case Against Pilots Dropped. Judge Rules Insufficient Evidence.'

One day later, Graham sat high above the clouds in a London-bound jet, with the boys dozing at either side of him. He laid his head wearily against the headrest, the deeply disturbing images of the past weeks still whirling behind his closed lids. In view of Nicholas's troubled state the previous night he was more than ever convinced something bad had happened during his time in Prasad's company. On returning to the hotel his son had been almost hysterical, refusing to be left alone with Ranjan and begging to be allowed to sleep in his father's room. Fearing he would be ill, Graham had agreed at last, despite the misery he glimpsed on Ranjan's face. Going along to the court next morning, Ben having already departed for London, Graham had found the press on the steps of the courthouse, cameras at the ready, and they had surrounded them at once shouting questions.

'What do you think the verdict will be?'

'Do you think they'll do a deal for the gold?'

'What will you feel if forced to return to this country where you were imprisoned?'

This last question was directed at Graham closely following the defense counsel as they forged steadily ahead of him into the court. He had not answered but grimly taken his seat on the bench. In the course of the next two hours the most alarming accusation had been the prosecutor's suggestion that young and all as Nicholas was, Captain Pender's son was being primed to join the liberation movement, for why else had he been brought so far to sit in upon an arms trial? Despite some glaring inconsistencies and what plainly amounted to circumstantial evidence, Graham was being accused of conspiracy, collusion, grand larceny, and murder after the fact. And then, when all had seemed lost, Benjamin Sakalana had gone on the stand and turned the whole thing around with his sworn testimony.

Captain Pender still could not get over the miracle and when the judge declared him a free man, relief and gratitude flooded his soul. Safely aboard his flight home at last, Graham's muscles gradually unclenched and within minutes of the cabin lights being lowered, he fell into a deep dreamless sleep.

***

The news of Captain Pender's acquittal quickly spread about the airport and amongst his colleagues in Celtic Airways there was a general feeling of rejoicing on the pilot's behalf. So much had happened to him in the space of a few short years that most people were relieved to see him come successfully through this latest ordeal. In the pilots lounge only very few made uncharitable comments about there being 'no smoke without a fire' or cast doubts on Graham's innocence. These were mainly pilots who had done a stint with East-line Airways themselves at one time or another and would not have been averse to picking up a few extra rupees given the opportunity.

Ben Higgins, having so recently come from the battle front, so to speak, was less tolerant of pilots with attitude than he might otherwise have been. Crisply, he put down a brash Second Officer who had the ill-luck to remark in Ben's hearing that Pender was 'a snooty over-rated pilot obsessed with flying by the book' still rankling over a reprimand administered by Captain Pender coming out of Kennedy Airport for his failure to run all the pre-take-off checks. Not only had Second Officer Pearson got the dressing-down of his existence but he was required to present himself and his flight manual immediately to the Chief Pilot for inspection, and there he learned that he would be checked out on his next two Atlantic flights by no less than Captain 'Hurricane' Hogan, who visibly exacted pleasure from flunking pilots he found wanting, reducing them to a quivering mass of indecision and lacking confidence to fly a kite without assistance, much less a Boeing aircraft.

Ben, having trenchantly dealt with Pearson, felt somewhat soothed until he happened to hear from Andy Hegarty that Oliver McGrattan had voiced in public his sneering opinion that Captain Pender had been clearly engaged in 'extra-curricular activities' while flying for Eastline Airway.

'I'm afraid he's out to make trouble,' Andy stuffed tobacco into his pipe and regarded Ben over it with a frown. 'You say Pender was acquitted of all blame?'

Ben nodded. 'So I believe. I'm afraid I wasn't present for the summing up. From what I hear it had something to do with one of the prosecution's witnesses switching sides at the last minute and revealing a conspiracy to frame the Eastline pilots, including Pender.'

Andy lit a taper and touched it to the bowl of his pipe. 'How's Pender taking the strain?'

Knowing how the Chief operated Ben took his time in answering. 'Very well considering. Look, I think he has already proved himself, don't you? Surely he doesn't have to go through all that psychology stuff again?'

'He has been exemplary,' Andy agreed, 'But this is a make or break situation, Higgins. Pender's honour and integrity have been questioned, paraded before the world and not for the first time either. Intolerable position for an upright man and bound to have repercussions. You are familiar with what was said of officers under continual fire during the war?'

'What was that?' Ben said tersely, not liking the drift.

'Their valor or their stamina was never in question when under constant attack, in fact they coped heroically. It was only when the intolerable strain was lifted that they were hit by post-traumatic stress disorder and went to pieces.'

'What are you suggesting?'

'We need to bear in mind that Pender has been through a helluva strain over the past few years and this latest could be the unhinging of him.'

'Well, a week or two off the roster should set him straight.'

Andy shrugged. 'Mightn't be so simple, not if McGrattan's kind of thinking reflects the majority of public opinion. He can be a soulless little swine at times but he does have the airline's interests at heart.'

'Meaning just what?' Ben demanded.

'Well, the paying public can be very broadminded about any sexual scandal in an airline but where the ability of its pilots is in question they tend to worry. The idea that the captain of their flight might ditch them all in the drink in order to make off with any lolly on board makes them uneasy.'

'But that's ridiculous,' Ben was outraged. 'Pender is the soul of integrity and a damn fine pilot to boot. Surely you haven't forgotten his masterly handling of the Cuban hijacking some months ago.'

'No, I haven't. Most impressive but the public have short memories,' Andy said cynically.

Ben felt he had had enough of the conversation. 'Let's just wait and see, shall we,' he said crisply. 'It's a nine day wonder and will blow over just as quickly.'

'They said the same about Vietnam,' Andy said soberly, and Ben kept a tight rein on his tongue lest he prejudice Graham's case further. But that evening relaxing at his own fireside he waxed indignantly to Linda over what he termed as the unmistakable beginnings of a 'witch hunt'.

Kay was overjoyed by what she read in the papers. Just as Graham had predicted, everything worked out all right. She was so relieved that she almost forgot she was pregnant. Judy had been following the Colombo trial also and was equally relieved at the outcome, although not so optimistic as Kay for she was aware that McGrattan had hastily summoned a meeting of the board of directors to discuss the situation. Pete Kenny had been most informative when he dropped by her office. Yet again. Judy could not ignore just how often this was happening. For goodness sake, the man was married with children and, according to gossip, there was another baby on the way. He had no business to be wooing her like this. But she tolerated him anxious to hear all about the kidnap of Graham's boys in Colombo.

'Gone for three whole days,' Pete said, having got the details from Ben Higgins. 'Pender was nearly demented and who could blame him,' adding with a soppy grin. 'You worry so about your kids.' Not that Pete seemed overburdened in that respect, Judy thought cynically, not if the number of times he had left poor pregnant Prue caring for their brood on her own was anything to go by.

Christy Kane was also privy to Pete's confidences, and interested to learn that the Chief Executive was doing a character assassination on Pender. He whistled through his teeth, glad these days he was beyond McGrattan's spite. Over the months, Captain Kane had come to view his own sacking from CA as a blessing in disguise and now, free of the strain and subterfuge he had been required to practice for so long to conceal his drinking and preserve his career, he was the happiest since his school days. He had invested his gratuity in buying a half share in an up-and-coming flying club a few miles beyond the airport which he managed these days and had, besides, the chance to impress young female wannabe flyers with his flying skill, life had never been better.

***

Dave's conference in London had been extended by another week. When he rang to tell her, Kay tried to keep the elation out of her voice saying, 'Not to worry, Dave,' brushing aside his apologies at leaving her so long on her own. 'It can't be helped.'

All evening Kay had been hoping that Graham would ring and they could arrange to meet. It seemed so long since they were together and a long, lonely time without him. In the afternoon, anxious not to waste a precious moment of the coming week with duty visits, she had decided to slip over and see her aunt. Two months earlier, Molly had been moved to Dublin to the old people's home and Kay

180

only been to see her a couple of times. Now she was shocked at the change she saw in her and concerned to hear she had not been well.

'Didn't get a wink of sleep last night with the oul chest,' Molly told her plaintively, and on impulse Kay left Sinead happily playing on the floor at her aunt's feet and went to have a word with the sister in charge.

'Mrs Begley was in bed all week but she's a lot improved today,' she was told.

'When did the doctor see her last? She's coughing an awful lot. I'm really worried about her. She has always had a weak chest, you know.'

'Oh, you need have no fears, dear,' the nurse assured her. 'Doctor saw Mrs. Begley only yesterday and he prescribed another course of antibiotics, to be on the safe side. At her age, he's not taking any chances.'

Kay was somewhat reassured and went back to the sitting-room where Sinead was leaning against Molly's knee, the pair of them looking at her picture book.

'Isn't she the great girl,' Molly smiled up at Kay, 'She won't be long reading,' and Kay laughed at such foolishness on her aunt's part. 'It's good of you to come and visit me when you have so much to do and you needing your rest.'

Molly was almost pathetic in her gratitude, making Kay feel sadder and guiltier by the minute. On the way home she promised herself she would ring the nursing home that evening to ask how she was doing and would try and visit her aunt more often. But as soon as Sinead was gone to bed Kay could only think of Graham, and dialed his number.

When he picked up, her delight rendered her speechless. 'Oh, darling it's so good to hear your voice,' she said at last. 'I've been so worried about you.'

'Oh, it's you, Kitty,' he said, as though from a long way off, and she was struck with compunction when he muttered something about having been asleep.

It appeared he had arrived back that day and only been in bed a couple of hours. 'Yes, it was tough,' he sighed. 'But thank God it's all over now.'

'When can we meet?' the question was on the tip of her tongue but she restrained herself, merely saying he could ring her at home next day. 'Dave is away for another week. Oh, and I'm not due out again until Friday,' wanting him to know how available she was.

'Talk soon,' he said automatically, almost asleep as he spoke.

When Graham awoke during the night he wondered if it had been a dream hearing Kay's voice. He had little or no recollection of having answered the telephone. He was worn out after the long flight and the trauma and emotion of the trial, and felt as though he could sleep for a week. Indeed, if it was left to him it would be as long again, he knew, before he felt rested enough to get out of bed.

However, he was aware that life must go on, he had a job to do and the boys must go back to school. Next morning early he got on to rostering, wanting to know how soon he was expected to resume duty.

That was when the first shock came.

'Can you hold one minute please,' her voice sounded muffled as though she had her hand over the receiver, and then she said, 'I'm sorry, Captain Pender, but you don't seem to be on the roster.'

'That's okay,' Graham said tiredly. 'I expected to be left off until I had checked back in again. I wasn't exactly sure what date I would be returning.'

'I mean your name isn't on the roster at all.'

Graham was puzzled, 'Oh, I see. That's unusual,' and waited.

'Must be some mistake,' she sounded flustered. 'Look, would you mind leaving it with me, Captain Pender. I'll get back to you.'

'Sure, take your time.' Graham was just as relieved. He could do with a few extra days, he thought, some clerical oversight, no doubt.

'Dad, do we really have to go back to school today?' Nicholas demanded, stumbling down the stairs, looking pale and exhausted.

He shot ahead into the kitchen and kept filling glasses of water at the sink and drinking thirstily as though he had been in the desert for months.

Graham followed him. 'You'll have to go back soon, Nicky, so it might as well be today,' conscious of how much of the term the boys had already missed. Yet he wondered as he spoke if it might be wiser to keep them at home for a bit, both boys looked worn out. Regrettably, they were no friendlier towards each other than before. Maybe they just needed a little more time to adjust, he thought.

'Forget school for now,' he relented, and Nicholas looked relieved. 'We're all tired. Perhaps we shouldn't push ourselves too hard. Okay?'

As Nicholas nodded gratefully, the telephone rang and Graham went out to answer it. It was the Chief Executive's secretary.

'Captain Pender, Mr McGrattan has asked me to notify you. There is a meeting of the board of directors at 10 a.m. tomorrow morning. He hopes it's convenient for you to attend.'

Graham was startled, but under no illusion it was anything other than a summons. 'Well, I only got back from Colombo yesterday but yes, I can make it.'

'Thank you so much,' she said smoothly. 'Mr McGrattan will be pleased.'

What the hell was McGrattan up to? Graham lifted the receiver again and dialed Ben's number, only to have Conor tell him his father was away in New York.

'He'll be back tomorrow, Captain Pender. Can I take a message?'

'Not to worry,' Graham said wearily. 'I'll ring again.'

As he put down the phone, Ranjan passed him on his way to the kitchen. 'Sleep okay?' he asked, and the boy nodded. Like Nicholas he looked washed out. Graham followed him into the room and came to a sudden decision.

'Look, I've something to say to the pair of you and I'd like your full attention.' Aware of their surprised glances, he pressed on. 'Now I know that you've had some difference of opinion lately and you're

183

not the happiest with each other, but I want you to put aside your grievances and make up your quarrel.'

Ranjan lifted his head. 'I have no quarrel with Nicky,' he said simply. It was clear he was speaking the truth.

'Very well. Can you say the same, Nicky?'

Nicholas looked uncomfortable, then angry. 'That's not fair, Dad. You're putting me on the spot.'

'I know I am.' Graham ignored the mute plea in his son's eyes. 'Please just answer the question. I want this resolved now and I want to see you shaking hands.' His voice rose in exhaustion. 'Look, you haven't spoken to each other in days. Put an end to this stupid misunderstanding or whatever it is, and make it up.'

His tiredness was making him irascible, at the back of his mind he was thinking, why is McGrattan calling a board meeting, what charge is he going to make against me? Doesn't he *know* I was acquitted?' He wondered if he should contact Andy Hegarty and try and find out what was afoot, then he realized the boys were waiting for him to speak.

'Okay,' he said wearily. 'What's it all about?'

'You ask him,' Nicholas cried hysterically, pointing at Ranjan. 'Ask *him* why he was carrying a gun and got blood all over him.'

With a sense of shock Graham's brain registered gun... blood... what on earth was Nicky talking about?

Ranjan stood stolidly, neither affirming nor denying, while Nicholas continued excitedly, his voice cracking with strain. 'I *saw* him! He and that man...they were carrying guns I tell you... and Ranjan,' he gulped heartbrokenly. 'Ranjan was all covered in blood. Don't deny it,' he hurled at the Indian boy. 'You *know* you were.'

Graham looked at Ranjan and saw his expression. So something had occurred. He laid a gentle hand on his shoulder. 'Ranjan, do you want to tell me about it?'

'Please...not before Nicky,' Ranjan begged. 'It is not fitting that he should hear what I have to tell you.'

And so it had turned out to be, something more dreadful than Graham had ever imagined. Horrified, he listened to Ranjan recounting it all in the privacy of his study, the shooting of the bodyguard and the woman who had killed his sister, confessing how ever since in his dreams he had been besieged by demons, haunted by bloody images of his dead victims, and all of it mixed up with his Hindu religion and his loyalty to Harinath Prasad.

***

Dave sat having a drink with Anne Stack in the hotel bar. He knew he should make his call to Kay but after their last conversation he felt a great reluctance to speak to her. It still rankled the way she had reacted when he had told her he wouldn't be home for another week. It had been downright unflattering to say the least. He might have been telling her that his plane would be delayed an hour in getting into Dublin, not that it would be another seven days before he returned and he already away a fortnight!

Obviously, she was getting on rather too well without him, he felt angry and not a little depressed. Maybe he would find Sinead equally disinterested when he returned. He was so appalled at the prospect, he considered flying home at the weekend and charging the cost to the company. The only thing putting him off was the uncertainty of Kay's schedule, not much point in making the effort if she was away flying.

He was aware that Anne was not making much headway with her first drink and he was drinking too fast himself, but he felt like knocking them back tonight. He was sick of being careful and sensible and reasonable. With another drink, unhappy thoughts of Kay receded and he was filled with the reckless desire to go somewhere and have fun. He could not face the thought of going back up to his room after dinner, to sit before the television with work on his knee. Not tonight!

'How would you like to go out on the town?' he interrupted Anne, aware of what he might be letting himself in for, but with no will to stop it.

Kay was drinking more than she should too, but for different reasons.

Two days and not a word from Graham! All too soon, she would be out of contact, away in New York, and then Dave would be home and her freedom curtailed. All those precious days wantonly wasted, she sighed, in an agony of frustration, feeling worn out with thinking and regretting. Eventually, she decided there was no convincing excuse he could give her for his continued silence. She could not have been clearer about her movements. Didn't he love her at all? Oh Graham, she cried desolately, for our child's sake do not desert me.

Graham lay gazing dully at the drawn curtains, with no idea what time of the day or night it was. He had no inclination to look at his watch or to get up and shave the two-day stubble from his chin, he was not going anywhere. Earlier, Ben Higgins had collected the boys and driven them back to Mellwood College. Graham had been glad to be saved both the trip and the pain of observing the continued hostility between them. All day the telephone had been ringing but he had no desire to answer it.

'For God's sake, Dad,' Jeremy had exploded when they had spoken earlier, 'Why didn't you tell us you'd been sacked from the airline? You are going to fight them, aren't you?'

'No,' he admitted.

'But they'll think you're guilty. I never thought you were a quitter, Dad.'

'You don't understand,' Graham said tiredly. 'Does Nicky know?"

'Yeah, and the whole school. It was on television during recreation. Nicky's in a bad way but he won't talk about it and he's no long friends with Ranjan. Hey Dad, what did Ranjan do that was so awful? Must be something really bad,' he reckoned, adding with chilling perspicacity. 'Anyone would think he'd murdered someone,' and to Graham's relief he rang off.

Graham's ex-wife had rung too, and Sile was not sympathetic. 'You brought all of this on yourself, Graham,' she told him. 'It was outrageous subjecting Nicky to danger like that. Just don't expect me to allow the boys stay with you again.'

'But surely they'll come at Christmas,' he protested.

'No, not even for one night. You're lucky to be allowed see them at all.'

After that Graham had ignored the telephone, letting it ring away, unable to bear any further analysis of his situation. But then the thought that it could be Nicholas or Ranjan desperate to talk to him made him lift the receiver. Lord knows only a totally selfish and irresponsible parent would deny them that opportunity.

Setting aside her pride, Kay had kept doggedly redialing Graham's number until her efforts were rewarded at last. Earlier, in her extreme unhappiness, she had drunk a couple of glasses of wine. She knew that she was putting the child within her at risk but in her misery thought maybe it might be better all round if she were to lose it, until remembering that a miscarriage would be every bit as hard to explain to Dave.

'Graham?' she said when he picked up at last. 'Graham? Is that you?' and heard him sigh, 'Kitty, Oh Kitty,' sounding so despairing her heart raced in alarm.

'I need to talk to you,' she told him. 'It can't wait any longer.'

'I'm afraid I'm not the best of company, Kitty, but of course we must meet. I would have been in touch but…well, rather a lot has caught up with me since returning.' It was an explanation or apology of sorts. 'You'll come here?'

'I'll come straight away,' she said, although she had no idea if it would be possible to get anyone to watch Sinead at such short notice.

She was bitterly reminded of the sacrifices she had been forced to make all summer to allow their affair to proceed smoothly, and asked herself what if any sacrifices had Graham ever made? Almost at once she was filled with panic for the disintegration of the love she had felt so long for him, and which had sustained her all unknowing through the years of his captivity and rehabilitation. Oh,

187

Graham forgive me, darling, she thought contritely, as she rushed to get herself ready, but I'm frightened, desperately frightened. Hastily, she renewed her lipstick, shaping her mouth with unsteady fingers. Oh God! Supposing she couldn't get anyone to mind Sinead. But thankfully when she ran next door the eldest girl obliged. In less than forty minutes Kay was standing on Graham's front step. Except for a faint glow showing through the curtains in an upper room, his house was in darkness, even the porch light was out. After some delay, he opened the door.

'Kitty, come in. You'll have to excuse me but the place is in rather a mess.'

Following him into the sitting-room, she saw that he was in his bathrobe, his bare feet stuck into leather mules. On the table there was a bottle of wine and two glasses. When he switched on the overhead light, she was shocked by his appearance, unshaven, his hair tousled. Disconcerted, she sank into a chair as he poured the wine, hurt that he had not kissed her, something must be very wrong.

'So how have you been?' He placed the glass before her.

'Fine.' Kay tried to answer him just as casually, but it was an effort. 'The usual run back and forth to New York.' She registered that the wine was warm and again felt surprise, he usually paid attention to such details. He wasn't expecting me, she excused him. But he had at least thirty minutes to chill it, said the critical little voice in her head. Ah but, he's not himself, said the kinder one. And it was true. Something had happened to radically alter him.

Looking at him more closely, Kay saw the blank look in his dark eyes, the tremble in his hand. Oh my darling, what's happened to you, she cried silently, coming out of her own self-absorption, her immediate problems forgotten in her loving anguish for this gaunt white-haired man who appeared to have aged in the weeks since she had seen him. On impulse, she got up and knelt on the carpet before him.

'Graham, my dear,' she said, laying her hand on his knee. 'Tell me what happened? The papers said you were acquitted.'

Graham turned his head and gazed at her, his dark eyes strangely vulnerable. 'Kitty, I'm finished,' he said at last. 'Yesterday I was suspended. McGrattan used the link with the terrorists against me and the board went along with him.'

He thought of the atmosphere in the board room, the pity and the reserve as the directors strictly avoided meeting his eyes, staring down at the stapled sheets on the table before them, loth to break the silence. McGrattan had been both judge and executioner, ponderously preparing the ground before delivering the *coup de grace.*

'And so, Captain Pender, you maintain by the end of the trial you were completely exonerated, cleared of all charges of conspiracy against the Ceylonese state. Surprising when as recently as the previous day the case against you was looking black...very black indeed?' a note of incredulity in his tone that was deeply offensive.

It had been a complete travesty of justice and Graham had refused to go along with this rehash of the trial. His anger had risen swiftly and savagely, and he was hard put not to get up and walk out of the room. In the hands of the Chief Executive it was more an inquisition than an interrogation, and in this he was joined by members of the board who relentlessly put their own questions.

How could a pilot of your experience, Captain Pender, permit an unknown man, possibly a dissident, access to the flight deck of an airliner under your command? Such an irresponsible action is in direct convention of airline safety regulations.

Was it prudent against all advice to bring your son and the Indian boy you had adopted back with you to a country known for its political unrest, a foreign boy moreover whom the evidence has since shown had all along kept in communication with a notorious terrorist leader?

Could it be, Captain Pender, you were not so naïve as you appear and this relationship had not only your knowledge but your full approval?

How do you think passengers travelling with Celtic Airways might feel knowing that the captain of their flight has links with known terrorist groups?

Why, Captain...But, Captain...Don't you think, Captain...

Endless questions, smugly self-righteous voices, all of them judging him and finding him wanting. Oh God, why did I survive that plane crash? Graham wondered in despair. It was a question he had asked himself many times these past weeks, but this was the first time he found himself wishing that he had perished with his crew.

As it sank in what Graham was telling her, Kay stared at him in horror, the pit of her stomach seemed to have dropped away. Graham disgraced, no longer employed by CA. She caught her breath struck by what it must mean to such a proud and able man, with a brilliant flying record behind him.

'What will you do?' she asked him. 'Surely the pilots will stand by you?'

'There is some talk of it,' he said indifferently.

Hearing the dejection in his voice, her heart was filled with compassion and pity, and instinctively she reached up to console him. His arms came about her at once and she lay against him, her heart aching for all he was going through

'Oh darling, what have I done to you?' The anguished words were muffled by her hair. 'I have destroyed your life. I should have died in that plane crash. Oh God! if only I had.' And he began to weep. It was terrible.

Kay trembled at his appalling grief. After a few moments he recovered himself enough to go on speaking, and he told her things that seared her brain and over it all was apparent his terrible guilt and regret for having brought the boys with him.

'I'll never ever forgive myself,' and there was a lot more she could not understand about terrorists and killings, and it was too much for her to take in. Could he really be saying that his adopted son had committed a terrible murder? But he was only fifteen or sixteen, she thought horrified, her mind sheering away from it.

'My only hope is to go abroad, get work with some small airline. But there's the boys' education to think of.' He rubbed a hand tiredly over his eyes. 'Jeremy is in his last year...Nicky and Ranjan have two more years to go.'

Her heart stricken by the thought of him going far away, she felt a sudden stabbing fear for herself. What would happen to her now?

Putting her gently from him, he stood up. 'Enough of such gloomy talk,' he said with forced cheerfulness. 'I should not have burdened you like this but you have caught me on a bad evening. Here, let me pour you more wine.'

She watched as he topped her glass, wondering how she was going to live without him and he went on in the same unnatural tone, 'So what has you so urgently needing to talk?' and at once she knew it was imperative that he never find out the real reason for her visit.

'It was nothing. I just wanted to see you,' she lied, smiling flirtatiously up at him, and he frowned. 'Surely you don't need an excuse to see me, Kitty?'

She lowered her eyes. 'That's true but when you didn't ring I thought you were avoiding me.'

'Why would I avoid you?' He sounded bewildered. 'Are you sure there's nothing the matter, my dear? You sounded very upset on the telephone,' and she shook her head, resolved that no matter what hardships lay ahead she would not add to his feelings of guilt and remorse by telling him she was carrying his child. She had no idea what she was going to do but that was something she would have to sort out on her own. Of that she was certain.

'Come,' she said, taking his hand and pulling him gently on to his feet. What she most wanted was for him to make love to her. Oh God! Just to feel him deep within her. 'Let's go to bed. Everything will be better then. I've missed you so."

With a sigh, he allowed her to draw him up the stairs. In his room, she turned off the ceiling light and, switching on a table lamp, she pushed him down gently on the bed. He watched her as she shed her clothes and she was suddenly shy of his gaze and the way he looked at her breasts, fuller and more enticing than ever with all the changes taking place in her body. Her nipples no longer pink but a rich wine color. But if he was aware of the significance or had noted the slight swell of her stomach he gave no sign as he gathered her into his arms and pulled her down to him.

Indeed, he seemed almost in a trance and she realized that he was still suffering the shock of recent events. She would have turned out the light but he stopped her. 'It has been so long,' he whispered. 'I want to see you…enjoy you, darling. These past weeks have been like a nightmare. Some time I will tell you, but not now. Ah, but if you only knew how often I thought of you… and longed for you.'

His words comforted and reassured her but she did not let them give her any hope, as she gazed into his eyes and saw in their dark depths the same love that had warmed her and brought her back to him time and again. Instead, she concentrated in remembering every little detail of their last lovemaking, and gave herself up to the enjoyment of his lips on hers, his caressing hands and tongue, the wonder of his body with every sensation heightened after this long lonely time without him.

When he slept at last, she got up and dressed herself. Crouching beside the bed, she stroked his hair, gazing her fill at him in the lamplight he wouldn't let her extinguish so that he could see her, as he'd said, in all her beauty. Sadly, she luxuriated in the beautiful mouth, the arched brows and the silver wing of hair falling on his forehead. At this point, she almost woke him, prepared to beg and plead and plot a future in which she and their child would have a share, but some residue of that earlier strength returned to her and she resolutely turned away.

As she drove away from Graham's house she knew that all her life she would carry with her the image of him lying there with that amazingly youthful look about him in the aftermath of lovemaking, and then the tears began to flow as though they would never stop.

***

Next afternoon Kay arrived in Kensington and headed for the hotel where Dave and his colleagues were staying. Only thoughts of Graham's baby kept her courage high as she prepared to carry out the plan that came to her after a sleepless night. She was still full of sorrow and regret for the way things had turned out but her mind was made up. By the time Eileen arrived at the house Kay's overnight case was packed, and she had already contacted rostering with the excuse of a grievously ill aunt in London. Fortunately, there had been no bother getting on a flight to Heathrow at midday, the story of her dear aunt's sudden illness evoking sympathy and cooperation on the part of the ground hostesses who got her a seat on the midday flight.

On enquiring at the hotel reception desk Kay was told that Mr Mason was not in the hotel and she went out again to find herself a modest Italian restaurant off the High Street. There she ordered pasta, lingering over a Cappuccino to pass the time. Gazing in the washroom mirror she was dismayed to see how pale and strained she looked.

Oh God! She wanted to seduce her husband not frighten him off, she thought, pinching her cheeks to improve her colour and applying fresh lipstick. With a last tired glance in the mirror she went back to the hotel somewhat heartened by the hot food and only hoping she would not throw up.

Disappointed on learning that Dave had not returned Kay went to sit into a comfortable winged chair in the foyer, with a clear view of the entrance. Sometime later she came out of a doze in time to see him coming through the revolving door, talking animatedly to someone over his shoulder. After a moment, she recognized Anne Stack close on his heels and felt immediately uneasy at the way the young woman was laughing and hugging Dave to her, as though conceding some point under discussion. Kay stared at their backs as, with his arm about her, Dave walked Anne over to the reception desk to collect their room keys. The gesture was intimate and way too familiar, and as the couple got into the lift together she had the disturbing notion that her husband and this woman were even now on their way upstairs to go to bed together. It came as a shock for it had never crossed her mind that he might be unfaithful to her. Her face burning with mortification she was thinking, maybe that's why he hadn't made love to her in a month. And she had an impulse to leave the hotel as quickly as she could. Wavering unsteadily on her feet, she grabbed for her overnight bag. She would go back to the airport in the hope of getting on standby for a late flight home, she told herself, and felt a rush of nausea. With a hand before her mouth, she almost ran to the washroom and rushing inside, threw up into the lavatory.

As the lift ascended to the third floor Dave was no longer laughing, still puzzling over the fleeting glimpse he had got of the woman sitting below in the foyer before stepping with Anne into the lift. Was it Kay or had he imagined it?

'Your room or mine?' Anne was saying. 'I think there's a tee-ny-weeny bit of gin left in the mini-bar we didn't guzzle last night.'

Dave spun around. 'Listen Anne, you go on. I've just remembered something I have to do,' and before she could protest he hurried back to the lift and pressed the ground floor button. As the doors opened he was in time to see Kay walking towards the exit and rushed after her.

'Wait! Kay, wait!' he called, and at the sound of his voice she turned and stared at him with startled eyes.

'I thought it was you. Is everything all right?' He wanted to ask why she had been leaving without speaking to him, but some part of him had already answered that question. She must have seen him with Anne and added up wrongly. Maybe not so wrongly, Dave conceded uncomfortably, reaching for her case. 'Why didn't you let me know you were coming, Katie?'

'I didn't know until this morning,' Kay said truthfully, feeling a great weariness descending. 'I just took a chance and came.'

'What a pity I didn't know. We could have gone out for a meal and now the night is almost gone.' Dave sounded upset and Kay made a huge effort to laugh as though he had said something funny and sexy.

'Not the best part,' she said meaningfully, and Dave put his arm about her and laughed in relief.

'True,' he grinned. 'Let's go make up for lost time, shall we.' Then remembering that she might be hungry. 'Do you want to have a bite of something first?' but she shook her head, murmuring she had already eaten.

In the bedroom Kay took out her wash bag and, after a second's hesitation, her nightie too, not wanting to risk her husband's scrutiny unclothed. With the bathroom door shut she slumped down on the rim of the bath, then rousing herself climbed in and took a quick shower before putting on the new diaphanous nightie she had been saving for Graham, her eyes filling at the thought. Well, Dave might as well enjoy it, she mused bleakly, then sighed. Oh dear! This would never do! With an effort she made herself smile as she went back to the bedroom.

Dave had lowered the lights and was on the telephone, but he quickly finished his conversation and turned to look at her. 'Wow!' he said staring,

'Come here to me,' he enfolded her in his arms. 'How did I ever last all these weeks without you?' he asked wonderingly. 'It has been a hell of a lonely time, Katie. I should have tried to get home even for a night and to hell with the expense.'

'Forget it,' Kay murmured, eagerly seeking his lips and pressing seductively close. Now that they were almost there she did not want to waste time soul-searching. She made little mewling needy sounds and Dave began breathing heavily.

'God, Katie,' he gasped. 'I'd forgotten how beautiful you are. We mustn't ever be parted so long again,' and a moment later, 'Won't be able to hold out I'm afraid.'

Before blanking into sleep, Kay thought: Thank God for that!

***

Two evenings later Kay met Florrie coming off her Paris flight and hugged her close. Never had she felt more in need of a confidant. Seated in the canteen, Kay wasted no time in tell her that she was pregnant and Dave was not the father, they had not slept together in weeks. Holding nothing back, she confessed how she had gone to London in order to sleep with him before it was too late. She could see that Florrie was shocked but there was relief in unburdening herself at last.

Florrie was horrified, she could only suppose somewhat cynically that Captain Pender was the one to blame or to be congratulated, whichever was in order.

'Kay,' she said at last. 'What are you going to do?'

'Wait a while before telling Dave I might be pregnant. What else?' Kay met Florrie's eyes. 'I know, I know but it's that or be cast off.'

'Yerra, Dave would never do that to you.' Florrie felt she would burst if she did not hear what Graham Pender thought of it all or whether he even knew, but she could not bring herself to ask. Since Kay was being so painfully honest she would probably get around to it in time, she decided, forcing herself to be patient.

'Maybe he would …maybe not! I don't know anything anymore. I can't risk losing Sinead.' Angrily, Kay brushed away a tear. 'You know the doctor never warned me that the antibiotic he gave me for my face rash could wipe out the Pill. You would imagine it was *my* fault instead of his, and now all my plans to work full time are down the drain. I mean Sinead isn't two yet!'

Florrie was slightly taken aback by Kay's cold-blooded mention of her work plans, but knowing how much her own independence meant to her she tried to be fair.

'Look, I know how much you were counting on signing the work contract,' she began, but got no further.

'Yes, I was!' Kay interrupted bitterly. 'I told Judy Mathews that I would definitely sign up at the end of the summer and now I'm going to look a right fool. But I suppose that's the least of my problems.'

Florrie winced at her abrasive tone. 'Okay, I can see that on top of everything else it must be a shocking blow. But from all you told me it would have been difficult getting Dave to go along with your working full time. Maybe after this baby is born he'll be better disposed to the idea.'

Kay looked away. 'Or maybe I'll just go on having babies,' she said dully. 'And *never* get a chance to do what I really want.' She fell silent, lost in thought, and then she heaved a sigh and reached across the table to take hold of Florrie's hand.

'I'd like you to be godmother, Flo. God knows, in the circumstances, the poor mite will need someone special,' and Florrie saw that her eyes were heavy with unshed tears. Once more her sympathy was fully engaged and she stroked the hand holding hers. Poor Kay, she sighed, what a terrible plight to be in.

***

Somehow Graham got through the days. Each one seemed to bring with it some unexpected new low, until he gave up nurturing even the faintest hope there would ever be an improvement in his circumstances. Unemployed, with no hope of getting work, he was beset by feelings of inadequacy, acutely bringing back memories of his hostage years. Was this to become the pattern of his life, he wondered in despair, dogged by ill-luck for the remainder of his days? In that moment he believed it was.

Most of all Graham missed the routine of flying, the welcome distraction it brought. But even when Ben Higgins had assured him that the Pilots Association voted to back him one hundred percent he refused to even consider appealing the Board's decision. He had seen the cold look in McGrattan's eye and knew it would be wasted effort. Without a doubt Oliver had scuppered his chances from the outset, Graham reckoned, more than likely he had reminded the members of the Board of their earlier generous, but misguided, act in reinstating a pilot who had not only originally crashed his plane, but been involved with terrorists all along. Bitterness tinged Graham's thoughts when he remembered how none of the board of directors had spoken out for him at the meeting that day. At one time he would have counted one or two of them as his friends, he thought, but there was truth in the saying you only discovered your real friends in time of trouble.

As the weeks passed Graham's mood sank lower. In retrospect, it seemed to him in every area of his life he was overwhelmed by misfortune and regrets. He got in the habit of going for long, solitary walks and sat up late at night listening to opera on his stereo. More often than not the composer he chose was Puccini. He had bought the Maria Callas version of *La Bohème* in the Metropolitan Opera House on the night that he and Kay had attended the opera, and it was rapidly becoming his favourite, most often played piece of music. In those grim days music was one of the few consolations afforded Graham and *La Bohème* always brought the memories rushing back. He would see again Kay's entranced face and remember how she had genuinely loved the music on that memorable night at the Met. What a gift it was to share similar interests with someone you loved, he often thought, especially something so passionate and deeply satisfying as opera. But there was a certain sadness in reliving that happy time. Despite the two letters he had sent to Kay care of her friend Florrie, she had not written back.

Graham was puzzled at her silence, not at once did it strike him that she might have been upset, even disillusioned by his conduct on their last meeting. When another week brought no response from her it merely occurred to him that Florrie might be away on winter leave, for it was that time of year again. Well, if that were so he would just have to wait until she returned, he told himself, or else write directly to Kay, but the last thing he wanted was to compromise her in any way.

And then he began dwelling more and more on the night that Kay had come to his house. Small details came back to him and he shuddered imagining what she must have thought of his frowzy appearance, his unmanly behavior, and his mind sheered painfully away from the images conjured up. And now Graham was conscious of having painted too bleak, too hopeless a picture to Kay of his prospects, or lack of them. No wonder she had been scared away.

But in Graham's more realistic, less emotional moments, he knew that he had not exaggerated the seriousness of his situation nor his poor chance of re-employment in the damning circumstances. Reluctantly, he acknowledged, that in this respect his prospects were every bit as poor as he had implied to Kay that night, and there had been no improvement since. Desperate for some lightening of the blackness surrounding him, he resolved to write again to her at her friend's address. Once again he poured out his heart to her then waited, not at all patiently, to hear back.

***

The letters were piling up. Three now, Kay thought, her heart twisting painfully as she put Graham's latest missive into the brown envelope she kept hidden at the very top of the hot press. She had to exercise great discipline not to open any of them and yet she could not bring herself to destroy them.

'What! You haven't read them yet!' Florrie cried in amazement. 'But surely you should at least see what he has to say?'

But what was the point? Kay knew it would only tear her apart, weaken her resolve. Since making her painful decision some weeks before, she was aware the situation had not altered. At the airport it was the opinion that Captain Pender's only option was to go abroad. While secretly forced to agree, this pessimistic outlook was a double-edged knife piercing Kay's heart. She wept inwardly for him and for herself, felt reaffirmed in her decision to spare him the additional burden of the child they had inadvertently conceived together. But although she had put his letters out of sight, Kay could not put them out of mind. It was as though Graham had entered her house and taken possession of it. She found herself constantly imagining the words he might have used, the incidents referred to, savoring like a bittersweet potion the memories evoked.

It was not until sometime later that Kay heard the wild rumours about Graham's son, and was horrified by the speculation that the boy had tried to kill himself. 'I don't believe it. No, it can't be true,' she protested, when Florrie gave her Graham's latest letter and solemnly confirmed the story.

'They said in the restroom it had something to do with knives or swords,' Florrie said, and Kay shuddered.

'No, you must be mistaken, Flo. He's crazy about his children and they about him. They would never do anything like that. I just *know* they wouldn't.'

But later when on her own again, Kay remembered something that Graham had said about one of his boys killing someone in Colombo and how terribly shocked he had been. Who knows, she thought, maybe his son had gone into a depression or something

199

afterwards. Suddenly, Kay was no longer sure; the more she thought about it the stronger her conviction that she must lose no time in reading Graham's letters and learning the truth. While Sinead was taking her nap, she tore open the first envelope with shaking fingers and began to read.

'Forgive me, darling, did I frighten you with my pessimistic words about the future and all the other nonsense I spoke that night. But I felt it was only fair to let you know how poor my prospects were and still are, I fear. In that respect nothing has changed. But I feel unable to continue without seeing you now and then. Selfish I know but I hope you feel the same.'

Kay lowered the letter in dismay, clearly he did not realize what he was asking of her. Yes, she had been frightened at seeing him weep before her, but only because she had never seen him as anything but in control, and few others had either, she suspected. With a troubled expression, she opened the other letters, certain lines jumping out at her, 'I want only the best for you and Sinead.... I don't care what I work at so long as I can make a living and we can be together...telephone me and put me out of my misery...believe me, darling, I am suffering.'

Kay was suffering too. He had always been so proud, she thought, and here he was almost begging her for a reply, prepared to make a go of things, anything not to lose her. But the possibility of having a life together after all only confused and unsettled her. Apart from anything else she could not see Graham content to engage in anything not connected with aviation and planes Oh darling, what am I doing to you? she thought in distress, turning to the letter Florrie gave her that day.

'My dearest, perhaps you rang in my absence. I was away at my sons' school. Nicky, my youngest lad, had an accident at fencing but thank God he's all right. Slipped and fell. Just a touch of concussion, but deeply worrying at the time. You are a parent yourself and know all about it.'

Kay shuddered and read on. Despite his relief at his son's recovery, the whole tone of the letter was despair and disillusion. The wounded words leapt at her from the page. 'I can't understand why

I haven't heard from you...I have laid my soul bare to you...can it be that you no longer care for me,' until the final bitter accusation. 'I did not realise my high profile job meant so much to you but it would seem that you have been more taken with the status of an airline pilot than the man himself. Oh my beloved, I am in a hell of your making and one word from you can save me...'

Kay could hardly bear to read on. She put up a shaking hand before her face as though warding off blows. She found she was weeping and got up unsteadily, to pluck tissues from a box. What terrible hurt he was enduring and all because of her selfish and cowardly refusal to be honest with him. But I am only trying to protect our child, she told herself. And if I tell him the truth he will only take on any job no matter how menial in order to provide for us, and this would eventually destroy any love between us. No, this has to be the best way. Dave would never let Sinead go, she told herself. He would make very sure I didn't get custody of her.

Waking at 5 a.m. for the fourth night in a row Graham sat up smoking one cigarette after the other, and knew there would be no more rest for him that night. As the darkness gave way to the wintery dawn, he was remembering his chat with Judy Mathews the previous day, during which she had let slip that Kay had given in her notice. 'Not the career girl after all,' Judy had said. 'I had such high hopes for her,' and Graham winced, for so had he.

'Oh Kitty, have I completely lost you?' he groaned, unable to believe after all they had meant to each other that she could so easily give him up. Utterly cast down, he told himself no matter how much he loved her he would not allow any woman reduce him to the point of having to beg. If she did not reply to his last letter, he told himself with weary finality, it was over, he was finished with her.

***

All along Kay knew that she should have at least done Graham the kindness of writing back but the impossibility of satisfactorily explaining to him how she had let four letters go unanswered daunted her. With Dave back home again wanting to take up where they had left off in London, she was forced to play the part of loving amorous wife. She was like an actress playing her saddest role and never was Kay sadder than when in the marital embrace, unable to forget how Graham had kissed and loved her and nothing her husband could do or say ever came close.

And then tragedy struck.

Dave's father was missing for three or four days before he was found floating in the Liffey, and there was talk of suicide. Given his drink problem, it was not the first time he had failed to come home but he had never been away so long before. Dave took it very hard. When Kay tried to comfort him he pushed her away, refusing to talk about it, then overcome by grief he had turned to her at last. Usually so reserved, he spoke emotionally of his great need of her and what it meant to him having her and Sinead to come home to. Without them, he told her brokenly, he wouldn't want to go on living.

Kay still longed to put things right with Graham but worn out by sorrow and hassle, the debilitating sickness she was experiencing with this second pregnancy, she held off contacting him. Held off too long, she realized. Never had it been truer that procrastination had been the thief of time. She had not had the courage or the honesty to call a halt to her marriage when Graham had begged her to come and live with him, and now it was too late! The moment for understanding or believing was long past.

***

The following year, after months of unemployment and much soul searching, Captain Pender was offered the position of Chief of Flight Operations with MacDoolAer, the low cost airline run by the controversial owner and Chief Executive, Tim O'Callaghan.

This was the turning point for Graham and to celebrate his change of fortune he booked two tickets for *La Bohème* at the Gaiety. Maybe Judy Mathews might like to go with him, he thought, but in the end he went alone.

The months had been lonely and fraught following his breakup with Kay. Graham had agonized over the mess he had made of his life, telling himself despite the many severe life-lessons he had been taught, he had not learned anything at all. Christmas had come and gone, the miserable time on his own with Ranjan only slightly alleviated when Sile, relenting at the last moment, allowed Jeremy and Nicholas to stay with him a couple of nights. Only because, he suspected, she was going to a house party on New Year's Eve and it suited her. Still, their presence was salve to his loneliness and he rejoiced to see the Indian boy smiling and happy; much of it due to Nicky and himself becoming friends again after their bitter falling out. Nicky's unfortunate accident following their not-too-friendly fencing match had signaled the end of the feud and the beginning of a stronger, more balanced relationship. The incident in Colombo was never referred to again. Graham felt there was a lot about the Tamil leader's part in the execution of the Sinhalese woman who had betrayed Ranjan's sister remained unexplained, but he was prepared to leave it that way. Better for Ranjan to try to get over the trauma, he considered, if only this were possible for the scars had gone deep. It worried Graham that the Tamil leader was a sinister force in the boy's life, using him for his own ends, as well as his own part in allowing himself to be coerced into agreeing to return the boy to his homeland when his education was complete. But that was still a long way off. In the meantime circumstances had changed and in view of the crime committed, Graham believed that such a promise might not even be binding. He was aware that Ranjan needed protecting from the Tamil leader, and to the best of his ability, he intended doing just that.

He was aware too, how much he owed Andy and Ben. At the lowest time in his career, when he was friendless and alone, they had strongly supported him and working on his behalf to make sure he got a good financial settlement from the airline in compensation for the Board's unfair and prejudicial treatment. He knew that Ben could never understand why he had not challenged the decision to suspend him. 'You have a very strong case, you were acquitted in the Ceylonese court on all charges,' Ben had stated. 'You are within your rights to bring a suit against the airline for unlawful dismissal and defamation of character. With the full backing of the Pilots Association you cannot lose.'

But Graham had no heart to go to court again, once had been enough. If he had not lost Kay he might have taken on the battle but, as it was, he left it in the hands of his lawyers and he was not sorry. From the money he received in settlement he was able to take up Christy's offer when approached by his former colleague regarding investing in the M & K flying club along with Marty Mullen and himself. As always, before making an investment Graham sought advice from his accountant. On receiving a good report of the company he met up with the Marty Mullen to discuss the offer and find out exactly what it entailed. He realized that in his new capacity as managing director Christy needed to remain sober if the club was to continue to thrive but Captain Pender did not have a lot of confidence in Kane staying off the booze for long, he never had been able to in the past. However, it appeared that Christy was a changed man and determined to make the most of the opportunity afforded him.

On meeting Mullen, Graham was impressed by the shrewd business man, he was clearly an entrepreneur with a talent for making money and a very likeable fellow besides. The wonder of it was what he had seen in Christy but when Graham thought about it he realized it was just another of Marty's shrewd hunches that had paid off. Kane was undeniably a good pilot and would not only manage the club but give flying instruction too. He was a gregarious fellow and if he could keep off the beer, he could be a real draw with his flying stories and ready wit. Already a colorful figure swaggering about the airfield in his airline cap and leather jacket, Christy was popular with members, chatting and joking as he served them their drinks. Graham went very thoroughly into every aspect of the business and was satisfied on learning that Marty was a major shareholder in the company and Christy a director, being paid a salary for his part in running the club. He himself would have a seat on the board and be appointed the company's financial advisor, answering only to Mullen, which was what Graham wanted. Despite himself, he took confidence in Marty's shrewd judgment, his obvious liking for Christy and his belief in the man. He decided to go ahead and invest in the company, and found himself looking forward to teaching his boys to fly, maybe in time he might even purchase his own light aircraft, Graham thought. It was a good feeling after the tough days he had endured.

It was about this time in early spring that the job offer came from MacDoolAer's owner, Tim O'Callaghan. Initially, on receiving O'Callaghan's phone call Graham had had certain reservations. The man had a reputation for his tough approach, boasting of a service devoid of frills – no complimentary drink or sandwich snack between Dublin and London to ease the hunger pangs - but without the usual hefty air ticket either, it had to be said. Graham's only concern was how far O'Callaghan's cost-cutting extended and whether it affected the servicing and maintenance of aircraft and, indeed, any other aspect of crew and passenger safety.

For him that was a no-go area.

On meeting Tim, however, he was pleasantly surprised. O'Callaghan might be a trifle blunt in his manner but Graham judged him to be sincere and straightforward.

'You'll suit us very well, Pender,' he said, firmly shaking his hand. 'Think over my offer and let me know. We can have your contract drawn up and ready to sign by the end of the week.'

To be honest, Graham could very well have given his answer there and then, there were not many job offers coming his way, but he decided it would be no harm to check out O'Callaghan first with Andy and Ben. When he did, they both agreed that O'Callaghan was a tough man but he insisted on all aircraft inspections being regularly carried out in strict accordance with safety regulations. Graham was relieved to hear it. As he told his former colleagues he would prefer to resign himself to a lifetime of transporting livestock than align himself with any airline not operating in accordance with IATA and PTSB. At that Andy related some funny, and not so funny, cargo stories in which animals went berserk when the engines started up and tried to savage their way into the cockpit.

'You'd be damn glad of the crash axe in a situation like that, Pender,' he said thoughtfully. 'Not to mention a length of rope to truss the beast.'

'Or you could always go on oxygen and depressurize the aircraft,' Ben suggested with a grin. 'That usually puts 'em to sleep.'

205

'I'll bear it in mind,' Graham told them gravely, but he enjoyed the crack and lost no more time in accepting O'Callaghan's offer.

Now as he took his seat in the theatre dress circle he was relieved to be back working again and to have a job that had been worth waiting for. Listening to the overture of *La Bohème* Graham was acutely reminded of the night he and Kay had attended the opera in New York. By the time the curtain fell at the interval all his love and longing for her had resurrected, and with the confirmation of his new appointment with MacDoolAer, he wondered if there might yet be a chance for him.

This was very much on his mind as he entered the bar and glanced about for the gin tonic he had ordered earlier. All at once his heart suffered a painful constriction for there, across the small crowded room, stood Kay and she lovelier than ever in a filmy gown the deepest shade of rose. The bodice was low-cut and draped over her full breasts in the Empire style and while Graham might have been long out of touch with maternity fashions, he could not be blind to the fact she was pregnant. He was so shocked he could only stare. Turning her head and perceiving him across the room, Kay's tranquil expression became stricken. For a moment her startled green eyes met his and all the wealth of feeling and regret was in their locked glances before her returning husband claimed her attention.

Graham, much shaken by the encounter, escaped into the corridor. Stumbling down to the foyer, he doubted he could ever listen to Puccini again. So that's why she couldn't leave him, he thought anguished. That's why she hadn't answered his letters or phone calls. Graham's heartbreak was complete. That it was deliberate, he did not question for one moment. He was aware that she was taking the pill, he had seen her swallowing it often enough before making love. Hurrying out to the street, he was conscious of the bitter irony in the ill-timing of the new job and the new life within her. He wished he could bring himself to hate her, but he couldn't.

*****

PART TWO
(May, 1972)

The baby came almost three weeks before the rough date that Kay had given Dave, but in actual fact Dervla Annabel Mason was right on time. By a fortuitous coincidence Sinead had been a couple of weeks early, so everyone assumed this to be the case with the new baby. In the midst of Kay's overwhelming joy in Dervla was the fear that after his first cursory glance Dave would come to suspect the truth, for in looks the child did not resemble him at all. Then she remembered the baby's cleft chin belonged to her as well as to Graham, and with growing relief she attributed the dark hair to herself too. Fair-haired and fair-skinned, Sinead took after Dave, so it was quite in order for their second child to resemble her. Just so long as no one commented too closely on the baby's brown eyes, they were deep and dark like Graham's.

Suckling the child in the early hours – she was feeding this one herself – Kay experienced another wave of relief remembering that Molly's eyes were hazel. And then she gave up trying to deny all resemblance to Graham and wearily allowed herself to take extreme pleasure in the fact. In fact when the nurse placed Dervla in her arms and Kay gazed down at her beautiful, dark-haired daughter, her heart had turned over at the likeness of the child to the father and, in those first unbalanced emotional moments, she had been swept by the crazy notion of urging him to come see his child, even going so far as to ask the nurse to bring her some writing paper. But the madness soon passed and Kay let it lie in the locker drawer deciding, however, that she would name the child after Graham's mother. He had often spoken of her and she had sensed the deep loving bond between them. It seemed fitting that the woman's only granddaughter should be named in her honour. What Dave might want did not greatly seem to matter but, for the sake of appearances, Kay invested a mythical cousin on her dead mother's side with this name, no longer bothered by such duplicity.

It was just one more deception in so many.

The relationship between Dave and Kay had never really got back on to the old lighthearted footing of the early days of their marriage. Since the time of his father's death Dave had taken to coming home later and later from work. Often he had a smell of drink on his breath and Kay suspected he had got in the habit of fortifying himself on the way. The unhappy atmosphere between them made her regret anew her failure to end her marriage when she had had the chance. Clearly, by staying with him she had not made Dave any happier nor could she claim any great degree of happiness for herself. As for Graham, on the night of the opera his expression seared her and she would have given anything to have been able to tell him the truth and ease his pain. Over the months there had been times when Kay had felt she must surely break down under her sorrow. In deeply troubled moments the only course appeared to be honest with both Dave and Graham and accept the consequences. But something always stopped her. If it were not for the totally unsupported conviction that one day Graham would come to know the truth and she would somehow be vindicated, she would have found it impossible to go on. But for now his baby sustained her, the little girl would make up for it all, so Kay believed.

Florrie took her time before giving her opinion when she visited, remembering Dave's phone call to say that her goddaughter was born and seeming to see nothing strange in a baby three weeks premature weighing over eight pounds. But when Florrie turned back to face Kay there was no doubt what she was thinking, and Kay was relieved there were no witnesses as she demanded, 'Well, what do you think?'

'She's a stunner,' Florrie said, adding bluntly. 'There's not a trace of Dave in her. As to the other, she's the spitting image of *him*!'

Coming from the one person who knew the truth her honesty gave Kay the confirmation she craved, and she leaned back on the pillows with a sigh.

'When are you planning to hold the Christening?' Florrie was saying. 'You know we are heading off to the sun next week, Brian and myself?'

'I'll get Dave to ring you tonight,' Kay promised, aware that Florrie had broken up with Danny and was giving Brian another chance. 'Oh Florrie, how long will you be gone?'

'Sure I'll be back before you know it …if we don't get heart failure from those hot passionate nights.' She gave her limpid grin and rolled her eyes. 'Two weeks tops. Then it's back to being bossed about by Ciara. 'Twould almost drive me to marriage.'

'Oh yeah, knowing you that's a long way off.'

'Well, you could be right but Brian is sticking around this time. I could do worse.'

And you could do a lot better, Kay thought, but smiling she said, 'Enjoy your freedom while you can and may the passion and delight never grow less.'

'Oh Kay, I wish *you* could get back your delight,' Florrie cried. 'You were happy with Dave at one time. Yes, you *were...* You're well suited in many ways, you know.'

'Yes, but once you've known the other there's no going back,' Kay admitted with sad finality, her gaze resting on Dervla. 'At least I have her. I'm very lucky.'

Florrie was getting ready for bed when Dave rang. 'Tuesday suits best for the Christening,' he told her. 'Sorry I can't give you more notice. Hope this doesn't present any problems, Florrie.'

'None I can't get around,' she said cheerily. 'I have a Cork/Paris that day but sure Angie here would do it at a pinch,' glancing at her flat-mate who smiled and nodded. 'And sure why not? Full of the joys and she getting married shortly,' ignoring Angie's scandalized, 'Florrie!'

'That's great!' Dave was relieved.

'Oh, and congrats! on your new baby,' Florrie hurried to say. 'She's gorgeous, the image of Kay and it's only right because Sinead is the image of you, Dave,' feeling a bit bothered by her insincerity but knowing it would please him.

'Sinead is nice enough,' he agreed, as if he didn't think her the most perfect little girl on earth. 'I think Dervla will be quite nice too.'

Quite nice! Florrie almost reeled at the inadequacy of the word. She wanted to say, 'She's a beauty and she'll always outshine Sinead, no matter how lovely you think your own daughter.' But some sixth sense warned her from too openly praising the new arrival. She felt a sudden better understanding of what Dave lacked and Graham Pender possessed in abundance. Poor Kay, she thought for the second time that evening. You could live on bread but how much more enjoyable was cake.

***

By the time Dave had made arrangements with their parish priest to have Dervla Christened that Tuesday he received word from the nursing home that Kay's Aunt Molly had died in her sleep. Kay was devastated and Dave decided it best to postpone the Christening and explain the situation to Florrie.

'Sorry to mess you up,' he told her. 'We'll have it when you get back from your holidays,' and she agreed, 'Of course, Dave. Give Kay my sympathy.'

It was only when Dave dropped over to the hospital soon after speaking to Florrie that he found Kay collapsed in tears watching the lunch time news and learned of the tragic crash of the Celtic Airways Cork/Paris flight that morning.

'Oh Dave, God help them,' sobbed Kay, turning a distraught face towards him. 'What a terrible thing. Thank God, Florrie wasn't on it. Only for swapping flights to attend the Christening she would have been.'

Dave sank down on the bed and took Kay in his arms, soothing her with a gentle hand. What if she got so upset she couldn't feed the baby? he worried, glancing helplessly down at the sleeping child. It seemed selfish to be bothered by such considerations in the face of the enormous tragedy, but the fact remained that Dervla was only a few days old and would suffer if Kay lost her milk. He sighed and felt the first stirrings of love for this child that produced in him such a welter of emotions.

The plane crash was the main topic of conversation between incoming crews and a pall hung over the airport. Florrie only learned about it when she checked in that evening for her London flight, the one she had swapped Angie for when her flatmate agreed to do her Cork/Paris. So far there was no word of any survivors.

Trembling with delayed shock, she went on board, the tears streaming down her face. Poor, poor Angie, how terrible, she mourned, only for agreeing to oblige her, she would still be alive. And she herself, Florrie shuddered at the thought, right now could be at the bottom of the sea. .

Captain Pender heard about the Celtic Airways crash early afternoon and thought it was ironic he should hear about it from a MacDoolAer pilot. He had just finished reading the newspaper in the pilots lounge and learned that Ceylon had been renamed and would now be known as Sri Lanka. The dreaded name of Lanka had brought the past rushing back to him but what Captain Jameson had to tell him returned Graham to the present with a jolt. Only for the fact he had been overseeing pilot training on Jumbo jets all that week he would have been in the air like Jack, and tuned into the same radio frequency.

'Poor bastards,' Jameson was saying, 'Jim Lee and a young chap called Mannion. On their way to Paris. You probably flew with them, Pender?'

Graham nodded. Not the young First Officer, but he remembered Jim Lee well enough. He had come straight to CA from the Air Corps and often co-piloted with Graham in the days they were still flying turboprops.

Jameson looked at him curiously. Cold fish, he thought. Not a trace of emotion and one of his former colleagues just gone into the drink.

Graham was not unaware that the florid-faced pilot with the truculent stance harbored resentment against him. He had encountered the same stolid opposition from some of the other MacDool-Aer pilots since joining the airline and most of them, he had to say, were a mediocre lot. Maybe he was prejudiced, Graham thought, but the intelligence and application of the junior pilots in CA was far in advance of any of their counterparts in MacDoolAer. He often compared it to working with carthorses after dealing in thoroughbreds, but it was a job and bringing in good money, he reminded himself, determined to make the best of it. He sometimes thought how different it would have been if he were doing the same job, even with all its limitations and the less than satisfactory attitude of its pilots, if only Kay were sharing his life. At the thought, his mind immediately sheered away but only momentarily. By this Graham had learned to live with the disillusioning manner in which his hopes had been cruelly dashed and, if not always successful, he had done his best to move on. It was only later that he saw Molly Begley's death notice in the paper. Oh dear, Kitty would be heartbroken. He knew how close she had always been to her guardian and his heart swelled with compassion. Maybe he should set aside the past and convey his sympathies. It was the least anyone would do in the circumstances.

*＊＊

Dave was conscious of the need to find Molly's Last Will and Testament, already her daughter Winifred had been on to him, irked by the fact her mother had not seen fit to give such an important document to her instead of her cousin.

He had just begun his search when the telephone rang. Hurrying to answer it, he was surprised to hear a man asking to speak to Kay.

'She's not here just now,' Dave told the caller, and was about to ask his name when he realized whoever it was had already hung up.

Frowning, he returned to the search conscious of his need to visit Kay in the hospital before heading back to the office. In the end, Dave came upon the document by accident, when he dislodged it from between the pages of a cookery book. But this happy discovery was not made until he had first unearthed two objects in the course of his search. One was a medical invoice for a pregnancy test he found at the back of Kay's dressing-table drawer, the other a small object wrapped in tissue paper and concealed beneath lining paper on the wardrobe shelf. On opening it out, he was dumbfounded to find a spectacular solitaire diamond set in a band of heavy gold.

Cradling it in his hand, Dave wondered just where his wife had come by such a valuable ring, and felt suspicion clutch at his heart. He was reminded of the pilot she had been in love with and the phone call earlier took on a new significance. It seemed only logical if she were having an affair with anyone it would be with him. At first, Dave rejected the unpalatable thought, but as soon as he was ready to explore this possibility, he found other things requiring answers.

Troubled and confused, he went downstairs to sit at the kitchen table and stare out dully at the overgrown garden. Perhaps he was jumping to the wrong conclusions, he told himself unhappily, just because Kay had not mentioned the pregnancy test did not necessarily mean anything. After all, she was so keen to keep on flying it was understandable that she must have occasionally panicked thining she might be pregnant. For all he knew it was not the first time she had gone for such a test.

As for the ring, there was probably some innocent explanation, maybe some friend had given it into her safe-keeping, who knew. Maybe even Florrie, whose flat-mate Angie was soon to be married. At the thought, Dave's anguished expression lightened. He was almost ready to retreat under the mantle of happy ignorance once more, when two days later the post brought in a bundle of baby cards and, amongst them, a letter of sympathy to Kay on her aunt's death which fondly began, 'My dearest Kitty' and was signed with that oh-so-familiar name at the bottom, taking away any doubt in Dave's mind about the relationship between his wife and this man.

With no knowledge of Graham's letter, her husband having taken the precaution of burning it, Kay took her seat in the funeral car behind the hearse carrying her aunt's remains to the cemetery. In the back window she had put her tribute to Molly's memory, a dozen long-stemmed red roses. Red roses for love, Kay thought sadly, and Molly was all love. She would never forget how her aunt had given her a home and shown her unfailing kindness, even when Winifred and others were quick to find fault.

'Oh Molly, dear Molly,' she cried inwardly, only managing to control her grief for fear of frightening the child in her arms.

. At the graveside, Kay recognized Molly's old sea-going friend and former lodger, Bill Norton, looking a bit worse for the years and unashamedly mopping his eyes. 'She was a grand lady, none better,' he murmured, shaking Kay's hand. Poor faithful old man, she was saddened to see him so shabby.

Nearby, Winifred snuffled into a handkerchief, Cahal held two-year old Emma in his arms staring morosely at the ground, and the older children whispered together. Kay's eyes moved bleakly from face to face, anything to keep from seeing the lonely-looking coffin poised over the freshly dug earth. Memories kept striking her, and she found it hard not to break down.

Laying the roses on the coffin, she turned blindly away, devastated by the knowledge that the two people closest to her heart were lost to her forever.

***

By the time Dervla was three Kay had still made no move to go back to Celtic Airways. She told herself that she was being overly protective and if she ever wanted to get on with her career she would need to make a start. The fact that the government had finally recognised women's right to work after marriage and be paid a proper wage was a big incentive, but even though the whole employment issue had improved for married women, Kay still hesitated, unable to bear the thought of leaving Dervla a minute sooner than she must. In the end, she had decided to wait until the little girl was going to school, secretly relieved to have more time to enjoy her baby.

It was true whenever Kay looked at Dervla she felt her heart turn over with love. She was such a beautiful child, with a mop of dark curls framing an exquisite little face, and big brown eyes gazing trustingly up through sooty lashes. She seemed to have inherited the best features of both her parents and the result was arresting. Even strangers were drawn irresistibly to her, stopping to engage her in talk for she always seemed to be quivering on the brink of laughter. Dervla's sense of fun often got her into trouble but so penitent and regretful was she for any little naughtiness that within seconds she had won everyone around. Even Eileen was not proof against her innocent charm but from the beginning she had determinedly resisted her, as if sensing something not quite orthodox in her makeup. Maybe because Dervla looked too much like herself, Kay mused wryly, knowing this would not recommend her to Eileen. But there was another factor; Dervla would always outshine her older sister and Sinead was her grandmother's favourite, no question about that.

Sinead was the replica of Dave, the opposite of her younger sister and a rather serious, practical little girl given to perceptive comments but no flights of fancy. By contrast, Dervla was a most imaginative and creative child, given to drawing artistic pictures but not at all drawn to her grandmother. Kay had noticed how Dervla never ran blindly to Eileen like her older sister did whenever she hurt herself, not even when the predatory marmalade cat slipped under the fence and eyed her balefully through the tall grass. Secretly, she was glad the little girl kept aloof from Eileen and meanly applauded her good taste. For it was mean, she knew, after all Eileen would surely never harm Dervla, she was kind to both children even if she did openly show her preference for Sinead. And why wouldn't she, and Sinead the image of her father?

From Florrie, Kay learned of the changes in CA and the mixed reactions to the official report on the crashed BAC1-11 when it was finally published three years after the tragedy. Sadly, the provision of the international agreement gave miniscule compensation to the those bereaved families and badly injured survivors who had made application within the two year limit, before the Inspector of Accidents official report was published. When it was filed after three years it did not confirm that the plane was struck nor did it rule out pilot error and consequently there was no compensation forthcoming to the injured and bereaved. All of which greatly added to the suffering of all those involved. Angela Liston had survived the crash but her back was badly injured and she was confined to a wheelchair, her family continually striving to raise funds to pay for her treatment. Kay knew that Florrie kept in close touch with Angie and her friend had never ceased to blame herself for having asked her to swap flights that day. Kay herself was troubled knowing it was because of her baby's Christening that Angie had been on board at all on that fatal day.

When Dervla turned four and attended Montessori school Kay still remained at home looking after her children, claiming they kept her occupied and her days full. Each year up to this she had stretched the return to work date a little further knowing she would never have Dervla all to herself like this again, and secretly including the little one's father in this calculation. Only to herself would Kay ever admit that she could never look at Dervla without seeing Graham, and understandably the amount of petting and hugging she indulged in with her youngest child was in proportion to the emotion she still felt for him.

Watching Kay breastfeeding Dervla in the early months and seeing her absorption with her child, Dave was saddened to see how satisfied and fulfilled she appeared to be in a way that she had never been with Sinead, and he worried that their eldest daughter might feel neglected. But he kept his opinion to himself for fear of making too much of it. He and Kay had become a little closer as the unhappy memory of Reggie's and Mollie's deaths receded. These days they busied themselves in various ways, Dave as always with his work, spending more time at the office – even on Christmas Eve he would work late and when he finally came home and Kay would think, 'This is it. Now Christmas is starting' there would be more calls from his boss. Indeed, her husband seemed to welcome them, never happier than when talking business with Tony and strategically planning new deals for the company.

For Kay more money coming into the house meant that Dave replaced her first car with a younger model, although it was still secondhand. When Florrie had moved in with Brian, Kay felt she was selling herself short. What a pity she had let Danny McCarthy go, he was a much nicer, kinder man than Brian who struck her as a bit of a know-it-all. Over controlling too, but Florrie just shrugged, too obsessed by him to get free.

By the time Dervla turned five Kay was ready to suss out the prospect of returning to the airport, and felt fairly hopeful of getting her old job back. Surprisingly, Dave made no objection, merely heard her out then changed the subject. So Kay went ahead and phoned the airport, her heart lifting when the Super said warmly, 'Of course, I remember you, Kay. Come any time it suits you and we'll have a chat.'

Kay brought Dervla with her to the airport that day, although she could have left her with her grandmother, but then Dervla was never any trouble. If she grew tired she would just drop off to sleep in her car seat, with her chin resting comfortably on Nellie, her favourite

217

doll, the sweep of her dark lashes fanning her cheeks. Besides Kay always looked forward to showing the little girl off and Judy's reaction was most gratifying.

'What an absolutely beautiful little girl,' she cried, astonishing Kay by swooping up the child and placing her on her knee. 'And what's your name, pet?'

'Dervla Annabel Mason,' the little one replied sunnily, not at all shy.

'Well now, Dervla Annabel,' Judy cooed. 'You play with these while I talk to your Mummy,' lining up an assortment of treasures plucked from her desk and cubby-holes, while chatting over the child's head.

Kay learned that inevitably changes had taken place in the years she had been away, in addition to the Jumbo CA's fleet now consisted mainly of B737s, 113-seater short to medium-haul jets operating to the UK and the continent. It appeared these would be the routes she would be flying on her return. Kay was not sure how she felt about being back on Europe, apart from having three days off between flights on the Atlantic there had always been a certain status about being on the Atlantic and exchanging it now struck her as a bit of a comedown.

At Judy's suggestion, the Chief Hostess Europe was asked to come down to her office but, when she appeared shortly afterwards, Ciara was hesitant and doubtful in direct contrast to Judy's encouraging manner regarding Kay's return to work.

'I can't see how it would work out,' she said flatly, making Kay feel anything but welcome back. 'A lot has happened in the past few years. I mean we've all moved on. It's harder, more competitive now. Not everyone is able to keep up.'

'Nonsense,' Judy said bracingly. 'Kay was one of my best girls on the Atlantic. She flew quite a bit on the 747 and will easily pick it all up again. Anyway, we are constantly running refresher courses.'

'But the expense! She would have to be retrained on all our aircraft.' From her look of aversion she might have been talking of potty-training, Kay thought in disgust, 'Mr McGrattan's recent memo *expressly* requested that we reduce our expenditure.'

Judy looked bored. 'Yes, yes! Nothing new about that. We've been getting memos of that nature since before we moved into our new hostess quarters.'

On her way out Ciara cast a glance of dislike at Kay, Dervla might not have existed, and Kay found she was not at all drawn to working with her.

'I do hope you will bring Dervla to see me again,' Judy said, getting to her feet. 'She's a lovely child. You are very lucky, my dear. Do you know that?'

'Yes, I do.' Kay was surprised by Judy's wistful expression.

'Make your application to the personnel officer and tell him you have been to see me. There'll be no problem, I assure you.' She held out her hand to Kay. 'I'm delighted you are thinking of coming back. I was sorry when you changed your mind before but now I think you did the right thing,' her gaze straying back to the child.

Stooping down, she said, 'Goodbye, my pet. You'll come and see me again, won't you?' and Dervla nodded solemnly, setting the silky curls dancing.

Pleased at how the interview had gone, despite Ciara's attitude, Kay started back down towards the lift with Dervla by the hand. She had only a minute to wait before the door slid back, and when it did she was startled to see a tall familiar figure stepping briskly out; one she had not seen in a long time, except in her dreams. Equally taken aback, Captain Pender paused in his stride and they stared dumbly at each other.

'Kitty!' Graham sighed, as though he had been saving it up all this time, and she blushed. 'What brings you here?'

'I...I was visiting Judy Mathews,' Kay stammered, in her confusion letting go of the child's hand, whereupon Dervla immediately trotted towards the open lift.

With a dismayed sound, Graham started swiftly after her and just in time swung the little girl clear. Startled, she looked up at him, her mouth quivering with upset.

'There, there,' he said hurriedly. 'Back you go to your mother.'

As Kay reached for her, Graham's gaze moved to the new smart haircut, shorter than he had ever seen it, the layered waves emphasizing her high cheekbones, then to her mouth softly parted and the green eyes that were locked in his.

'Oh God, how I've missed you,' he breathed.

'And I missed you.' The frank admission was torn from her and they stood taking their fill of each other in a way not possible with others present.

Momentarily, Graham glanced at Dervla before saying, 'She's delightful, so very like you,' and Kay felt like saying, 'Ah, but even more like you,' convinced he could not fail to see the resemblance.

For those few moments while the child had been close held in his arms she had seen how Dervla's exquisite little face, with the shapely winged brows over intensely dark eyes, was a tiny replica of the face above hers. Thrilled and saddened, she had wanted to let him know what pleasure the resemblance had given her from the start.

'What name did you call her?'

Her heart thudded. 'Dervla.'

Graham drew in a deep breath and folded his arms tightly across his chest, as though keeping his own heart in check. 'That was my mother's name.'

'I know.'

In anguished tones he said, 'I've made a lot of mistakes and missed a lot of opportunities but none that I regret so much as seeing you now with...with Dervla and having no part in your lives.'

'D..don't say that, Graham,'

'It's only the truth.'

'Graham, I'm sorry.'

'Not anything as sorry as I am, believe me.'

She swallowed, wanting to reach out and console him, wondering if it was merely a matter of time before she revealed the truth about the child. At the thought, she felt a wild anxious fluttering in her chest and took a backward step, involuntarily seeking a safe distance from him.

Graham's pained gaze moved to the child regarding him gravely over her rag-doll and Kay knew what he was thinking. *She could have been theirs*, and felt more cowardly and deceitful than ever.

'I have to go,' she told him, remembering Sinead. 'I have to pick up my older child. She'll be upset if I'm late.'

At once, Graham turned and pressed the button recalling the lift and all the previous sad partings Kay had ever shared with this man seemed to come together to form one unbearable ache. Their eyes locked for a long moment and then Graham leaned forward and caressed the child's petal cheek with his fingers.

'Goodbye, Dervla, your grandmother must be very proud of you.'

Before the lift doors slid shut his eyes met Kay's, and the sorrow she saw in their dark depths was repeated a hundredfold in her own heart.

***

As Judy sat across from Graham drinking coffee, she wondered if he and Kay might have bumped into each other in the corridor; nothing else, she thought, could have accounted for his tortured expression on coming through her doorway. Remembering how lovely Kay had looked in the linen suit the shade of ripe greengages, Judy was surprised she felt so little jealousy. But then to her, Kay had always appeared like a younger sister or even a beloved, slightly naive daughter, neither whom she would have dreamed of entering into competition with. But then the fact she possessed neither sister nor child doubtless accounted for the Hostess Superintendent's somewhat unreal perception of sibling rivalry, once sex entered the quotient.

And Dervla! Judy's gaze softened, remembering the charming child. Just what was it about her that had so entranced her, she wondered, not often taken with children and undoubtedly bowled over by this one. Even as she was thinking this Graham raised his dark eyes from the paper knife he was fiddling with, and met hers apologetically.

'Judy, my dear, forgive my distraction,' he said, getting to his feet. 'I've a lot on my mind. I'd better be going.'

Behind his back, Judy's hand flew to her mouth in a gesture of astonishment. Oh, my goodness! she thought, why didn't I see it before? She was all at once remembering Dervla's exquisite little face, her smile, those arresting eyes. Was it any wonder Graham was troubled and the child the image of him. Stunned by the realization, Judy wondered if he was aware that the child was his, and would have given a year's salary to know this herself.

Walking back to his office Graham's mind was still whirling with poignant images of Kay and her lovely child. He felt overwhelmed, conscious of jealousy, hatred even, for the man that Kay had opted to remain with, but most of all he felt the resurgence of hurt at the cruel manner in which she had ensured that he should have no further part in her life. On top of that he was suffering the shock of hearing the child's name. That Kay should have named her child after his mother was upsetting and cruelly misleading. Graham's first reaction had been a sudden flare of hope. On reflection though, it seemed merely an indulgent and whimsical action for it had opened up wounds, emphasizing his loss and making him mourn what he could never have. Ah, but what a striking child, he mused, knowing he would never forget her face so like Kay's, and yet possessed of something else again. He was aware the little one's sweet trustful gaze had stirred some deep emotion in him, and he tried to shrug it off. Maybe because she reminded him of Nicholas as a baby, his youngest son had the same sweetness of expression, so innocent and open. Yes, it was surely that.

Sifting through the pile of flight reports on his desk he was two thirds the way towards coming to a decision that was on his mind for some time now concerning his friendship with Judy Mathews. Seeing Kay with her child, so composed and lovelier than ever, it had been brought home to him just how barren his own life had become, without any close relationship to ease his loneliness. He asked himself in sad frustration if he were destined to spend the rest of his days hopelessly languishing after her. It was something he would have to make up his mind about, and very soon.

Not long afterwards Judy was pleased to receive an invitation from Graham to dine with him at a newly opened, exclusive restaurant in town. She dressed up for the occasion and when he collected her at her apartment she considered that he was looking very smart himself, approving the pale lavender shirt and the striped tie perfectly knotted beneath his chin, the well-cut navy blazer.

At the restaurant it was gratifying to see quite a few well-known faces amongst the diners, the food was superb, there was a very good wine list and they both agreed it would be a success. At the start of the evening, the chief topic of conversation between them had been Captain Lee's widow and son and how they were struggling to survive since the findings of the crash investigation had been made public some years earlier. The invalided air hostess. Angela Liston, came in for discussion too. By all account she was not doing too well, her medical expenses were heavy and there was too little money forthcoming apart from what the airline had paid out in compensation.

Before long the couple gladly turned to other more cheerful topics until falling silent at last, they eyed each other thoughtfully in the suddenly charged atmosphere. And then Graham signaled to the waiter to bring champagne.

'To us,' he toasted unexpectedly, and lifted his glass.

Judy's heart did a little double-take at the words. Could it mean what it sounded like and, even more, what she hoped it might mean?

But she gave no indication of her turbulent feelings as she lifted her own glass murmuring, 'To us!' And when later they arrived at her apartment in Dalkey, she was not too surprised when Graham accepted her offer of a nightcap, nor when he later suggested that he might stay the night.

***

By the time Kay eventually took up the offer made to her by Judy Mathews some years earlier, Dervla had already made her First

Communion and would soon be turning nine. The reason for Kay's tardiness had been her shock on hearing about the affair between Graham and Judy Mathews. She was out one night with Florrie and some hostess friends when, one of them, Jocelyn, spoke out about the hottest airport romance of the moment, if not the decade. Prior to that Kay had been quite enjoying her witty observances and then it transpired the couple in question were none other than Judy and 'that pilot, you *know* the one everyone thought was dead, only he wasn't.'

Kay had tried not to listen, finding the details Jocelyn insisted on giving them too painful and explicit. Meeting Florrie's compassionate glance, she had smiled bravely back, trying to convey the message she was okay, really she was. But she was far from okay, desperately trying to deal with the emotion tearing her apart, regret and jealousy a big part of it. It was a relief when it was time to call it a night. Arriving home, she found Dave in amorous mood, he had succeeded in pulling off some advantageous business deal that day and was already well into a bottle of good Merlot. She had joined him in a glass but her heart was not in it, still stunned and distracted by what she had heard. Dave had made great efforts to arouse her that night in bed, but nothing could have done that if he had only realized, and it became another routine lovemaking, soon over. Kay knew he had put down her lack of response to tiredness, but heart-break not fatigue was at the root of her trouble.

On her return to the airport after the long gap Kay found CA in the throes of change, there was a new Chief Executive, Taylor Duval, an American management consultant formerly with Arthur Anderson in Atlanta. According to the rumours, Duval had been personally head-hunted by the chairman of the board and offered twice McGrattan's salary as an inducement to join CA. To save it, some said. By all accounts he was a vast improvement on his predecessor. In other respects, the changes in the airline were not for the better. Although Judy had lived up to her promise to secure a better financial deal for hostesses who had resigned on marriage in the years before the marriage bar had been officially removed by the government, to-day's married hostesses were only marginally better off than before. They were still employed on a temporary basis and had, besides, lost their original date of entry. As some people said they felt like displaced people. Although experienced cabin crew they had no particular status, although fully committed to their careers they had no voice. Anyone it seemed from the newest of the new automatically got priority over them, whether in line for promotion or on standby travel. Most stressful, Kay considered, was the atmosphere aboard flights these days; gone was the lighthearted camaraderie of the past. In its place existed an off-putting competitive spirit that would not have been out of place in a big corporate finance group, with no one caring whom they crushed in their unseemly scramble to the top. Another change in keeping with the times and carrying its own stress factor was the employment by CA of male flight attendants. True, only thirty had been taken on so far and, admittedly, this was a small number when compared with the large number of air hostesses already rostered. Kay found the guys pleasant, and even fun to work with, but she could not help being aghast by one of the young men she was working with on the drinks trolley and the joking, slightly vulgar patter, he kept up to passengers. He was what her Aunt Molly would have called, 'playing to the gallery' and, of course, he had them in stitches. Kay could just imagine Judy's disapproving face. Not that he was representative of his fellow flight attendants, she had to admit, but they had their grievances too, not least being under the jurisdiction of women and required to report back to the Hostess Super. Their constant complaint being they 'hadn't a hope in hell' of being promoted to cabin manager, not with all the competition they were up against.

'Try being female *and* married,' Kay felt like saying. Still, she told herself, this was what she had wanted - to make a comeback and fly again with CA - and despite Ciara's earlier pessimism Kay had experienced no difficulty in effecting this. Her retraining completed, she was passed to fly on all jets. The only blot that Kay could see was Ciara's undisguised bias against the married hostesses, accusing them of using marriage and children to excuse their lack of commitment to the job. Unfair and untrue, nonsense in fact with no evidence to support it, but Ciara had the power to make life unpleasant, if not downright impossible. Kay knew if she wanted to succeed she must be prepared to accept whatever Ciara dished up, *and* work twice as hard. Like her married colleagues, she volunteered to work two days a month in the hostess office, this was the way to go if she ever wanted to be considered for promotion. She found the first weeks back to work a bit stressful but knew there was no use complaining to Dave about any of it, he was as career-conscious as ever and had made it clear that his own work would always come first, no matter what. Indeed, on her return to the airport Kay was unsure if he would be willing to help out with the girls like he had done in the past, but she was determined not to let it put her off.

It was not long before Kay crossed swords with the Chief Hostess, Ciara having decided to ignore the roster and dispense with her help in the office on the appointed day. When the crew of an already delayed Paris/Rome was down by one hostess she put Kay's name forward, without consulting her, of course!

'Oh dear, does it interfere with your domestic arrangements?' Ciara asked with mocking emphasis, her supercilious expression defying Kay to protest at the high-handed action at unacceptably short notice.

'Well, it's not exactly helping,' Kay said mildly.

'Oh, what a pity.'

'Yes, it is. I'm down for ground duties today and this sudden change presents me with a few problems I hadn't envisaged.' Now they were sure to overnight and with Dave away on business, it meant ringing Eileen and asking her to sleep over.

'It may come as news to you but married hostesses aren't the only ones with problems,' Ciara smiled without humor. 'We all have them, you know. You surely don't expect special consideration, just because you happen to be married?'

'Well, yes, some consideration wouldn't go amiss.'

'Are you refusing to do this duty?'

'No,' Kay's tone was cautious, obviously the whole thing was calculated. 'But I would like to know why one of the reserves can't do it.'

Ciara flung up her hand. 'Look, I can't stand around all day discussing this. Are you going or not?'

Kay shrugged. 'Put like that I'm going, but I'd like to make it clear I'm going under protest. I intend taking the matter up with the Hostess Superintendent.'

'Why don't you do that!' Ciara's smile conveying, much good may it do you!

One thing Kay hated was arriving late and breathless aboard a flight that was obviously only waiting for the last crew member to arrive before closing the doors. Not easy to be the only married hostess on board either, and all the others junior to her. More trouble, Kay sighed, when confronted by a hostess who had clearly believed that she would be in charge until Kay had put in an appearance.

'Will you make the announcement or shall I?'

'Why don't *you*?' the young woman said pointedly. 'You're obviously the oldest,' and Kay flushed at her tone. But even as she picked up the handset another hostess came up the aisle.

'Can't seem to get the back door to close,' she said worriedly. 'Would someone *please* come down and check it with me?'

Seeing her way out of the dilemma, Kay offered to go. The door was probably okay but it was easy to become rattled. 'Better to be safe than sorry,' she told Niamh, and the girl smiled gratefully.

That there was a fault was not immediately discernible. Kay opened out the door several times and swung it shut again, firmly pressing down the locking lever. When it did not move as smoothly into position as it should have, she knew that she had to report it to the captain, and the flight was delayed even further while the co-pilot checked it out. Mark Mannion agreed with Kay and while they waited on the Chief Engineer Kay was given a hard time by some of the hostesses, but grimly stuck it out.

Eventually she was called to the cockpit by the captain who told her, 'Well Madam, I suppose you are aware that thousands of gallons of expensive aviation fuel are just wasting away while you refuse to allow this flight to get underway?'

Kay croaked, 'I'm terribly sorry, Captain. I really thought the door was faulty and...and...'

'And you were quite right,' his tone had changed from blustering severity to jocular goodwill and Mark gave her a conspiratorial wink.

It appeared that the engineer had discovered a dent in the rear door, possibly the result of being hit earlier by the loader's van and, according to his grim verdict, the door would have almost certainly blown off in flight. They had had to change aircrafts and when the truth filtered out only Niamh's sincerely voiced gratitude meant anything to Kay, who was still wondering where she had got the courage to stand up to them all.

Word of the incident quickly got about the airport and speculation was rife. As always, with regard to anything involving crew safety, Ben Higgins was the first to hear about it and Judy Mathews came a close second. What interested Judy most was the reported clash of wills between members of the cabin crew and she already knew, from Ciara, about the dispute over the roster change and judged it to be inconsiderate, without good reason, to swap any member of th hostess team on to a flight that might overnight. But to do it at short notice to a married hostess with a young family only aggravated an already inflammable situation, as Judy crisply informed Ciara.

Graham had heard about the Paris/Rome incident too, although a little later in the day than those in Celtic Airways. As usual his informant was Ben, and on hearing that Kay was the air hostess involved Graham was conscious of surprise, he had not realized she had returned to CA, indeed with the passing years he had come to believe that she never would.

'She stood firm before them all,' Ben crowed. 'Didn't budge even when the skipper came near to blowing a gasket and you know how shirty Ronnie Devlin gets if he thinks he's going to be deprived of his overnight pint. Has the timing down to mega seconds, not like others I could mention, fifty feet from bottle to throttle guys!' Ben laughed. 'No doubt but she saved them all. No harm that Mannion was the co-pilot, he certainly wouldn't want to risk being in the headlines again.'

Graham knew that Ben was referring to the Cork/Paris crash that Mark Mannion had crewed with Captain Lee who died in the crash, and he was appalled at the thought of the tragedy repeated with Kay on board. Going back to his office, he was aware that the occasional glimpses of her he would almost certainly be granted from time to time would only serve to deepen the heart ache he still felt. But thankfully with time his bitterness had been replaced by more compassionate thinking. Only the terrible regret remained – if only he had received O'Callaghan's job offer earlier, he would never have lost her.

Graham's decision to work for Tim O'Callaghan had proved to be a good one and he had no regrets about joining MacDoolAer. From the beginning, Tim had made it clear he regarded CA's loss as his gain, and in turn Graham had found whatever about his reputation for being a hard man O'Callaghan had his head screwed on. His no frills policy was paying dividends and the airline showing a tremendous turnover in profits. Graham had come more and more to like and respect the man, and indeed to share in the wealth of the airline, in time he had become a director and major shareholder of the company. Another venture that had proved most lucrative for Graham had been his decision to invest in the M & K Aeroclub when approached in the early years by former CA pilot, Captain Christy Kane and his shrewd business partner, Marty Mullen. Before taking up his position with MacDoolAer he had checked it out with O'Callaghan and been given the go-ahead.

'No problem, Pender. What you do in your spare time is your own business,' Tim was nothing if not unconventional.

Graham's involvement with the flying club had helped him during the lonely years without Kay or the hope of her, his life and happiness once more on hold. His sons learned to fly at the club, becoming flying instructors in their spare time, all of which had helped to shape and guide them towards the careers they eventually chose. Nowadays, Jeremy was doing well in the Air Corps and been promoted to the rank of captain, Nicholas and Ranjan had graduated from college with engineering degrees, and Nicholas had recently been accepted for pilot training by CA. Graham had to confess he had mixed feelings about his son's choice of airline, fearing his own past history might adversely affect Nicky's chances there, but he took heart from the fact Ben Higgins was CA's best chief pilot to date and would undoubtedly look out for him.

Graham was very proud of his sons and he would not have been human if their achievements had not afforded him satisfaction; so much had already been taken from him and his family meant everything to him. Sitting back at his desk. he found himself thinking again of Kay, his feelings unaccountably stirred knowing she was back once more working at the airport. Philosophically, he accepted the fact he was never going to be able to forget or entirely give her up. The recognition that some part of him must always be free to love her had come some two years into his relationship with Judy and stopped him from making her his wife, although she and everyone acquainted with them was clearly expecting it. Even in the face of Judy's hurt and dismay, he had stubbornly kept to his decision, feeling sad for the inevitable ending to their relationship. But strangely, it had not come to that. With her usual tactful restraint Judy had 'cut him some slack' and they had continued on much as before, but without the forward planning of earlier.

Deliberately turning his thoughts away from his personal life, Graham pulled a file towards him and resigned himself to getting down to work. But before he could open it a knock came to the door and First Officer, Conor Downey, bobbed his cropped head into the room.

'Ready whenever you are, Captain. The lads are all lined up.'

'Good God!' Graham exclaimed. 'I'll be there at once.'

'Thank you, sir.' The First Officer grinned as he stepped smartly aside to let Graham past. 'The lads thought you had forgotten all about us, sir,' he said tactfully, 'But I thought it was more likely you had forgotten the time.'

***

Kay found her husband's reaction to what might have been a dangerous situation aboard her Rome flight disappointing. She quickly gave up trying to claim his attention, she could see that he was not listening, all her earlier exhilaration and pride of achievement vanishing as he raised his eyes from the newspaper and muttered,

'Honestly, Kay, if I were to worry about what *might* happen every time I took to the road I'd be a nervous wreck.'

Surely lovers cared about what *might* have happened to the other, Kay thought sadly. What were all the love poems and songs about after all if not *what ifs?* She would save it for Florrie, she decided, if anyone could appreciate near misses *she* could. And Graham, she was struck by the thought she wouldn't have to beg for *his* attention, her heart suddenly stricken with loneliness. Kay knew that Dave was a bit fed up at having to ask his mother to sleep over with the children when she had unexpectedly overnighted in Rome recently and he away in London. 'Nice to have a wife who would be around when needed,' he griped. It hurt, so too had his sarcasm. 'Maybe we should ask Ma to move in altogether. Save her making the journey every time you're away.'

It was so unfair, Kay thought. These days, there were few times when she had to ask Eileen for anything. And then she thought of the Super's note, 'Come see me on Monday.' But surely Judy knew she was off that day? Kay frowned, it had to be about herself and Ciara. Talk about stress!

And then Kay learned that on Monday she would have to drive Sinead to the airport; her class had their school trip to the Lake District. Just to be awkward the nuns had given the whole school the day off too, which meant Dervla needed minding.

'I did tell you, Mummy,' Sinead said, and Kay sighed thinking she probably had. Trouble was she was trying to do too much lately. Half the time she was too distracted to hear what the children were telling her. Since the faulty door incident she had been bothered with scruples about Dervla's parentage, wondering if she should leave something in writing to be opened after her death. Not to do so, Kay believed, would be unfair to Graham, yet what about Dave who believed he was the child's father? Supposing she wrote the letter and it was opened ahead of time?

Judy was aware it was Kay's day off that Monday, but not too bothered. She had put in a lonely weekend without Graham, while he spent time with his sons, before Nicky's departure to Florida with his training group. Left on her own, Judy had dwelled overmuch on her conversation with Ciara and all that the Chief Hostess had had to say about Kay's uncooperative behavior. Good gracious! Judy thought, things were coming to a pretty pass when hostesses felt they could challenge authority in this way. She was reminded of one of the Senior hostess's recent revelations about hostesses on flights hitting and calling each other names. What in God's name had got into everyone? Judy decided it was time to redefine the rules of behavior. Starting with Kay, she would make it clear once and for all just what was acceptable and what was not! That was until she saw Kay standing at her office door with the child.

'Dervla, isn't it?' She was rewarded by the little girl's singularly sweet smile that had made such an impression on her before. 'You see I remembered. You were to come back and visit me and you've taken a long time in getting around to it, haven't you?' seeing the quick gratified glance she gave her mother, as if saying, 'And *you* thought she'd forgotten me.'

'I'm sorry but I had no other option but to bring her today,' Kay muttered, obviously stressed. 'I only learned at the last minute that Dervla had no school today. Not a lot of notice.'

She was sounding harassed, Judy thought, not really surprised. Up to her neck in hot water, was the phrase that came to mind. Yet she found herself saying, 'I'm afraid I didn't give you a lot of notice either,' and then was annoyed at herself for being so accommodating. What was she thinking? Judy asked herself. She really would have to adopt a firmer line. Ah, but it was the child, she thought. The child was affecting her. At five she had been an enchanting scrap but four years on, she was really quite striking. Those dark eyes with the impossibly long lashes, the cleft chin and the smile! That devastating familiar smile! Judy felt suddenly breathless. Whom did it remind her of? Oh dear, need she ask!

'Look, why don't we send Dervla to sit in the restroom?' she suggested, trying to regain control of the situation but shaken by the child's uncanny resemblance to Graham, hugely distracted by it.

'Well, if you're sure she won't be any bother.' Kay turned to Dervla. 'I won't be long, darling,' although in view of the circumstances she really was not the one to say it, the Super considered haughtily. If anyone prolonged or terminated this interview it would be her!

Still, in the presence of the child she couldn't be too severe. 'Of course, she won't be any bother and besides the reserves will keep an eye on her. You'll amuse yourself, won't you, Dervla?'

All the time she was talking, Judy was getting a better look at the child. Why, she's the image of him, she thought, familiar with all his mannerisms; this one now, she knew by heart, the way the little girl was pushing her index finger thoughtfully into her cheek as she gravely contemplated the question, before giving her answer.

'I could look at magazines, couldn't I?' Dervla suggested. 'But if not,' she said hastily, catching Kay's eye on her. 'I could do some drawing.' She glanced at Judy's desk. 'I could use jotter paper,' she added helpfully. 'I don't mind.'

Judy tore her eyes from the flowerlike face. 'Oh, I'm sure we can come up with something better.' Without a pang, she sacrificed a pad of expensive notepaper and impetuously swept up copies of House and Garden from off her shelf. 'There you go! You'll enjoy looking at the pictures.'

'I can read, you know,' Dervla said reprovingly. 'I've been able to for ages.'

Judy's involuntary laughter rippled forth. 'Oh, I'm sure you can and read very well too, I've no doubt.' What a quaint little thing, she was thinking. And she can stand up for herself too. She gave the child a reassuring pat. 'Here, pet, put this coin in the machine and get yourself some lemonade.'

Dervla accepted it with a dip of her head and, following her mother's pointing finger, she went tripping towards the restroom, clasping the magazines to her chest.

'She'll be fine,' Judy said, glancing at Kay's doubtful face. 'She knows where you are if she needs you. Shall we sit down,' waving her towards a chair. 'I'll just pop this on the door so we won't be disturbed.'

The notice in place, Judy sat back at her desk but somehow all she had intended saying no longer seemed quite so urgent or even relevant, and she had difficulty keeping her mind on the subject. Even Ciara's rather presumptuous insinuation that she might welcome the chance to be rid of someone who was once her rival had lost its sting, and no longer had the power to unsettle her.

Now Judy felt in a better position to judge the situation; if not with complete impartiality, at least with something approaching fairness. Something, the child most likely, had helped defuse the situation.

***

Graham was feeling a bit guilty that Monday morning as he headed over to share his coffee break with Judy. Under his arm he carried a peace offering in the shape of her favorite Godiva chocolates, conscious of having neglected her that weekend. On Saturday he had had an enjoyable night out with his sons. Predictably, they had all drunk a bit too much, even Ranjan, who seldom touched the stuff; and on returning home they had drunk some more. Graham accepted the blame for this, he had been the one to get out the Glenfiddick, even pouring them all seconds. But soon Nicky would be gone to Florida and it would be months before they were all together again.

Even Jeremy became emotional, most unusual for him, pressing a load of dollars on his brother, 'My dear bro, take it. You won't get anywhere with those American broads without it.'

On Sunday they had gone with Nicky to the airport to see him off and then Jeremy had returned to Baldonnel and Ranjan went to Galway, where he had accepted an internship with the ESB. Graham had promised Judy to drop by but he had not been in the mood for company and went instead to sit in the garden. Some years earlier. when he had got the opportunity of buying back his old home in Blackrock, he had had the house renovated and extended. The builders had done a good job and, while they were at it, they had landscaped the garden, making it his favorite place to be. Sitting there that Sunday evening in the scented surroundings, conscious of the empty house, his sons far away, the softly illuminated garden had done its usual healing magic and he had been loth to break the spell

Now seeing the 'Do Not Disturb' sign on Judy's door, Graham was thinking maybe he should have rung her after all, when a voice sounded behind him.

'She's busy talking to my Mummy,' and he swung around to see a little girl regarding him over the sheet of drawing paper clutched to the bodice of her dress.

'Oh, is that so? Your Mummy is in there now?' he queried, with raised brows.

She nodded, and something about the big brown eyes and the way she was staring at him triggered a memory. Wait a bit, Graham thought, he knew this child. Surely, this was Kay's little girl but how she had grown.

'Dervla, isn't it?' he said, her name coming to him without effort.

'How do you know my name?' she asked with interest.

'Ah, but we've met before, haven't we?' Graham smiled down at her. 'You were only little though…about this high,' he put his hand at a certain level.

'Just a baby,' Dervla agreed. 'I'm nine now,' she said it with evident pride. 'Or I will be very soon. My birthday is next week.'

'So you're a Gemini. That's your zodiac sign,' he explained, seeing her mystification. 'It's determined by the date you were born. You see I was born in September so mine is Virgo.'

'And I'm jemma?'

'Gemini,' Graham corrected, thinking she was quick on the uptake. The thought of Kay only a few feet away behind the closed door was unsettling him.

'Did you do that drawing?' he eyed the paper she was clasping.

Holding it out to him, she said deprecatingly, 'It's not very good, is it? But then I only have this…' showing him the biro. 'My pencil got broke.'

Graham felt in the inside pocket of his jacket and drew out a silver propelling pencil. 'Why don't you take this, when the lead is used up you just give it a twist and more pops up.'

'That's brilliant. Can I try it?'

'Go ahead.'

She placed the paper against the wall and carefully drew a box and into it she put a load of little crosses. Graham was reminded of aptitude tests he had been required to do when applying to the Air Corps and wondered what the psychiatrists would make of this one. 'Good pencil, isn't it? You can have it if you like.'

'Could I really?' She gazed up at him in wonder. 'For keeps?'

'Why not?' He smiled at her pleasure.

All at once the glow faded. 'Oh, but I couldn't. It's too good,' she said doubtfully. 'Mummy would never let me keep it.'

'Why don't you borrow it then? You can always give it back another time.'

Her face brightened as she considered this. 'Yes, that would be all right. I mean it wouldn't be like for keeps, would it?'

'Not at all,' Graham agreed. She really was extraordinarily bright, and so very pretty. She was going to be a beauty when she grew up. Like her mother, he thought with a pang.

'I'll do a drawing especially for you,' Dervla was saying. 'That's only fair, isn't it, seeing as it's your special pencil I'm using. What would you like? I'm quite good at cats…well, they are easy, aren't they? Just a circle and whiskers.'

'That would be very nice. I look forward to seeing the finished product.' At her puzzled look, he laughed, 'I mean I look forward to seeing your cat when you have him pinned to paper.'

'Pinned to paper…that's funny,' she laughed back at him. 'But you know,' she went on in that sedate, grown up voice. 'You said him but I might just decide to draw a girl cat, mightn't I?'

Graham was captivated by the merry mischievous look she gave him. 'Indeed you might,' he answered gravely. 'Either way I'm sure it will be a very good drawing. And now I'm afraid I must go for I have work to do.'

She skipped beside him towards the swing doors and he got quite a start when she asked in the polite tones of one making conversation. 'What work do you do…I suppose you are a pilot?'

'Yes, I am as a matter of fact but I don't fly very often these days.'

'That's a pity. My mummy loves flying. I'm going to be an air hostess like her when I'm big.'

Graham paused with his hand resting against the door. 'Well, this is where we part. You mustn't come any further,' he cautioned, suddenly concerned she might get lost. 'Your Mummy will be worried.'

At that, she hung back and Graham was filled with sudden fear for this beautiful captivating child, who was too open and trusting for her own good. Supposing someone other than himself, someone unscrupulous, had stopped to chat with her, would she have gone so trustingly with him just because he had known her name?

Graham was swept by sudden irrational anger. How irresponsible of Kay to bring the little girl here and then leave her on her own like this. 'You must go back now,' he said gently, taking her to the door of the restroom.

On impulse, he presented the chocolates to her with a flourish. 'I just happen to have something here for a little girl who is soon to have a birthday.'

Dervla was speechless, but only for a moment. 'But how did you *know* they're my favourite of *all* chocolates,' she said reverently. 'Mummy brings them back as a special treat when she goes away.'

Graham just smiled, before beckoning to a hostess. 'This young lady shouldn't be wandering off on her own,' he told her. 'Can you take her under your wing?'

'Certainly, Captain, I was just coming looking for her,' but before she could take hold of Dervla's hand the child turned and hugged Graham quite spontaneously.

'Thank you very much. Wait till you see. I'll do a lovely picture for you,' she promised earnestly.

'Bye, Dervla. I look forward to seeing it,' he called back over his shoulder, and to his amusement overheard one of the hostesses saying, 'Gosh, aren't you a lucky girl having a Daddy who spoils you like that,' but what the child said in return he didn't quite catch. Something telling, he had no doubt.

Kay was amazed at the chocolates and worried about the handsome propelling pencil. 'Oh Dervla,' she sighed. 'You shouldn't have accepted it. You know I told you never to take things from people you don't know.'

'But I told you, Mummy. He knew my name. Anyway, it's only a lend. I knew you wouldn't want me to take it.'

'But how can you give the pencil back when you don't know who he is?'

'Maybe the lady will know,' Dervla said helpfully. 'She was nice too, wasn't she, giving me the drawing paper and everything. She said I was to be sure and come and see her again. Can I, Mummy?'

But Kay was busily negotiating the lunchtime traffic and grappling with the identity of Dervla's unknown benefactor. It was only when they were almost home that Dervla said, 'He said he knew my name 'cos we met before when I was little. Oh, I wish now I'd asked him *his* name but I didn't want to be rude.'

Kay wished she had too, but she was beginning to think it had to be Graham. Who else? He must have been coming to see Judy, she thought, and was disappointed at having missed him. If only she had gone out to check on Dervla but she hadn't liked to interrupt Judy's lecture on the importance of treating one's superiors with respect. But all in all, Judy had been less severe than she had expected, even commending her for her part in the faulty door incident. Of course, when Judy had insisted she must apologize to Ciara there had been nothing for it but to agree. Kay frowned, not at all happy about that, telling herself it was only because she had to!

Once home Dervla never stopped talking about the mysterious stranger, running to show her father the chocolates when he came in from work.

'What's she going on about?' Dave said shortly. He was not in the best of tempers and Kay prudently bundled Dervla into the sitting-room to watch television, since she had no homework to give up next day.

As soon as he had finished his meal Dave dropped the bombshell. His mother was selling her house and he was thinking of asking her to come live with them. Indeed, the way he said it suggested to Kay that he might have already done so. By this, she knew his method of breaking news, first the soft lead-in followed by the truth.

'Ma has been lonely this long time,' Dave avoided Kay's incredulous glance. 'The house is getting too big for her and this seems the most sensible arrangement.'

'Well, all this is news to me,' Kay's tone was cool. 'I don't remember hearing before about your mother's loneliness, or anything else.'

Dave shot her an equally cool glance, she could see he was not pleased, but then he had never approved her habit of frank speaking, he was always measuring his own words. The way of the business world, he often pointed out.

'How could she not be lonely with Reggie gone and Breda away from home?'

Kay's expression was doubtful. 'I would have said she was relieved on both counts.' But here again her honesty was not appreciated, she saw it in the broody pitying look he gave her. 'It isn't easy being old, Kay. It will come to us all. Anyway, she has been thinking of making a move for some time. When she sells her house she can invest the capital and live on the interest. Living with us will mean she won't be on her own and can see more of her grandchildren. '

Kay was dismayed by his decision, even disillusioned for Dave had always maintained how important it was for married couples to live on their own, away from their in-laws. What Dave neglected to tell he was the option his boss had given him to subscribe for company shares in Maxwell's. For days Dave had been wracking his brains on how to raise the necessary cash, before he had got the idea of selling his mother's house. Once he had persuaded Eileen to come and live with them, he could set it in motion, he thought. He had already lined up an estate agent to handle the sale.

**

The Hostess Superintendent sat frowning at her desk. Only that morning disturbing reports had reached Judy's ears about continuing aggression aboard flights, with provocative push and shove between the married and unmarried hostesses. It would seem that morale was steadily deteriorating. At the Union meeting the previous night there had been two hours of heated discussion whilst the prevailing mood had become more embittered on the one side and vindictive on the other. Beattie Burgenhoffer was a Union representative for the hostess body, Barbara Brennan another. As Judy was aware since the beginning of her career Beattie had been as active in the Union as Barbara, but while Beattie had always sought the general good, Brennan had worked assiduously to improve her own standing with management. By continually currying favor and routing on the side of the permanently employed single hostesses she was now voted their official spokeswoman. This was as much to do with Brennan's sleeping with Tommy Cleary, the head union man, as her ability to handle the job. The Hostess Administrator, Elinor Page, had attended the meeting and had all the facts to give Judy when they met that morning in her office. Elinor had described Brennan's newest proposal carried with Cleary's backing, which stated that only permanently employed air hostesses could become Cabin Supervisors; in future, all candidates would be obliged to sit exams and attend interviews, thereby making the previous system based on a good work record and length of service obsolete. It was just one more discrimination against the marginalized married air hostesses. Most of those who attended the Union meeting had come away angry and talking of bringing it to the Labour Court for resolution. Beattie, having worked so hard to give the married hostesses a better deal, now felt she had failed them miserably.

This morning as she hurried towards the Hostess Superintendent's office intent on informing Judy of the disastrous ending to negotiations, she was dwelling bitterly on her rival's duplicity. Too late, Beattie had seen Barbara's treachery and vigorously protested against it, but to her chagrin the motion had been carried by the majority for Brennan had already managed to get the bulk of new hostesses on her side.

In her present raw state Beattie was determined not to allow herself to be fobbed off any more by weak, unconvincing arguments or bewildering notions about 'not rocking' some boat. Her frown deepened. No, today she intended speaking her mind, she would say to Judith, 'This issue has become crucial, the problem urgently needs addressing,' and having seized hold of Judith's attention she would then impress upon her the need for doing, and for doing *schnell*. In moments of stress Beattie, who possessed a German mother and an Irish father, was apt to revert to her mother tongue, resulting in a confusing mix of languages. It was not unknown for her to say to new trainee hostesses, 'Brostaig schnell,' when they dawdled between classrooms. Only when she heard the muffled laughter was she aware that she had uttered some bloomer. But she took it all in good part.

Arriving in the hostess corridor, Beattie found the Super's office empty and went to sit in the restroom, unsettling the Reserves by her brooding presence as she impatiently awaited Judy's return. But she was in for a long wait.

At that moment Judy was closeted with the new Chief Executive in his office. What Elinor had to tell her that morning had been graphic and disturbing, alarming enough to send her hurrying off at once to seek Taylor Duval's advice. Judy had met Duval only twice since he had joined the airline and had yet to form an opinion of the man. According to the grapevine, he was not married at present but whether this meant he was between marriages no one knew, only that his hobby was wind surfing and he was as proficient at flying tow-planes as gliders; this piece of information volunteered by one of the Atlantic hostesses who had briefly dated him. 'An all round guy,' she reported enthusiastically, but volunteered not much else.

From Judy's limited contact with Duval she could see that he was quite the charmer. Even as he ushered her into his office he was complimenting her on her appearance, Judy having chosen that morning to wear her white linen suit and navy polka dot blouse.

'Mighty fresh-looking, m'dear, in this warm spell,' his smiling gaze lingering overlong on her shapely ankles, her tiny feet in four inch Italian heels bringing her head level with his shoulder.

Judy smiled back at him, guessing Duval was a leg man. Relaxing into the leather armchair angled cosily near his desk, she crossed her legs and was not at all fussed when her short skirt rode even higher. Judy did not believe in maidenly tugging at neck or hemlines, such gaucheries she left to teenagers. Besides, she had some angles of her own to pursue and Taylor in pliable mood best served her purposes.

'My profound apologies for keeping you waiting,' he was saying. 'There wasn't a damn thing I could do or believe me I'da done it.'

'Of course,' Judy smiled. 'I won't take up too much of your time.'

'You take all the time you want, Judith. I may be one helluva a man to pin down but once you got me pinned, I'm all yours.' He gave his big expansive grin. 'So how can I help you?'

Judy would not have been surprised if he had added 'little lady' and hid a grin of her own. The Yankee, as she had privately dubbed him, was really quite cute.

'Well, what I've come for is your advice,' Judy rested her chin thoughtfully on her hand, and fixed him with her remarkable eyes. 'It has to do with the situation between cabin crews.'

'Only too happy to help, Judith.'

With that, she proceeded to pass on all that Elinor had confided, stressing how the married hostesses who had originally joined the airline at a time when the marriage ban still existed had a legitimate grievance and were only defending their corner. As Duval listened without interrupting, Judy could not help thinking how the former Chief Executive would have tried to bully her into preventing the married hostesses from taking action. Not for the first time she rejoiced that McGrattan's double-dealing had landed him out of a job.

'Seems to me you have quite a situation on your hands,' Duval commented, his sandy brows meeting in a frown. 'This affair looks pretty ripe to me. The married stews have had enough and are ready to take it further, it could all end in court with the married stews bringing an action against the airline When something similar happened way back in the States between some of the more mature stews and the younger uns, we didn't hesitate to hand it over to our attorneys. They straightened it out between them. Involved a deal of money but the airline had no choice but to settle.'

'Is there an alternative?'

Taylor shrugged. 'Not that I can see. The Employment Equality Act needs to be considered. Been in force over here just how long now...two...three years?'

'Four,' Judy confirmed, adding anxiously. 'So what will the procedure be?'

'My guess would be the Union will take this case to the Labour Court and the officials there will investigate the various alleged acts of discrimination and refer them to an equality officer. And then if *they*consider they have a legitimate case it will go forward from there.' Duval sketched the air with his hands. 'Very likely it will come under a lawsuit headed 'Celtic Airways versus Cabin Crew' or vice versa.'

'Oh dear,' Judy sighed, there did not seem any way of avoiding the hassle. For a craven moment she wished it did not have to happen during her administration.

On looking up, she found Taylor eyeing her with an expression she found hard to define. Interest most definitely, but mixed with something that might have been tenderness. She felt the blood warming her cheeks.

'Hey, you don't want to let this thing get on top of you,' he said, leaning over to pat her hand, and then he was all business again. 'Best thing we can do is set up a meeting with the Union and hear what they have to say. Okay with you?'

'Good idea!' Judy met his glance with gratitude. She should have been ashamed at being caught off-guard but, strangely, she was not.

He was a good sort, she thought, straightforward with no subterfuge or pretension about him, not like his predecessor. It was a refreshing change. Tapping her way back across the concourse to her own office on very high heels, Judy realized with a sense of surprise that she had somehow agreed to have dinner with Duval that evening. Well, naturally there was a lot to discuss about the case, she mused, best to get it over with.

***

Dave was greatly relieved when he received the estate agent's cheque for the sale of his mother's house. Once Eileen had endorsed it, he lodged it in his bank account and straightaway discussed with his boss the purchase of the coveted company shares. He thought how easily it could have eluded him, remembering how Eileen kept changing her mind about selling. 'I've been in this house forty years, David,' she had protested. 'It's a big step to take and I'm not sure I'm ready for it,' refusing to be hurried.

Dave had no idea what had made her suddenly capitulate. He did not ask, only too relieved that she had done so whatever the reason. In the fury of the thwarted moment he had even considered forging her signature on the documents. On reflection, he thought it might have been the visit from his sister one evening to talk sense into their parent, if it was he owed Breda one. Then he reminded himself the boot was on the other foot, that she was the one who would benefit by his action without any effort.. After all, he was the one taking their mother into his home and prepared to look after her for the rest of her days. Too right! If anything, Breda *owed* him.

It seemed to Kay that one minute Dave was talking of asking his mother to move in with them and the next Eileen was ensconced in Dervla's bedroom and looking all set to stay. That first evening to Kay's horror her mother-in-law placed her galoshes in the vegetable rack, her sticky cough bottle and arthritic tablets on the mantelpiece. She had a habit of hanging her handbag and cardigan over the backs of chairs and her library book she left on Kay's polished coffee table. There were reminders of her presence everywhere. Dave had brought in a load of black plastic sacks containing the overflow of his mother's clothing and belongings, and piled them in the front sitting room. Kay despaired of ever keeping the house tidy. Before long the nightmare of drilling started and there was rubble everywhere, gaping holes in walls, plastic sheeting flapping in the wind, and a fine layer of dust over the furniture. She sighed, convinced she would go raving mad before ever the extension was finished.

On the advice of the architect it had been decided to build a fully self-contained Granny flat which, he said, would be a good investment and add to the value of their home. Of course, it would be a lot more expensive than the original plan. In an amazingly short time the decision was made to go ahead with it Not her decision, Kay thought resentfully, having already protested long and loudly and been overruled by Dave. She might not have spoken. It had been the same with her protests about his mother moving in with them, it had all gone ahead anyway. Dave adroitly avoided discussion whenever he could, usually by absenting himself from the house but he was becoming increasingly irritated by his daughters grumbling about having to share a room and Kay nagging on about the bank loan.

'You surely don't expect Ma to pay for our house extension?' he snapped at last, deciding attack his best defense.

'Well, if it wasn't for her,' Kay retorted, 'we wouldn't need the loan.'

'I told you. It's just to bridge the gap until the sale of her house goes through.'

At that Kay looked dubious, from earlier remarks he had let drop she understood the buyer had already handed over the cheque. She did not speak to him for a time but then she wearily called a halt to hostilities, keeping up a vendetta was too exhausting. Nothing had changed but, at least, the atmosphere gradually lightened, and the girls grew noisy with relief, having been worried at their parents constant wrangling.

Sometimes Kay felt her husband had suffered a complete personality change in the years since she had married him, and rarely discerned anything familiar or lovable about him anymore. It saddened her. The old feelings of guilt that it was all her fault returned.

She immersed herself in work and after a while it succeeded in distracting her as she familiarized herself on every aspect of the case they proposed taking to the Labor Court. Even Dervla's continual pleas fell on deaf ears.

'But Mummy, I promised to draw him a picture. He'll think I only said it to get the chocolates,' Dervla wailed. 'You're always saying you *have* to keep a promise... and what about his silver pencil? I only borrowed it...'

But even that failed to galvanize Kay into action.

'Not now, Dervla,' she sighed. 'We'll talk about it later,' conscious of her child looking pitifully at her with Graham's eyes. 'Truly we will but *not* now!'

Dervla despaired of ever gaining her mother's help. When her grandmother was out pegging clothes on the line one afternoon, she quietly closed the kitchen door and dialed the airport. By the time she put down the phone it was all sorted. Judy promised to call by the house after work and pick up the silver pencil for the pilot, and now that Dervla knew his name she would write him a letter.

That evening when Kay arrived in late from the airport she found the house in uproar. It seemed that Dervla was in dire trouble having cheeked her grandmother when reprimanded for disobedience. Dave had backed his mother and sent her to bed.

Poor Dervla! Kay had guessed something must be wrong when only Sinead came running to greet her, and then she had glimpsed the forlorn pajamad figure on the stairs. On hearing Eileen's continual references to some woman who had called to the house Kay was confused. She could only deduce that Dervla had cheeked this woman too. What an atmosphere to come home to, she thought, going upstairs to question the little girl, before she even had a cup of tea.

'Oh, Mummy, Mummy,' Dervla clung to her sobbing. 'I thought you were never coming home. Granny was horrid to me. I didn't cheek her, not really, but she shouldn't have spoken like that about Judy.'

Kay was completely bewildered. 'Do you mean Judy Mathews?'

Dervla raised her tear-blotched face and nodded. 'She came 'cos I rang her. She said that she would give the pilot his silver pencil and the pictures I drawed for him. There was the one of the cat and the one of you in your ball gown.'

Kay sighed and hugged her close.. Graham had made a big impression on the child, she could see that, and it hurt badly knowing the true relationship between them and unable to own it. It was only later as she went downstairs to make a sandwich for Dervla that the significance of the crayoned pictures her child had drawn for Graham struck Kay, and her heart faltered. *The one in your ball gown.* Oh dear! she thought mortified. He would think that she had put the child up to it.

Graham was puzzled when Judy placed an envelope in front of him saying. 'One of your girlfriends asked me to give you this.'

Mystified, he registered the clunking metallic sound through the thin paper, then recognition dawned as he lifted out the contents. His face lit with amusement on beholding the crayoned drawing of the plump tabby supporting a flashy bejeweled medallion about its neck.

'Hey! Not bad!' he exclaimed, holding it up.

'I rather fancy the medallion,' Judy smiled.

Graham laughed. 'Yes. This is no ordinary feline is what she's telling us. This is a mix of Dick Whittington's cat and the one that went to London to see the queen.' On picking up the other drawing his amusement was replaced by a more serious expression as he stared at it for a long moment without speaking.

Judy had already anticipated this reaction for, naturally, she had seen and praised the drawings when the child had proudly shown them to her. Yet she was unprepared for her own feelings as she observed Graham examining Dervla's portrait of her mother. He didn't hold it up for inspection like he had the other, but Judy already knew that the smiling dark-haired young woman with a glossy bang of dark hair falling on her forehead was wearing a red, low-cut evening dress, with long matching gloves, and about her throat another version of the tabby's bejeweled necklace. The drawing was amateurish by any standard, even so the child had strongly captured the look of the mother. Maybe captured it *too* well judging from Graham's fraught expression, Judy thought in dismay, as he slotted the drawings back in the envelope.

Graham found himself dwelling on the child's cat drawing with amusement but, much as Judy had suspected, the portrait of the mother inspired a deeper emotion. He wondered if he would have been quite so taken with Dervla's artwork if she had merely drawn the cat. Finally, he had to admit it was the portrait of Kay that had captivated him. He propped it in front of his dressing table mirror, where he saw it every time he knotted his tie. Couldn't *avoid* seeing it.

Before long, Graham scrawled a few words of thanks to Dervla, saying how much he liked the drawings and hoped she might do another for him soon. He chuckled at the memory of the medallion, Nicky had been like that, Graham mused with a pang. Always playing jokes and knocking fun out of everything. He sighed, thinking the house was like a mausoleum without him. God! how he missed him. True, Nicky had returned in the autumn to spend a week at home, before heading back out to finish his training on jets. His departure had left such a gap behind that Graham would almost have preferred if his son had stayed in America until it was time to come home.

'Remember, I'm not your only son,' Nicky had laughingly reminded him as they embraced at the foot of the aircraft steps, Graham having exercised his pilot's privilege to accompany him thus far. 'There are two other leaves to your shamrock, don't forget.'

Graham had refused to comment, these days he saw very little of either Jeremy or Ranjan but at least, thankfully, all three would soon be home for Christmas.

Now his pen hovered over the letter to Dervla wondering how he should sign it, reckoning she would show off to her friends. His eye was caught by an arty postcard on his bookshelf, and he took it down. It was of a painting by William Osborne of two little girls building card houses, always one of his favourites. On impulse, he enclosed it with the letter suggesting that her mother might one day bring her to see the original in the National Art Gallery.

Judy was the recipient of artwork from Dervla too, as a thank you for helping her but beyond casting an occasional amused glance at the cheekily grinning feline astride a rather downtrodden hound bearing the title 'Supercat rides again,' she remained immersed in her work, busily preparing what she would say at the hearing of 'Celtic Airways versus 32 Married Air Hostesses' due to take place at the Labor Court the following week. Going back over the past made sad reading. The Hostess Super was further disturbed by Beattie's graphic reports of increasing dissention between cabin crews. 'Every day the new insolence and the name-calling on flights after which they are giving the *hausfraus* the blows, ja? All of them making war, the one against the other and the passengers too, they are hitting and injuring the *hausfraus*.'

Judy sighed, remembering Beattie's description of an incident aboard involving an intoxicated passenger. When refused more alcohol by the hostess the man, who had been secretly imbibing from his own store, landed the unfortunate young woman a blow (as luck would have it one of the married hosties) putting her flat in the aisle.

'And did the Union support this hostess, did they?' Beattie had demanded, with irritating rhetorical inflection. 'I ask you did they look for justice and compensation for the indignity suffered by this employee?' slapping down her hand hard on Judy's desk for emphasis. 'Did they?'

At which point Judy had done a bit of desk-slapping herself, tired of having to endure all this repetitive torture. 'No, they did not!' she snapped, aware that the Union's unsympathetic attitude was one of the truly appalling things about the present situation. Encouraged by Barbara Brennan, their toady, the Union was not even bothering to hide its lack of interest in the married hostesses' plight, and giving scant attention to individual complaints. The pilots too, most disappointingly, were unashamedly admitting their preference for young, unattached hostesses walking their aisles, clearly not sympathetic to the cause. Such an attitude disgusted Judy. For crews to work smoothly and efficiently together, she argued, all members must be prepared to work as a team. She sighed, wondering how anyone as kindly and courteous as Captain Brennan could have produced such an objectionable offspring as Barbara. To put it charitably Babs, as she was known to her friends and Barb to her enemies, must have been a changeling at birth. Judy smiled reluctantly, but really it was no laughing matter. She could only hope the Labor Court would speedily sort out their differences.

Gladly, she turned her attention to more frivolous matters. Like what she would wear on her dinner date that evening? Judy was conscious of feeling quite giddy these days, and it was all due to the disturbing effect her illicit liaison with Taylor Duval was having on her; to be honest she was loving every guilty minute of it.

Dave was enjoying his new status as a major shareholder in Maxwell Tailoring as he pondered whether or not to take the remainder of his mother's house purchase money and invest it in the stock Tony had tipped him off about. Before long he was of the opinion it would only be to Eileen's advantage to do so. If the shares did well he could then begin giving her back what he had borrowed. Of course, the new stock would have to do very well indeed, Dave knew, to make any impression on the huge amount involved. There were, besides, certain attendant risks. Still, it was the kind of gamble his boss was continually making and, undoubtedly, Tony's enthusiasm was infecting Dave with a similar rich and reckless feeling, the only difference being that Tony actually *was* rich and Dave was not!

Kay could only welcome her husband's brooding distraction in view of the amount of secrecy involved regarding Dervla's friendship with the pilot. Since receiving Graham's arty postcard, the child was all the time obsessing about paintings and visits to art galleries. Kay's one fear was that Dave might suddenly come out of his reverie and actually hear what the child was saying. Actually, she need not have worried, for whatever voices her husband was tuned into these days weren't human. Even when his mother addressed him he was slow to hear her, and when his attention was finally caught it had the frustrating habit of quickly veering off again. Life was too short for such hassle, Kay decided, and chose to concentrate instead on the final court briefing of the married hostesses scheduled to take place the following day.

***

Despite all their efforts to be cheerful there was a subdued air about the small group of air hostesses one week later as they walked away from the Labor Court. Ahead of them Union officials, accompanied by a jubilant Barbara Brennan, moved briskly in the direction of their parked cars; Brennan's laughter floating back to her vanquished opponents, only added to the bitterness of the moment.

Sneaky little toad! Judy thought contemptuously, but aware such comments were not appropriate for the Hostess Superintendent to voice, she kept them to herself as she walked in the company of Ciara and Beattie. Behind them the other senior hostesses, who had come along to the court that day to hear the judgment, followed more slowly. Like Judy, they were angry and disappointed at the judge's ruling, venting their feelings in no uncertain manner.

The air fairly bristled with acidic comment as Taylor Duval swiftly passed them, merely slackening stride to call, 'Real tough luck, ladies!'

'Don't suppose he'll lose any sleep over it,' Ciara sneered, but Judy had seen his look of commiseration as the judgment was read out, and taken comfort. She knew Taylor was as disgusted as any of them by the Union's biased attitude and this knowledge crisped her tone as she said, 'Duval has his job to do like anyone else. Don't forget he turned up each day to support us. He didn't have to, you know.'

'Yes... he is a kind man...*gemutlick,*' Beattie came unexpectedly to her support, remembering how Duval had listened to her proposal that the married hostess' date of entry should be immediately restored, readily conceding it was galling for hostesses of some years standing, often travelling with young children, to be forced to take their place at the end of the standby queue. But, of course nothing would be done about *that* now!

Ciara said nothing but she flushed at the implied criticism and increased her pace, as though wishing to distance herself from them. She had not been at all affected by the court's decision and Judy had no doubts that her sympathies lay with the opposition. Seated behind the wheel of her BMW, Judy's mind kept slipping back to the events of the previous few days. From the start Taylor had made it clear whatever she did was all right with him. 'I understand you have to fight your corner, Judith. That's swell with me. You go do what you think best and let Celtic Airways take whatever you have to dish out.'

Indeed, much of the stress of the hearing had been offset not only by Taylor's impartial attitude, but by the pleasure of regularly seeing him at close quarters. Seated in the courtroom, she had pretended not to notice how often he looked her way but inwardly rejoiced in the knowledge he was as interested in her as ever. If only she did not feel the need to keep reminding herself that the fling had gone on longer than she had ever expected, and must end before Graham discovered she was cheating on him.

Kay was as disappointed as any of her married colleagues over the court's decision and busily taking part in the general postmortem in the restroom, when she saw the Hostess Super's note on the noticeboard. Vainly searching her conscience, she entered Judy's office only to learn that the Hostess Super wanted to check with her if it was all right to take Dervla on a Christmas treat the following weekend.

Kay supposed she should have been expecting it for the child had been talking of little else for weeks but with a mother's gift for separating wishful thinking from fact, Kay had decided early on it was all in Dervla's imagination, at the same time doing her best to keep the little girl's rhapsodizing to a minimum in Dave's presence. But now it seemed as though her mother's intuition had let her down. By all accounts the treat was already laid on, with expensive tickets purchased for the much publicized Christmas Bazaar in Dun Laoghaire town centre in aid of homeless children.

Kay stood with a smile pasted to her face as Judy spoke enthusiastically of the official lighting of the twelve foot Christmas tree and the other festive treats that would undoubtedly appeal to children. She was conscious that so far the only time she had been out to celebrate the Christmas season had been to share a brief lunch with some of her own flying group. Like her, their children were waiting on them at home and their popular executive type husbands out with their colleagues doing the social round as usual at this time of year. Kay and her flying buddies had ended up in the staff canteen trying to whip up some festive cheer with a glass of wine and platter of smoked salmon, but sadly their surroundings lacked atmosphere, despite an abundance of inflated plastic Santas and snowmen. Well, it was better than nothing, their shrugged comment.

Seeing that Judy was waiting for an answer Kay brought her mind back to the present declaring, 'What a lovely idea. So kind of you. Dervla will be thrilled,' before taking her leave, almost, but not quite, backing out of the august presence.

Judy noticed Kay's somewhat unenthusiastic response but put it down to the pervading gloom amongst hostesses since the court's ruling. Having acknowledged her own need to engage in something joyful and distracting, she had judged that an afternoon spent in Dervla's company would be just the thing. She had so enjoyed the letter accompanying the cheeky puss drawing, and signed with rows of grateful kisses.

Yes, Dervla would banish the blues, Judy was thinking, when Beattie arrived hotfoot with the news of the married hostesses unanimous decision to appeal to the High Court. Judy had not realized they were so determined.

'All week they are holding the meetings,' Beattie reported, barely able to contain her excitement. 'And now they are putting into readiness the requirings for victory.'

Ah, yes, Judy pondered uneasily, but were they also storing up more stress and heartbreak for themselves? She couldn't but feel for them, they had got a raw deal.

The minute Beattie had departed, having declared her own intention of supporting the married girls through *durch-und-dunn,* Judy reached for the telephone, interested in hearing Taylor's views on the matter. Of course, the appeal would mean a lot of extra paperwork for him, she realized, but his opinion would be valuable. He suggested meeting for cocktails in the airport lounge.

Seated with drinks before them, Judy updated him as to the married hostesses decision, finally putting the question. 'So what do you think of their chances?'

'Not a lot, Judith, but it's to be expected. And you?'

'I'm not sure it won't be a complete waste of time,' she admitted. 'I'm afraid they will end up even more demoralized and dispirited, and still no better off.'

There! She had said it! She wondered if she were being disloyal speaking so openly before Taylor who represented management, after all.

The Chief Executive rubbed his jaw reflectively. 'Well, in that case, Judith, I'd advise you to try and talk those married stews out of it, even though you'd be wasting your time, I reckon. Our own lawyers have been on to us and suggest we begin preparing ourselves.'

'Isn't there any way you could meet their requirements?' Judy asked, reminded of Beattie's 'requirings' for victory. 'They have been treated very shabbily, you know.'

'Heck, I'd be the first to agree with you on that score,' Taylor owned with disarming honesty. 'But it's not that simple. Look, would you mind if we discussed this again?' glancing at his watch. 'I gotta be somewhere real soon.'

Judy was disappointed, knowing from their earlier talk he would shortly be taking off for the States. To spend Christmas with his family no doubt, she had heard the gossip about him but the fact he had never mentioned a wife had encouraged her to hope the lady in question was at least out of the picture.

'Fine! I must be going too. Have a wonderful Christmas, darling,' out of pride turning the endearment into a shallow, social sort of thing.

As Taylor took off with his loose-limbed stride Judy decided to include Graham in the weekend treat with Dervla. Why not, she salved her conscience, the gesture cost her nothing and would afford them both pleasure. Not as if there would be any competition for *her* festive favours, she acknowledged glumly, not with Taylor returned to the bosom of his family.

Graham had been busy preparing for Nicholas's return all week. He found himself marveling at the transformation that took place the minute his youngest son came through the front door, their house magically became a home again with his return. Popping the cork on the bottle of Krug he had been saving for the occasion, he enjoyed the expression on Nicholas's face as he foamed champagne into the elegant crystal flutes and handed him one. Oh, but it was good to have him back.

'And it's good to be back, Dad.'

Together they went out to sit in the conservatory, Graham bidding Nicholas to bring the ice bucket along. 'Criminal not to keep this stuff at the right temp!'

'Heinous!' Nicholas agreed with a grin, 'Can't wait to see what you've been up to, Dad,' and Graham chuckled, 'I'm afraid you know me too well.'

'Some things never change,' Nicholas was amused, aware there would be at least one new statue somewhere and exotic trailing plants. He lowered the ice bucket to the floor of the conservatory and looked expectantly about him.

'Wow!' he gasped reverently, catching sight of the Neptune, his father's latest acquisition for his conservatory. When Graham pressed the switches bringing the fountain and the exterior lighting into play, Nicholas gazed out at the patio and murmured, 'Double wow!' catching his breath at the beauty of the softly illuminated Japanese Maples, planted in triangular formation amidst the paving stones, the delicate tracery of reddish leaves thrown into relief against the pewter sky. 'Gee Dad, you don't do things by halves, do you?' he said awed.

He met his father's pleased gaze, before crossing over with a fascinated expression to examine the Neptune at closer quarters. 'Where did you pinch this from - the Trevi Fountain?'

Graham lowered himself into his favourite seat, wedging a cushion comfortably behind his back. 'Not quite,' he grinned. 'But I did have it shipped over from Italy on special order. Like it?'

'Most impressive,' Nicholas pronounced, taking a distracted sip at his glass, 'Has Jeremy seen it?'

'Not yet,' Graham sighed. 'I'm afraid your brother hasn't a lot of time for sculpture.'

Nicholas chuckled. 'That's your polite way of saying Jerry is a philistine. Oh well, we can't all be connoisseurs of art. He's too busy making his mark on aviation.'

'Wouldn't be surprised if he's in line again for promotion.'

Nicholas whistled. 'Let's see …Comdt. Jeremy Pender?'

'Right…unless he jumps rank and then it will be Lt. Colonel.'

Nicholas looked appalled. 'You're kidding!'

'Well, maybe …but give him a few more years.'

'I'm relieved to hear it.' Nicholas got up to top his father's glass. 'So how's business? MacDoolAer becoming a serious rival to us yet?'

'Oh, we're getting there. Although I have to say since Duval joined CA he has given us some stiff competition in the European market.'

'Never thought I'd see CA actually dropping their prices.'

'Still nowhere as low as MacD but they really don't have any choice, you know, according to Ben they have been losing too much lately to ignore the signs.'

Nicholas looked curiously at his father. 'Have you ever regretted joining the opposition?' he asked quietly.

Graham shrugged. 'Let's say, I would never have done it if circumstances had been different but well, after almost a decade with O'Callaghan I can honestly say it was one of the better decisions of my life.'

'And yet you never tried to influence me when I was dithering between airlines.' Nicholas cocked an eyebrow at him.

'I quite understand you have your own way to make, Nicky. At any rate, with your ability you don't need any special favours. You were wise to choose CA. They are a good outfit to work for and you'll get a first class training. Mind you, I'm not denigrating Mac-DoolAer, but they just aren't in the same league.'

'Not even with you as their Chief of Ops?'

Graham merely smiled and went to root out his old log books. He was soon back and telling his son about the tremendous discovery he had made when coming across them in the attic, neatly stacked away in a corner, along with family photos and his mother's paintings believed irretrievably lost. By some miracle they had survived Sile's sale of the house, lying undiscovered under the eaves until Graham had bought back the house and had the attic converted.

'Wow, Dad, what a treasure trove!' Nicholas slowly turned the pages.

'Bit of luck finding them again, eh? Chance in a million you know but...' the ringing of the telephone interrupted him. 'I'll just get that,' he went off to answer it.

Graham was away for a few minutes and when he returned he was smiling as though he had just received good news. Not that he shared it with his son, merely sat down again waiting for Nicholas to put down the log books and come fill his glass.

As he poured them more champagne, Nicholas thought his old man was looking mighty pleased with himself, probably a hot date, he mused tolerantly, and topping his own glass sat down again. Nicholas was right about one thing, Graham did have a date that coming Saturday. It seemed that Judy had laid on a whole series of treats for Dervla and needed his help in entertaining the little girl. As he had told her, 'Nothing would give me more pleasure,' and it was true.

**

Dervla was entranced by everything she saw at the Dun Laoghaire Bazaar from hoop-la to toss penny, her visit to Santa Claus, with the switching on of the Christmas tree lights the afternoon got better and better. Judy was enjoying herself too, and she hugged the little girl closer to her side as they moved from stall to stall.

'Yes, of course, you can try everything, darling,' buying double amounts of rings or balls, and chuckling at Dervla's wild, extravagant throws.

She even took ten pennyworth herself, and felt absurdly pleased when she managed to score at the rifle range, the little girl gazing in awe at her as if she were Clint Eastwood. When Dervla guessed 'Diana' as the name of the beautiful china doll Judy, not to be outdone, wrote down 'Grace' after another glamorous Royal, telling herself that she hadn't felt such youthful exuberance since her own childhood.

Their day was made when Dervla's lucky guess won the beautiful doll. Before long the pair were strolling along the pier, Dervla happily clutching Princess Di when surprise, surprise they bumped into Captain Pender.

'Graham! How nice to meet you out like ourselves taking a stroll.' Judy exchanged conspiratorial smiles, enjoying the child's delighted confusion.

'Imagine meeting you like this,' Dervla gasped, her cheeks rosy with shock as she looked up at the tall, smiling figure of the pilot. 'As a matter of fact ... well, gosh! I have a present for you,' she gabbled happily. 'I was going to give it to Judy but now I can give it to you myself.'

'That wouldn't be it now, would it?' he remarked slyly, indicating the doll.

'Nooo, I won *her* in the raffle. Isn't she nice?'

'Very! But this present now you have for me?'

'It's in the boot of Judy's car.'

'Whatever can it be?' Graham teased. 'Would it be a cat by any chance?'

Dervla shouted with laughter. 'No, you silly! I made it in art class.'

'Intriguing,' Graham winked at Judy. 'Well, I have a suggestion that hopefully might meet with Miss Mason's approval.'

'Oh, what's that?' Dervla looked interested.

'That you ladies might accompany me back to my house and give me your opinion of my Christmas tree. Not sure if I've underdone or overdone the decorations. And besides, there's a splendid chocolate Yule log just lying there and no one to eat it. You'd be doing me a great favour ...' he shrugged and spread his hands

'Oh yes, please,' Dervla said eagerly. 'I love chocolate log.'

'Well, that's settled then. Shall we be on our way?' Laughingly, Captain Pender offered them an arm each and shepherded them back to the road. Within minutes, they were sitting in his car and on their way to his house.

Nicholas caught the flicker of car headlamps as his father's car turned into the driveway and glanced out the window in surprise. From his lengthy toilette before leaving the house, he could have sworn the old man was out for the night. Peering through the slatted blind, Nicholas was surprised to see a little girl in a red anorak climbing out of the Porsche, an elegantly familiar figure stepping after her. So Dad was meeting Super Lady, Nicholas thought with an affectionate grin, their teenage nickname, Jerry's and his, for Judy. And who was the child?

Nicholas craned his neck the better to see but the trio were already entering the house and out of his line of vision. Closing over the flight manual he was studying, he went down to meet the visitors. Hearing the child's high infectious laugh he headed for the conservatory, guessing she had come upon the Neptune! There he saw that the child had not only discovered the statue but removed her shoes and socks to dabble her feet in the trickling water. Three laughing faces turned towards him and at once he was impressed by what a strikingly beautiful child this was, and then he was moving forward again.

'Judy, good to see you!' Gallic style, he kissed her on both cheeks.

'Nicky!' Judy broke off her amused contemplation of the child to return the embrace. 'My, but you look well. And why wouldn't you out there in all that gorgeous Florida sunshine.' She drew him towards the child, as though introducing him to a distinguished guest. 'I'd like you to meet Dervla Mason. She shares your passion for flying and is going to be an air hostess when she grows up, isn't that right, darling?'

Nicholas was amused to see how shy the little one became all of a sudden, dipping her head and hastily hopping back out of the fountain. He gazed at her with a friendly smile and thought the sudden startled drop of dark lashes over the fabulous eyes quite captivating. Give her a few more years, he predicted, and she'll be an enchantress.

'How'ya doing, Dervla?' he grinned. 'Don't pay any heed to Judy. She only wants to recruit you into her lot. I'll bet you're going to be a pilot.'

At that the child lifted her gaze and nodded eagerly. 'Yes, yes…I do want to be a pilot but how did you know?'

'Ah now,' Nicky laughed back at her, 'We pilots have a way of recognizing one another,' and was pleased to see her gaining confidence and talking back.

'Takes one to know one,' she said wisely. 'That's what my granny says but she doesn't mean anything nice by it. *The opposite!*'

Nicholas couldn't help laughing and glanced over at his father, inviting his amusement, only to see that he, like Judy, was regarding the little girl in doting fashion. It was obvious the pair of them were mesmerized by her. Who was she? As far as he knew Super Lady was not married.

'Dervla's mother is an air hostess,' Judy explained, guessing his thoughts. 'One of my best hostesses too,' she added quickly, and Dervla smiled proudly. 'Almost certainly Dervla is going to follow in her footsteps when she's a little older.'

And now Graham chipped in thoughtfully, 'Do you think so? Well now, Judy, it's a matter for some deliberation. I mean Dervla could be an air hostess or a pilot but I think it's more likely she'll be an artist. She specializes in cat art, Nicky. Take her 'Juggling Cat' for instance. He sits for his portrait wearing a very fine medallion and that portrait, believe me, would fetch a small fortune were it put up for auction.'

Dervla collapsed into helpless giggles. 'No, it w…wouldn't,' she protested. 'It's only done with crayons,' she explained to Nicholas. 'I mean it's very ordinary. Not like real pictures in the art gallery.'

'Oh, have you been to the gallery?' Nicholas asked interested.

'No, not yet. My Mummy says she'll bring me when she has

time but well...she does have a lot to do,' she defended her absent parent. 'But I'd like to go some day.'

'Well, we must do something about that, mustn't we?' Graham glanced at Judy for confirmation. 'Perhaps after Christmas...'

Nicholas saw Judy's smiling nod and wondered at his father's interest in this child to the extent of taking her to an art gallery. He never brought any of us, he thought. And then the little girl wandered into the living room. Hearing her cry out and fearing she had hurt herself, he hastened to join her. But to his relief she was merely standing by the sideboard, holding a silver photograph and staring at it in surprise.

'Look at that,' she said mystified. 'It's my Mummy!' And with an amazed expression, she held it out to him.

Kay was only thankful that Dave was out when Judy brought Dervla home that evening. On hearing the double ring at the door she hurried out to find her daughter on the doorstep clutching a beautiful china doll she had won in a raffle, and had just time to call 'Thanks Judy,' as the Super's BMW pulled away from the kerb.

Struggling out of her anorak, Dervla was full of the wonderful things she and Judy had done, the people they had met. 'Guess what, Mummy, who do you think we bumped into just by chance,' bubbling over with excitement at having met her pilot. 'Just by chance, Mummy,' she kept repeating, causing Kay to seriously doubt it.

Catching sight of Eileen eavesdropping, Kay hustled the child upstairs.

'He...the pilot...invited us back to his house,' Dervla was saying. 'And his son was there and, Mummy, he's a pilot too. Nicky was really nice and said he would bring me up in a plane some day. I can go, can't I? Oh, do say I can,' she implored, 'Just imagine, Mummy ...'

On and on it went. Kay was filled with panic with Dave returning at any minute, but short of gagging Dervla there was no way of stemming the flow. And then her panic turned to anger. What was Judy thinking? she groaned.

It was only when Kay had calmed herself and managed to impress upon Dervla the need to keep her lovely afternoon to herself,

'Sadly, Daddy is not over fond of pilots and might even ban such outings' (hating herself for saying so although it was true) Kay felt the danger past.

'Cross my heart, Mummy,' Dervla told her solemnly. 'I won't say a word. Only about Princess Di…fabulous, isn't she?'

Not until Christmas Day was over and done with had Kay a moment to dwell on what Dervla had told her about her visit to the Penders' house. Standing at her dressing table unpinning the ruby and pearl broach, Dave's gift to her, did she think again of their conversation. All in all it had been a happy day despite Eileen's irritability, no doubt she was missing Reggie.

Lying beside her sleeping husband, Kay stretched her toes and wiggled them luxuriously, her legs aching from hours of standing. She thought how she and Dave had slipped away in the late afternoon to have a brief nap, and how they had made love. Something they had not done in a very long time. She had felt quite daring slipping away under Eileen's nose, so to speak, and getting under the duvet with him. He had really been quite different, more loving and seemingly better tuned to her needs. She had not realized just how much she had missed lovemaking.

As always when dwelling on that particular subject Kay's thoughts turned to Graham, but she quickly moved on from past delights to the more recent ones enjoyed by Dervla. How ecstatically her daughter had described the magical lights in his garden, the fountain inside his house with cascading water, and his son Nicky so nice to her. All a bit jumbled, but it was obvious they had made a fuss of her and she had loved every minute! Kay told herself that she was not envious of Dervla, certainly not. It was only right that she should have had such a happy time with her father and her half-brother, if she did but know it. But undeniably, all of it deepened the ache of loneliness that was never absent from Kay's heart these year. Even with ruby broaches and love in the afternoon, she thought. Bunching the pillow under her head, she dropped off at last to sleep.

***

There was something to be said for the cold grey skies of January, Kay thought, if only with fewer flights in the slack post Christmas period there was less occasion for stress, and regrettably stress played a big part on every CA flight these days. It was something all the married hostesses shared in common.

Going on board, Kay took seriously the Hostess Super's recent memo warning them all to be on their guard against sloppy pre-take off cabin checks, aware that the new breed of hostesses she regularly flew with would have sooner let a flight take off without having cross-checked the aircraft doors than report back to any of the married hostesses and they undoubtedly with more service than any of them. Well, maybe that was a slight exaggeration, Kay conceded, striving to be fair, as she raised her head to meet three pairs of eyes coolly regarding her from beneath penciled brows.

'Hi everyone, I'm Kay Martin,' she kicked off, knowing if her wedding band did not alert them to the fact she was one of the married hosties, her more mature appearance would. 'Want to toss a coin or will we check our D.O.E's?'

Blank stares greeted this remark, and Kay tried again, 'Date of entry,' she explained helpfully, 'You know, so we can work out who does what.'

Actually, they were not all that bad, she amended her earlier view, as a girl with razor short blonde hair responded to her overture by offering to check out the toilets and sick bags, and a heavyset girl with thick brows over startlingly blue eyes agreed to give herself indigestion, by stooping the length of the cabin to ensure the life-jackets were in position. And then the third hostess went and spoiled it all by saying pertly, 'So what do *you* propose to do Kay Martin…lie back and do your nails?'

Kay regarded her for a moment, before asking with deceptive meekness, 'So what do *you* suggest?'

'Stop giving orders for starters!' The unpleasant young woman was already known to Kay, she had had one or two run-ins with Connie in the past.

As Kay was choosing her words, she was distracted by the arrival of the Captain and First Officer, but it was the dark-haired young Second Officer swiftly following on their heels who instantly grabbed her attention, and she was momentarily struck dumb as he turned his well-shaped head and his dark expressive eyes locked with hers. Kay was conscious that she knew him from somewhere. It was that, or else he strongly reminded her *of* someone – she couldn't decide which - as she returned his glance with a faintly quizzical look. He smiled at her before ducking his head to enter the cabin and she was unsettled all over again by the beauty of that smile. Of course, she thought, with an agonizing jolt, he must be Graham's son, the one that Dervla never stopped talking about, saying he was the image of Captain Pender.

She got a chance to speak to him in London having coffee during turnaround.

'Hi,' he greeted her, sliding into the seat beside her, and again giving her that heart-stopping smile. 'You're Dervla's Mum, aren't you? She's very like you.'

Kay returned the smile. 'Nicky...I mean Nicholas, isn't it? '

He laughed. 'Nicky is fine. It's what my family call me. Dervla is a lovely child,' he went on warmly. 'I don't think I've ever seen anyone that size so self-possessed, and yet so unaffected. She has a great sense of fun and yet she can be so shy at times. She's amazing,' giving Kay a rather shy look himself.

'Seems like she made quite an impression,' Kay was very conscious of the fact this gorgeous young man was Dervla's half-brother. She wished there was an opportunity to examine his features more closely in order to discover greater resemblances between them. And then Connie drew his attention away from her, no doubt feeling married women had no business monopolizing attractive single men.

On their way back on board Kay was stopped by one of the ground girls who needed someone to keep company with an elderly passenger until a wheelchair was available to take her out to the aircraft. 'There's two of us out sick with the 'flu and would you believe four Jumbos have just landed.'

'Of course,' Kay told her. 'Glad to help.'

When the wheelchair was available there was no one to take the woman out to the aircraft, so Kay readily obliged glad to know their aircraft was parked not too far off. Glad of her winter gaberdine too, and only regretting the discontinuing of the airline cap as she pulled her scarf closer about her throat. Exchanging encouraging words with her elderly passenger she set off briskly, on lookout for the distinctive green and gold of the CA jet.

Drawing close before long, she glimpsed an irate Connie out on the steps with her hand dramatically shading her eyes against the dying rays of sun.

'Where have you *been?*' she yelped, as Kay off-loaded her charge into the care of the ramp hands and started wearily up the steps. 'I can't *believe* you've taken so long. This will *all* have to go down on the flight report,' her dire pronouncement.

All what? Kay moved past her into the cockpit. 'Sorry for the delay, Captain,' she told Noel. 'They're shorthanded inside and one of the ground hostesses asked me to bring out our wheelchair passenger.'

'What will they require of us next?' wondered Captain Lavin good-humouredly. 'Our hearts and our livers too, I don't doubt.' He grinned back at Kay. 'Not to worry, Kay, we'll soon make up the time. Reassure that lot back there they'll make their connections all right, and you might bring coffee as soon as we're airborne. Bring it yourself, there's a good girl.'

'Will do,' she caught the eye of the First Officer and he winked. 'Skipper's afraid of falling into Connie's clutches.'

Kay was saved a reply as Connie thrust her way past Kay reporting officiously, 'Doors closed and cross-checked, Noel.'

Kay could have kissed him when he replied, 'Thank you, Miz Coughlan. You can leave it to Miz Martin to bring us coffee after take-off. I'm sure you have more important things to do.'

Kay did not linger to hear Connie's reply, pleased he was not like some pilots encouraging familiarity in hostesses in the hopes of making it with them. Glad too, of his support at a time when most pilots were slow to side with the married hosties.

Connie emerged on her heels, her face a tell-tale red. Not that she stayed squelched for long, though. She was soon busily bossing Kay again, and when it came to the flight report she told her. 'I've got it all down here. How you delayed the flight fifteen whole minutes.' Kay might have been off enjoying herself, not helping a little old lady to make her flight.

'And naturally I will write down the reason for the delay,' Kay told her coolly,.

She ignored Connie as she busied herself caring for the passengers particularly her old lady who confessed she was that thirsty she could drink Lough Eireann dry.

On landing, Kay was pleased when Nicholas lingered in the aisle to say, 'That was a very nice thing you did back there for the old lady,' and then he was bounding down the steps in the wake of his crew. Kay stared after him, his approval salve to her self-esteem, his sincerity warming her through and through. On tucking Dervla in that night she let drop how she had crewed with Nicky Pender and her daughter's enthusiastic response was all she could have asked.

'Gosh! Mummy!' Her brown eyes alight with flattering interest and delight. 'He's really nice, isn't he? But that Connie…ugh! Sounds just like Imelda Donovan at school, Mummy,' she said indignantly. 'She's a right bossy pain always telling us to clear up the room after art class… and she isn't even a class monitor.'

'Exactly like Connie,' Kay agreed amused.

'Did Nicky ask for me?'

'Of course!' Kay patted her cheek. 'We did nothing but talk of you and how good you are at drawing.'

Dervla was delighted. 'First thing tomorrow I'll draw him a picture.'

'Good idea!' Kay kissed her goodnight. 'Get your beauty sleep now, sweetie.'

On arriving home Nicholas, like Kay, felt moved to speak of his day. It was his second time flying with CA and he had found Noel Lavin an easy skipper to work with, although the First Officer had been a bit of a know-it-all. All in all, not a bad day, he judged, just thankful he had not done anything foolish. Not been *let*, Nicholas thought wryly, but given his newness that was to be expected.

Nicholas could see by the old man's expression he was enjoying hearing about it all and, as he expected, his father was soon asking the kind of technical questions the Chief of Ops. invariably got around to before long.

Nicholas grinned to himself and did his best to give intelligent answers. But was relieved when his father ceased the inquisition and returned to his newspaper.

But no sooner did Nicholas casually mention that Dervla's mother had been part of his crew, than his father was all attention again

'Did she know who you were?' Graham lowered his newspaper.

'Well, she did when I introduced myself. Not hard to imagine what Dervla will be like when she grows up, I ouldn't help feeling like I've met Kay before.'

Graham said nothing aware that Nicky had met Kay ten years back when they were living in the house he had purchased with the court settlement money. 'Well, as to that I can't say. I haven't seen her in quite some time,' he admitted, his expression pained. 'So she's back on Europe.'

Oh, interesting! Nicholas thought. The old man still cares!

It was no surprise to Kay to be called into Judy's office a day later, nor to find Connie there before her. She took a seat when bidden, fully prepared to speak up in her own defense, but soon realized there was no need to justify her Samaritan act, Judy was merely assembling both parties in order to pass judgment verbally, which she did at once in her usual forthright manner.

'I must confess that I'm surprised, Ms Coughlan, that you should waste my time in this way. I'm quite satisfied Ms Martin acted in the best interests of the elderly passenger and the airline.'

'But she delayed the flight by fifteen minutes and if you calculate this in terms of cost to the airline...'

'Ah, very good,' Judy said sweetly. 'You were obviously paying attention at your induction program...delays to the airline work out at £1000 per minute. But I really don't think you need concern yourself with such matters. The captain and his co-pilot are more than capable of working it all out for themselves. At any rate, the lost time was happily made up in flight and no one any the worse for the delay.'

'Maybe so,' Connie persisted. 'But I *told* Kay that she should let the London ground staff do their *own* work but she just ignored me and went ahead.'

'Quite right too,' Judy said firmly. 'Let me remind you that passengers *are* your work, Ms Coughlan, whether you are on home ground or abroad. I have seen Ms Martin's explanation of the incident and I'm satisfied she cooperated with our London girls, showing not only compassion but foresight. I think you owe *her* an apology.'

Connie glared at Kay. 'Sor-ree,' she got out, making it sound like an insult. But Kay nodded graciously, feeling she could afford to. At the same time, resolving never to be on her own with Connie in the washrooms at night without a can of hairspray.

Taylor Duval paused outside the Super's door about to knock when all at once it opened abruptly and a furious-faced young woman in hostess uniform pushed past him without apology. Eyebrows raised, he stared after her mentally making a note to remember her. Duval was not unfamiliar with raging stews, but not since his American airline days had he seen one in quite such a temper. And those American 'gals' sure could light a fuse when riled, he told himself, having dated quite a few high-steppers in his time. The young woman that left just now was in a right stew over something, he decided, enjoying the pun. He would sure as hell like to know what Judith could have said to her to produce that kind of rage. Intrigued, he entered her office smiling.

Judy greeted him pleasantly but distantly. Since his return from America he had not said a word about how or with whom he had spent his Christmas. Not good enough. True, he had gone all out to woo her with candy and flowers but his attentions were too calculated to be of much value, she considered, and strengthened her resolve to resist the man. Not easy. He had never appeared more attractive nor her own body more eager to betray her. Using the excuse of all the work she must get through before the High Court appeal, she politely thanked him for his gifts and showed him the door.

Kay had a spring in her step as she left the Super's office and returned to the restroom smiling, elated even, for according to Judy there was a newly created appointment for a hostess guidance counselor and she believed that Kay would be just right for the position. Kay could not help feeling flattered, if not entirely convinced. She wondered if the Super believed she was totally right for the position or if she were in the running because of Dervla?

She would have given a lot to know the answer.

***

Nicholas soon found himself on Dervla's mailing list and realized how seriously she had taken his promise to bring her flying. The first drawing arrived in the shape of a grinning feline in cap and goggles. 'Can't wait to zoom into the sky with you' the banner read.

Nicholas enjoyed a good laugh. When it was followed by a grinning pilot puss holding up a placard with one word, 'When?' he pinned it on the wall above his computer, telling himself he would soon have as good a picture gallery as his old man. No doubt about it she was a character, Nicholas mused with a grin, was it any wonder Dad was so fond of her. She had all the charm of her mother, he decided, thoroughly beguiled by the pair of them.

Two days later he received the picture of a sad looking flying cat shedding copious tears into a voluminous hanky, and felt stricken with guilt. Poor Dervla, he had promised to take her flying and let her down. Vividly, he remembered his own childhood disappointments and knew he would have to make it up to her. He would take her up some Saturday very soon. Maybe Judy might come along with them.

But when he asked her, Judy said that she would love to help out but she was up to her eyes preparing for the High Court Appeal. 'You've got me at a very bad time, Nicky. Yes, I agree you can't take her to the flying club on your own but I really cannot spare the time.' But Nicholas would not take no for an answer, and her voice tailed weakly away for he was at his most charming and persuasive.

'The thing is, Judy, I did promise her and she won't let me forget it, not for one minute.' He sounded rueful, but she could tell he was smiling. 'Persistent little monkey. She keeps sending me zany drawings to remind me and funny, pathetic little notes that only a stony-hearted monster could resist.'

'Well no one could accuse you of that, Nicky,' Judy protested. 'I can see the little imp has you wrapped around her finger.' Like all of us, she acknowledged wryly. 'Okay! count me in,' she sighed. 'I'm sure it'll be fun!' With Dervla it usually was!

Going into Nicholas's room to borrow shaving gel Graham discovered his son's rapidly growing picture gallery. He peered closely at the crayoned pictures and scribbled words, mystified as to what Dervla was begging him to do. But there was no time just then to find out, he had a meeting with the Board of Directors at 8.30. With a last curious glance, he hurried back to his own room to finish dressing.

Taylor was another mystified man when Judith continued to resist him. But he told himself that he was not one to give up without a fight. From here on in he would use a more dashing line of wooing, he vowed, something to make those pansy eyes widen in delight, accepting that he had been bowled over the moment she had turned them on him. And now Taylor was prepared to use every means at his disposa, even going so far as to make promises no woman could resist, for with the most recent communication from his lawyer he was free at last to utter them. Regarding the small package wrapped in the distinctive black and gold paper he had purchased from a leading city jeweler, Duval reckoned flowers and candy were out but diamonds were always in. Later, sipping champagne in Patrick Gilbaud's elegant restaurant, Judy's reaction on opening her gift was every bit as gratifying as he had envisaged.

'How absolutely beautiful,' she gasped, obediently bending her head as he came around to her side of the table to fasten the sparkling trinket about her neck.

There were more treats in store for her.

'I've booked us into Dromoland Castle next weekend,' said this master of surprises. 'And, honey, are we going to have ourselves a ball.

Judy was impressed.

'So tell me it's okay with you, Judith me darlin' so I can start anticipating.'

'More than okay,' she assured him. Graham believed that she was working on the High Court appeal all weekend, accepting that she really needed time to complete her report. So Judy graciously agreed to go to Dromoland Castle with Taylor and began pleasantly anticipating herself. She forgot all about her promise to go flying with Nicky and Dervla, and by the time she remembered it was too late to cancel. As for Nicky, she shrugged, he would understand something had come up.

***

Kay had been only too pleased to grant permission for the Hostess Super to take Dervla on a treat that Saturday, knowing how delighted her daughter would be, but taken aback when Florrie protested, 'Is it daft you are, Kay? To be letting Dervla go off with her, and after all you said. Surely, it isn't wise to be encouraging these outings?'

Kay squirmed uncomfortably under Florrie's steady blue-eyed gaze. 'Don't look at me like that,' she said feebly. 'I'd feel really mean if I told Judy that she couldn't go and only think how disappointed Dervla would be.'

'Not if she didn't know about it,' Florrie said practically.

'But what would I say to Judy?'

'That Dervla was doing something else that day.'

'But she isn't.'

'Now, Kay,' Florrie looked skeptical. 'How would she know that?'

'Anyway, she would only suggest taking her out another day?'

'Then tell her the truth.'

Kay looked horrified. 'Which is?'

'That in view of your former association with Graham you think it might be better *not* to get too chummy. She would surely understand that.'

'Yes...but wouldn't she wonder why I had never objected before?'

Florrie shrugged. 'Well, I just think you're building up trouble for yourself. You can't have it both ways, Kay.'

Kay knew she was right, but felt she would look foolish if she were to object at this late stage. Next time she would say no, she promised herself, in the meantime she would let Dervla enjoy her trip to the Zoo. The child was planning to bring her sketch pad, she eased her conscience telling herself it would be educational.

But for all that Dervla had talked about bringing her sketch book she was under no illusion that they were actually going to the Zoo, having already received Nicholas's note and his pen and ink drawing of two agile, very brawny-looking pilot cats, holding up a banner with the words 'Come fly with me'. Giggling, she stuffed it deep into her schoolbag. Gosh! It was really good, she thought, and heaps better than anything she could do. She felt a bit silly, not knowing he could draw. Taking it out again at break, she saw there was a postscript she had missed in her rush to get to school. Reading it, her heart sank.

'Be sure and clear with your Ma that it's okay to come flying with me,' Nicky wrote. 'Otherwise it's off!'

Her initial excitement dying down, Dervla bit her lip in distress. Oh, dear, what was she to do? No, she couldn't possibly tell them, her father was bound to forbid her. To fly with Nicky was worth any trouble, she finally decided, her mind made up. Mummy and Daddy might be cross but they would surely get over it.

Nicholas turned in the entrance to the airfield, thinking how much he was enjoying the Saturday afternoon with Dervla. Maybe it was as well Judy had cried off at the last minute, he thought, it gave him a chance to get to know the child. He had been sorry not to see Kay though, apparently the grandmother was in hospital and she had gone to visit her. Nicholas told himself that Dervla was a great kid and tremendous company too, well able to hold her own in any conversation, whether it was about the boredom of school or the pleasures of creating new captions for cartoons.

'So what gave you that idea?' he asked intrigued, it was something he enjoyed himself.

'Mummy did! I draw cartoons too, that's even better!'

'Yeah, it is!' Nicholas agreed, having named his own collection 'Pender originals.' No doubt but Dervla was an interesting child, he mused. Probably be a lot of fun growing up with a sister like her, he thought.

'Nicky, indicator still flashing,' Dervla called him smartly to attention, and he amended his earlier thinking. Oh, Lord! Probably be a right pain in the ass, like having another Jeremy on his back. But, of course, he didn't mean it.

'Who's your lady friend, Pender?' Christy Kane came to meet them. 'A bit on the young side, isn't she?'

Nicholas laughed. 'Dervla, say hello to Captain Kane.'

'How's it going, Derv?' Christy gave her a mock salute. He had been out sick for a while but was back running the club since the middle of March and looking a bit pale and bloated. No doubt the effects of chemo, poor guy, thought Nicholas.

Dervla smiled shyly at the older man.

'Relative of yours, I reckon,' Christy probed. 'Looks just like you.'

Nicholas ignored him, knowing his reputation for gossip.

'So what'll it be, young lady? Coke…lemonade…name your poison.' Christy donned his pilot's cap at a rakish angle and leered at her. 'Not on the sauce yet, I reckon.'

Dervla giggled. 'Coca-cola, please.'

'Polite as well as pretty. Wow! That clinches it. Couldn't be related, Pender.'

'Make it two cokes,' Nicholas threw down a note.

'Save your money.' Christy flicked it back at him and set down the drinks. 'Reckon you're taking young Dervla up for a spin?'

'That's the general idea.'

'Okay. Take your pick. The Cessna was overhauled recently.'

'What's the weather doing?'

'It's fairly okay. Talk to the new guy. Long-haired chap in canary-coloured overalls, an ice lolly stuck in his gob.' Christy sniggered. 'Can't miss him!'

'Sounds like it'

'Aiming to be up for long?'

'Nope.' Nicholas glanced at Dervla who was following the conversation intently. 'Fancy a spin to the Isle of Man?' he joked.

'Could we?' Dervla was excited.

'We could but whether we should…that's another story.'

'Oh, do let's go, Nicky,' Dervla was already planning how she would tell her class mates 'That would be brilliant.' She started jumping up and down.

'Hey, don't play the kid,' Christy frowned.

'Oh, didn't you mean it?'

'Maybe some other time,' Nicholas resolved to watch his words, seeing Christy fairly bristling with curiosity. He and Dervla related. Huh! he almost smiled.

'Ready for your inaugural flight, Miss Mason?'

Dervla nodded, and gulped at her drink, her throat gone suddenly dry.

Maybe she was nervous. 'Nothing to it. Right, Christy?' He cocked an eyebrow and Christy caught on at once.

'Piece of cake…with gooey chocolate icing,' Christy embellished, banishing Dervla's worry lines and making her giggle again.

'Okay, let's get weaving.'

Nicholas led the way, with Dervla alternating between hops and skips in an effort to keep up with his long stride. He cast his eye over the three turbo-props lined up, and rejected the Socata TB-9 and its slightly older sister craft, opting instead for the Cessna 150 that Christy had recommended. It had seen about fourteen years service, unlike the other two with twice as many years in the air. Even so, Graham was a stickler for safety (as well he might, Nicholas mused) and consequently maintenance had always been a strong feature of the flying club. The M & K Aeroclub was lucky besides, in its chief engineer, Pat Ryan, who was a whizz with anything that flew. He had a reputation for taking aircraft up in weather when even the birds were walking.

Catching hold of Dervla's hand, Nicholas ran with her to the waiting aircraft, crying, 'All aboard, all aboard for the ride of a lifetime.'

Graham was out on the golf course that afternoon. With Judy tied up all weekend going over work in connection with the High Court Appeal he was having dinner with Ben and some others after the game, and quite looking forward to it. When the first drops of rain fell, he glanced doubtfully at the sky, thinking with only another few holes to play, they should be back safe and dry in the clubhouse before the heavens opened. All in all, it had been a good day, he mused, waiting for Ben to tee off on the 16th green. It would have been a whole lot better without Dan Tully, of course. Pity Ben could never bring himself to exclude the man when making up foursomes. It was more than Tully deserved, that's for sure.

As always, with Dan in their midst, there had been the usual brash stories and lewd ogling of any females crossing the fairway. Tully was at his most obnoxious, constantly referring to the Hostess Superintendent and casting sly glances around as if he knew something no one else did. Graham frowned. Given his close connection with Judy he found it distracting, and was unaware he was holding everyone up until Ben called him to attention.

'Your shot, Graham.'

'Sorry!' Graham bent down to press his tee into the turf. Angling closer, he adjusted his grip and then swung his shoulders powerfully, sending the ball soaring.

'Wow! Nice shot,' Mark commented, and Ben said, 'You *are* on form today, Pender,' followed by, 'Here comes the rain...knew it couldn't last!'

Once Nicholas had made a few circuits of the airfield he was tempted to do aerobatics, not something he would have considered for a moment if Dervla had not been such an enthusiastic passenger. Maybe he would swoop down over the Blessington Lakes and give her a thrill, she would love that. And sure enough, as they skimmed the water she showed no fear, uttering delighted oohs and aahs at the sudden descent. 'That was soooo brilliant!' she cried. 'Again please, Nicky.'

Nicholas laughed and soared back up into the sky. Such enthusiasm was infectious and he gave into her pleading with another hair-raising swoop.

'My tummy was in my mouth that time,' she gasped. 'Golly! I felt as though I could put out my hand and touch the water. Can we go again, Nicky?'

Of course they could! 'Hold on to your hat,' he called, and down he zoomed, grinning as he listened to her delighted shrieks. The kid was a natural, he rejoiced, not a nerve in her body. Little daredevil! He wished the old man was there to witness it.

'I can't wait to tell Mummy all about it,' Dervla crowed, and then grew quiet remembering the only person she could actually tell was her best friend, Gemma.

Nicholas did not notice anything amiss in her sudden silence, too busy regaining height and keeping an eye on his instruments. Thank goodness, it was a fairly good day and some sunshine about. Still, better not stay out too long, he decided, first flights should be short and sweet and, besides, he had forgotten to get an up-to-date weather report before taking off. Chatting with Christy had driven it from his mind.

'We'll go around one more time,' he said. 'Then we'll head back, okay?'

Dervla nodded but she was disappointed, not wanting it to end. Nothing in her life had been as exciting as this first flight and she was eager for more thrills. 'I know you were only joking about the Isle of Man but could we go to Wexford and see the train chugging out to Rosslare?' she coaxed.

Nicholas thought about it, no real problem, he had enough fuel for three hours. At the same time, he was conscious of slight unease, really they had been out long enough. Reluctant to disappoint her, he weighted it up and nodded.

'Well okay, just a quick flyover. But only for a look-see, mind. No trying to get around me to land on the beach and go paddling,' he teased.

Off they went, as though it had been ordered especially for Dervla the train was passing below on its way to Rosslare as they flew down low over the coast.

'Satisfied?' he asked, as the threatening rain spattered the windscreen.

Dervla smiled and nodded vigorously. 'Home, James,' she ordered regally, like she had heard Mummy saying to Daddy after a pleasant lunch out.

'Aye, aye,' Nicholas grinned, despite his disquiet at the massing cloud and sudden rattle of hail on reaching cruising level.

Only seconds later, the Cessna was rocketing about, the sky had grown dark and hailstones lashed the windscreen. Immediately, he tightened his harness and turned to give an extra tug on Dervla's belt. Whew! Who would have thought the aircraft could reach 2000 ft without even touching the throttle!

'We're experiencing a bit of turbulence,' he said quietly, not to alarm the child. 'Just keep your belt on tight and we'll soon be out of it.' Time to contact the Flight Information Regional Controller, Nicholas told himself, as he cautiously climbed another few feet, all the while keeping an eye out for other aircraft in his area.

He gave his position over the radio and waited. Ruddy hell! Nicholas clamped his jaw and tried changing frequency but the radio was dead. For the first time he noticed the "Off flag" on his VOR. He changed to his Number 2 set, with no better results. This was getting serious. And now he was raging at himself for his stupidity in not checking the weather, if he had he would have been aware of the expected deterioration.

Back at the flying club, Christy saw it was getting on for 5 o'clock. He strolled across to the door and frowned up at the gathering clouds, they were in for a downpour. Nicky was staying out a bit, he thought. He would have expected him back long before this. Maybe the little minx had got around him and they had gone to the Isle of Man after all. Not ruddy likely, he grinned.

Graham was almost finished his first pint when the barman came across to where he and the other pilots were sitting and swapping yarns, and told him he was wanted on the telephone. 'Shall I bring it over to you, sir?'

'No, don't bother. I'll take it at the bar.' He got up, wondering who it could be. The golf club was still predominantly a male stronghold and usually safe from domestic calls. 'The only place I'm safe from the ball and chain,' Dan declared facetiously. Graham had sympathy for Charlie wishing she could go somewhere safe from him!

He lifted the receiver and straightaway recognized Christy Kane's voice, but it took longer to understand what he was saying, and the rowdy shouts of laughter coming from another party of golfers nearby was not helping.

'What's that, Kane? Bit of a racket going on here... can you repeat it?'

'I said that I'm going home soon,' Christy shouted into the phone. 'Think you should know that Nicky took up a crate this afternoon. Said he was going for a short spin. Don't want to worry you but that was some time ago and we haven't heard from him since. And now the weather is closing in and visibility down.'

Graham felt the clutch of fear. 'What was he flying?'

'Cessna 150. Just been overhauled, so I told him Oh, yeah, he had a passenger with him... real cute kid.'

'Are you saying he had a child with him?' Graham was astonished.

'Yeah, little girl. Debbie or Deirdre,' Christy hazarded. 'She was on at him to take her to the Isle of Man but he wasn't having any. Look, he'll probably turn up any minute.. just wanted to let you know.'

Graham cut across him, 'I'm leaving *now*.' Dear God, let them be all right, he thought, as he hurried back to inform the others he would not be staying to dinner after all, and almost ran from the club.

The child could only be Dervla Mason, who else? Graham's acute anxiety turned to rage. What in God's name was Nicky thinking to take Kay's little girl joy-riding, and not a word to anyone?

Kay finished applying her makeup and glanced at her watch in concern. By this, she would have thought the Super would have had her fill of the animal kingdom. Oh well, maybe they had gone in somewhere to eat. Kay was familiar with how single women often forgot time and the need to keep parents informed of their children's movements. Not that Judy was irresponsible exactly, she told herself, but it would have been good if she had brought Dervla back on time on this particular Saturday. With Eileen in hospital since breaking her hip and they dining out that evening with Dave's boss and business associates, she had had to find a baby sitter. Better get changed, Kay decided, hurrying to the wardrobe. Let's hope Cate wouldn't be late, and Dave nagging all afternoon about leaving on time. That's all she needed!

***

With a rush of relief, Nicholas found that the circuit breaker for the Number 1 set had somehow popped out. It simply needed re-setting, and once he pushed it back into place the radio crackled to life. So the Cessna had been recently overhauled, had it? No doubt the fault of the lollipop-loving, long-locked Liam, he thought with cynical alliteration, Pat Ryan would never be so careless. But when he had calmed down Nicholas was forced to acknowledge that he had been at fault too, for not testing the radio when taxing down the runway. Not to mention not checking with the met, he mused guiltily, as he tuned the radio and gave his call sign.

Turning, he saw Dervla watching him. Poor kid, she looked really sick.

'Hang on tight,' he told her. 'We'll be out of this turbulence in a jiffy.' He wished now that he had brought some mints or even chewing gum she could suck on, he just hoped she would not be sick. God! He'd made a right hash of things, probably turn the poor kid right off flying for life.

Soon Nicholas was listening to the calm voice of the ATC and being directed away from the turbulence and into clear air at 2500 ft. He was relieved to see Dervla's colour returning. For the first time, he glanced at his watch and was appalled to see how late it was. Jeeze! Christy would be doing his nut. Better get on to the club and give an ETA. But first he needed to check his fuel, he told himself.

What he saw made Nicholas stare in shocked disbelief for the needle was pointing to near empty. No way, his mind protested, they were not yet in the air 90 minute. Automatically, he eased back on the throttles to save petrol, struck by a new chilling possibility. Given the new engineer's unreliability what if he had not actually put enough fuel in his tanks for three hours flying?

With that, Nicholas made the decision to retrace his flight path and land at Baldonnel Aerodrome. Immediately, he felt a whole lot better. At least there were proper runways at Baldonnel and an ATC to guide him safely in, not to mention fire engines standing by. 'Once we land I'll ring your Mum,' he told Dervla. 'She'll be worried at not hearing from us.' But almost at once his tension returned hearing the child begin to gabble and he listened to what she had to say.

'Nicky, you're not going to like it, but please, *please* promise me you won't be angry at what I have to tell you.'

'Okay,' he said uneasily. 'Shoot!'

'Mummy and Daddy don't know where I am. I didn't tell them.'

'What! But don't they know you're flying with me today?'

'No,' Dervla said miserably. 'They think I'm at the Zoo with Judy. My Daddy hates anything to do with flying. I was afraid he wouldn't let me go.'

Nicholas absorbed this in silence. The prospect of an angry parent coming the heavy on top of all else was daunting in the extreme. And they were not out of the wood yet, the fuel gauge was now registering empty, there was only what was in the reserve tank keeping them in the air.

In the Baldonnel Tower, with his bird's eye view of the runways and surrounding countryside, ATC Comdt. Joseph Little eased back his headphones and stretched his cramped muscles. 'Cover for me while I have a smoke,' he said to his duty partner, fumbling in his trousers pocket for a fag.

'Sure!' Capt Alan Deegan angled Joe's monitor so he could keep track of his aircraft, and then his eyes immediately returned to his own screen, where he was guiding in the Cessna 150 on its final approach to the airfield. The ambulance and fire trucks were standing by and the pilot alerted to cross-winds. Alan did not envy him having to cope with twenty to thirty mile winds, and a critical fuel situation. The guy sounded cool enough though, he'd give him that.

Recalling their brief conversation, Alan wondered what it was that struck him as familiar. Pleasant voice, no particular accent, en route back to M & K Aeroclub in County Meath. Of course! realization struck, Nicky Pender, Jerry's young brother.

'Hey Brian,' he turned, on impulse to Flight Sgt. Connors, the third man on ATC duty that Saturday evening. 'Isn't Jerry Pender on duty watch this evening? Ring down and tell him his brother is requesting permission to land, critical fuel situation.'

'Sure thing,' Connors punched out the extension number and spoke into the receiver, then turned back to tell Alan. 'He's on his way up.'

***

Kay was slipping on her rings when she heard the telephone. At last! That must be Judy ringing to say she was on her way. Better let Dave answer it, she decided, he had been ready for ages and she would only waste time running downstairs. Eyeing her reflection in the mirror, Kay rather liked what she saw, then reached for the orange chiffon scarf, draping it about her shoulders to take the bare look off of the new daringly low-cut black dress.

'Didn't you hear me calling you?' her husband burst into the room. 'There's someone on the phone about Dervla. Isn't she back yet?' And then taking in the dress he said doubtfully, 'You're not wearing that, are you?' to which Kay replied, 'Well yes, I had rather thought I would. Don't you like it?'

'Bit low, isn't it?'

Kay shrugged and draped the chiffon across the offending area, before heading downstairs. She was darned if she was going to change now and, anyway, she knew she looked great. Sometimes Dave was a real prude.

'I knew it! I just knew we were going to be late,' he was saying, as he followed her down. 'Couldn't we just for once leave on time? Is it too much to ask? Now I'm going to have to kill myself racing across the city…and where's the baby-sitter? I thought you had one lined up.'

'And so I do,' Kay said calmly. 'Anyway, Sinead is old enough to stay here on her own till Cate arrives.'

But Dave had already gone out to the car and was backing it on to the road, all ready for a quick getaway. Why did he always have to create such tension? Frowning, she spoke into the receiver. 'So sorry to keep you waiting,' and was taken aback when a familiar voice tersely cut her short. Her heart pounding in shock, Kay recognized Graham's voice.

'Kay, I'm sorry to ring you like this but I just heard and I don't want to alarm you but I feel you should know…'

It took her a full minute to understand what he was telling her and then she told him hurriedly, 'No, no, you must be mistaken. Dervla is with Judy Mathews. She took her to the Zoo this afternoon. It was all arranged. Well no, I didn't see her. Could you hold on a moment,' and she beckoned frantically to Sinead.

'Sinead,' she croaked, her voice almost failing her. 'Didn't Judy Mathews pick up Dervla while we were out?'

Sinead shook her head. 'No, Mummy. It was someone called Nicky…Dervla seemed to know him. '

'But why didn't you tell me?' Kay's voice rose. 'You should have *told* me.'

'I meant to Mummy, but I forgot when Daddy asked me to go for the paper.'

Kay turned hastily back. 'Graham, it appears you're right,' she said in a strained voice. 'I had no idea. I understood she was going to the Zoo with Judy.'

'You must believe me when I say that I knew nothing about it either,' Graham's own voice was stiff with tension. 'Look, I'm going down there now. Try not to worry, Kay. I'm sure they'll be back by the time I get there.'

Kay's throat swelled. Dervla, her beautiful child. Oh, God! she thought, if anything happens to her I'll die.

'Kay, are you still there?' and she managed a choked, 'Yes.'

'My dear, I can't tell you how sorry I am. I wouldn't have had it happen for the world. Look, I have to go.'

Kay felt her head begin to spin, her knees go weak. 'Please,' she whispered. 'Please, I must go with you,' and, after a moment's hesitation, she heard him say, 'Very well. I'm on my way. I'll pick you up in fifteen minutes.'

***

Graham made good time along the northern road. Fortunately, the traffic was mainly coming against them, more people travelling towards the city than going the other way that Saturday evening. He was very conscious of Kay lost in her own private misery beside him, and felt responsible for the anguish she was suffering as a result of his son's irresponsible act. Graham had been deeply affected by his first sight of Kay as she had hurried from the house, accompanied by her oldest child. It was several years since he had last laid eyes on her and he was immediately struck by her beauty and her distress. His eyes taking in the elegant black frock, the careful make-up, he realized she had been on the point of going out for the evening, and he found it still caused him a pang after all this time to think of her dressing with such care for anyone except himself.

Kay was conscious of Graham too, even while plunged into the depths of misery and apprehension at the thought of what they might learn on reaching the flying club. She was aware of his strong, well-shaped hands gripping the wheel, his stern profile, the profile she had once termed 'beautiful' in the early days of their acquaintance. This at a time when she had been a besotted young air hostess barely out of training. Was Graham thinking of this now she wondered, and found herself grateful for Sinead's presence, otherwise she might have said or done something for which she might afterwards be sorry. Yes, it was just as well there was someone else present to keep a check on them, she told herself, for he was having the old mesmeric effect on her. It both frustrated and angered her. It was because of him, or rather his son, she reminded herself, that she was in this deeply worrying situation.

No, Kay thought a moment later, if anyone should be blamed it was Judy for arranging to take Dervla out, then failing to show up. She could have at least rung to say there had been a change of plan, Kay told herself, it was having the whole thing sprung on her like this without warning, that was the worst. But what upset and shocked her most was Dervla's deceitful behavior. Kay had always believed her child was completely open with her but, in this instance, it seemed that she had fallen under Nicky's spell. Kay drew in a shuddering breath. Well, the young man *was* charming, no doubt about that, he had charmed her too, she acknowledged honestly, and felt doubly betrayed. Suddenly chilled, she pulled the chiffon scarf closer about her throat, unbearably reminded of the way Dave had driven off at once, rather than risk being a few minutes late to the restaurant, not even waiting to find out what had delayed the child. She blinked back tears. It was all he ever cared about his blessed career, she mused with a tinge of bitterness, work first, family last, it had never changed.

As Graham turned in the entrance to the airfield and drove straight up to the clubhouse door, he saw Christy standing out on the step.

'Any news?' he shot the question as he got out of the car, his anxiety easing when Christy nodded, only to flare again when he heard him saying,

'Yeah, but that was forty minutes ago and still no sign of Nicky.'

'But surely you were in touch with him again?' Graham glanced back at Kay and Sinead, wanting to shield them from hearing anything to further alarm them.

'Yeah, but he's not responding,' Christy growled. 'Could be he's run into some kind of trouble. Beats me though,' he frowned, looking white and exhausted, reminding Graham that he was a sick man. 'That crate was fully serviced only last week. The new guy gave it a thorough going over. You met Liam when you were down here last time, he came with great references.'

'That's right you told me,' Graham agreed, and refrained from adding, 'But only when you had already engaged him.' His own first impressions of the man had not been good. Frowsy hippy-type of individual, he considered, but, as Kane said, he carried good references.

Might be an idea to run another check on him, make contact with his previous employers, Graham decided. Once inside the clubhouse he ordered brandy for Kay. Glancing at her strained face, he wondered unhappily at the terrible luck that kept dogging him and this beloved woman, whose happiness was all he had ever wanted.

Sitting in the bar mother and daughter were going through their own private misery as Sinead kept repeating 'Sorry, Mummy,' over and over.

'Look darling, I'm not blaming you,' Kay whispered to her. 'I was just a bit upset earlier. I didn't mean to be cross with you. Dervla should have told me of the change of plan but she wanted so much to fly. I suppose she was afraid I'd say no.'

Sinead glanced up with haunted eyes. 'It's all my fault. I should have told you it was not the hostess lady. Oh, if only I'd told you,' and she began to cry again.

'Hush, hush,' Kay put her arm around her daughter and rocked her against her side, conscious of Graham's watchful eyes on them. 'Look at it this way. I should have asked *you*. Have you thought of that?'

Sinead shook her head, gulping in her distress. 'N…no.'

'Well, think of that now. You did nothing wrong, pet. I was just upset thinking she might be hurt… '

Kay's lips wobbled and she felt a rush of tears that kept threatening to overwhelm her. Oh, Dervla, Dervla, she sent up the soundless cry now, Why, Oh why, didn't you tell me what you were planning, the tears beginning to drop fast and unstoppable down her cheeks.

'Kay, are you all right,' Graham was at her side in a moment and his steadying arm went immediately about her, but she just kept her head down so that he wouldn't see how completely unhinged she was becoming.

'The washroom,' she got unsteadily to her feet. 'Where…I don't see …' and at once he walked with her across the bar and indicated a door. 'Through there,' he pointed. 'And then down to your left.'

Kay took her time and managed to get a grip on her emotions as she mopped her eyes, relieved in spite of herself that her mascara had not run in black pools, yet sickened by her own superficiality at such a time. When she eventually emerged, she was only marginally more composed than when she had gone in.

Further along the passage, Graham stood staring out a window, and he turned towards her at once, speaking with infinite gentleness. 'Ah, Kay, my dear, there you are. How are you feeling now?'

Kay gulped at his tone, stared back at him with tragic eyes, not answering.

'Darling…' the endearment broke from him and his breathing was as distressed as the dark eyes watching her so intently. 'Isn't there *any* way that I can be of help to you? Anything I can do. I feel so helpless, so angry this should have happened.'

And now Kay's breathing was ragged with upset. 'The only way you can help me,' she said in a breaking voice. 'Is to bring back my child safe and sound, she's not yet ten. What was she doing up in a rickety old plane without a proper radio and too little petrol? What kind of club is this anyway?'

Graham said nothing, just stood there looking at her with a troubled expression, and Kay was instantly sorry. Why was she attacking him like this, she thought bewildered, and he only trying to help her. 'I'm s...sorry,' she faltered. 'I shouldn't have said that. After all, we are both in the same position and you must be terribly worried about your son.' She was shocked at herself for having so completely forgotten that Graham stood to lose every bit as much as she, even more if he only knew.

'Let's try and keep things in perspective,' he was saying. 'Nicky is a good pilot and he has been well trained...although the best trained pilots, even one's own flesh and blood, 'he added, 'encounter circumstances over which they have no control.'

As he said this, with an expression of resigned acceptance, Kay felt immeasurably moved, remembering all he had gone through himself. And with another unpredictable swing of her already overcharged emotions, she reached out blindly to comfort him, murmuring, 'Oh, my dear, my dear!'

Graham stared down into her upturned face with a startled look and then his arms closed around her and his lips came down hard on hers, giving and receiving comfort, blotting out their present misery and the dread of what might yet come to be.

Sinead glanced at the door her mother had gone through, wishing she would come back. She took another sip of orange and was wondering if she should go look for her when the telephone rang. She saw Christy unhooking the receiver from the wall.

'Yeah...yeah, thanks for telling us. Yeah, no sweat. We'll get straight back. Ciao!' Hanging up, he called, 'Hey, kid, news at last. Go tell your Ma, there's a doll.'

Sinead jumped eagerly to her feet and ran to the door leading to the washrooms. News, he had said, not good or bad news, just news. Oh please God, let them be all right, she was praying as she pushed open the door. She was about to go in further when she saw her mother a little way down the dimly lit passageway, standing very close to the pilot who had driven them to the club. They were deep in conversation and she hesitated, not wanting to interrupt them.

Then remembering the urgency of Christy's voice she went nearer, calling tentatively, 'Mummy, you are to come at once, Christy says. There's news of Dervla,' and all at once they pulled abruptly away from each other and, with a sense of shock, she realized they had been kissing.

***

Despite all Nicky's reassurances, Dervla felt afraid. Closing her eyes tight, she clung on for dear life to her seat, trying to ignore the horrendous clunking sounds, the retching gasps of the engine as though it was about to die on them at any minute.

She stole a look at Nicholas's grim face and knew better than to say anything. Earlier when she had asked him what he was doing he had roared at her to be quiet, and she had been so shocked by this unexpected reaction, so unlike his usual gentle bantering manner, that she had been hard put not to cry.

True, a moment later he had put out his hand, saying in a more reasonable voice, 'Sorry! Can't talk now, Dervla. Need all my wits here,' which was even more alarming and showed he was having difficulty handling the plane.

At times Dervla was not sure which was the most frightening – to be horribly injured in a plane crash and end up dead, or stay alive like Auntie Florrie's friend Angela and have no legs. Worst of all to escape unhurt and have to face her father's terrible anger, for he was almost certain to blame her, even if Mummy did stick up for her. And why should Mummy do that after all her lies? Dervla swallowed miserably over the lump in her throat convinced they were going to die, after her deception even God wouldn't want to do anything for her.

Nicholas was having trouble keeping calm himself. No petrol in his tanks he could understand and the way the engine kept coughing and spluttering due to the low fuel situation, but what he could not understand - and was alarming the hell out of him - was the way he was skidding off course unable to line up the Cessna with the runway.

Looking down he could see the springs of the rudder-control moving but not the rudder itself. Damn! It was stuck fast. Even as he got on the radio to alert Baldonnel Tower to this new hazard, Nicholas began battling with the aircraft, giving it full throttle and then sliding it gradually back to see if by crossing the controls, in effect keeping the stick forward and to the right while the rudder was still locked to the left, he could keep the Cessna in a mild slip and still *have* control. And then came the shock of his brother's voice.

'Nicky listen, this is Jerry. Keep coming and watch out for cross-winds – gusting twenty…thirty miles – emergency equipment standing by. Good luck!'

Nicholas looked down and saw they were indeed prepared below, with the fire trucks and ambulance in strategic positions near the runway. What was Jerry doing in Baldonnel, he wondered inconsequentially, he had thought he was based this month at Gormanston. Funny hearing his voice like that, comforting too. They may have had their differences growing up but he was his big brother and there was a strong core of affection and trust running through their relationship.

So here we go! Nicholas said a fervent prayer, and dismissing all else from his mind he came around with full left rudder on and managed to push the stick far over to the right, calculating as he did so that this would be the same as slipping towards the ground; he was banking his hopes that in this fierce wind the manoeuvre might just hold the Cessna straight till he could get the wheels on the ground. It was a brave hope, and the only one now he had to hang on to.

***

Graham left the flying club and using his knowledge of the countryside to cut across from Meath to Kildare in the quickest possible time, he drove as fast as was safe towards Baldonnel. He took to back roads and avoided town areas where traffic might be building up that Saturday evening. He spoke little as he drove still upset that the girl had seen them. He would have given anything for it not to have happened that way although he was unable to regret the kiss, that wonderful kiss that gave the lie to the myth that Kay was indifferent to him. It had felt so natural and so right, effectively wiping out the lonely in-between years as if they had never been. But his euphoria had been quickly dispelled by Jeremy's phone call and now he was uncomfortably aware of the strained atmosphere in the car, the girl huddled in the back and Kay sitting silent and stricken beside him. He wished he could have eased her distress with consoling lies but knew better than to do that. He could only hope and pray that the situation was not be as bad as Jeremy had led him to believe, remembering his grim tone as he said, 'We pulled a young child out of the wreckage, Dad. What was Nicky *thinking?*'

What indeed, Graham thought heavily.

At Baldonnel, Jeremy was there to meet them at the gate and he told them that the ambulance had already left with Dervla and Nicky on board. Kay wanted to rush at once to the hospital but Graham persuaded her to come into the barracks and drink a mug of hot sweet tea; only then did they drive the remainder of the way.

In the ICU of Naas Hospital Dervla was lying white and still, her head swathed in bandages and an array of tubes and wires linking her with the monitor positioned beside the hospital bed. Kay put up a hand to her mouth to stifle a cry of anguish and hurried forward. Somehow, the little girl seemed smaller as though the accident had robbed her of stature, her cheeks usually so rosy were devoid of all color, reminding Kay heartbreakingly of a bumble bee that had lost its glorious markings in death.

Leaning down to her unconscious child she whispered, 'Dervla…darling…this is Mummy,' picking up the small hand and stroking it ever so gently with her thumb.

Overcome with sorrow, she lowered her head and pressed her lips against the cool skin, and at the touch all her pent-up emotions spilled over and tears began to fall. She caught her breath, aching with the effort of trying to control her sobs.

At the other side of the ICU Graham's eyes were anxious as he leaned down to speak a few cheering words to Nicholas, bruised and bandaged and muzzy from medication, only able to mouth, 'Sorry, Dad,' before slipping into drugged sleep. But not before acknowledging with the ghost of a grin Jeremy's, 'You did amazingly well, Nicky, in the circs.'

Despite his anxiety, Graham's lips twitched too. From Jeremy that was praise indeed. And when he reluctantly left Nicky's bedside at the nurse's bidding and went across to where Kay sat by her child, he was shocked to find her huddled over with her face buried in her arm, giving way to her grief and despair.

Graham had no wish to intrude upon this intensely private moment but his very real concern ousting such considerations, he advanced closer and was more distressed than he could ever have imagined by the altered appearance of this child whom he had never seen as anything but vibrant and bonny.

Moved by pity and love, he stooped over Kay and whispered, 'Don't cry, Kitty, please don't cry. She'll be all right, you'll see. They are doing everything possible for her. She's a healthy little girl. Just give her time.'

Kay lifted her head, her tear-stained face as deathly pale as her child's and she stared at him so long and hard that he felt suddenly concerned that the shock had turned her mind, as she said harshly, 'Too much time has been wasted already, Graham. Time we will never have again. This might be all we will ever have with Dervla, these few hours and you still don't see it, do you?' It was almost an accusation.

'See what?' Graham humored her, more than ever convinced the shock had unhinged her, and then it occurred to him if he had not eaten since lunch time, the chances were she had had nothing either and they should visit the hospital cafeteria.

But before he could make the suggestion she said again, almost angrily, 'You really have no idea, have you? Not even an inkling of what I'm talking about, not even now when you are in danger of losing your child?'

Still he stared, nonplussed, imagining she was speaking of Nicholas. He had never seen her like this and was seriously contemplating calling the nursing sister, when Kay's next words arrested him where he stood. 'But then I suppose it never occurred to you that you might have more to lose here today than just your son?'

Something about the angry, sorrowful way she stared at him, and then glanced pointedly at the unconscious child, jolted Graham into an awareness of what she was suggesting. And now it was he who looked from the mother to the child and comprehension slowly dawning, he said aghast, 'What are you suggesting, Kay? Surely you're not saying...'

'I could never understand how you never saw it for yourself.' She spoke without emotion now as though the revelation had taken the last of her strength. 'God knows you've had opportunity enough. In the beginning I even thought you had some suspicion that she was yours and it was why you kept on writing to her and arranging meetings. Judy Mathews knew the first day I brought Dervla to her office. I could tell by the way she looked at her. Didn't you ever wonder at the resemblance between Nicky and Dervla when they stood side by side, as they must surely have done when she visited your house? They are just *so* alike,' she gulped on a dry throat. 'She even has *your* eyes and they are Nicky's too, and she has his gift for drawing. But if none of that struck you didn't you *ever* wonder why I called her after your mother?'

'Was that the reason?' Graham felt as though he had been in an accident himself, confused and deeply shocked. He sighed deeply, it was all too much to take in. 'Yes, I did wonder that time I met you both in the hostess building,' he told her unsteadily, remembering the anguish he had felt on believing she had been intentionally cruel, it had only been with time that he had recognized it for the consolation it was.

'I couldn't get over the resemblance when you took her up in your arms and your faces were so close together,' Kay said in a breaking voice. 'It seemed so obvious...the likeness between you so strong.'

Graham stared at her stricken, feeling the foundations of his whole world quaking. If only he had had some inkling of the truth that day, if only he had realized he would never have let her walk away from him. But why had she never told him? Why had she kept it from him all this time?

'Seeing you that day I was tempted to tell you,' Kay admitted, as though reading his thoughts. 'I almost did but...I didn't have the courage.'

'Oh my dear, how I wish you had.' Graham's voice was husky with regret. Oh God! To think he'd had all the aces and not known. 'I thought she was the most beautiful child I'd ever seen and afterwards I couldn't stop thinking of her,' he spoke almost dreamily. 'Strangely, she reminded me of Nicky at that age. I distinctly remember thinking that! How very stupid I've been.'

After a moment he said. 'What I don't understand is why you found it impossible to tell me,' and now his voice was heavy with hurt. 'Surely you realized there was nothing could have made me happier than to know a child - this beautiful child - had come from the love we felt for each other? Surely you knew once I became aware of the true situation I would never have let you go?'

'Oh, Graham. I see now that I have made a terrible mistake,' Kay gasped, overcome with contrition and regret. 'But supposing even now it's too late, supposing this here and now is *all* you are ever going to have of her?' Inwardly she was crying, 'Oh God! Ten short years.... is that all *I'm* going to have?'

At the bleak thought nothing could stop her anguished tears, and she cried in earnest now while he looked helplessly on.

***

Jeremy stayed on at Nicholas's bedside, unable to get over how concerned his father had been about the little girl. What was the relationship between Graham and the attractive dark-haired woman? he wondered. Certainly not platonic, not if he read the signs aright. And another thing, how come his brother had brought the child joyriding in the Cessna and their father had known nothing about it, nor the child's mother either? The whole business left much to be explained, Jeremy frowned. Someone would need to come up pretty soon with some answers. He was remembering the beautiful little face like a waxen effigy, the closed eyelids fringed with long luxuriant lashes and the huge poppy bruise on the forehead, partially hidden under the silky tangle of curls.

'Still breathing but only just,' he had told his father on the phone, hearing him let out an audible sigh of relief. 'Thank God for that!'

The pair of them had had a lucky escape, Jeremy mused, how the child would fare remained to be seen. Luckily, Nicky had kept his cool and got the plane down. Jeremy felt proud of his young brother. Four broken ribs and a broken collar bone was a stiff enough price to pay for someone else's gross incompetence, Comdt. Pender considered, but he supposed it was a small enough price to pay when compared to your life. The whole thing could so easily have ended in a burning heap of twisted metal, and no survivors. At the mental image this conjured up, he gave an involuntary shiver.

First thing tomorrow he would instruct the Corps' mechanics to strip down the Cessna. For a recently serviced aircraft, Jeremy told himself grimly, a helluva lot of things had gone wrong with it.

*** *

Kay finally got through to Dave at the restaurant and told him what had happened, trying to keep her voice steady and speak coherently. Bur it was all she could do not to break down and sob, putting it into words made it all the more real and terrible.

'Are you telling me that Dervla was in a plane that crashed?' Dave said bewildered, he had thought Kay would never ring, was tired of making excuses to his boss for her non-appearance. 'But I don't understand. What was she doing in a plane? You told me she was going to the Zoo with that woman from the airport.'

'That's what I understood to have been the arrangement,' Kay gripped the telephone hard, dizzy from emotion and painfully conscious of Graham standing within earshot. 'Dervla didn't tell me that the plan had been scrapped and she was going instead to some flying club.' How she hated exposing her deceitful behavior before Dave and he already so censorious of the little girl, but what had happened was far too serious to cover up. 'I'm afraid there was a very bad accident.' Even as she spoke she was conscious of music at his end of the line, the babble of talk and laughter. People having a good time, she thought dully.

'Oh, my God!' Dave was horrified. 'How serious are her injuries?'

'She's unconscious and she has head injuries...until she comes out of the coma they won't know just how bad.'

There was silence as Dave digested this, and then he said, 'Do you mean to say she never said a word to you about where she was going?'

'No, she didn't,' Kay said shortly, not up to an inquisition at this stage. 'Look, Dave, I've got to go. There are others waiting to use this 'phone.'

'Will you be much longer?'

'What!' She wondered if she had heard aright.

'We've just started dinner. Kay! You really need to be here.'

'I'm afraid there's no way I can leave Dervla...and Sinead is with me.'

'Couldn't you at least come for a drink? This is a very important dinner, there's a lot resting on it.'

Kay took a deep breath. 'No, I can't,' she said shortly. 'I'm much too worried about Dervla to be any company. She...she's so white and still. I'm afraid to leave her in case ...' the tears thickened in her throat preventing her from completing what she was saying, aware of Graham's involuntary movement. He was angry, she knew, intolerant of what he considered her husband's insensitivity. She knew him so well.

'Well, if it's as bad as you say I suppose Tony will understand and overlook your absence.' Now she grew angry herself. Unbelievable, she thought. He's more concerned with what Tony thinks than their child's welfare. 'Look, Kay, I've got to go. We'll speak of this later,' and he rang off.

Couldn't wait to get back to the party, Kay thought, turning wretchedly to face Graham, ashamed that he had overheard the conversation.

'Are you all right?' he asked gently, regarding the over-bright eyes and wounded expression. 'Was that your husband you were speaking to now?'

She nodded. 'He doesn't mean to be unfeeling,' she tried to excuse him. 'It's just that he's in the middle of a very important business deal and I should be there.'

Graham said nothing. It seemed patently obvious to him that Kay had stressed the seriousness of the child's condition. What kind of man would not rush at once to join her at the bedside of their critically injured child? He felt the slow burn of anger.

***

Sinead could barely keep her eyes open on the journey home from the hospital, but the minute she was in bed she felt wide awake. She had been so glad to be home, relieved when the moment came say goodnight to her mother when she could close the bedroom door and be on her own at last. It had been a dreadful day and she needed time to think about all that happened. Sighing, she knew she could not put off the moment any longer, she just *had* to think about the strange scene at the flying club. Could she have *imagined* that her mother was kissing the pilot? It had been really dark, too dark to see properly, she told herself. But if she had only imagined it, why then did she feel so upset? It just didn't make sense. She lay there mulling it over for a long time and then mercifully she slept. Kay's mind like her daughter's was full of disturbing images of what had taken place that evening and, over all, the terrible weight of fear pressing down on her. *What if Dervla's condition worsened during the night and she were to die?* At the terrible thought she began to shake.

Now she knew that she had been wrong not to stay at the hospital or, at least, somewhere close-by. She sat on the edge of the bed for a long time, still clad in the low-cut dress that in the early evening she had been determined to wear in defiance of Dave's rather conservative views. Meeting her eyes in the mirror, she stared in dismay at her woebegone face, her tousled hair. God! She looked dreadful. What must Graham have thought! That she could even care about her appearance and her child so ill sickened Kay. How shallow she was, she thought in despair. But where Graham was concerned Kay had always cared too much. She thought how concerned he had been at her distress, how shocked when she had finally revealed to him what she had kept secret from him all these years.

Bestirring herself at last, she went through the mechanical motions of removing her makeup and splashing her face with water. She got into her night clothes and lay on the bed a while, before getting under the covers. She did not expect to sleep and lay tense and still, listening for Dave's key in the front door, dreading the inevitable conversation that would take place between them. She was growing drowsy when at last she heard the click of the front door lock, but her husband was so long in coming to bed that she eventually fell into an exhausted asleep.

Downstairs, Dave slumped in a chair with whisky glass in hand, moodily sipping his drink and reviewing the events of the evening. Business-wise it had been a success, he reckoned, but the pleasure and satisfaction this should have afforded him had been negated by his wife's absence and Tony's frowning displeasure. Clearly, his boss didn't really take seriously that their youngest child had been in an accident, it was merely an inconvenience to him. This was partly because of the way Dave had told him, playing it all down, saying the hospital was keeping Dervla under surveillance for the night and not taking any chances. It was not as if he had not stressed the importance of this meeting with the British bankers and how important it was for Kay to be there. He sighed and acknowledged that she had never really like going out to dinner with Tony and the Maxwell wives, regarding it as an onerous duty.

Dave got up to fill his glass again, mindless of how much he had already had to drink, not caring if he got sloshed, wishing only to wipe out all memory of the unhappiness he felt and much of it due to the troubling phone-call from Kay, the telling details regarding the pilot suppressed. He had returned to the table, feeling deeply upset because of past connotations, only to find Tony discussing the new merger and the possibility of Anne and himself working together with their British associates. He did not know whose suggestion it had been but suspected it was Anne's. After his frequent lamentable lapses with her over the years he had made an effort lately, going out of his way to avoid any working partnership with her, successfully teaming her up with one or other of the junior managers. But now with this new deal they were smack back together again and what lay ahead was bed, booze and big biz in that order, he told himself, with cynical exactitude.

Dave was conscious that his irritation with Kay was the reason he had gone back with Anne to her apartment. That and too much to drink. What in God's name had possessed him to go up for a nightcap? he groaned. It was an ill-judged decision. He could have known what would happen, and happen it did! God! She was one hungry female. She'd had the clothes off him even before he was through the doorway, and he had let her, even helped her, Dave thought sickened.

He sagged hopelessly in his seat and the glass fell from his hand, seeping a golden pool on the pale Aubusson rug. He buried his face in his hands, and in the privacy of the dark sitting-room he cried for himself and for Kay and for the injured child whose birth had raised such terrible doubts in him and whom, he knew, would always mean more to Kay than himself.

***

Early next morning Graham drove to the hospital to visit Nicholas, and to look in on Dervla; he was not yet able to call her his daughter, not even in his thoughts. He was glad to find Nicholas a little stronger, but troubled to find that the little girl was still unconscious. It had been late the previous night before Graham had finally slept, his mind endlessly going over what had passed between Kay and himself; even now a day later he was still trying to come to terms with it. He only wished he might have been able to discuss it with her more fully, but in the circumstances this had been out of the question. One good thing, she had promised to sit down with him at the first opportunity and discuss the past; there was so much they needed to speak about.

The previous evening walking in the garden and thinking back over the day, Graham had been reminded by what Kay had said

about Judy having instinctively made the connection between himself and the child the first time she had laid eyes on her. Struck by
how much time must pass before he met Kay again and desperate for answers, he had decided to go over to Judy's apartment and
have a chat with her. By this, she would have surely caught up with
the backlog of work. But when he stood outside the door of Judy's
apartment and rang the bell, he was disappointed to get no answer.
Too bad, he thought, she must have gone out to get some air. He
went downstairs and slipped a note into her postbox, before heading
back to his car. He had almost reached it when he caught sight of
Judy some distance away getting out of a car and was about to go
towards her, when he saw that she was not alone, her companion
was Taylor Duval. Frowning, he had watched as Duval lifted Judy's
elegant pigskin case from the boot of his car and then, putting his
arm closely about her, he began walking with her in the direction of
the apartment block. Incredulously, Graham stared after them, even
at a distance there was no mistaking the intimacy between them and
the fact they must have been away together. When he recalled Dan
Tully's remarks on the golf course, he realized what he had all along
been too blind to see.

Judy was appalled to hear of the flying accident and felt apprehensive even before Graham came storming into her office next day,
knowing from the note he had left in her mail box that he had called
to her apartment the previous evening. Oh God! he must have seen
us, she thought dismayed, her offer of coffee savagely rejected and
her secretary unceremoniously bundled out the door with the command. 'See that we are not disturbed and do *not* come back in here
until sent for.'

Shutting the door on Colette's disillusioned face – she had been
one of his most ardent admirers –Graham told Judy in the same de-
cisive tone, 'Hold everything for the next thirty minutes. We need
to talk!' before settling down opposite her, obviously determined to
have it out.

'I presume by now you are aware that this ill-judged expedition
you were initially involved in, ended most tragically with a child
badly injured? Not to mention the fact that my own son is in much

the same sorry state in hospital. And to think that *no one*,' he raged, 'no one had seen fit to inform *me* of the proposed outing.'

'Hold on a minute,' Judy protested, feeling as though she had somehow landed herself in front of a war tribunal, but Graham swept on, his eyes cold and unforgiving.

'I consider it highly irresponsible of you to arrange an outing of this nature and, then, to back out at the last minute without informing the child's mother.' Disgustedly, he shook his head. 'Do you realize that Dervla's parents had absolutely no idea where she was and if they had known, they would have been exceedingly slow to give their permission?'

Judy stared at him mesmerized, unable to reply as he coldly continued. 'In all good faith they had agreed to allow their child go with you to the Zoo so how do you think they felt on learning late on Saturday evening that she had been involved in a plane crash? And how do you think I felt,' Graham grated on, 'when it was my unpleasant duty to have to tell them the bad news?'

Judy paled at the torrent of words, accusation in every syllable. 'Well, in all fairness, Graham,' she found her voice at last. 'I really had intended taking Dervla to the Zoo. It wasn't my idea to take her flying, not my idea at all,' she stressed, fixing her eyes desperately on him. 'That was all Nicky's idea and when he asked me to go along with them I could hardly refuse… but something came up I simply couldn't get out of.'

'Ah yes, as you say something came up,' Graham unpleasantly pounced on this piece of information, making her sorry she had mentioned it. 'I trust you enjoyed your weekend *away* from your crushing workload. I was concerned to think of you slaving over the backlog of work you were so insistent upon dealing with this weekend.' His laughter chilled her. 'Seems it wasn't the first time you have been trysting with that womanizer Duval. I would have expected better of you!'

There was a wealth of contempt in his tone that brought the hot color surging to Judy's face, and she stared at him in outrage, for his jibe had slid under her armor and shredded her pride, which was not inconsiderable. Even at a time when her self-esteem was one hundred percent reinforced by Taylor's recent avowals she suddenly felt like the undiscerning slut Graham called her, and not particularly an attractive or intelligent one at that!

'How …how dare you,' she said weakly, but she had no real defense and she knew it. She had played him false and he was too fine a man to be treated in that way. After a few more hard-hitting home truths, he took the keys to her apartment from his jacket and she felt a sudden shock of loss as he tossed them on her desk.

'Hardly needs saying… I have no further use for these,' and before Judy could rally he had gone out the door leaving her feeling thoroughly demoralized, and not a little shocked to think she had not uttered one word in her own defense, nor had she told Graham that Taylor Duval had done what *he* had never done and asked her to be his wife. But it was too late for such disclosures.

That same afternoon Jeremy strolled down to the hangars to see how the work on the Cessna was progressing. Earlier, he had checked in with the duty engineer and been given a rough estimate of when he might expect the overhaul to be completed.

'Save yourself a journey, skipper,' McBride advised. 'The earliest we'll be done around here is four if you want her stripped down, give or take an hour.'

'Sure thing,' Jeremy accepted this equably enough. There was no rushing McBride, he knew. Not a man to ever underestimate the workload, he always did a good job and Jeremy would put his trust in any airplane he serviced

Now ducking into the hangars out of the sunlight, he hailed him, 'So what have you got for me?' and the engineer rooted about in the pocket of his overalls.

'There's your culprit, skipper,' McBride extended his hand, palm up, revealing four small plywood sticks. 'Found them jammed in the rudder pulley, these little beauties are what kept it fully locked.'

Jeremy stared. 'Good God, man. How do you reckon *they* got there?'

McBride shrugged. 'Looks to me like somebody at the M & K Aeroclub has a passion for iced lollies. What else!'

***

It was ten days before Dervla came out of her coma, every hour up to that moment was agony for Kay, all the time fearing the worst. Dave was so taken up with his work and the proposed merger that he had made only one visit to the hospital and, after that, she had been free to sit down with Graham as promised and have their discussion. Soberly, they had discussed the past. Mutual hurts and grievances were acknowledged and finally put aside, having come to a new understanding of that fraught situation ten years before when Graham had been suspended from the airline, with little or no prospect of reemployment. And Kay, finding herself pregnant, was forced to make the decision she had made at the time, faced with the very real danger of losing Sinead should her husband learn the truth. Graham had seen Kay's precarious position in quite a different light, and generously acknowledged if she had been guilty of not showing enough trust in him it was understandable given how little faith he had exhibited in himself at that catastrophic time. With the welfare of their child uppermost in their minds now, both saw the importance of letting go of the past and looking to the future.

With Dave so occupied with his work Kay was glad when Graham, having spent time with Nicholas, crossed the unit to support her vigil at Dervla's bedside. At this point, the pattern of Kay's days was very much the same, talking continually to her unconscious child about anything that came to her mind, past holidays, special birthdays, her great love for the child and how Sinead was badly missing her little sister. Kay's main objective was to somehow get through to Dervla's subconscious mind and motivate her with the desire to recover. Sometimes she felt a little desperate, even ridiculous to be making so much effort and getting no response. But in this she was again helped by Graham who did his own share of talking to the unconscious child, referring to her drawings and warmly speaking of something called 'Juggling Cat' - whatever that was - and which had the effect of making him smile even as he besought her to get well and draw for him some more of that amazing feline's adventures.

Listening, Kay had to smile herself, liking this strangely boy-ish side of Graham she wouldn't have known if it weren't for the accident, and her joy soared when almost two weeks after Dervla was rushed by ambulance to the hospital the little girl opened her eyes and whispered, 'Mummy, Mummy,' the sound coming softly to Kay's ears, as she stood staring glumly out the window of the ICU. It seemed fitting that Graham was also present at this heartwarming moment and so the two people in Dervla's life who cared most for her were able to rejoice in her blessed return to consciousness. It was a few more days before Dervla was strong enough to hold a proper conversation but when she did, it was evident from subse-quent remarks that she had a fairly clear memory of the accident, up to the moment of impact.

'I tried to do what Nicky told me, Mummy,' she told Kay ear-nestly, her dark eyes so like her father's appearing huge under the white bandage. 'But I was afraid, really afraid. Is Nicky okay?' her voice rose anxiously and she only calmed down on being reassured that he was recovering well and soon to be discharged.

But she was still a very sick little girl and the doctor told Kay it would be some considerable time before she would be up and about again. In the meantime, they would be running tests to assess what damage had been done.

'Until then, Mrs Mason, we'll just have to wait and see.'

'In other words,' Dave said dryly, when he heard. 'They aren't going to commit themselves one minute sooner than they have to.'

Kay tried not to let this remark put a damper on her relief. Dave meant well, she told herself, he just did not want her to get her hopes too high. By contrast, Graham's optimistic viewpoint did much to sustain her, and she took heart each time she heard him saying, 'Dervla will be fine, Kitty, believe me. She's a fighter and, to me, she seems as bright as she ever was,' adding with a bashful grin, 'I'm not just saying this because I'm her father but I've always thought her an unusually intelligent little girl. Once they run the tests, we'll have all the reassurance we need.'

Kay loved it when he said 'we' and even more to hear him own-ing his child. It was enough to boost her spirit while waiting for the results. Earlier, she had sought and been granted compassionate leave with Judy falling over backwards to facilitate her in this respect, as well she might. So far the Super had not discussed her own questionable part in the ill-fated outing but Kay knew Graham had held her accountable and taxed her with irresponsibility. She was only glad *he* had been the one to do it. It was not *her* place, Judy was her boss. She had heard too, of course, about Judy's engagement to the Chief Executive and was quick to tell herself it made no real difference to her, for the revival of her friendship with Graham was not something they would be taking to the next level, he knew it and she knew it, and so no ambiguity existed.

More than ever since Dervla's accident Kay had accepted that her children needed her to be in a stable marriage, regardless of how unsatisfactory that marriage had become. But even with such clear thinking she did not find it easy seeing Graham every day. If anything she was coming to love him all over again; spending so much time in each other's company it would have been impossible not to. Sometimes she found herself comparing it to being on a rack, the emotional screws tightening a little more each day and Kay assumed that once Nicholas left the hospital to recuperate at home Graham's visits to the hospital would cease. This did not happen, however, and she began to realize how seriously he took his commitment to his daughter, assiduously visiting her each day and thoughtfully bringing her a good supply of drawing paper and pencils to keep her from becoming bored. When Kay remarked on how good at drawing Dervla was becoming, she heard the pride in his tone as he quietly affirmed,

'Yes, I'm happy to say that she has inherited this gift from her grandmother.'

Judy also visited the little girl, despite her earlier fall from grace she loved the little girl, doted on her from the beginning. 'Darling, so good to see you,' anxious to make amends. 'I've been worried out of my mind about you,' keeping hold of the hot little hand. 'What a dreadful ordeal. I heard you were terribly brave. Never mind who told me,' entrancing the wide-eyed child. 'I so *wanted* to come and see you but I was given strict instructions to keep away until you were strong enough for visitors.'

Judy hugged the ecstatic child, aware her emotional breakup with Graham and backlog of work on the High Court appeal had prevented her visiting sooner. Aware too, her engagement to the Chief Executive when eventually announced had caused quite a stir at the airport. Since the first sighting of her huge diamond, the number of carats in the fabulous solitaire had steadily increased with each retelling.

Now she asked Dervla, 'Was it very scary, darling and would you fly again?' Then seeing the child's expression she said quickly, 'Not fair... not fair! Sorry, pet,' but Dervla gravely considered the question,

'Yes, I would, Judy, if Nicky was flying the plane. I always feel safe with him,' and Judy was struck by the unwavering faith in those big dark eyes.

Florrie had paid her godchild a visit too, appalled at what had happened, and bringing board games - Ludo and Snakes and Ladders and colouring books. She played several games, letting Dervla win, not always intentionally, for like Judy she was somewhat distracted these days have finally broken up with Brian and taken up again with Danny McCarthy, who it appeared had never stopped thinking of her all this time. The relationship was beginning to look like it was serious. When Kay heard, she was really glad for Florrie's sake; she had always liked the sound of Danny and her friend seemed so much happier with the controlling Brian gone from her life.

When the day came at last for Dervla to be discharged from hospital Graham made a point of being there early, even before Kay, wanting to make his goodbyes to the child on his own, and when the nursing sister told him, 'We are all going to miss your little daughter, such a lovely child,' he felt elated at this, not so mistaken, assumption. He felt sad too, at the inevitable ending to the enjoyable visits shared with this child he had come to love. Kay too, was conscious of sadness as the trio stood making their goodbyes, seeing from the melancholy look in Graham's eyes as they touched cheeks that he was just as sad over the termination of their special association. Dervla, of course, he hugged hard, releasing all his pent-up feelings in that prolonged embrace, laughing to cover his emotion as he was hugged back every bit as enthusiastically. And then with a toot on the horn he was gone, leaving Kay to follow him more sedately on to the motorway.

***

Kay found it difficult to adequately express how happy she was at having Dervla back home again and the stress of the past few weeks finally over. The doctor continued to be pleased with the little girl's progress, not, however, to the point of agreeing to let her go back to school. Dervla was disappointed, she had been so sure she could get around him. Earlier, with devious intent, she had crayoned a picture for him of a rather stern-looking, white-coated feline with his stethoscope about his neck and the caption 'Puss Doc at work'. But beyond having a good laugh at his portrait, and rather flatteringly asking if he might take it home to show his family, he had not relented.

'Next visit, Dervla,' he said firmly, but with a smile. 'We'll see then.'

'Oh, if only he'd let me, Mummy,' she cried. 'I'd work so hard Sister would have to make me a class monitor,' glowing with the zeal of the converted.

Kay had chuckled at her scheming, but on hearing Eileen's dour comment, 'The path to hell is paved with good intentions,' she had set about praising Dervla as if she had already secured this distinction and seen the way her mother-in-law's expression darkened. But then Eileen was not in good form. Since returning from her fortnight's convalescence she had made one or two disagreeable remarks in Kay's presence about the way things were run in her son's house, even going so far as to suggest that moving in with them had been a mistake. She found fault all the time with Dervla, continually bringing up the subject of the accident and scolding her for deceiving her parents. In her grandmother's opinion Dervla was every bit as guilty as if she had lied outright about the Zoo trip, and to Kay's dismay this was Dave's sentiment too.

When the time came to return to work Kay was unhappy about leaving her little girl in her grandmother's care, but glad to be back flying again for it proved to be a distraction from the worsening friction between herself and Dave. These days neither of them saw to eye over the disciplining of Dervla, although in Kay's opinion that was too strong a word, but not in Dave's, determined to impress upon the child the folly of her ways. Kay could not ignore the frequency of the nightmares disrupting Dervla's sleep or the stammer she had developed in her father's presence and attributed it to his over strict attitude. But when she said so, he brushed it aside.

'That's nonsense! I'm merely trying to ensure the safety of our children.'

'Safety is one thing,' Kay agreed. 'But we don't want to make her so scared that she's afraid to go anywhere.'

'Given Dervla's wilful character the chances of *that* happening are negligible,' he said dryly. 'She is far too fond of getting her own way. From now on she'll do what she's told and there will be no more pandering to her.'

Kay was struck silent at this unflattering portrait of their child. One of Dervla's most endearing characteristics was her sense of fun, her all embracing love of life and people, qualities that Graham had been quick to appreciate from the start. Her own promise to contact Graham made on the day that Dervla was discharged from hospital, continued to weigh heavily on her. She was very much aware of his rights as a father and knew there could be no going back to the way things had been before the accident. But although she went to the phone a number of times she never got around to making the call, too conscious of being overheard by Dave, or Eileen who was always hovering, hoping to hear something incriminating.

More than ever Kay found herself worrying about the effect of their unhappy household on Dervla, still nervous and traumatised after all she had been through, and she counted the days until the doctor would allow her back to school. She also tried to make allowances for Eileen who was finding her convalescence difficult and refused to exercise her new hip on the grounds it was too painful. She sat about all day and in the evening took to joining them in front of the television, sitting in Dave's favourite chair and not budging until the television station had closed down for the night. In retaliation, Dave went out most evenings and returned late having had a few drinks. With his mother retired to bed he would often open a bottle of wine or pour himself more whisky at which point Kay would leave him to it and go to bed herself. And then, at the tea table one evening, Eileen dropped her bombshell.

'I've said it before and I'm saying it again. I'm tired staying where I'm not wanted. Just as soon as I can find somewhere to live I'm leaving!'

Kay could not understand why Dave got so upset. If the woman wanted to go, she thought, why not let her? But her husband just kept trying to reason with his mother until at last, with his shoulders bowed, he had given up and gone out to drown his sorrows. The phone call later from Breda set the seal on it.

'You'd better believe it, Kay. Ma's very unhappy living with you and she wants to move out.'

When Kay passed on Breda's message Dave looked positively ill. 'For crying out loud, Kay. She can't mean it,' slumping, ashen-faced. 'You must have said something to upset her.'

'No, I didn't!' Kay was astonished, his mother was an impossible woman, only a hypocrite could pretend to be sorry she was leaving. 'Look, it's not the end of the world,' she tried to cheer him. 'Maybe it's for the best. She could get an apartment in one of those complexes for the elderly, and still have enough money to live comfortably. Anyway, she'll probably change her mind,' only praying she wouldn't.

'You don't understand...she can't go,' Dave croaked. 'My mother *has* to stay!' It was then he told her what he had done.

'But...but it wasn't your money to take,' Kay was shocked. 'How could you!'

'I was going to put it back. Anyway, that money will eventually be mine, you know that. Whatever Ma has will come to myself and Breda.'

Not if she discovers what you've done, Kay thought dubiously. 'Look, maybe if you were to tell her the truth...'

'Are you mad!' Dave's head shot up and he glared at her. 'Don't you go saying anything to her. It would kill her if she knew.'

Kay doubted that. But she knew it would kill Dave to be toppled off the pedestal his mother had placed him on since his childhood.

***

Graham was missing the little girl terribly. He was very concerned to know how Dervla was recovering after the accident. As the weeks passed, he kept hoping that he would get the promised phone call from Kay, if only to let him know whether the doctor had allowed the little girl to go back to school yet. But so far she had not rung.

He kept remembering conversations that he and Dervla had shared at the hospital and knew that he would never forget the time he had hugged her goodbye at the end of a visit and she said wistfully, 'I like it when you do that. My Daddy never kisses me,' and wondered how anyone could possibly withhold affection from such a lovely child. Was it because the man suspected that she might not be his? It was the only explanation that Graham could see for such unnatural behaviour. And then he found himself wondering how his own sons would react when they learned the truth. Nicholas was fond of Dervla but how would Jeremy feel about having her as his sister? The more Graham thought about it the harder it was to tell them about his past indiscretion knowing that was the way his sons would regard it.

The old man sowing his wild oats.

He grimaced at this trivialising of his long-standing love for Kay. And yet he was only being realistic, he knew. The youth of the day might not condemn babies born outside marriage, or the fact that many couples sought happiness with partners other than their spouses, but his sons looked up to him and were bound to be shocked.

At last, knowing he could not put off the moment any longer, he prepared the way for the disclosure by inviting Jeremy to join himself and Nicholas for dinner one evening, choosing fillet steaks and a good bottle of burgundy to accompany the meal. All went according to plan. With the truth out in the open at last, Graham gained certain comfort from Nicholas's joyful reaction to the news that he had a little sister and that she was, in fact, Dervla of whom he was already so fond.

'Well, well, Dad,' Nicky shook his head amazed, and then he smiled. 'I suppose I should have guessed. Somehow I felt as though I knew her all my life. So that's what it was! We're related.' His smile was full of wonder.

'You can't be serious, Dad,' Jeremy burst out. 'Do you mean to say that child ...the little girl we pulled out of the wreckage...she's your *daughter?*' And then, 'She's how old? Ten, eleven? I mean this didn't happen yesterday.'

Graham regarded his eldest son thoughtfully, thinking he would not care to be a young cadet being interrogated by Commdt. Jeremy Pender, and told him crisply,

'No, it didn't! Suffice to know it did happen and I'm telling you now!' which effectively ended the discussion.

All in all, it had gone better than he feared.

Coming away from the canteen some days later Kay was deep in unhappy thought, her mind taken up with problems, still trying to come to terms with Dave's shocking disclosure and Breda's upsetting phone call. The reason for much of her husband's distraction and ill-humour over the months had become clear and while originally Kay's heart had leapt at the thought of Eileen living elsewhere, she had soon realized this was impossible, not with her money tied up in stock and they in debt to the bank. It worried Kay that there might be other debts that Dave had not told her about and she was just thinking what a sorry mess their affairs were in when she heard a voice calling out a friendly, 'Whoa there!' and with a shock of happy surprise saw who it was she had almost bumped into.

'Graham!' she exclaimed 'How nice to see you.'

'And you,' he smiled. 'Have you time for coffee?'

'Well, I've just come from the canteen,' Kay hesitated, and he said quickly, 'That's okay. We might take a stroll instead.'

Even as he spoke, Graham was steering her towards a private walkway behind the MacDoolAer building, not overlooked by windows. On reaching the stone bench, he removed his jacket and spread it out for her.

'You don't have to do that,' she protested, patting the warm stone

'Go on,' he urged. 'Might as well be comfortable,' and she lowered herself down, momentarily distracted by the fact the cloth still retained heat from his body.

'How is Dervla? Tell me! I can't help worrying, you know.'

Kay hesitated, longing to share the burden and confide her worry that the troubled home atmosphere was delaying the child's recovery, but unable to bring herself to speak of Dave's harsh attitude.

'Kitty!' Graham said quietly. 'Come back to me.'

Kay coloured at the ambiguity of this remark, and seeing him regarding her with furrowed brow and overcast look, realized he was imagining the worst.

'Well, the doctor seemed pleased enough at Dervla's last check-up but...' she said carefully, 'but the atmosphere at home is a bit tense at present.'

'But why so tense?' Graham frowned. 'I would have thought it would be a lot lighter if only from the relief of having her home safe and sound.'

'I'm afraid it's all a bit complicated,' Kay said unhappily. 'Dave is still very angry at her deception.'

Seeing Graham's thunderous expression she shivered. 'It's just that he's anxious it shouldn't happen again. That's why he's making such a big thing of it.'

'For God's sake, Kay! You surely don't mean to say he's continuing to blame the child after all she's been through. What kind of man is he! She was nearly killed, she could be dead and buried right now.'

'I'd better go,' Kay said miserably. How could she expect him to understand what she could not understand herself, just how cruel and hateful Dave was being. 'Maybe this wasn't such a good idea,' she got to her feet.

Graham stayed her with his hand. 'Please don't go yet,' he pleaded, his anger evaporating. 'You haven't told me anything about our little girl,' emphasizing the pronoun while gently stroking her hand. As if to claim ownership of her too, Kay swallowed, feeling suddenly dizzy.

'I'm very conscious of her birthday coming up,' Graham was saying, 'I'd like to give her something special to mark this first birthday I have ever been aware of.'

But actually, it was more than that, he wanted to give thanksgiving in some special way for this tenth birthday his daughter had come so close to *not* having

Slowly Kay sank down again. 'Do you know I had forgotten,' she confessed. 'Can you believe that?' And looking into his eyes, she said in altered tones. 'Has it really been ten years? No, even longer,' and he knew that she was referring to the last time they had made love.

They fell silent, each remembering how it had been and, in the intimacy of the moment, Graham asked quietly, 'Am I going to be able to see her regularly, Kitty?' It was a question burning his brain for weeks and he really needed to know the answer.

Kay was moved by the entreaty but helpless in the face of it. Was it to be a lifetime sentence, this long drawn-out punishment for loving him, she agonized, and was Dervla to suffer because of it too?

In that moment she made up her mind.

'Yes, of course you are, Graham,' she told him firmly. 'Just give me time to sort something out. Okay?' And felt her heart lifting at his evident joy.

Kay was determined that nothing must be allowed to prevent the little girl from enjoying precious moments with her father and she agreed to celebrate Dervla's tenth birthday at the Zoo with Graham, all three of them together. Graham had booked lunch in the members dining-room and hinted at all kind of surprises that he had in store for them. Kay entered into the fun, was even the one to suggest that she accompany them, although this had not originally been her intention.

At home the tension had not eased nor had Eileen changed her mind about leaving. Dave had revealed that he had gone back to his old neighbourhood to visit his mother's bosom friend, confident that May would talk sense into Eileen.

'She'll get around Ma if anyone can.'

'Wouldn't place too much hope on that,' Kay said honestly, his mother was still determinedly repulsing all overtures. 'Strikes me she's set her heart on going.'

Getting dagger-looks in return, she realised that she should have kept her opinion to herself. By soliciting May's help, Dave was merely revealing how desperate he was to keep his mother from learning the truth. But then if she had misappropriated Eileen's money, Kay mused dubiously, she would probably be every bit as desperate.

Now strolling in the sunshine on Dervla's birthday, Kay could almost feel jealous of the rapport between Graham and the child, the way the little girl was coaxing him closer to the cages, encouraging him to toss peanuts to the monkeys.

'Hey, what about that notice over there, young lady?' Captain Pender protested, his dark brows drawing together in a mock frown. 'Doesn't it say no feeding the animals?' But the next moment he was tolerantly offering to 'keep nix' while Dervla indulged them on the sly.

Watching them, Kay wished that she could video-tape the day to remind herself of the amazing difference in Dervla when away from the repressive home atmosphere. She was a changed person, happy and mischievous, the way a child had every right to be. Kay wished that she could always be like that and felt a mixture of sadness and joy.

When it was time to have lunch, Graham firmly steered Dervla away from the snake house towards the restaurant, saying, 'We'll visit them later. I'd like to keep my appetite.' Kay's sentiments exactly! 'I could eat a monkey or two though,' he admitted, drawing an appreciative yelp from the little girl.

'Or maybe even a tasty rhino. What do you say, Derry?'

Derry! Kay was startled. When had he started calling her that?

'Ugh! I don't think so.' Dervla wrinkled her nose and giggled. 'But I'm starving too. I was too excited to eat any breakfast, wasn't I, Mummy?'

Kay hugged her. 'I'll say! Half a triangle of toast and two sips of orange juice. Let's go eat, darling. You're not the only one skipped breakfast.'

'There's a pair of you in it,' Graham chuckled. 'Okay, it's agreed. After lunch we'll go see the seals and next whatever the birthday girl wants to look at.'

'Don't forget the otter,' Dervla said excitedly. 'I just love the way he disappears into the pipe then comes whooshing down the slide.'

'Oh, I don't think I've seen that particular trick. Okay, we'll take in the otter first thing after lunch.' Graham held open the restaurant door. 'After you, Madam.'

With the rest of the afternoon satisfactorily mapped out Dervla confidently followed the waiter to their table and perched on the chair he pulled out for her.

'You must love working in the Zoo,' she said chattily. 'Fab seeing the animals any time you want.'

'Quite makes my day.' He winked at Kay. 'Especially, the two-legged ones!'

Lunch was a great success, finishing up with Dervla's favourite Black Forest Gateau carried to their table by a waiter, ablaze with ten candles. Once she had made her wish and blown them out, Graham had produced the birthday gift.

'Nicky's idea really,' he admitted, revealing it was a family trip to Disneyland, with flight tickets and accommodation for four in a Howard Johnston for one week.

If Kay had not already loved him, she would have been totally won over by Graham's kindness to the child that day.

'Should be a great trip,' he said, meeting Kay's grateful glance. 'I don't mind admitting how much I'd like to be going with you.'

Kay had been thinking the same thing herself and veiled her eyes, almost wishing that something would prevent Dave from accompanying them so that Dervla might experience this special birthday gift in the manner intended. And then, feeling guilty at entertaining such thoughts, she raised her eyes to see the elderly woman in the woolly hat wildly waving at her.

'Kay, I thought it was you.' The screechy voice was vaguely familiar but Kay had no idea whom the gaunt, pale-faced woman could possibly be, and then, as she spoke again, she recognised her mother-in-law's friend.

'It's May, isn't?' Struggling with her dismay, Kay was aware of Graham greeting May's companion who could only be the housekeeper he had mentioned from time to time. Smiling, he had stopped to chat to her.

'I see you had the same idea as ourselves, Rita.'

'Well, you know what they say, Captain Pender. Great minds think alike,' she chuckled, with a sidelong glance at Kay. 'I don't know when I last set foot in the Zoo. Second childhood, I suppose. Next thing I'll be getting out my bucket and spade and going paddling.' She laughed heartily, as Dervla, finding they were no longer following, came running back.

'Mummy, Mummy! Come and see the otter,' she cried, tugging at Graham's hand too. 'Come quick before he disappears again.'

'All in good time.' Graham laughed good-naturedly, but with a cautious glance in May's direction, the woman was staring at him as though he had two heads.

May averted her gaze. Real ladies man, she judged, and he chatting away so friendly-like to Rita. 'How's it going, Kay?' she asked, and seeing the stiff smile pasted on the young woman's face, took in the situation. 'Ah, would you come on outa that, Rita,' she cried, 'an' not be standing around gassing all day.'

Yanking her surprised friend by the arm, she hurried her away thinking that maybe Eileen had good reason for wanting to leave her son's house, and maybe she might be wiser not to get herself involved with any of it.

***

Graham was relieved to find the chance encounter with the women had not altered Kay's decision to allow Dervla to meet him on a regular basis, nor dissuade her from sometimes accompanying the child on the outings. Although pleased and relieved, he could not help wondering if it would actually be feasible. As he had suspected, Rita's companion had turned out to be a close friend of Kay's mother-in-law, and despite Kay's apparent calm handling of the meeting, her fraught expression continued to haunt him. In the meantime there was the worry her husband might get to hear about the encounter. Graham resolved to have a discreet word with his housekeeper; in short to warn Rita to be careful of what she said to her friend, if it was not already too late! Of course, he did not have the same fear of discovery as Kay, the only thing Graham feared was losing Kay herself. Indeed, he would have actually welcomed exposure if it had somehow brought him his heart's desire. But even that pleasure he would have gladly eschewed if it meant that Kay or the child might suffer in consequence.

The need for discretion was on Kay's mind too, as they neared home. 'It might be better not to say too much in front of Daddy or your grandmother,' she warned the child, struck by how often lately she seemed to be issuing that warning. 'It was quite a treat, wasn't it, and Captain Pender so kind.'

'Yes, I had a lovely day,' Dervla agreed enthusiastically. 'It was my best birthday ever and he's my nicest and best uncle ever. Amn't I lucky!'

Kay did not contradict her, for he was the nicest and the best.

But really there was no need to put Dervla on her guard for she had already learned for herself in a most painful manner how angry her Daddy became at any mention of pilots. Although clearly over the moon after the wonderful birthday treat and equally wonderful birthday present, she knew better than to jeopardise future meetings with Graham and Nicky, and solemnly told her mother, 'My lips are sealed,' making Kay smile, if a little sadly, at the lengths they must go to maintain the peace.

But if Dervla was discouraged from talking before her father she could at least confide in her sister, and Sinead proved to be a willing, if slightly envious, listener.

'Oh, you are lucky, Derry,' she said, examining the flight tickets to Florida. 'Imagine! To be going to Disneyland. What a fab birthday present!' But she cheered up when Dervla pointed out the tickets were nost just for herself but for the whole family.

'All of us, Sinead,' Dervla said firmly. 'Mummy, Daddy, *you* and me. Oh, just think of the fun we're going to have.'

As the little girls hugged each other, Dervla thought how wonderful if she could openly take delight in this great birthday gift, and even better if Graham could go with them to Disneyland. How great that would be.

*** *

The High Court appeal was scheduled to take place at the end of May, and after enduring three tough days of questioning at the hands of the airline's lawyers, morale amongst the married hostesses was at its lowest. Was it any wonder some of them hesitated or stammered under pressure, Judy thought dismayed, and some of them had even begun contradicting their earlier statements.

By contrast the Union reps were blessed with total recall and seemingly possessed of photographic memories as well, regarding times and dates.

Between sessions, Judy did her best to bolster the spirit of the hostess body, encouraging them to keep a positive and optimistic outlook. But it was not really surprising when it came to the summing up that anxiety was their chief sensation.

That last evening they parted company in subdued fashion and went home to await the verdict with a feeling of anti-climax that was even worse this second time around. They were all aware with the judge's decision there could be no more appeals, they would just have to accept her ruling and make the best of it. Some of the hostesses were even beginning to bitterly regret having entered so wholeheartedly into the business of defending their corner, aware their disappointment would be proportionate to all the effort and belief they had invested in their fight for justice. The more philosophical amongst them consoled themselves with the thought that at least they had had the guts to bring their grievance into the open and make management sit up and take notice. These were the married hostesses who made a thing of congratulating each other in *not* having cravenly withdrawn their accusations, even when it had provoked management into petty retaliation.

'By taking it to court we sent a clear message to the Ciaras and Barbaras and all the other bullies like them that we are *not* prepared to take such treatment lying down,' they told each other. 'So let them not even *think* of trying it on again.'

Fighting words which proved small consolation next day on hearing that the judge had ruled against them on several counts. This was the deeply disappointing outcome to their legal action against the airline, much as Judy had earlier suggested it had to do with timing. It seemed had they only spoken out on the matter of unfair discrimination, not just months but years earlier, it would have made all the difference. In short, they had lost their case by having put up with the intolerable situation for too long. According to the Equality act passed some five years earlier they would need to have lodged their complaint within six months of the passing of the act or, perhaps, within six months of the commencement of the abuse; no one really understood the intricacies of the case, only that they had been unfairly treated once again.

In her ruling the judge said that any other cases of abuse or unfair discrimination that occurred subsequent to the present hearing would, of course, be reviewed. Which was a fat lot of use, they all agreed, what they wanted was for the present injustice to be put right, not some hypothetical future abuse. And without a doubt, the sceptics agreed, that *too* was on the cards. As someone dourly commented, 'Once a victim always a victim.'

Judy was aware of the dejection in the restroom and was debating on whether to allow them more time to get over their disappointment before addressing them, when Beattie arrived at her door, determined on carrying out her own post-mortem.

'*Gott in himmel*! Just who do those people think they are!' her anguished cry.

Oh dear! Judy sighed, sitting back and letting Beattie have her head, but not for long, she vowed, and soon found herself flinging up a protesting hand. 'Yes, yes Beattie, I understand how you feel. Believe me, I'm just as upset as you over the high court decision. So very disappointing.'

Now it struck Judy that Beattie had been totally unprepared for defeat. Much of her anger was directed at Barbara Brennan whom she seemed to believe had used her wiles on the irreproachable Maeve Rogerson, S.C. and somehow 'got' to her.

'Nonsense!' Judy protested. 'Rogerson is an extremely able barrister with an impeccable reputation.'

'That Brennan has ways of making people to do her will,' Beattie said darkly.

'Well, it's true Barbara is ruthless but it's preposterous to even think such a thing!' Judy sighed, convinced disappointment had derailed Beattie's mind.

Kay was every bit as disappointed as her married colleagues, like them she had centred her hopes on Rogerson obtaining a judgement in their favour.No one could avoid noticing Brennan's ill-concealed triumph as she passed in and out of the restroom, accompanied by her supporters, 'Jolly tough luck!' she called out, with a big smirk, annoying them all with her burnished tan and unmistakable air of having had a fantastic holiday. 'Too bad it went against you!' as if she had not worked overtime to bring it about.

It would have afforded them some small satisfaction had they been present in the airport bar that evening where Brennan and her cronies repaired to make the most of their victory, the gin fairly flowing. But to Barbara's chagrin Tommy Cleary had failed to appear. This time he has gone too far! she raged. But in Captain Brennan's opinion it was his daughter Babs who had gone too far, turning up at the house each evening to give gloating descriptions of the opposing counsel's relentless battering of the already battered married hostesses, boisterously slapping his arthritic shoulder,

'We've as good as won, Pops. Nothing...but *nada* can save them now!'

It was then John Brennan, goaded beyond endurance, had decided he could no longer await divine retribution, the time had undoubtedly come to drop a word in the right ear and, by God, drop it he damned-well would!

As a result of his direct intervention, one married Union head was not to be seen out on this particular night celebrating with a certain aggressively suntanned air hostess, nor for that matter on any other night either.

***

Early June there was the Celtic Airways gala ball to cheer the air hostesses and take their minds of the failed High Court appeal. The ball was held to mark the 35th anniversary of the airline since flight operations had commenced at Dublin Airport. Judy's time was busily taken up preparing for the event and she relaxed somewhat once the gilt-edged invitations had been sent out. On the guest list there were some illustrious names of former pilots and members of the management board dating back to those far-off pioneering days, it promised to be a very glamorous and nostalgic night.

Thankfully, the excitement generating at the prospect of the forthcoming jubilee was doing its work and lifting the spirits of the air hostesses in general and the married hostesses in particular. At least on this occasion Judy could ensure that the married hostesses would be favoured over their unwed colleagues, each one allowed to bring a guest, presumably spouses, and maybe even children over a certain age. The latter had still to be confirmed but Judy had already indicated to Kay that Dervla would be most welcome. But although Kay had nodded and smiled she had no intention of bringing Dervla, not unless it was made clear beforehand that all the other married hostesses could bring a child too; there had been enough talk already of favouritism since word had leaked about her new appointment. The official announcement would be made on the night of the ball, Judy assured Kay when the Super summoned her to her office to request a favour. Another one, thought Kay dubiously.

'It has to do with Dervla,' Judy said, making Kay ask the silent question when ever did it not. 'It would make me very happy, Kay, if you would allow her to be a flower girl at my wedding. I do hope you will say yes.'

'But of course!' Kay said faintly. 'How lovely!'

'Splendid!' Judy beamed. 'And her dress...I was thinking wild silk...a ruched bodice, perhaps, with a very full skirt...long... and with an apricot sash and matching slippers. Quite lovely, with those dark eyes and rose complexion.' And then it seemed she had another outing much closer in mind, some fashion show. 'Little girls do so adore pretty clothes. Actually, it's rather a special night,' Judy admitted coyly. 'It will be the first showing of the summer bridal collection, the very latest gowns from our own couturiers as well as London and Paris. All very glam, I assure you, so do let her wear her prettiest frock.'

Again Kay weakly nodded, if Judy had suggested taking Dervla on the honeymoon it would not have surprised her. She decided to say nothing about the wedding to Dervla until later, and was in two minds about giving Dave an invite to the reception knowing how he felt about her job. Besides she would enjoy it far better on her own. But in the end she relented and left it on the hall table.

Drawing ii out of the envelope he said, 'Your big moment, Kay, your new appointment made official. I'm quite looking forward to it.'

'You are?' She was unable to hide her surprise.

'Why wouldn't I be? I'm proud of you, Katie.' He seemed unusually pleased with her, affectionate too, as he squeezed her waist on the way to the sink to get himself a glass of water. Had he been drinking?

'Not every day my wife lands an exciting new job. Good pay and even better prospects,' Dave chuckled. 'Might even take early retirement,' convincing her that he must have indulged in a few. But then she realised it could be that in his own fashion Dave actually *was* proud of her, and she scolded herself for her suspicions.

There was a buzz of excitement on the night of the ball and great glamour and style amongst the hostesses, not only the present air girls but former high fliers, even those more mature ones still managing to retain vestiges of former glamour and good looks, despite long hours on the golf course. Amy Curtis, former Hostess Superintendent, was present, of course, looking a little older but still mobile.

With his southern twang Taylor Duval was quick to compliment all the air hostesses in his welcoming speech, 'Here's to all you lovely stews out there in your glamorous gowns,' before turning to Judy with his expansive smile. 'And now, folks, I have pleasure in handing you over to the queen of 'em all, Miz Judith Mathews, your Hostess Superintendent,' retiring to his seat amidst much applause.

Beforehand, Kay and Dervla had been required to take part in a photo shoot. It had been Judy's idea that Kay should wear uniform complete with the traditional flat airline cap, and that the child, also wearing an airline cap, should be snapped mid-cabin offering her mother a drink. The notion was a bit contrived for Kay's taste but she had good-naturedly gone along with it. At least the Super had not suggested that she and Dervla sit in a huge jet engine, swinging their legs, like other air hostesses were required to do in earlier years. The photographer was a professional with a job to do, polite but firm, and Kay could not fault him although vastly irritated by the amount of shots he insisted on taking. Privately, she wished he would go annoy someone else but suppressed her impatience, reminding herself this was Dervla's moment too. Of course, the photographer was aware of Kay's irritation but he had been told how important these mother and daughter pictures were in the scheme of things and was determined to make a good showing.

'That about wraps it up,' he eventually told Dervla. 'You've been a real trouper,' winking at Kay. 'Miss World next stop! '

Kay had had to laugh, and with the easing of tension she and Dervla exchanged smiling glances. 'He was nice, Mummy,' Dervla passed benign judgment, catching hold of her mother's hand. 'Can we please go talk to Judy now?'

'Sure,' Kay smiled. 'Just let me change into mufti first.' She had bought herself a new black dress with a beaded jacket and giving herself a quick critical glance in the powder room mirror, decided she would do.

'Mummy will Graham be here?' Dervla was asking.

'Oh yes, and your Daddy too,' although not too sure of the latter, business as usual taking first call. 'Come on! Let's go see can we spot them.'

Joining the group around the Super, Kay was reminded of Dave's phone call earlier. Apparently, the bankers were over from London and an impromptu meeting had been called before they drove to Cork. Dave would be taking the early train next morning to meet up with them, and complete his business. At present he was taking them on a tour of the factory and not sure what time he would be free to join her at the airport. 'Sorry!' he said, sounding genuinely regretful. 'I know this means a lot to you...but if I don't make it on time good luck with everything.'

'Don't worry. I understand,' Kay assured him, but she had felt a bit cheated all the same. It was not every day she was being singled out in this way, she told herself. One's husband *should* make an effort to be there.

Kay forgot Dave as her eye was caught by the sight of three more pilots entering the crowded room, Graham amongst them. Dervla tugged at her hand, suddenly shy.

'Look Mummy,' she whispered. 'There's Graham. Do you think he sees us?'

'Later, darling,' Kay gave her a little push towards Judy, suddenly shy herself at the sight of him. All at once she found herself wishing that Dave would *not* come, it would leave her so much freer. To do what she wasn't sure.

As Dervla twirled about showing herself off to Judy and some of the married hostesses, enjoying all the compliments on her new dress, Kay caught sight of Graham pushing his way purposefully in their direction. On reaching them, he laughingly swung Dervla up in his arms and Kay caught her breath in sudden anxiety, convinced everyone present must mark the resemblance between them. She glanced down, unwilling to meet anyone's eye, telling herself she was probably imagining it.

Dave thought the bankers would never finish up their business and leave. They lingered in the factory examining all the equipment and insisting on speaking to the different machinists. Dave had already introduced the supervisor and the foreman and the bankers had been brought through to the cutting room and anywhere else they expressed an interest in, chatting to the quality controller who went to great lengths to describe the work in progress and which styles and materials were proving most popular this season. Diligently, they had produced the order books to view advance orders, the demand for certain materials and their due delivery date. It should have been enough but the bankers then progressed to the engineers wanting to be given a run down on the age, function and life expectancy of each set of machines. As more time passed, Dave grew increasingly impatient. Would they never stop putting questions? He began fretting over the delay aware that Friday evening traffic would be building up and his chances of making the reception on time growing less. Maybe Kay' s speech would be the last one on the agenda, he thought, he could almost have recited it by heart having heard her practicing for days. Well, despite everything he was determined to put in an appearance, it was better to arrive late than not at all. So with an effort, he bit down on his tongue and kept a tight hold on his temper.

At last the two men were ready to leave and got into their rented Ford Cortina saying, 'See you in Cork tomorrow, David. 11 o'clock sharp. We're booked on the 4.15 to London and we have a lot to get through before then.' As if he didn't know! But he smiled and nodded. 'Look forward to it. See you then.'

'Oh Dave, have you a moment?' Tony detained him.

'Sure,' Dave's heart sank, it could only be about the money he owed him.

Some months earlier, he had been desperate enough to mention to Tony how he needed to sell shares in order to buy some prime property he had put his eye on, and his boss had shown extreme displeasure. Nearer the truth had been that Dave was in arrears on the bank loan and the outstanding household bills. It was only recently, with Eileen pressing him to find her a house, that he saw the irony.

'Out of the question, Dave,' Tony had said sternly. 'How do you think it will look if a company director puts his shares on the market? Well, I'll tell you. Not good, not good at all.' It was then he had suggested giving Dave a personal loan to tide him over and Dave had grasped it thankfully. But now payment was overdue.

'No problem. All be sorted by the end of the week,' he assured his boss, and could see by his dubious expression that Tony did not believe him.

Driving fast for the airport Dave was gloomily aware there was no way he could pay back the loan. To make matters worse the stock he had invested in had not done well. Oh hell, he sighed, knowing he was terribly late. Still, he kept on going, wishing he had not drunk so much wine at lunch.

Kay thankfully surrendered the microphone as the applause burst out and stepped to where Florrie awaited her with a welcome glass of bubbly in her hand.

'Great speech, you've earned this, Kay!' she chuckled. 'So you see yourself like a kind of Agony Aunt, do you? Wonder what Judy made of that!'

Kay laughed, thinking that's what her new job would undoubtedly be. Counseling new, and not so junior hostesses, encouraging them to confess their troubles and hopefully help them to put things right. On her way back to where Graham stood holding Dervla's hand and chatting with Ben Higgins, she found herself stopped and congratulated many times. One of the well-wishers was Captain Chris Canavan, an attractive pilot new to CA, with whom she had shared a flight recently.

'Congrats! Kay,' he warmly kissed her cheek.

'Thanks, Chris,' she smiled, recovering herself quickly.

'I hope this new appointment doesn't mean you'll be spending all your time on the ground nurse-maiding those lucky new hosties,' he told her in comic dismay. 'That would be a terrible waste!' and Kay laughed, exhilarated by the look in his eyes.

'Oh, I imagine I'll still be flying a fair bit of the time. Got to keep an eye on them in the air too, you know,' she said, moving on.

'Glad to hear it!' he called after her. 'I'll be watching out for you.'

Nice, Kay thought, wondering if he were married. Not all that old, late thirties, she guessed. All a bit of fun, she thought, elated at having succeeded in getting this plum job, whatever about her colleagues' jibes about favouritism.

'Heartiest congrats! Kitty,' Graham told her warmly, and Dervla hugged her. 'You were terrific, Mummy!'

Meeting their glances, Kay thought this must be the most satisfying part of it, the love and pride she saw glowing in Dervla's dark eyes, and glowing too, in those other dark eyes with such intensity that she had difficulty in breathing.

It was at this precise moment that Dave hurried breathlessly into the crowded ballroom and a sudden shift in the packed assembly revealed his wife laughing up at the handsome white-haired man he had seen at the hospital at the time of Dervla's accident. And then Dave saw that the child was holding the pilot's hand and laughing fondly up at him too, as if he were a very close friend. He stared at them in a daze and his heart pounded in sudden shock as the truth of what he had all along suspected hit him, before the shifting crowd once more hid them from his sight.

***

It was nearing midnight as Kay arrived home from the reception with Dervla. Helping her daughter prepare for bed she was unable to shake off her unease at the unpleasant ending to the evening. With Graham already gone some time earlier, she had made her goodbyes to Judy and left the ballroom with Dervla chatting animatedly by her side. Passing the bar, Kay had happened to glance in the door and been startled to see Dave sitting inside with a glass of whisky in front of him. She was taken aback having long ago given up on him joining her at the reception. Yet here he was. But why hadn't he tried to find her?

'Dave, when did you get here? 'she called, going towards him. 'I was on the lookout for you all evening.'

'Were you?' was all he said, and it was immediately apparent he was very drunk. Deeply disquieted, she suggested that he leave his car at the hotel and come home with them, but he ignored her. Helplessly, she had watched him driving rapidly out of the car park, almost colliding with the entrance posts. Only then did she get into her own car, having first put Dervla into the back for safety.

The little girl had been frightened and tearful, intuitively picking up on the tension between her parents. 'Why is Daddy cross, is it something I did?' she asked plaintively.

'No, no, not at all. He's just not feeling well, that's all. Did you enjoy the night?' she diverted her, and Dervla nodded enthusiastically.

'The best of my whole life, Mummy.'

Now Kay was increasingly aware how late it was and Dave still not home. She should never have let him drive off in the state he was in, she told herself, but knew there was no way she could have stopped him.

Dervla fell asleep the minute she was in bed but Sinead was still awake, and came in to Kay's room to ask how they had got on. Kay was relieved to find her over her earlier upset at not being brought to the reception. Uncharacteristically, she had cried, 'It's not fair, Mummy. Why is Dervla going with you? I'm older than her, it should be me.'

Now it occurred to Kay that maybe she could ask Judy if Sinead might go with Dervla to the fashion show. It would help to make up for her disappointment tonight and when Sinead asked wistfully, 'Was the food lovely?' Kay was pleased to produce the slice of Jubilee cake she had saved for her.

As she tucked into it, Kay glanced at the book her daughter was holding and saw it was 'Tess of the D'Urbervilles.' It was many years since she had read it herself and she knew the story well.

'It's good, isn't it?' She tapped the cover and Sinead, her mouth full of cake, nodded. 'It's sad though, I mean how could Angel Clare blame Tess for what happened with the horrid Alec. It wasn't *her* fault and then to go and leave her like he did and they only married that day.'

Kay sighed, unable to answer her. Kissing her daughter good-night, she went to bed, increasingly worried by Dave's absence. What could have happened to upset him, she wondered, but tired out she was soon asleep. It was only when she awakened some hours later to the quiet sound of his voice in the darkness that she realised what it was all about, and was frightened by the intensity of his tone.

'Katie,' he was saying, his voice full of unshed tears. 'Why did you never tell me Dervla was not my child. What happened to us that you could conceal it from me all these years, leaving me to find it out tonight when I saw the three of you together.'

'No!' he stopped her as she struggled up in the gloom. 'Leave off the light. I just want to know the truth. Let's have no more deceit, no more lies between us.'

And feeling shame and a strange kind of sorrow that she had hurt him so terribly and that anything she was to tell him now would only wound him even further, Kay had put into stark words the whole in-excusable story of her marriage on the rebound, and the subsequent return to life of the man who had totally possessed her heart and whom she had believed dead.

***

Dave's thoughts were tortured as he stared out of the train window next morning on its way to Cork. Never again would he experience happiness or be able to trust another person, he told himself bitterly, reliving the disillusion of Kay's halting confession, the agony of hearing spelled out what he had avoided confronting all these years. He was aware of Anne's stony face opposite as she worked on her report and knew she was still resentful at his coldness towards her that morning, his heart too torn by Kay's searing admission to make any effort to be sociable.

When later Anne went to the washroom to freshen her makeup, Dave worked away on his own report for the bankers, keeping his head down for an hour, only then realising that she had not returned to her seat. Frowning, he told himself she was still sulking over his earlier remark. He set off down the violently swaying train, keeping an eye out for her, aware they still had things to discuss before meeting up with the bankers. He came upon her further down the train, deep in chat with some man, not seeming to notice him as he passed. Typical! Grimly, Dave continued on to the restaurant car, badly needing a drink.

When the train stopped in Thurles and half a dozen bikes destined for the Ras Tailteann in West Cork were labelled and loaded into the guard's van, Dave had almost finished his second whisky. He was aware of the ticket inspector passing his seat, heard him asking the steward to pour him tea. After a moment they were joined by the train driver. Absently, listening to their conversation, Dave heard the driver complaining of having pulled a muscle in his shoulder the evening before while chasing his young fellah over the fence. 'By God! Tis killing me,' he admitted. 'Only for the pain killers I'd be off my head altogether. Barely closed an eye all night.'

You aren't the only one, thought Dave grimly, haunted by the memory of the darkened bedroom, the question he had steeled himself to ask. 'Are you still seeing him, this pilot?' and Kay's hesitant admission, 'Well, yes, I see him from time to time... but only for Dervla's sake.'

For Christ sake! Dave had felt like shouting. Does the child *know* I'm not her father? That would be the last bloody straw. But apparently she did not. He was thankful for that at least knowing that he had not been kind to the little girl in a long time. In a way, he blamed Kay for this. If only she had been more open and honest with him, he agonised, he would never have been so petty as to take it out on Dervla, he would have tried to set aside his resentment and accept her as his own. In the end, he had flung out of the bedroom, ignoring her anguished cry, 'It was over a long time ago. I was never with him again like that...not ever!'

Maybe not, but she had continued to see him nevertheless, Dave told himself miserably. Staring out at the passing landscape, he wanted to put his fist through the glass, knowing the pain would be as nothing compared to his agony just then.

'Really going it, aren't we?' the pleasant-faced woman sipping coffee across the table from him broke into his thoughts. 'We should be on time at this rate.'

'That'll be no harm.' With an effort, he answered her.

She was right though, Dave thought, the train was fairly belting along. His smile grew fixed as she chatted on about her job in textiles but he hardly heard her, his mind still on his wife's betrayal. Oh God! If only it could all be wiped away, if only none of it had ever happened.

He became aware the woman had grown quiet and was watching him with a kindly expression, and then to his surprise she laid her hand briefly on his.

'Forgive me, I can't help noticing how troubled you are. You know sometimes it helps just having someone to listen.'

Dave stared back at her in shock, and then he drew a breath to chill her off with a few well-chosen sentences. But he was suddenly unable to go on, feeling an absurd desire to cry, sudden tears stinging his eyes as he fought desperately for control.

'Let me get you a drink,' she turned tactfully away, saying nothing more until it was before him on the table.

Dave drank the whisky gratefully, and gradually the trembling subsided in his limbs. He supposed it was some kind of delayed shock, coupled with having had so little sleep the night before. 'You are very kind,' he told her. 'I had some rather bad news before coming away and I'm still trying to come to terms with it.'

The woman nodded. 'I thought as much. But look, you don't have to say any more. My name is Maria,' offering her hand.

'Dave!' He shook it briefly, felt obliged to offer some information about himself. 'I suppose I should have seen it coming but I didn't. I blame myself for that.'

'Don't be too hard on yourself. Of course, I don't know the circumstances but often we hold ourselves responsible for actions and events that in reality have their roots in something quite outside our control.'

Dave was surprised at such astuteness. It was true that Kay had married him on the rebound, something he had never wanted to admit to himself, for it was too painful to think she had never loved him like he loved her. But with his rival dead he had believed the danger was past and they could make a life together.

'Can't you begin over again?' Maria said gently. 'It's never too late, you know, or so they say.'

'I'd give anything to believe that but I don't know. I'm afraid I said a lot of things this morning, things that I wish now I'd never said.' Dave was driven to honesty by what he saw in her eyes, neither censure nor judgment only sympathy.

They talked some more. Dave was conscious of the need to finish his report, relieved when she said, 'Look! I'd better be getting back to my seat. Goodbye, Dave. I do hope it works out for you,' holding his hand a moment before releasing it.

'Thanks, Maria, I'm sure it will. Oh, and for the drink...I owe you one.'

She smiled back. 'No, you don't. Take care of yourself.'

Dave waited a few minutes then got to his feet, aware the other passengers were discussing the excessive speed of the train. Lurching towards the door, he almost lost his footing. Maria was right, the train *was* going fast. Too bloody fast, Dave told himself uneasily, and grabbed hold of the seat-back to steady himself.

Anne bid Niall, an old boyfriend, goodbye and went looking for Dave, aware they would soon be in Cork when all at once the speeding train sent her stumbling into a woman coming against her.

'Hey! Sorry!' she muttered. 'The driver must have a hot date,' and heard the woman chuckle, 'Hope it's worth it!'

Not really funny, someone could get hurt, Anne mused, proceeding more cautiously. Suddenly, she spotted Dave through the glass dividing door, his expression anything but sunny. She clung to a seat-back waiting for him to come through. He was in a right mood this morning, she thought, still resentful of his casual treatment of her.

Glancing out of the window as she waited for him to reach her, she saw up ahead the engine and front coaches coming into view. Idly, she noted the way the carriages were veering precariously as they followed the steeply curving track, and with a sudden presentiment of danger her heart began pounding and her hand flew to her mouth in horror. 'No! Oh please. No-o-o!' she whispered.

Dave stretched out his hand to slide across the partition door, when without warning the train shifted violently on the track and flung him off balance. Landing on his back, he lay stunned, unable to move or catch his breath when all at once the train lurched again and he felt the impact as it went ploughing headlong into the embankment. It jumped the rail and there was a hellish, grinding sound, followed by a succession of loud bangs. Trapped and helpless, Dave was aware of the compartment ceiling collapsing, the walls folding in on top of him, and he felt agonising pain in his chest before mercifully losing consciousness.

***

As Kay walked into the convivial atmosphere of the canteen she knew that she had made the right decision to take a lunch break. The first morning on the new job she had spent looking through files, but it was impossible to concentrate. She soon felt the need to be amongst people, if only as a distraction from the guilt and sorrow eating into her.

She had gone to work that morning shocked and remorseful, after a near sleepless night. She and Dave had talked until the first light filtered through the curtains when he had risen grim and white-faced to take the early train to Cork. After he had gone she had lain there feeling utterly wretched, convinced that he would never be able to forgive her for it was not in his nature to condone what he termed her 'immoral' conduct. Arriving at the airport, she had found everyone talking about some RAF pilot who had been shot down three times in the Falklands conflict and survived.

'They are saying he's a hero,' the reserves told Kay. 'Probably get a medal.'

Kay nodded, heartsick and distracted, and went to sit behind her desk in the tiny space partitioned off from the Chief Hostess's office, more of an annexe than a proper workroom, and far too close to Ciara for comfort. Opening a hostess file, she had striven to immerse herself in the details but her troubling talk with Dave kept intruding. She was unable forget the scene in the early hours or the cutting words he had used before rushing off, without giving her a proper chance to explain that she had never strayed again, no matter how great the temptation. If only she had had more time, she might have convinced him. But then honesty kicking in, she admitted that she wouldn't, not if she were given a thousand years. Somewhat naively she had imagined she could get it all over with in one go, confess and be forgiven, start afresh. Crazy, she realised now. There was no quick and easy fix. She had sinned and would have to atone. Oh God! she groaned, hadn't she suffered enough already, more than she had ever believed possible? Bloody awful years knowing she had made a terrible mistake in marrying Dave, and all of it compounded by Graham's miraculous re-entry into her life, another chance for happiness that had come too late.

She glanced at the canteen menu trying to decide between fish and chicken, wondering if she should be bothering with food at all with so little appetite. She glanced up undecided, and caught sight of Ciara purposefully making her way down the table towards her. Oh Lord! Kay's heart sank and she made a valiant effort not to scowl. Last thing she needed was Ciara plonking herself down beside her. But to her surprise the Chief Hostess merely beckoned to her. What in the world? Exasperated by the royal summons, Kay got up and went reluctantly to join her.

Not until they were outside the canteen did Ciara speak, laying a hand on Kay's arm in a strangely sympathetic gesture. 'Kay, there was an urgent phone call for you and I'm afraid it's not good news. You need to ring this number at once,' holding it out to her. 'We'll go back now and you can use my office.'

Kay stared at her stupidly, unable to make sense of what she was saying, struck less by the words than the absence of any self-importance in Ciara's manner. For once, the Chief Hostess seemed genuinely sincere and a terrible foreboding crept over Kay. Oh dear! She began to tremble, convinced now that something had happened to Dervla or Sinead. Panic rising, she almost grabbed the piece of paper and began running back to the hostess office. Almost there, she glanced down and was surprised to see the name and telephone number of Dave's boss. What on earth could Tony want with her, Kay wondered, and why hadn't Dave rung her himself? And then, in her hurt and upset, she thought: Oh, for goodness sake! Holding a grudge like that. How childish can you get!

**

Mid-afternoon, Kay flew in to Cork Airport. Ever since learning that her husband had been involved in a train crash she was in a state of shock. Danny McCarthy was waiting for her in the arrivals hall, Florrie having rung him earlier to request the favour.

'Danny will take care of you,' Florrie had told her at the foot of the aircraft steps, promising to join her in Cork as soon as she could, which was comforting.

So was Breda's offer to pick up the girls from school and to stay overnight at the house, agreeing to hold off telling Eileen for the moment. Everyone was being so nice, Kay thought bleakly, yet she had never felt so alone.

Deep in her thoughts, as Danny drove rapidly along the road to Mallow, she was remembering her fraught telephone conversation with Tony who admitted there had been no word of Dave, only that he was believed to be at the front of the train when it crashed. On learning that Tony had offered to drive Kay to Cork Judy had said immediately, 'Not at all, Kay. You will fly down. I have already booked you on the 3.15. Once you collect your ticket you can be on your way.' She had arranged for tea and sandwiches to be brought to her office, insisting that Kay eat something before leaving. She couldn't have been kinder and Kay had struggled with her tears, afraid if she broke down she would never be able to stop.

All she could think of was the terrible manner in which she and Dave had parted, no matter what she did nothing could ever change that. She became aware of ambulances speeding past them on their way to Cork city and wondered if her husband might be in one of them, or whether he was still in the train wreckage, her mind veering away from the frightening image this conjured up. No point in dwelling on any of it until she really had to. After all, you never knew, she thought, even now he could be somewhere safe, drinking hot tea and soon to tell her how foolish and irresponsible she had been in leaving the girls and his mother and come all this way. And then her mind swung into another scenario in which Dave was pleased and thankful to see her, grateful to know she cared enough to come, ready to forget the appalling night spent in recrimination. On arriving at the site of the crash she and Danny found a wide swathe cut into the earth to facilitate rescue operations. Choosing her steps carefully, Kay followed the big Cork man along the mucky path into the middle of a busy rescue operation, where no one had time to do more than point them on to someone else who might be able to answer their questions.

'Try the St John Ambulance,' a medical orderly paused in the act of bandaging a woman's badly gashed hands. 'They might remember bringing your husband to hospital.'

'I will, thanks!' But after more time spent in fruitless enquiry, Kay looked helplessly at Danny. 'This is getting us nowhere,' she sighed, glancing irresolutely beyond him to where further up the railway line men could be seen clearing the area about the main wreckage. She forced herself to look at the carnage telling herself this was no time to be squeamish. 'Danny, I'm going on over. Maybe those men can tell us if my husband was one of the injured...or ...or dead,' she faltered.

With a blanket wrapped about her, Anne Stack squatted on the ground in the company of other shocked survivors. She looked white and shaken, her eyes huge in her pale face. She had no idea how many hours had passed since their rescue from the train. She only knew that she had gone to pieces long before that had happened, screaming and out of control, until someone had taken her in hand, slapping her face with shocking force and curtly ordering, 'Get a grip on yourself, for God's sake!'

Niall found her there and he had hunkered down to talk to her, his arm in a sling, guessing from her dazed looks she was still shocked and disorientated.

'Thank goodness you're all right.' He gazed at her in concern.

'Your arm...you've hurt your arm,' Anne was finding it strangely difficult to form the sentence.

'Got a bit of a bang but it's nothing.' He made light of it. 'I was sitting way back and, luckily, escaped the worst of the impact. I say, did you ever find him?'

'Find who?'

'Your boss, don't you remember?'

Anne struggled to clear her thoughts. What Niall was saying struck a familiar chord. She stared at him but all at once she was seeing Dave, remembering how he had suddenly appeared at the far side of the sliding door. He had been trying to get to where she was clinging on for dear life to a seat back as the train lurched and rocked.

'Oh, my God!' she whispered, remembering everything. 'Dave!' she whimpered piteously, scrambling awkwardly to her feet, unaware she had grabbed hold of Niall's injured arm. 'Quick... Oh, quick! My boss... Dave.' Her voice rose hysterically. 'He's down there now buried under all that wreckage.'

*****

Another body had been discovered and the muffled cry sounded from the depths of the wrecked train 'This one is still breathing, only just about. We need a doctor here.'

As those at the entry took up the cry, the doctor came hurrying over, with his stethoscope about his neck, and began crawling inside to where the victim lay.

'There's a ton of stuff on top of him, Doc,' sweaty and bare-chested the members of the rescue team made way for him in the cramped, airless space. 'Reckon it's about crushed his chest. Won't know for sure though, not until we dig him out.'

Kay and Danny stood anxiously waiting to hear back from the workman who had gone to make enquiries. 'Thanks for your support, Danny,' Kay told him tremulously, aware she could not have managed without him.

'Tis nothing, Kay. I'm only too glad to help.' He glanced around, becoming aware of voices nearby and saw a couple walking towards them, the man with his arm in a sling, the woman with a bandage about her head. At the same time, the workman reappeared and Kay hurried to meet him.

'Did you find out anything?' she asked fearfully. 'Is my husband in the train?'

'Can't say for sure, Miss. Only that the injured man being brought out any minute now is around the same age as your husband. He's in a bad way, I'm afraid. 'Twill be helpful if you can identify him.'

Kay kept her eyes fixed intently on the stretcher as two men in yellow rescue gear emerged, supporting it between them. In some trepidation, she moved closer and stared hard at the unconscious man, his bruised face partially obscured by the oxygen mask over his mouth and nose.

'Is that your husband, Miss?' the workman was asking, but before Kay could answer the woman with the bandage about her head pushed past them sobbing,

'Oh my God! Oh my God! Dave! Dave!' she cried. 'I didn't mean what I said. I'm sorry, I'm sorry,' leaning over him, her tears falling on his face.

Kay froze where she stood as the woman went on hysterically pouring out endearments, and her head spun with the combined shock of having found her husband at last and this new and unexpected development. And then she realised the woman was familiar to her and recognised Dave's colleague from work. All at once she better understood Dave's moodiness and excessive drinking over the years, and when Kay's head eventually cleared, all of it made sense to her at last.

***

By evening Dave had not regained consciousness. In the hospital's A & E the doctor told Kay, 'We are doing everything we can for your husband, Mrs Mason, but his bloodstream was flooded with toxins when the weight of the wreckage was eventually lifted off his chest. This is a very dangerous situation; elevated levels can lead to kidney failure and cardiac arrest. Despite our best efforts I'm afraid his condition is deteriorating. I think you should prepare yourself.'

Kay felt her knees beginning to shake and her senses cloud. She drank the water the nurse gave her and felt a little better. At the same time, she did not trust herself to get up yet. She looked at the doctor with stricken eyes. 'But...but surely there's something you can do?' she said pitifully. 'I mean he's so young.'

The doctor gazed at her for a moment. 'Mrs Mason are you aware your husband has a heart condition?

'No...no! I didn't know that.' It was one more shocking surprise about a man she had thought she knew all about.

'He is suffering from an enlarged heart, the condition is hereditary, passed on to children from one parent or the other, in some cases it skips a generation. Did your husband's father have this condition, do you know?'

Again Kay shook her head. Maybe he had, she thought, maybe that's why Reggie's death could have been suicide. But the autopsy would have shown the condition of his heart, her thoughts ran on. And if it had, surely Dave would have mentioned it to her. Suddenly, Kay was not so sure, remembering something her husband had said about renewing his life policy, but first needing to reduce his cholesterol and cut down on alcohol.

Could he have known he would not pass the health check?

'Was your husband a heavy drinker?' the doctor was asking. 'We found very high alcohol levels in his blood.'

'Well, he has been under a lot of strain lately,' she defended him, feeling sudden shame. No doubt they knew about his mistress too, she thought bitterly.

338

'Alcohol is the worst thing for a man with congenital heart condition.' The doctor said it mildly but Kay felt he was judging Dave, herself too. Oh God! she mourned, how had her marriage deteriorated to the point when strangers knew more about her husband than she did herself.

It was nearing midnight when Florrie arrived into the A & E having driven straight to Cork on finishing her last duty. She brought with her toiletries for Kay and a change of clothing that Jocelyn, her flatmate, had loaned her, she was about Kay's build and height. By then Kay had phoned Breda and asked her to contact Judy Mathews and see if she would put the girls on a flight to Cork next morning; they would need to come at once if they were to be in time to make their goodbyes to their father. When she spoke to Breda again Kay was relieved to hear it was all arranged and they would be with her by midday.

'That's the plan,' Kay told Florrie tearfully, as they sat huddled together on the uncomfortable seats in the waiting room. About Anne Stack she said nothing, it was all too raw and painful to share with anyone, even Florrie.

Breda was not looking forward to breaking the tragic news to her mother. She got the girls up to bed and packed a few items of clothing into the small overnight case that Kay kept conveniently in her wardrobe, jeans and tee shirts and a sweater each.

'Get some shut-eye now,' she told them. 'I'll wake the pair of you in good time, don't worry.'

Seeing their downcast looks, Breda came back into the room to give them another hug. Reassured, they clung to her. 'Rough and ready Breda,' as Dave styled his sister, had a generous, caring streak and now she felt deeply for her little nieces she loved so much but never, as was her wont, with any great outward show of emotion.

'Chins up,' she braced them. 'Remember you were in a coma, Derv, and look at you now, not a bother on you.' Downstairs again, she said goodnight to her mother deciding to let her have her sleep, and gently closed over her door. It would be time enough to tell her in the morning, she thought, when the girls had left the house, Judy having promised to pick them up and bring them with her to the airport.

In the kitchen she poured herself a generous measure of gin and was just adding the tonic when she heard a sound behind her, and turning saw her godchild standing in the doorway.

'Sinead!' she exclaimed. 'What are you doing downstairs? Are you worrying about your Dad, is that it?'

Sinead shook her head. 'It's Dervla, Auntie Breda, she's crying. I don't know why, she won't tell me.'

'Okay. Let's take her up some cocoa and find out what's bothering her.'

Dervla raised her tear-stained face from the pillow as they came into the room, and began crying again. 'I'm s...sorry, Auntie Breda,' she sobbed. 'But I can't go to Cork tomorrow. I just c...can't. Please don't make me.'

'What is it, Derry?' Could she be afraid of going into the hospital with all the injured people from the train, was that it? 'Of course, you don't have to go if you really don't want to.' Breda stroked the damp curls away from the child's hot forehead. 'I won't make you but your Mum asked for you two especially. You wouldn't want to let her down now, would you?'

'N...no,' whispered Dervla.

'She's down there on her own and don't forget your friend Judy has it all arranged for you to fly to Cork in a big airplane. You're going to love it.'

But Dervla just shook her head frantically under the caressing fingers, and began to sob with a trace of hysteria, making Breda even more anxious.

'Auntie Breda,' Sinead tugged at her blouse. 'I think I know what's the matter. Derry is afraid of flying since the accident. She told me but I've only just remembered. She keeps thinking of the time with Nicky in the plane just before it crashed. That's why she doesn't want to go, that's why she's so upset.'

Oh dear, Breda thought in dismay, if that doesn't rightly mess things up!

***

During the night Dave's heart arrested, the doctors managed to get it going again but he had been down forty minutes and he had to be put on a ventilator. What the prognosis might be they would not know until they had run tests. But at least he was still alive, Kay thought, badly shaken and besieging heaven that he might live until the children arrived. She was glad of Florrie's company and support in the long hours until dawn. Her friend had always been fond of Dave and was very upset now at the rapid deterioration in his condition. Kay wondered what Florrie would think if she knew about Dave's affair - she had always been ready to make excuses for him even at those times when Kay had admitted to being very unhappy, wanting out of her marriage. But although it was the night for confidences, she found that she still was not ready to talk about Anne Stack, and wondered if she ever would be.

As Florrie dozed beside her, Kay's thoughts wandered back to earlier in the evening as she had sat with Dave. She had been reminded of the time following the accident when Dervla had been in a coma and she had hoped her daughter might somehow hear her voice and derive comfort from it. But in the present circumstances Kay's lack of confidence was such that she found herself imagining it was the voice of Anne Stack her husband would want to hear, not hers. At no time could Kay forget the young woman's intimidating presence nor dampen down her anger at the way Anne insisted on hanging about the A & E long after her own injuries had received medical attention. It had been a relief when the young woman's companion had persuaded her to go and get something to eat. Thankfully, she had not returned since.

The sky was paling beyond the dusty windows of the A & E while Kay was still trying to work out in her tired brain just what she would tell the girls when they arrived. Utterly worn out, she fell asleep at last, her head drooping on her chest, and for a time she was blessedly lost to the world and her troubles. Until at eight o'clock Danny came walking into the A & E and woke her and Florrie, suggesting they all go and have breakfast, after which he would check them into a B & B to shower and change. It was a welcome break and Kay was surprised how hungry she felt. On reflection, she realized she had not eaten anything since Judy's tea and sandwiches the afternoon before. In the end all she had was tea and toast, her appetite deserting her as quickly as it had come. Danny dropped her back to the A & E waiting room. When he suggested driving Florrie to her home, which was only a few miles out of the city so she could visit her mother, Kay urged her to go.

' I'll be all right, go with Danny. I'll see you when you get back,' so with an apologetic glance Florrie allowed herself to be persuaded, and off she went.

Kay went back out to the corridor wondering if she should go have a word with the doctor when, all at once, she saw Graham coming towards her with Sinead and Dervla at either side of him. Her heart leapt in a mixture of joy and relief, she had been expecting them to come by plane. Meeting Graham's look of commiseration, she turned to her children and flung wide her arms. At once, Dervla dashed into them. Kay reached out to pull Sinead to her too, and held the pair of them close.

'Darling!' she breathed, seeing the look of misery in those grey eyes so like Dave's, and thinking: Oh dear! She knows! She's expecting to hear the worst.

Graham saw Kay's stricken expression and murmured, 'She's bearing up well. They both are. Why don't we go sit down and the girls can get cans from the soft drinks machine.' Once they had run off, he explained, 'Judy phoned me to say that Dervla was upset about flying so I thought it best to drive them. Maybe this isn't the time to talk about it, Kitty, but later I'll help Dervla get over her fear. She'll be fine, you'll see.'

Kay nodded absently, her expression sorrowful, her eyes without animation.

So it was bad, very bad, Graham deduced, his concern flaring. 'I'm so sorry, Kay. What terrible misfortune that your husband was on the train. Now that I'm here I'll do whatever I can to help,' aware delicate handling of Sinead would be required, without a doubt she was her Daddy's girl!

Kay blinked back tears, 'It was a dreadful shock, of course.' She hesitated, desperately needing to confide the burden she was carrying and who better than he. 'You see we had a terrible row... it seemed he actually came to the reception and must have seen the three of us together. I think something clicked... maybe it was the resemblance between Dervla and yourself. I don't know but it seemed he had always worried she might not be his. Anyway, he didn't come home for hours and when he did, he began to talk about it. He was dreadfully hurt. It...it cut me to the heart.' Kay confessed, covering her eyes and looking away remembering her husband's searing words, his reproaches, knowing she would probably never have a chance now to gain his forgiveness or to ease his hurt.

Graham took her hand in his, he could only imagine how it had been.

'His heart stopped during the night,' her voice quivered. 'Oh Graham, I'm so worried about Sinead. I don't know what to do... what to tell her. She loves him so much. If he dies, I don't know what it will do to her.' And now the tears came.

Graham just let her cry, watching her with a pained look in his own eyes. And yet he took a certain comfort from her grieving because all her love and emotion was for her child. He did not doubt her strong feelings for her husband, but her first care was for her children; that much was very clear.

***

Kay was glad when Graham had suggested that they should speak to the girls together. In the end he had done most of the talking as they sipped their drinks. In every way he had been in control of the situation, lifting just enough of the weight from her to make it supportable. When Kay brought Sinead to see Dave she was glad to be able to leave Dervla with Graham and to give all her attention to the older girl.

'Mummy,' Sinead's voice shook as she looked down at the still figure, frightened by her father's deathly pallor, his bruised face, the strange clicking sounds coming from the different body monitors in the small cubicle. 'He looks so white ... not at all like Daddy. He's going to die, isn't he?'

Kay held her close, not denying it. 'Darling, don't cry. Please don't cry,' she begged, tears blinding her own eyes, her heart torn.

'Mrs Mason,' the nurse hovered. 'The doctor would like a word in private,' and with a last sorrowful look at her father, Sinead went ahead of her out of the cubicle,

Telling the nurse she would be back in a moment, Kay hurriedly followed her daughter into the corridor. 'Darling, I hate to leave you like this. Are you okay to go back now to Derry and Graham?' and when she nodded, 'Good girl! Tell them I'll be along just as soon as I can.'

Kay watched her setting off, head bent, valiantly struggling with her tears. Then with a sigh, she went to hear what the doctor had to say. It was shocking and explicit, the tests he had carried out revealed that her husband's brain was not responding, there was no sign of activity, which meant the ventilator he was hooked up to was circulating his blood and doing his breathing for him, but clinically he was dead.

'I realize this is very painful for you and the decision to turn off the machine not an easy one to make, but sooner or later it will have to be faced.'

Kay was horrified. 'B...but can't we just wait until he goes naturally.' She could not believe it had come to this, they were talking of letting Dave die.

'You must speak of this amongst yourselves, Mrs Mason,' the doctor advised. 'If no one feels able to do it one of the hospital staff can assist you. Again I'm very sorry.'

Hurrying back along the corridor Kay's thoughts were sad and chaotic as she desperately tried to come to terms with this additional burden, not at first aware of the woman in her path trying to attract her attention.

'Forgive me stopping you like this but by any chance are you Mrs Mason?' she was asking. 'Dave Mason's wife?'

Deep in unhappy thought, Kay kept on going, but at the mention of her husband's name she hesitated and turned back. 'You know my husband?'

'We had a drink together on the train, Mrs Mason. That's what I wanted to speak to you about. Do you have a moment?'

'I really have to be getting back to my children.' Kay said uneasily, wondering what it was about, afraid this might be another woman friend of Dave's she knew nothing about and feeling unable for any more unpleasant disclosures.

But when the woman explained, 'You see, I must have been the last person your husband spoke to just before the crash,' Kay knew that she must hear what she had to say, if only to gain some insight into Dave's state of mind after leaving home that morning in such rage and sorrow.

'Very well,' she resigned herself.

'Perhaps we could get a cup of tea in the canteen?' Maria suggested. 'I have an appointment at 12 o'clock so I don't have much time.'

As they followed the sign for the cafeteria Maria was remembering her conversation with Dave, how he had said that he would give anything to believe there might still be a chance for his marriage. Now she held fast to that thought, feeling it would be some consolation to his poor wife to know how much he had regretted the manner in which they had parted, perhaps, for the last time.

***

Just after midday Graham took Kay and the girls to a restaurant for a meal. Knowing how reluctant she was to leave the hospital in case Dave came out of the coma he had had to use all his powers of persuasion to get her to agree.

Not surprisingly, following the doctor's grim news and Maria's revelation about Dave, Kay had not felt much like eating.

'Look it won't serve anything if *you* collapse,' he told her, before appealing to the girls. 'The troops need feeding if they are to remain fighting fit. Okay, lads?'

Dervla giggled, 'Why do you keep calling us lads?' she choked with laughter. 'Do we look like lads? We're girls!' and even Sinead's wan features lifted in a grin.

But Graham merely chuckled, having achieved his objective which was to keep up their spirits on this traumatic day. Kay's thoughts were still dwelling on what Maria had told her, thinking none of it sounded one bit like her reticent husband. Apart from that last soul-searing talk before rushing away to the train she could not remember when Dave had ever opened up to her like that before. In the end, it was the unmistakable sincerity in the woman's tone that had convinced Kay that her husband had been regretful enough about the breakdown of their marriage to act in a manner foreign to his natural reserve, even to the point of confiding his acute misery to a virtual stranger. Earlier, when voicing her concern to Graham as to how she would tell her children and her husband's family that Dave had no hope of recovering, he told her firmly, 'You must tell them the truth, Kay. They need to know the situation as soon as possible and have time to come to terms with it.'

Of course, he was right, Kay thought, taking a few sips of the soup he had insisted in ordering for her, shuddering at the thought of Eileen's reaction. It was bound to be horrific. With that, her appetite completely deserted her. It was on their way back to the hospital that Graham suggested she might consider allowing Dervla to return to Dublin with him, he had a Board meeting first thing next day and was aiming to get back on the road before dark.

'Dervla can stay with Nicholas and myself,' he said. 'She'll be no bother. It will be easier on you, if you have only Sinead to concern yourself with, and she's going to need all your attention. In her own way, Dervla needs protecting every bit as much. She has been through a stressful time already these past months and, quite frankly, she doesn't need the added trauma of seeing her father die. It might be easier all round if she were safely out of this before your mother-in-law arrives.'

This was enough to convince Kay. 'You're right!' she told him. 'You must take her with you. She'll be thrilled, of course, '

'Good! That's settled then.'

All too soon they were getting into the car and preparing to leave. 'Don't worry,' Graham reassured Kay. 'I'll take good care of her. You can be sure of that.'

'I know you will.' She swayed on her feet, dizzy from lack of sleep. 'Thanks, Graham. Your coming has made such a difference. You'll never know how much!'

'Bye, Mummy,' Dervla was waving through the car window.

Kay lifted her hand to wave back, still fighting tears, and when Graham, with a last salute, drove off she felt an enormous emptiness and sense of loss that would not leave her, despite every effort to shake it off.

Breda arrived with her mother and May as it was nearing teatime. Their expressions were tense and drawn as they hurried into the hospital. After their initial greeting and tearful embraces, they followed Kay in silence to where Dave was lying connected to the monitors. What followed was an additional ordeal for Kay for Eileen's grief when looking upon her dying son was wild and unrestrained, wailing and sobbing and bleakly reminding Kay of how Anne Stack had thrown herself on the stretcher calling out endearments to Dave the previous day. For the second time in twenty-four hours she felt upstaged. Only she was so upset, she might have smiled. Deeply distressed, she took Sinead out of the cubicle and stood with her beyond the curtain, holding her hand and doing her best to soothe her. She could see that Sinead was unnerved by her grandmother's loss of control, the frightened tears running down her pale cheeks as she struggled to contain her own overwrought feelings.

Kay was wondering if she should take her daughter out into the corridor, out of earshot of Eileen's heartbroken cries, as the faithful May nervously beseeched, 'Come away now, Eileen, for pity's sake!' to no avail. In the end it was Breda who managed to bring Eileen out of the ICU. She was the only one who ever could manage her mother and, thankfully, she had not lost her touch.

'Come now, Mammy, you must be brave for David's sake. Let's all go and get a cup of tea in the hospital canteen and then,' trying to make a joke of it, 'we had better get ourselves checked into a hotel or we'll find ourselves sleeping in the car tonight.'

With Eileen calmer, Kay took the opportunity to leave Sinead with Breda and slipped away to make her own goodbyes to Dave.

Staring down at the inert figure, she was not immune to the beauty of the thick gold-tipped lashes fanning his pale cheeks. Bending down, she kissed his forehead, and blotting out the troubling reminders of his infidelity and other painful deceptions in their life together, she tried to reach out to his lingering spirit and give him release.

Stooping closer, she whispered brokenly, 'Dave, can we try now to forgive each other. Believe me, I'm so very sorry. I never meant to hurt you and I know you had regrets too, so go in peace, my dear, and let us both remember only the good things we shared, the happy times together.'

Having done what she considered necessary, Kay gained some measure of peace and hoped when the actual moment came next day she would be able to let him go. With a sigh, she headed to the canteen, knowing she could not put off the dreaded moment any longer. She was not looking forward to breaking it to Eileen that Dave's life support machine would have to be switched off but as Graham had said she must give them time to prepare themselves. She found the three of them sitting in glum silence over half-drunk cups of cooling tea.

Sitting down with them, she learned that Florrie and Danny had arrived in her absence and taken Sinead for a drive. Kay sighed in relief, she wanted to prepare Sinead on her own in as gentle a manner as possible. Taking a deep breath, she repeated to the others what the doctor had said to her, laying stress on the fact that the tests he had carried out proved that Dave was clinically dead and so free of any further suffering. Voiced out loud at last, it sounded even more shocking and explicit than when the doctor had broken it to her. Kay felt like an executioner as she beheld their stunned faces, Eileen's expression of horror, poor May blubbering into her handkerchief and Breda struck speechless for once.

'Oh, my God, you can't be serious,' Breda found her voice and then, suddenly recollecting how much more awful it was for her sister-in-law, she blurted, 'Oh God! I'm sorry, Kay, so terribly sorry. But surely it's not that hopeless?' she cried. 'Surely there's some chance of him recovering?'

Kay shook her head, wearily repeating it all over again, trying desperately to remember the doctor's exact words, her voice cracking with emotion.

'But that's barbaric,' Breda protested. 'Like asking you to dig your own grave.'

Now who was being shockingly explicit, Kay sighed, telling herself that her sister-in-law was not being intentionally callous.

'Wicked and cruel,' Eileen moaned. 'How can you even contemplate such a thing, your own husband? Oh, may God forgive you, Kay.'

May muttered, 'I'd never have thought it of you, Kay, heartless, it looks to me.'

Kay accepted that they did not understand the decision was not of her choosing. She tried not to take their criticism personally, feeling too sad to be able to deal with any of it just then. Best thing, she decided, would be to ask the doctor to come and speak to them himself, so off she went.

In the meantime, Sinead had returned and came looking for her.

'Florrie and Danny dropped me off,' she told her mother, pale and subdued. 'They said to tell you they'll come back to the hospital later.'

'Okay darling. I'll be with you in a minute.' Kay paused long enough to pass on her request to the nurse in the ICU. With an arm about Sinead, she walked her daughter up the street in search of a cafe where they could sit down and have coffee.

Kay was aware that she had the difficult and delicate task of preparing her daughter for what lay ahead, and she was anxious to get it over with before Eileen or Breda might further shock and upset Sinead by speaking of it to her. And it would be a shock, Kay thought sadly, even though her daughter already seemed to have guessed it of her own accord. But it seemed she had got it wrong.

'Oh no! 'Sinead wailed. 'You mean to say that I was right and Daddy is going to die? Oh no! I can't ...I w..won't believe it. It's too terrible. I was waiting for you to tell me I was wrong, Mummy,' and putting her head down, she began to sob. Kay stared at her in dismay, to think all that talk of Sinead's had merely been bravado while all the time expecting to be contradicted.

'Darling, I'm so sorry. But there's more you need to know,' grimly she continued on, determined there should be no more mis-understandings.

Sinead gulped and raised her head. 'You mean they want to take him off that machine and let him die?'

'Well, yes…to let him go peacefully.' Kay tried to soften it, tears starting to her eyes. 'I'd give anything for this not to be happening. Oh God, I feel it so terribly and so do Granny and Breda. I don't know how I can bring myself to do it.'

Kay was openly crying now, no longer able to conceal her dis-tress behind a balled-up handkerchief. All at once she felt Sinead's hand gripping hers, heard her voice full of emotion. 'Dear Mummy, please don't cry. You mustn't be the one to do this difficult thing. It's not right, not fair.' She gulped back her own tears and sat up very straight. 'Mummy, let's go back now. Maybe if we talk to Granny together she'll be able to understand and not be too unhappy. After all, if Daddy is gone already like the doctor says, it's better to get it over with, isn't it?'

Looking at her daughter, Kay saw how in her acceptance of this tragic reality Sinead had all at once left childhood behind her. Mourning the untimely necessity, she was conscious of a reversal of roles, with Sinead now the rock, the one to lean on.

***

It was close to eleven o'clock next morning as they all congregated in the ICU. Seeing Sinead hanging back, Kay decided there was no way she would allow her daughter to be present at the moment of turning off the machine, despite earlier resistance from Eileen. 'She'll regret it later on, Kay, you'll see, when it's too late,' her mother-in-law had stated positively, as if, Kay thought, anyone could have regrets about not watching her beloved father's life be-ing extinguished in this way

On returning to the hospital the previous evening Kay had been met by Breda in the car park anxious to make amends for the things she had said earlier.

'Just want to say I'm sorry, Kay,' she said gruffly. 'The doctor came to talk to us and I think we all understand the situation a bit better now.' It was then she had offered to be the one to turn off the machine. 'I know how hard it is for you, Kay, and don't forget there's Sinead to think of. You don't want her going through life remembering her mother was the one to do it.'

Wincing, Kay said, 'Are you quite sure, Breda? Maybe your mother will be the one with the long memory.' But Breda just shrugged and Kay was only too glad to accept, especially now that the moment had arrived.

As they took up position about the bed Kay knew that she was right to protect Sinead, her daughter's nightmares the previous night having brought it home to her the danger of allowing her emotional child be stretched too far. It had been a relief to find that the hospital chaplain was fully in agreement with her when she approached him for his advice that morning.

'Very wise, Mrs Mason,' Fr Costello had assured her quietly. 'In such tragic circumstances I always advise parents to go gently with their younger members, not forcing them into anything they are not ready for.' He was very understanding and had agreed to have a word with Eileen before asking, 'Anything else troubling you?'

So kind was his tone that Kay was hard put not to sob on his shoulder but she shook her head. 'Thank you, Father. I just want to save my daughter any further pain.'

'I see. Well, don't forget I'm here if you want to talk at any time. In the meantime, let me say that my plan is to read a passage from Scripture when we are all gathered together at your husband's bed-side, and follow up with some short prayers. Remember, the family is just saying goodbye for the present to a much loved member.' He laid his hand comfortingly on her shoulder, 'I understand how everything must seem terrible, even hopeless to you just now but remember that during a time of tragedy and change God does not forget those left behind. Be assured that you are precious to him and even now He is writing a new plan for you.'

Kay had held back tears, consoled by his words. True, she was feeling very alone, almost abandoned. Everything seemed to be about Dave, his life and death and compared to it she felt as though she was of no great importance. But the priest's words had restored her sense of balance and given her new personal hope in the divine scheme of things. Today Danny was present too, having come along with Florrie to give his support. The more she saw of him the more Kay liked him, and hoped Florrie might hold on to this one.

There was sudden quiet now as the chaplain entered the ICU with Eileen by his side and Kay was relieved to see her mother-in-law so much calmer. As they all moved after the priest into the cubicle, Kay whispered to Sinead,

'Just stay for the prayers, darling, and then it's all right for you to leave. Don't worry,' she stressed. 'It's okay,' fondling her hair. 'Just slip away when I tell you and wait for me outside.'

'Okay, Mummy.' It was obvious Sinead was relieved and Kay hoped Eileen would not say anything to upset her. But her mother-in-law merely turned around to murmur encouragement to her granddaughter and to press Kay's arm in sympathy.

Eileen had found consolation in the chaplain's words too, and even now her mind was dwelling on all he had said to her. Averting her eyes from the still figure of her son, her mind mercifully far away, she hardly heard the priest speaking of the tragedy of a young man cut down in the prime of his life. Not until some scriptural lines from Hosea suddenly brought her back to an awareness of where and with whom she stood. All at once, Eileen's mind was flooded with memories of her son's earliest years, and now she found herself listening intently, seeing her little boy of long ago like the infant in the psalm the Lord spoke of, reminded of that far-off time when she was the centre of his existence and he had depended solely on her for his every need, his every comfort. Silently, she mouthed the familiar words.

'I myself taught Ephrain to walk.... I led them with reins of kindness, with leading strings of love. I was like someone who lifted an infant close against his cheek; stooping down to him I gave him his food.'

With these evocative words, uplifting and sustaining her, Eileen was overwhelmed by an awareness of a greater power. Bowing her head, she accepted at last that what the Lord had given to her all those years ago he was now taking back to himself. The chaplain finished anointing Dave with the sacred oils and with a compassionate glance, he withdrew, leaving the family to themselves.

'Go now!' Kay whispered urgently to Sinead, and with a last dazed look at the body of her father, her eyes blinded with tears, she slipped beyond the curtain.

Breda looked after her niece hoping she would be all right. Too bad there was no one to go with her, she shouldn't be on her own. But there was nothing she could do for she had her own unenviable task to carry out now, and mustn't falter. She and her brother had not always been the best of friends, but she felt genuinely sorry she had not made more of an effort to get along with him. Going to the head of the bed, she eyed the knobs on the machine, identifying the one the nurse had pointed out to her earlier, the one she needed to turn to the off position.

Watching in silence with the others, Kay felt the tension mounting. She swallowed on a suddenly dry throat, remembering what the priest had said about Jesus and the many mansions in His father's house. At what point would Dave enter one of these mansions, she wondered, and when her time came to die would it matter if she were in a different abode? Suddenly, Kay felt suffocated, unable to breathe. More than anything she wanted to get away, to escape like Sinead from the morbid atmosphere before Breda took the irrevocable step, and she began to shake with apprehension. And then she felt Danny McCarthy grasping her hand, and at his warm comforting clasp she felt her courage returning. With that she reached out to Eileen and took hold of her mother-in-law's hand. Tremulously, Eileen found May's fingers, and then Breda seeing what was happening joined hands too, completing the circle.

Tentatively, Eileen began singing 'Abide with me' and first May and then the others joined in with her, taking comfort from the poignant words of the hymn.

In this way, the six of them were staunchly linked for those unifying and strengthening few moments, then Breda gently disengaged her hand and, taking a deep breath, reached out to click off the machine, and it was all over.

Dervla was unaware of the need to mourn as she wandered about exploring Graham's wonderful garden with Nicholas. She thought she had never seen anything so pretty as the crazy pavement laid out in a star-shape about the base of the bird bath, and it partially hidden behind the swaying clumps of bamboo. She had come upon it suddenly and, putting her finger to her lips, she alerted Nicholas to the blackbird splashing about in a few inches of water, before creeping closer to watch entranced.

'Look at him,' she whispered. 'He's having such fun!' True, he was dipping and fluttering his wings open and closed, sending the droplets flying. 'He's just like a dog coming out of the sea and shaking himself.' She laughed softly.

Not a bad comparison, Nicholas thought. 'The birds in this garden are very tame,' he told her. 'There's a robin that comes right down even when we're mowing the grass and, despite the appalling racket, he has been known to perch on the handle.'

'Well, this bird isn't a bit afraid either, is he?'

'Why would he be?' Nicholas chuckled. 'Isn't this his garden?'

'What about the robin, Nicky? Do you think he might come out while I'm here?' Dervla asked, and Nicholas was struck by the thought that if Dervla was enjoying the sight of the frisky blackbird he was enjoying the sight of her, even more. She really has a zest for life, he thought, she enters into everything with such gusto.

'Sure, why not. Just give me half a mo while I run out the motor mower.'

'Would that do it?' Dervla asked round-eyed. 'You mean once he hears the engine he'll come out from wherever he is?' Then hearing

Nicholas's laughter she slapped his arm reproachfully. 'Oh, Nicky, you're just teasing me, aren't you?'

'I suppose I was,' he admitted smiling. 'But if you stick around for a bit you're bound to see him for yourself and who knows he might come down on the seat beside you. He does that too.'

Ranjan, who was back from Galway and helping out part time in the flying club, came wandering down the garden to join them. Dervla was a bit shy of him and she kept her head down watching the blackbird finish his bath, before flying away. When Ranjan had returned to the house, she said to Nicholas, 'Graham says that Ranjan is part of your family. How is that, his skin is brown?'

'Dad adopted him, that's how.'

Dervla digested this in silence. Hadn't he got a mother and father? But she didn't like to ask, not just then. She wished that Graham might adopt her. That would be cool! Only then, with a guilty start, did she remember her own badly injured father, and wondered how he might be.

Up at the house, Graham replaced the telephone and went in search of Dervla. Finding her playing croquet with Nicholas he signalled to his son, then brought her into the summer house and sat her down. Positioning himself beside the little girl, he told her the sad news before drawing her gently back against his chest and letting her cry. Aware how far apart she had grown from her father over the traumatic months since the accident, Graham was surprised at the extent of her grief. He wouldn't have expected her to be so upset. But Dervla was crying for more than the loss of a father, she was crying in the belief that he had never loved her, certainly not the way he had loved her sister, he hadn't even liked her, she sobbed, and that could never change now that he was dead, and it was all too late anyway.

***

PART THREE

(June 1982)

In the weeks after the funeral Kay struggled to get over the shock and the tragic suddenness of Dave's death. When not at work she gave time to her children, helping them to adjust to the tragedy that had blighted their young lives. Her grieving mother-in-law talked continually about her dead son, glorifying him in the process. It was only natural, Kay knew, trying to feel more sympathy for her in those sad troubling weeks. But in truth, she was conscious only of irritation and resentment on discovering that their affairs were in even worse disorder than she had feared, none of it leaving her much room for tolerance or compassion.

It had come as a shock to Kay to learn that her husband had let his life insurance policy lapse and was in arrears on the bank loan he had taken out to finance the Granny flat. And that wasn't all. When Tony rang asking her to call over to the office for a chat, she had reached new depths of disillusion on learning that over the months Dave had borrowed heavily from his boss, an amount in the region of £20,000. When she recovered from the shock she asked Tony if the debt could be discharged from the sale of Dave's company shares, but he told her that nothing could be touched until Probate was granted and this could take anything up to a year. In the meantime, he was prepared to give her time to repay the loan, assuring her that he would not insist on immediate repayment. If nothing else, this humiliating discussion brought it home to Kay that her husband was well and truly gone and it was up to her to try and find a way out of her difficulties. Prior to that there had been a slightly unreal feeling about it as though it was a bad dream and she might wake up and find he was not dead after all. She still half expected him to put his key in the door after work or to hear his feet on the stairs coming up late to bed. She kept to her own side of the mattress out of respect to his memory, not wanting to make changes too quickly. Besides, there was usually one or other of her children climbing in beside her at night. More often than not it was Dervla but sometimes Sinead came too, and all three slept with their arms about each other. Thankfully, Sinead was fairly composed and making every effort to be cheerful. Kay supposed what she possessed, and Dervla lacked, was closure. Their daughter was a subject Kay needed to discuss with Graham when they met, whenever that would be. So far their only contact had been the warm consoling letter she had received the week of the burial. It was appropriate in the circumstances but she was missing him badly and in need of someone to confide in. So it was a relief when he rang at last and suggested they meet in the canteen.

'How are you coping?' Graham asked, concerned to see her drawn expression as he off-loaded the contents of his tray, deliberately placing a creamy chocolate cake before her. 'Eat up,' he urged. 'You look like you could do with something fattening.'

Kay smiled wanly. 'Don't let Judy hear you say that. She has some notion of me setting an example for the new hostesses. 'Perfect weight, perfect grooming, perfect role model,' she mimicked. But joking aside, Judy really *did* expect all three.

'I would say you more than fulfil her expectations,' Graham said gallantly, but he thought she was too thin and too pale to meet with anyone's ideal notion of the glamorous air hostess. 'So how are you coping?' he asked again.

'Oh, all right, I suppose.' Kay picked at the cake but soon laid down her spoon. Slowly she raised her eyes to meet his compassionate glance, 'Well, it's hell really,' she admitted on a rush of candour. 'Oh, the girls are good and even Eileen doesn't appear out of her room too much, but problems keep cropping up, stuff I knew nothing about,' she took a deep breath. 'All very worrying. You don't want to hear any of it.'

'And why would you think that?'

'Not your problem.'

'Maybe I could help,' Graham suggested gently. 'Two heads and all that.'

Kay began poking at the cream cake again, pushing it about the plate until a hand came out and firmly removed it to the far side of the table. 'You're obviously not going to eat it so let's get it out of the way.' He reached for the restless hand and held it a moment between both of his. 'My dear Kitty, your problems are my problems, don't you know that. So tell me how can I help?'

Nervously, Kay retrieved her hand, conscious of nosy glances.

'Well?' he prompted. 'Does Dervla feature in any of these problems?'

'Well, in a way,' Kay admitted. 'She's not sleeping well and comes into my bed most nights. But that's to be expected, isn't it?' casting him a tired look.

'Maybe, but she slept fine the nights she stayed with us. Do you think it has anything to do with the death ...' he was going to say 'of her father' but changed his mind, *he* was her father.

'I think there's a connection,' Kay admitted. 'Something is troubling her. I'm afraid it may do more harm to talk about it.' All the time she was conscious of his dark eyes watching her. 'If you or Nicky could talk to her, she just might open up to you.'

'Let me think about it.' Just then, Graham was more interested in finding out what caused the dark shadows under Kay's eyes. 'So one of our problems soon to be taken care of,' he joked. 'So what's next on the agenda? Your mother-in-law, poor woman – stressful I would say.'

Kay's face shadowed, he had got that right. Stress played a big part, even more since Eileen had set her heart on buying a house in her old neighbourhood, like the one Dave had grown up in. But, of course, there was no money now to pay for it, Kay felt an additional wave of hopelessness.

Seeing her expression Graham said urgently, 'Kitty! Won't you please tell me what's troubling you? '

But that was something she could never do. Her eyes filled with tears. 'Oh Graham, if only I could,' she sighed. 'If only I could but... but I can't,' feeling too ashamed to ever tell him about her husband's criminal misuse of his mother's money.

Some evenings later, Kay's worst fears were realised when Breda exclaimed jubilantly, 'Wait till you hear, Kay. There's a house for sale in Carrick Road. Ma's going to bid for it at the auction.'

'That's great!' Kay tried to inject enthusiasm into her tone, but was relieved when Breda left soon afterwards and Eileen retired to her quarters. Going back into the kitchen she sat slumped at the table, her appetite gone, not able for anything but tea and the melted cheese on toast that Sinead had prepared for her.

'Delicious,' she mumbled, munching away. 'Haven't tasted anything so nice in ages. You are a good cook, darling.' She poured tea for them both and they drank in silence.

'Gran is very excited about the house,' Sinead said at last.

'Yes, so it seems. Are you sad she's going?'

'Yes, I am. We've been having great chats about Daddy. I mean no one else ever talks of him.' Kay's conscience was stirred by her reproachful glance. 'There's so much more I want to ask her and now I won't get the chance.'

'But she won't be far away. You'll see her often.'

'Not once she goes,' Sinead shook her head. 'I'll *never* get to see her.'

'Don't worry, Sinead,' Kay said, before she could stop herself. 'It will be a long time before that happens, believe me.'

Sinead stared. 'How can you say that? She talked of nothing else during tea. Hasn't she enough money to buy a house?'

Kay hesitated, then admitted, 'It has to do with money, yes darling, and I'm desperately worried. But you must promise me not to breathe a word of this to your Granny or Aunt Breda. Not till I get a chance to sort things out. Promise me now?'

A few days later Graham rang to invite the girls to his house at the weekend. Ever since his talk with Kay he had been trying to figure out some way of helping her. He had been concerned that despite the opening he had given her she had not confided in him. Perhaps having some time to herself might help her to straighten things out.

'That's very kind of you, Graham. What time will you pick them up?'

'If three o'clock suits it will give us time to have a meal and play a few games of whatever they fancy. Nicholas and Ranjan will be there to help out and, believe me, they are both just as competitive as Dervla when it comes to croquet or boules.'

'Sounds fun!'

He caught the wistful note but said nothing. It wouldn't be appropriate to include her, not so soon after her husband's death.

The visit to Graham's house proved to be a great success. Sinead looked about her entranced as they trooped about the beautiful garden, thinking that she had never seen anything like it except in magazines. Every so often Dervla's laughter rang out and she found herself envying her younger sister the ease with which she got on with everyone, particularly the pilot and his son. Earlier, Sinead had shyly shaken Nicholas's hand and said, 'Hi!' to the dark-skinned young man mooching along with his hands deep in the pockets of his jeans, his name sounded like Randy.

'Okay, enough sight-seeing for now,' Nicholas announced. 'Let's play croquet.'

'Oh goody!' Dervla jigged about. 'I'm great at croquet, aren't I, Nicky?'

'Yes, you are. Not exactly modest though.' He grinned at Sinead. 'No fear of your little sister hiding her light under a bushel.'

Dervla tossed her head. 'If you've got it flaunt it, my Mummy always says.'

Sinead gasped. 'She never did! How can you say that, Derry?'

Graham looked amused. He could see that Sinead was an earnest upholder of truth and more than a little shocked at her sister's blatant manipulation of facts. No doubt but Dervla was a scene-stealer, he mused, wondering which of them she took after, his eldest son coming to mind.

'Shades of my brother Jerry,' Nicholas murmured, reading his father's thoughts. 'Highly competitive, usually wins, and does he let us know it.'

Sinead said loyally. 'Dervla is quite shy really.'

'Could have fooled me,' Nicholas laughed. 'Where has the little imp gone?'

'Into the shed I think.'

Just then Dervla emerged carrying the mallets. 'So who's going to be on my team,' she enquired, almost at once pointing at Graham. 'You, of course,' she smiled possessively. 'Together we'll knock the socks off them.'

Graham chuckled. 'What makes you so sure they won't knock the socks off us?'

'Cos we're much better than them,' Dervla said simply. 'What about him?' she pointed at Ranjan lazily stretched on the grass. 'Isn't he going to play too?'

'Maybe later.' Graham knew that Ranjan was expecting Carol to appear soon, the pair had been seeing each other again since she had begun flying with MacDoolAer. She was often included in Graham's hospitable invites.

To Sinead's relief, she soon got the hang of the game with the mallets and did not disgrace herself entirely. Croquet gave them all an appetite and they soon strolled back to the house. There Sinead found that the lavish tea laid on was every bit as spectacular as the garden. Rita, Captain Pender's housekeeper, had excelled herself and she went about the table offering them platters of smoked salmon, grilled spare ribs and crab claws. The claws were delicious, Sinead love them. She had only ever tasted smoked salmon, everything else was new to her.

'That's the lady we met at the Zoo on my birthday,' Dervla whispered.

Sinead nodded dumbly over a mouthful of exotic seafood, so that's who it was. She was really nice, she thought, and a very good cook too. She felt she had never eaten so much in her life and hoped they could rest a while after the meal. But she had reckoned without her sister.

'C'mon Nicky, let's have another game of croquet,' Dervla was saying enthusiastically, as she led the way back into the garden.

'Hey, give us a minute,' he groaned. 'I can't bend down I've eaten so much.'

'That won't save him,' Graham murmured and Sinead nodded shyly, familiar with her sister's determination once she got an idea in her head. Sure enough Dervla was soon to be seen hauling a reluctant Nicholas down to the shed, energetically planning, 'At least three games, Nicky, and some boules too.'

Graham took Sinead to look at the vegetable garden, knowing from what she had told him on the drive to Cork that she had dug a little plot in her back garden and planted it with lettuce and herbs. He could see she liked his neat orderly drills, and she asked him fairly intelligent questions about planting and fertilizing until he judged she was just being polite. He sat down with her in the summerhouse and changed the subject. 'You must miss your father, Sinead. Is it getting any easier I wonder?'

'Well yes,' she gulped, struck by his sympathetic tone. 'Some days it is and at others it's just like...like when it happened,' giving him an anguished glance. 'I kept praying all the time it wouldn't happen and...and when it did anyway, I couldn't help feeling angry.' She was surprised at herself for speaking about that nightmare time, normally she never did.

'I'm sorry to hear that,' Graham had no desire to upset her but he had a reason for his questions. 'It will take time to heal the pain and for the loss to become less acute. It's only natural...we're human after all.'

While Sinead was mulling over this he said suddenly, 'How do you think your mother is coping. She seemed troubled when we met recently.'

'Mummy is sad,' Sinead told him in a rush, glad to confide in the kindly man. 'She tries to hide it but I can see she's unhappy. Gran has her heart set on this house near where she used to live. She is going to bid for it at the auction next week. But Mummy told me... well,' Sinead paused, unsure if she should go on.

'You can tell me,' Graham reassured her. 'I won't say a word, I promise.'

'Well, it's just that there's no money for her to buy the house,' Sinead blurted. 'The awful thing is Gran doesn't know any of this and Mummy can't tell her. Not yet anyway. She doesn't know what she's going to do.'

Graham was startled. 'No money? I seem to remember your mother telling me that your grandmother got a good price for her old house.'

'Well, that's what Gran is always saying and how clever Daddy was to get it for her. I don't understand,' Sinead wrinkled her brow. 'I just know Mummy is very worried.'

'I see. I'm sure it will all work out.' So that's what was troubling her, Graham thought.. 'Why don't you come and see the quince trees, Sinead,' he diverted her. 'My mother showed me how to make quince jelly years ago. Hey,' he chuckled at her expression. 'Bet you never thought boys bothered with stuff like that.'

'No, I didn't. Did you really?' He had succeeded in his objective.

'Oh yes, there's quite an art in it, you know. Quite delicious. You must strain it through a muslin cloth and let it drip until it's all through, that's the secret. 'He chatted away and Sinead was clearly enjoying it. It was nice to see her laughing.

Then Graham suggested they go find the others. 'I told your mother I'd have you back by nine. But you'll come again, won't you? I like to think we might be friends.'

Sinead nodded shyly. How easy it was to talk to him. She hoped her mother wouldn't mind her telling him about their money worries. Might be better not to mention their conversation, she decided prudently, just in case.

***

Kay missed having the girls about the house and found herself wishing they were home. It had been a long day. When Breda had called over that afternoon she had been sorting through Dave's suits and jackets, but she had to stop what she was doing and cram everything back into the wardrobe, while she hurried down to make tea for her sister-in-law. She found Breda's conversation deeply upsetting. She wanted to know just how soon her mother's money would be available so that she could put a deposit on the house she had set her heart on buying. Not something Kay could answer. In desperation, she improvised, saying that she needed time to find a buyer for the shares that Dave had bought in Eileen's name. She knew that she was panicking, not wanting the disillusioning truth to be revealed and for Eileen to lose the high opinion she had always held of her son.

Breda was aggrieved. 'How come you never told me about the shares, Mammy?' she demanded. 'Didn't you think I would be interested to hear about something as important as that?'

'It was between my son and myself,' Eileen said grandly. 'He said it was no one's business but ours and best kept that way.'

'Thanks!' Breda's tone was bitter. 'I'm only your daughter. Maybe he should be the one going to the estate agent with you. Oh, but he's no longer here, is he?' she grimaced. 'You're stuck with me. What a pity!'

Kay had almost been sorry for Breda but felt she should have known better than to invest any emotional content in Eileen. When they had stopped berating each other she had offered to get in touch with Dave's stockbroker and see if he could put the shares on the market. For a while Kay had felt quite cheerful until she remembered there was no buyer and no shares in Eileen's name waiting to be sold. All she had done was delay the inevitable!

It was a great relief when Breda left and Eileen closed over the door of her flat. At that stage Kay was in no mood to go back to sorting and bagging clothes and began watching the clock instead. Eventually, she went into the front room and sat by the window so she would know the minute Graham arrived and parked outside.

Just after nine her daughters came running excitedly up the path, full of their wonderful day. Kay had the door already open to greet them, hugging them to her as Graham followed more slowly, from his wide smile he had enjoyed himself too.

'Here they are back to you in one piece,' he told Kay. 'Sorry we're later than I said but we got a bit delayed,' patting the top of Dervla's head. 'Took a while persuading a certain person here it was time to go home. Especially when she was intent on beating the socks off her competitors in what had started as a friendly game of tennis and changed into something else.' He smiled to take the sting out of it.

'That's not fair. It wasn't *me* wanted another game,' Dervla protested. 'Nicky swore he would get his own back 'cos we – Graham and me - beat him in the croquet match. He's such a bad loser!'

'No, he's not. Just look who's talking!' Sinead protested. 'You were the one went into the sulks when he beat you at the ball alley and, don't forget, you hit him over the head with his tennis racquet.'

Kay stared in surprise, not used to hearing Sinead speaking up so vehemently. She even looked different, her blonde hair straggling free of the hair band, a new dusting of freckles on her flushed cheeks. Dervla too, looked as though she had been romping about, her white shorts crumpled and stained with grass. Two ragamuffins!

'You never hit Nicholas,' Kay protested in horror, but Dervla only laughed. 'It wasn't hard and, anyway, he pinched me and pulled my hair. So we were quits.'

'Pinching and hitting!' Kay met Graham's eyes and he ran a hand over his own hair and cleared his throat. 'Sounds rather worse than it was,' he explained ruefully. 'I think she got as good as she gave. At any rate they parted friends.'

Again Sinead surprisingly spoke up. 'Nicky said next time he would spank her.'

'Just let him try,' Dervla growled.

Kay threw up her hands in mock surrender. 'Well, whatever about all the pinching and hitting a good day was obviously had by all,' she said dryly, her own had been so fraught with worry and tension she felt envious.

'Yes, you might say that,' Graham agreed, and Kay suddenly became conscious they were standing on the doorstep and any moment Eileen might put her head out to see what was going on. The thought spurred her to action.

'Do come in for a drink or... or coffee,' she found herself babbling, and almost dragged him over the threshold. Surprised, but unresisting, Graham allowed himself to be steered towards the kitchen. Once inside, with the door safely closed behind them, Kay apologised for almost kidnapping him.

'That's quite all right,' he said politely, but with a gleam of amusement. 'The snatch couldn't have been carried out by a nicer kidnapper.'

'That's funny,' Dervla giggled. 'Mummy's not a kidnapper.'

'Sinead, why don't you take Derry upstairs with you,' Kay suggested, thinking it time they got ready for bed. 'You must be tired, the pair of you.'

'Oh, I'm not a bit tired,' Dervla protested, rummaging in a drawer for playing cards. 'We're going to play 'Beggar my neighbour' aren't we, Graham?'

'Come on, Derry, let's go,' Sinead said, catching her mother's eye. 'I'll play one game with you if you get into your jammies quick. Okay?'

'Just one game,' Kay agreed relieved. 'Now say goodnight to Graham. And don't forget to thank him for a lovely day.'

Dervla ran over to put her arms about Graham and kiss him. 'Night, night,' she said softly. 'I had a lovely time. We beat the socks offa them, didn't we?'

Graham pinched her cheek. 'We certainly did! Up you go now and we'll play cards another time. That's a promise.'

Sinead waited until Dervla had joined her, then extended her hand to Graham. 'Thank you. I had a lovely time too,' she said earnestly. He shook it gravely then leaned forward and kissed her cheek. 'Sleep well, my dear,' he said.

Sinead flushed with pleasure. Catching hold of her sister's hand, she ran with her backwards out the door crying, 'Last one upstairs is a rotten egg,' and the pair turned and shot along the hall, in their haste leaving the door open.

'She's full of surprises,' Graham remarked, getting up to shut it with a smile. 'Most of the time Sinead is so sedate and conscientious, and then exhibiting that sudden impish streak.'

'She obviously had a great time,' Kay ladled coffee into the percolator, saying over her shoulder. 'How do you like it …with hot milk or cold?'

'Either way is fine.'

Kay switched it on and turned back to face him. 'Maybe you would like a drink. There's some wine in the fridge.' She had put in a bottle of Pinot Grigio in anticipation of this moment. It was slightly pricier than her usual buy.

Graham nodded. 'Sure, if you are having some yourself.'

'Yes, of course.' She got down two glasses and after a quick check to ensure they were clean, poured the wine. It was a good wine and she hoped he would like it. Leaving the coffee to perk she sat at the table with him. Outside the trees were silhouetted against the darkening sky but it was still too early to put on the light.

'This is very good,' Graham raised his glass to her, and she thought how strange it was to see him here in her kitchen, and then her expression changed catching sight of the black plastic bags Breda had hauled out of Eileen's bedroom and left piled against the back door, her mother having insisted on starting her packing that afternoon.

'Excuse the mess,' Kay started to say. 'I'm afraid my mother-in-law decided to clear her cupboards today even though ...'

'That's something I want to talk to you about,' Graham interrupted, turning his chair about to face her. 'Kay, you must know the last thing I want to do is interfere but I am aware for some time now something is seriously worrying you. No, don't say anything,' he held up his hand as she hurried into speech. 'Please let me have my say first. Well, today something Sinead said gave me some idea of where the problem may lie. I may be wrong but it seems to be a question of money.'

'Please, Graham,' Kay said in some distress. 'You need not … you *must* not concern yourself with this.' She was mortified that he had somehow guessed. Oh damn! What could Sinead have told him? She had promised faithfully not to say a word. But then in all fairness Kay remembered that she had only warned her about

Eileen and Breda, not anyone else. Ah, poor Sinead, she relented, only trying to help.

'But I *want* to concern myself,' Graham protested. 'Look, you don't have to explain anything to me or go into any details, just give me some idea of how much you need. Indeed, if I were in the same position,' he went on persuasively. 'I'd like to think you would want to help me.'

'You know I would,' Kay said in a low voice.

'Very well then. Let me share this with you now. It has to do with your mother-in-law, hasn't it?' Kay dipped her head in assent. 'I thought as much. Maybe money for the house she wants to buy?'

Again Kay nodded.

'So tell me what you need?'

'Far too much to be even talking about,' she said, between a laugh and a sob.

'Oh dear, this is obviously more complicated than I'd thought. I'm afraid we may need to rob a bank.' Graham succeeded in getting her to smile. 'Look, my dear, would it help at all to tell me about it?'

He leaned forward to take her hand and hold it while he talked. As always when he touched her she felt it hard to think, her senses stirred by the shock of his skin on hers. She shook her head to clear it and tried to find words to present the case without prejudice, not in any way malign the dead.

'I'm ashamed to talk about it,' she confessed at last. 'I'm afraid it doesn't reflect too well on my husband. When I first learned what he had done it made me feel angry... even betrayed. But yes, Oh yes, Graham, you're right. It's a relief...such a relief to be able to talk about it at last.'

As Kay began to tell him of the situation she had found herself on the sudden death of her husband she was glad of the gathering shadows affording them a privacy of sorts in the small room. Graham listened intently, his eyes fixed on her downcast face, his gently stroking fingers giving her courage to keep talking.

Once she had confessed the whole sorry tale to him she was aware of the need to pay attention to another wake-up call, recognising that the lifeline he was extending in pity, friendship or, dare she whisper it, love might be her only solution to the untenable, unbearable situation she had found herself caught up in.

'I can help,' Graham was murmuring. 'Won't you please let me?' His features were indistinct in the darkening room, making her wish for light to see him by, but wanting even more to preserve the intimacy created by the gathering dusk.

'Of course I want to,' she whispered, struggling with her longing to give in and accept, despite her own stubborn, if foolish, wish not to become the humiliating thing of pity she must appear in her extreme neediness.

'Kitty, Kitty, listen to me. Supposing I loan you the money and you pay me back whenever you are free to put the shares on the market? It means you can give the money to your mother-in-law now and she can buy her house without ever needing to know the true facts. It would be a compassionate thing to do,' he said softly. 'What you had in mind all along rather than bring heartache and disillusion to a grieving old woman. If you have her bank details I'll take care of it myself first thing on Monday.'

The ease with which he removed the burden that had been crushing her for so long made Kay's senses spin. She dropped her head into her hands and cried softly in relief and gratitude. 'Thank you,' she mumbled. 'It means so much that you want to help... and I'll pay you back...all of it... with interest.'

'Good!' was all he said, but she knew he was smiling, probably at her gauche mention of interest, but she didn't care.

The nightmare was over, she could breathe again. She felt dizzy with relief.

After a moment she felt his hand on the back of her neck and she shivered as his fingers dug deeply, caressingly into her hair, the slow sensuous movement inspiring the old languor in her limbs and making her forget everything, her children in the room overhead, her mother-in-law down the hall, the troubles so recently besetting her, and she allowed herself to be drawn upright until she was standing close against him. There in the shadowy room he bent his head and placed his mouth over hers, and she lost herself in the deep endless kiss that both stirred and consoled her, and was a lot more besides, reviving memories of the first time he had ever kissed her on a bridge in Richmond long ago on a London overnight. Kay was conscious of how much time and anguish had passed since those early days, but it might have been merely a few hours since her body had leapt with the same insistent hunger, her senses swooning at his sensuous touch.

It was the sound of feet running down the hall that alerted Graham to the fact they were about to be interrupted, and he suddenly put her from him and stepped back a pace, before Dervla burst noisily in the door wanting to know when they were coming up to say goodnight.

The money was deposited in Eileen's account and, within a few weeks, Kay's mother-in-law had moved out to stay with Breda until her new house had been painted and renovated and ready for occupation. Only Sinead was sad to see her grandmother go, but she took heart from Eileen's promise they would not lose touch, she would meet often with her favorite grandchild. And then there was all the excitement of Judy Mathews' wedding in July to keep Sinead from missing the old woman too much, Judy having invited her to attend the ceremony and reception along with Dervla. There was further delight when Graham gave the girls gifts of little gold lockets, imbedded with their birthstone chips. Aquamarine for Sinead born in March and emerald for Dervla born in May, and they planned to wear them on the day.

He had already given them so much, Kay thought, conscious of the holiday in Florida and more recently the house money for Eileen. He had assured Kay should the share price of her stock rise in the coming months any profit would be hers, brushing aside her tentative, 'But what if it falls, Graham, what then?'

He was being extremely kind, clearly sorry for all she was going through. But she did not want his pity, Kay told herself frowning, she had had enough pity shown to her during her orphaned years.

And now because of Dave's failure to provide for herself and the children she was once more on the receiving end of charity. She would have given anything for it to be otherwise. Naturally, Graham never by a word or glance put her under a compliment for the money. He could not have been better but Kay was conscious of the burden of owing so much money, of the need for such a loan.

On that morning of Judy's wedding the girls woke up early. Before long, Kay was awake too. Impossible to sleep with the giggling excitement generating between bedrooms, as the girls ran madly in and out. She gave up trying and eventually shifted over to make room for them, as they climbed into bed beside her. Across the room their wedding garments were hanging on the wardrobe door.

Kay was admiring the flower girl's silk dress with its wide apricot sash and the pretty Laura Ashley cotton she had chosen for Sinead, when she realized her eldest child was speaking to her, 'What's that, darling?'

'I wish you were coming with us, Mummy,' Sinead was saying, and Dervla agreed, 'Me too. Why can't you? Judy really wants you there.'

'I know, I know.' Kay hugged the pair of them. 'It's just that it's too early since Daddy died to go to anything so public yet. It wouldn't be right.'

'But Daddy wouldn't have minded, would he?' Sinead was puzzled. 'I mean he would *want* you to be happy.'

'Of course he would,' Kay agreed.

'So why not go?'

Why not indeed! After all, none of it could affect Dave one way or the other, Kay thought, and it was not as if she really cared what anyone thought. But it was too late to change her mind now and she roused herself to make a satisfactory response for her daughter's sake, if not her own. 'Well, it's out of respect and affection too, for your Dad's memory,' she said quietly. 'Not a huge sacrifice when you think about it.'

'You mean people will know you still think about him,' Sinead offered.

'Yes…something like that.'

'I think of him a lot. But not as much as I did in the beginning,' she admitted soberly, and Dervla piped up. 'If we don't think about him will he disappear altogether like Dorothy's grandparents in the Wizard of Oz? They began fading before her eyes.'

Kay smiled reluctantly. Trust Dervla to come up with something like that. 'Well, I don't know. That was just a story.'

'Well, there's no chance of Daddy ever fading in that particular way,' Sinead said staunchly. 'Not when we remember him like we do, and Granny most of all. No matter what happens *she'll* never forget him.'

This was so true that Kay was momentarily silenced. Then her eye fell on the bedside clock. Time was getting on. 'Let's go have some breakfast,' she suggested. 'With photos and speeches you probably won't get to eat until late so better fill up now.'

'Will you do pancakes?' Dervla asked, as they clattered down to the kitchen, still in their night things. 'I'd eat those,' as if nothing else could tempt her.

'Why not,' Kay got out the pan. 'Sugar and lemon, I suppose.'

'And honey too, please,' they chorused happily. It didn't take a lot to please them, Kay thought, as she set to work with a will. More than ever she wished she was going to the wedding. Wherever he was, she hoped Dave appreciated the gesture.

***

Kay drove the girls over in good time to the Penders' house dressed in their wedding finery. They were given a great welcome by Graham and Nicholas, both already attired in their morning suits. Feeling like Cinderella, Kay had made excuses not to stay and soon returned home, where she experienced regrets and anti-climax as she sat glumly drinking coffee and dwelling on how lovely Dervla had looked in the cream silk dress and apricot sash, with a circlet of rosebuds in her hair. She would carry matching blooms, mixed with angel's breath and trailing campanula, in a little beribboned basket up the church. Judy had great taste, she thought wistfully, wishing yet again that some outdated consideration for the dead had not prevented her attending the glamorous event. She sighed thinking how well chosen the little flower girl's outfit, how it suited the child to perfection. Kay had seen the fond way Graham's eyes had rested on Dervla as he complimented her and her sister, telling them they were visions of loveliness, the pair of them, in their beautiful dresses. Sinead did, indeed, look beautiful, her fair hair out on her shoulders in a silky curtain, Kay had brought her to the hairdressers the previous day to have it cut and styled. Dave would have been so proud of her, she thought with a catch in her throat.

Kay was still a bit bowled over by the memory of how splendid Captain Pender had looked in morning suit, not every man of his age looked so fit or possessed such an enviable figure. Of course, it had its usual devastating effect on her, reminding her how on this happy joyful day she was on a different planet to the rest of them, and although he had asked her to stay for coffee and tempted her with the mention of some delicious pastries to go with it, she had made an excuse about Eileen needing her help in her new home and driven off, out of temptation's way.

Now she decided, somewhat grimly, if she did not have the penitential cinders to clear out she still had her dead husband's wardrobe to sort through. And what better day to tackle such a delightful task, she mused cynically. But as before her heart was not in it, and she soon decided to enjoy the novelty of having no meals to prepare, no old lady's whims to cater for, and went outside to enjoy the day.

Dragging the shabby sun lounger through the wilderness to a sunny corner of the overgrown garden, she flopped down and soon drifted into a catatonic state. The clothes could wait, there was no immediate rush, after all.

When she awoke some hours later, Kay was amazed to find it was after four. By this they would all be at the reception, she thought, and went into the house to take a shower. When she had towel-dried her hair she left it to dry naturally, and changing into cool linen pants and a candy-striped shirt, she went below to make herself fresh coffee. Although she felt rested from her nap the task of clearing out her husband's gear was as distasteful as ever, but she managed to persuade herself with the girls out of the house it was the ideal time (if such a thing existed) to get it done.

Forcing herself to begin, her heart pounded suddenly as she came upon the invitation to the CA reception still in the inside pocket of the jacket Dave had been wearing the day before the crash. Sinking down with it on the overcrowded bed, she found herself dwelling on all the unhappiness that might have been saved had she only seen him arriving to the hotel, or if he had somehow not seen her with Graham. As regards the train crash, nothing she did or did not do could have prevented that! Maybe not, she thought, but at least he would have gone to his death in a happier frame of mind. And what about me, she protested, maybe I could have gone on living my life in a happier frame of mind if I hadn't had his affair thrust in my face. But what was the use of such speculation, it was all in the past now. She felt a wave of hopelessness and wearily moved on from the suits with their treacherous pockets to his highly polished leather shoes that he was so careful of.

She had just gathered them up and begun thrusting them deep into a bag, when the doorbell rang. Kay waited to see if the bell would ring again. Maybe if she stayed quiet, she thought, whoever it was would go away. But it rang again, a long peal.

Cautiously peering around the curtain, not wanting to risk being spotted, her heart jumped in her chest at the sight of the familiar blue Porsche parked at the kerb. Unless it was a huge coincidence, it belonged to Graham Pender. But what on earth was he doing here, she wondered, why wasn't he at the wedding?

***

Sinead sat taking it all in, the beautiful dresses, the picture hats and elegant heeled shoes, the dazzling broaches and earrings, unaware that much of it was costume jewellery, not the real thing at all. She touched the gold locket about her neck and her mouth curved in a smile. It was the nicest present anyone had ever given her.

Beside her, Dervla chatted brightly away to Nicholas who was sitting across the table with some of the other CA pilots. She was such a chatterbox, Sinead thought fondly. Although she knew none

376

of the guests apart from the Penders, she was really glad to be there and was busily storing up impressions to tell her mother later.

The meal had been delicious, starting with smoked salmon and asparagus followed by broccoli soup, sorbet and then medallions of beef in a delicious wine sauce. Sinead had eaten everything on the plate and realized she was really hungry.

Now someone was tapping a glass and gradually the buzz of talk died down. Turning her head to look at Dervla, she felt a bit forsaken when she saw that she had gone around the table to sit with Nicholas and the sandy-haired young man, and all three were having a great time. And then she narrowed her eyes in shock. Surely Derry was not sipping wine from Nicholas's glass? Oh dear! If Mummy knew!

Sinead looked away saying nothing, not wanting to be a kill-joy. There were a lot of toasts and she soon fell into a daydream thinking of the storybook heroine Tess and *her* wedding, and the disastrous ending to the day that had started out for her so joyfully. More and more, Sinead was beginning to identify with the ill-fated young woman and to mourn the ill-luck that had brought about Tess's downfall. She had used to believe she was so lucky and blessed but no longer did, not since her father died. Her eyes swam with tears at the thought, lately she found it was happening a lot and was ashamed anyone would notice. She was unaware of the band beginning to play popular tunes her mind still dwelling on the unfortunate timing of her father's tragic death. Oh Daddy! If only you had driven your car to Cork, if only you hadn't made the journey at all you'd still be alive. She was hard put not to sob.

'May I claim the first dance?' Startled, struggling to control her tears, Sinead looked up in confusion to see a smiling Captain Pender extending his hand to her.

'I...I don't dance,' she managed at last to say.

'Nonsense, of course you do. I'm sure you are a beautiful dancer,' and before she could protest any more, he had her on her feet and was bringing her out with him on to the dance floor as it began filling up. The music was lively and Captain Pender was a good dancer and a considerate partner, adjusting his movements to hers so that,

Sinead cheered up and soon found she was really enjoying herself, and even sorry when it was over.

'One of the best dancers I have ever had,' Graham told her gallantly as he brought her back to her seat, and Sinead smiled shyly up at him in gratitude. Almost at once Dervla pounced on him crying, 'My turn, Graham, my turn,' and he gave a mock sigh and good-naturedly took her on to the floor.

Trying not to mind being on her own, Sinead watched Dervla jigging about and Graham laughing in amusement at her antics, then she turned her gaze to the other couples. Gradually, she became aware of a noisy group of men sitting behind her. It seemed they were a group of pilots and before long she realized they were speaking about Graham and Dervla still on the floor. The music had jazzed up a bit and Dervla was giggling and going in and out under Graham's arm as he was twirling her about. They were having a lot of fun and Sinead felt a bit envious. Dervla never worried about not knowing how to dance, she just went ahead and tried it. Sinead looked away and began listening to the pilots again, if that's who they really were.

'Look at those two,' one of the men said. 'Now don't go telling me that child is not related to Pender. Did you ever see such a strong resemblance to anyone in your life? Sure she's the spitting image of him, same eyes, same colouring, well, before his hair went white, the whole shebang, right down to that dimple in her chin.'

'Oh, come on,' another voice protested. 'You're crazy, Dan. The child has dark hair and brown eyes, I'll grant you that, but so have loads of kids.'

Now Sinead was sure that they spoke of her sister. But don't they know Graham is our uncle, she thought proudly, no longer doubting what Dervla had told her.

'I kid you not. That little minx is from the same stable,' Dan was saying. 'And she's going to be a right little raver just like her mother. Oh, now fellahs, I could tell you a thing or two that went on in little ol' Noo York and any other location you care to mention between her Ma and the bold Pender, and to look at her you'd think butter wouldn't melt in her lovely gob.'

They were getting very rowdy, Sinead thought uneasily, she was about to change seats when Dan's next remark kept her rooted to the spot.

'You mark my words. Pender will soon be making his move on the little widow. She skipped today, by all accounts. Still in mourning, I reckon.' Another burst of laughter. 'Oh now, it's an ill wind blows nobody good, eh, fellahs, he's a lucky bloody bastard!'

Sinead turned white as the implication sank in. She sat silent and stricken as Dervla ran up to her, 'Come on, Sinead,' she cried. 'Graham has to go out for a bit and Nicky says you're to come and join us. We're going to do the Conga. It's great fun.'

Still shocked, Sinead allowed herself to be pulled out to the floor, her mind on the conversation she had just overheard, aware in some shameful way it involved her mother and Captain Pender, and maybe Dervla too.

Kay stood in Graham's lush conservatory and stood looking about her at all the exotic plants and statuary. Was that really the statue of Neptune, she wondered in amazement, remembering Dervla telling her how she had sat on the edge of the fountain and bathed her feet in the tumbling water.

Graham had thought she might be in need of company and had left the wedding and driven over to her house, so he had told Kay as he stood on her doorstep, urging her to come back with him to his house for a drink.. 'You shouldn't be alone, not today,' he'd said. 'Not with everyone enjoying themselves at the wedding. Please say you'll come.'

'Nice of you to think of me but I'm fine,' Kay had told him, thinking there he goes again feeling sorry for me. 'Shouldn't you be back there now with them all?'

'Not at all. I won't be missed. Nicholas is looking after the girls, and they'll be fine with him. So what have you been doing on this lovely sunny day?' looking concerned when she owned to clearing out her husband's wardrobe.

'Not an easy job! Don't you have anyone to help you?'

'Not really.'

'Well, leave it for now,' he urged, and suddenly deciding why not, she had locked up the house and gone with him.

Now she gazed about her in awe. She had thought the girls were exaggerating after their visit, but not anymore. The house Graham had owned years before and she had visited once or twice had not been anything so grand, she thought. This one was like out of a glossy magazine.

'Let's go walk in the garden,' Graham suggested, 'and then you can tell me what you think of it.'

'I can tell you right now it looks marvelous,' she told him, ruefully comparing it to the overgrown jungle behind her own house that Dave had never showed much interest after his initial effort with Ruari. 'You must have a team of gardeners.'

He chuckled, 'No, just one. He used to be my sergeant when I was serving in the Air Corps. He does it all himself, would you believe?'

As they made their way down the two flights of steps to the lower level Kay was remembering how on the drive across the city Graham had talked of nothing else but the bride, how beautiful, how calm and regal Judy had looked walking up the aisle on Ben Higgins' arm. Could it be he was regretting that she had married someone else, Kay wondered with a pang.

'Let's sit and watch the sun go down, shall we?' Graham said eventually, after they had done a round of the garden, and leading the way into the summer house

Once seated, Kay leaned her head back against the wooden wall to look out at the sky. It was still fairly bright. She reckoned it would be light for another couple of hours and felt suddenly swamped by sadness. The summer would soon be over and she had hardly been aware of it passing. Long weeks of mourning had taken their toll. Judy's wedding with Dervla as a flower girl should have been a highpoint for her. And it surely would have, she thought, if only circumstances had been different. As it was, it merely served to deepen her sense of aloneness. She did not begrudge Judy her happiness, but the knowledge that the other woman was on the brink of a new life with the man she loved had the effect of making Kay feel old, sad and bereft.

'What is it?' Graham turned her about to face him. 'I had thought to cheer you up but I don't seem to have done a very good job of it.'

Kay sighed. 'I would have liked to have been at Judy's wedding,' she admitted. 'I thought I was doing the right thing by staying away but...well, now I'm not so sure. I feel like I've somehow let her down.'

'Nonsense! I'm sure she doesn't think that. It means a lot to her having Dervla and Sinead there, especially Dervla. She told me so on several occasions.' But instead of reassuring her, this information only cast Kay further down. Obviously, he kept in close touch with Judy all along and still cared for her.

'Is there something the matter, Kitty?' Graham asked gently, and she turned away not wanting him to look into her eyes and see the hurt she was feeling. 'Come on! Out with it.' He drew her back against his chest, and said teasingly. 'You have the same look as Dervla when I took Sinead out on to the dance floor before her.'

Kay bit her lip in frustration aware that she was being irrational and insanely jealous of a woman who was safely married to another. But she found that she couldn't bear the thought of him caring so much for anyone else.

'Why didn't you marry Judy when you had the chance?' she suddenly blurted, before she could stop herself. 'I mean it's obvious you still care about her. '

'You think that?' He seemed unsurprised by her question.

'Well, you've been talking about her a lot,' Kay tried to keep her tone light and uncaring, 'It's just that I can't help noticing how regretful you sound.'

'Well, yes, in a way you're right,' Graham agreed seriously, making Kay's stomach lurch in desolation. 'Judy and I came close to marriage long ago but I married Sile instead. After I returned from Sri Lanka and learned of all Judy had done to have me freed I realized how much I owed her. Naturally, we grew close again and at one stage we almost became engaged to be married.'

Kay thought she detected that regretful note again and wished she had never started this painful discussion. Still, she could not leave it alone, masochistically probing the wound. 'I suppose you feel you have made a terrible mistake in *not* marrying her when you could have?'

The minute the words were out she wished that she could stop him from replying, knowing once he had put into words the confirmation of her greatest fear there would be nothing left for her to hope for ever again. She might as well lie down here in this heavenly scented garden and die, she thought miserably.

'I wouldn't quite say that,' came the ambiguous reply. 'My regrets lie in an altogether different direction, but now isn't the time to go into any of that.'

Although this was not the answer Kay had dreaded it was too obscure to give her any real comfort. Weakly, she contemplated probing deeper, but the time for such boldness (or foolhardiness) was past, and she trembled from anti-climax.

'I thought it might be nice to share a pleasant few hours uninterrupted by other people's cares and wants,' Graham was saying. 'Not something you have had an opportunity of experiencing these past few months, Kitty. So what do you say we stroll back to the house and I'll open a bottle of wine that's even now cooling. We'll drink a toast to Judy and Taylor and then forget all about them, shall we?'

'Sounds fine to me,' Kay said, just as lightly. Maybe she had been reading too much into all his talk of Judy, maybe his heart was not entirely lost to her after all.

'So tell me what you think of this Sancerre.' He poured wine into a glass and handed it to her. 'It's quite pleasant. I think you'll like it.'

Kay sipped and found it very good. But in the relief of the moment, even the sweetest Sauterne would have been acceptable to her. 'It's really nice,' she said inadequately, and he smiled. Oh dear, how gauche she must sound. She made an effort to redeem herself. 'I get the taste of gooseberries,' she hazarded.

It was a lucky guess.

'Clever girl! Have some more.'

Warmed by his praise, Kay began to relax and stop agonizing over beautiful brides, or what they had once meant to him. The atmosphere felt so friendly, so comfortable that she drank a few glasses without noticing and her spirits rose accordingly. She even found herself becoming quite giggly, some distant part of her wondering at the power of the grape.

'That's more like it,' Graham murmured approvingly, and she stopped feeling guilty about her dead husband and the sin of enjoying herself while still in mourning.

It was growing dark outside. Graham got up and pressed a switch so that soft lighting sprang up beyond the glass, transforming the garden into an even more magical place. When he gently took the empty glass from her and set it down on the low table, she turned quite naturally into his arms. The first kiss was gentle and drawn out, becoming gradually more urgent until the force of his passion bruised her lips. Giving him back kiss for kiss, Kay's own passion flared, making her cling closer to him and she was aware of a savage, all consuming body hunger that clamored to be satisfied.

Graham pulled her to her feet and she went with him eagerly. Swiftly they climbed the stairs, stopping once at the bend to fiercely kiss and then again on the landing to strain close together, before he took the last few strides, almost carrying her with him into the bedroom. By this, Kay was in a frenzy of wanting and he, with the same urgency pushed her down on to the wide bed. Gasping at the heavy satisfying weight of him, she yielded to him like parched earth that for too long had been deprived of moisture and nourishment, and when he entered her she strained hungrily towards the climax thundering towards her that nothing could stop, and her whole being exploded in an ecstasy surpassing anything she had known in a very long time.

Lying together in the near darkness, the soft illumination from the garden provided them with enough light to see each other by as they loved each other again and yet again, their heightened senses ever more tuned to the other's wants, and each time Kay felt taken up out of herself for endless stretches of enduring pleasure. Until the sudden shrill ringing of the telephone gradually recalled her to her surroundings.

Kay felt Graham reach to answer it and heard him speaking in a low voice, 'I'll come straight away. Yes, about ten minutes,' and she struggled upright, pulling the sheet about herself, aware from his urgent tone that something was wrong.

***

Kay often thought of the hours that passed after she had returned with Graham to where the wedding was being held and they had come upon Sinead in a dreadful nervy state, shivering and crying, stammering and hysterical, unable to tell them what had occurred. Most disturbing was her sudden aversion to Graham, turning abruptly away when he approached, no longer seeming at ease in his company. From her former adulation of the pilot it was a shocking, incomprehensible change of attitude that was wounding to him and deeply mystifying to Kay. In the end, it was Nicholas who had driven them home, and when Sinead did not open up at once to Kay when they were alone, nor later speak about what had happened, she despaired of ever finding out.

In the days following Judy's wedding Sinead continued to remain silent and withdrawn. Most disturbing was the change in her sweet-tempered daughter into the vindictive girl she became. Kay felt wounded by Sinead's ill-concealed animosity, at a loss to know how to deal with the sullen stranger, who without ever coming right out and naming him, managed to implicate Graham in her twisted innuendos.

Kay was shocked to notice that Dervla was also on the receiving end of her sister's spite and the little girl complained tearfully that Sinead was being mean to her. 'She tore my comic right in front of me, even though I begged her to stop.' Another time she sobbed in her mother's arms that Sinead had pushed her off her bike, the evidence in her bleeding knees and the depth of her sorrow.

384

But when her sister had deliberately broken the lockets that Graham had given them to wear at the wedding, the little girl was inconsolable.

'I'll have them mended, Derry. Please don't cry, 'Kay's own sorrow matched the child's as she tried to cheer her. 'Sinead is upset, she didn't mean it.'

Kay found the whole thing baffling and disturbing. She had her own problems. The memory of her recent intimacy with Graham was a torment and she convinced herself that she was responsible for inciting the passion that had brought them to make love with such total abandon. She blamed herself too, for not chaperoning her children to the wedding, acknowledging that out of some ridiculous respect for the dead she had put her little girls in jeopardy. Her misery was intensified by the fact that beyond one brief duty call enquiring after Sinead, she had not heard again from Graham that week. Even in those few brief minutes she was conscious of him showing more concern for his daughter than her own, and he had made no suggestion as to when they might meet again, nor any reference to what had taken place between them.

In her acute sensitivity, it was just another proof that Graham had only made love to her because of his sadness over Judy's marriage, and if it had not been for her own complete loss of control it would never have happened. Well, no way was it going to happen again, Kay vowed, and then almost laughed at her naivety. Not as if Graham was rushing for a repeat performance, she thought. With another week half over and still no word from him, she plunged herself into her work, trying to banish the image of that shadowy bedroom and the force of his lovemaking. She could only deduce he was regretting it every bit as much as she was, but for very different reasons.

And then one evening Kay arrived home from the airport to find that Sinead having gone out earlier still had not returned as it grew dark. Breda had been minding the girls and had her own disturbing story to tell of Sinead's behavior, obviously shocked by the terrible resentment she appeared to be harboring against her mother. Sinead, who was always so gentle and caring, Breda could not understand the change in her niece and was determined to have it out with Kay.

The last thing Kay wanted was to discuss something so intensely private with her sister-in-law. She had had a particularly stressful day starting off with the written notification in the post that morning of the date set for the investigation into the train crash. This was followed by what seemed like hours of listening to the gripes of disgruntled air hostesses, and now she longed for her tea. Besides, she had had her own talk with Sinead the previous night. Shockingly explicit, it had only confirmed her earlier fear that her daughter had overheard salacious gossip at the wedding. The lewd mention of her mother and Captain Pender, when coupled with reference to Sinead's betrayed father, had almost unhinged the sensitive girl. Hearing her impassioned outburst, Kay realized that Sinead's present resentment of Graham was only one degree less intense than her previous besotted crush on the pilot.

'How could you have hurt Daddy so,' she sobbed, pushing Kay angrily away when she tried to comfort her.

'Darling, please listen,' Kay entreated. 'It was all a very long time ago, you must believe me.' Weakly, offering this excuse in expiation, much as she had assured Dave the morning of the crash, and with as little effect on his daughter as it had had on him. There was little point in claiming her present relationship with Graham to be merely friendship, aware the recent passionate events of that unforgettable evening had removed the platonic element of a decade's standing in a few brief hours.

'Look, Kay, there's no point in covering up the truth,' Breda told her. 'I know something bad happened at that wedding. This Graham that Dervla keeps talking about - Well, I'd say there's more to this guy than meets the eye.'

'No, no, you've got it all wrong,' Kay was horrified. True, there was a lot about Captain Pender that her sister-in-law had no idea about and Kay wanted it kept that way. 'All I know is someone said something to upset Sinead at the wedding. I spoke to her last night and thought it was all sorted out.'

'Well then, why is she talking as though she hates this man? And it's all too obvious she hates you too,' Breda said bluntly, her speculative gaze resting on Kay's flushed face. 'I don't shock easily,

Kay, but if you'd only heard her! And where is Sinead now? Has she run away, is that it? Well, if she has you need to do something quick, anything could have happened to her.'

'Mummy, has something bad happened to Sinead?' Overhearing, Dervla put the question anxiously.

'No, no, she's probably called over to Patsy's or …or Rebecca's and forgotten the time,' Kay reassured her. 'I'll just go and ring around. I should have done it before.'

But Breda had other ideas. 'The neighbors can wait, let's go ring Mammy first. Sinead could be there.'

'But would she know how to get there?' Kay asked doubtfully, having only gone there one time in the car with the girls.

'Well, there's only one way to find out,' Breda stated firmly, but put down the phone almost at once shaking her head. 'She's not there!'

By this it was past nine o'clock and Dervla was in the front room watching television, useless to expect her to go to bed with her sister missing. Kay was about to go and look out the window again when the doorbell rang.

'Oh, maybe that's her now,' she cried in relief, and went running down the hall to fling wide the door crying, 'Sinead darling…' stopping short at the sight of Graham on the step, his hair clinging damply to his head, like he had come from the gym.

'What are you doing here?' Kay said faintly, as he stepped frowning past her.

'I got your message. Why didn't you ring earlier? I would have come at once.'

'What message?' Kay was bewildered, and then from behind her came a small voice, 'I rang Graham, Mummy. Well, somebody had to, hadn't they?' Dervla asked reasonably, but with a shake in her voice. 'He'll find Sinead. I know he will.'

Kay was conscious of Breda's pop-eyed stare. 'Graham Pender… my sister-in-law,' she introduced them, and saw her change of expression. Oho, the abuser! Only she was so upset Kay might have smiled.

In the kitchen the wine bottle came out of the fridge, this time Kay did not care what Breda thought. 'Not for me,' Graham politely refused, and Breda decided it was time for her to return to her apartment; in her car she had all Dave's clothing which she had packed that afternoon to deliver to the thrift shops, saving Kay the hassle.

'Let me know as soon as you hear anything.' she went out the door, judging Kay to be in competent, if questionable, hands.

'So what's this all about?' Graham demanded sternly, and Kay dropped her eyes, feeling like she was guilty of insubordination on the flight deck. 'Nicholas rang me at the gym to say it was a matter of life and death.'

'I told him that,' Dervla admitted. 'I knew you'd come when you heard that,' and Kay stared, not knowing whether to scold or thank her. 'But it could be a matter of death, c…couldn't it?' she earnestly defended her action. 'Sinead is gone hours and hours. We don't know where she is.'

Graham's expression became even grimmer, if that were possible.

'I knew nothing about Dervla telephoning,' Kay said hastily, feeling the strange need to justify herself, before this tall, stern-faced judge. This was not a side of Graham she had seen often, not since their flying days, the memory of the hi-jack coming suddenly to mind. With an effort, she dragged herself back to the present, horrifying enough in itself.

'Dervla did quite right to phone me,' Graham frowned. 'She would seem to be the only one with any sense here.'

Kay felt rebuffed. 'I didn't want to bother you,' she said stiffly. 'But I'm glad you came. So very glad,' she admitted on a sudden rush of feeling, and saw an immediate lightening of his expression. Could it be he had being missing her and was not entirely unaffected by their tempestuous lovemaking?

'That's good, at any rate,' he said dryly. 'All week I've been concerned about Sinead. When I didn't hear anything from you I thought she must have got over her upset. Now it would seem that's not the case at all.'

Kay's mood, lifting with hope that the silence of the past nine days might have been due to a misunderstanding, took a plunge with Graham's next remark.

'Just think of how this must be affecting Dervla,' he lowered his voice, nodding to where the little girl was gulping and wiping her eyes. So all he was really concerned about was his daughter, Kay thought disillusioned, she might have known.

'It's affecting me too,' she pointed out. 'Sinead has been very troubled ever since. I've tried but I can't seem to reach her no matter what I say or do.' Kay's voice took on a desolate note remembering the terrible hostility, the cold judgment in her daughter's eyes. 'I've tried ringing around her friends but no one has seen her... no one,' she repeated wretchedly, the strain combined with so little to eat all day causing her senses to swim, and she grew faint.

Graham was beside her in a minute and pressing her head down towards her knees. 'What's the matter with Mummy?' Dervla shrilled, the terror in her voice bringing Kay back to herself, and she struggled to sit up.

Graham poured some water into a glass. 'Drink this!' And you - keep an eye on your mother,' he ordered. 'I'm going to ring the Gardai.'

When it grew late and there was still no news of Sinead, Graham brought Dervla up to bed, promising to read her a story. Kay watched the pair of them climbing the stairs, hand in hand; the tall loose-limbed white-haired man and the pretty dark-haired child, so like him in so many ways, and her heart was wrenched by the look of contentment on the little tear-stained face looking back down at her over the banisters.

Going back inside to sit and watch the news, in case something might be broadcast about her missing child, the memory of Dervla's contentment was replaced by the image of Sinead's tormented accusing face, white with misery and rejection. Kay was struck by the inescapable fact that should her future ever become bound up with that of Graham Pender's the prospect would fill one child with delight, and be wholly unacceptable to the other. That being the case how could she even begin to hope for the fulfillment of her own dreams with the man her daughter judged to be responsible for destroying her father's happiness? Not something Sinead would ever forget, Kay thought miserably, not if she lived to be two hundred!

'She's asleep.' Graham was back. 'I got off lightly, one story was enough,' his dark eyes lit with pleasure at the simple fatherly act of putting his little girl to bed. 'Try not to worry,' he told Kay, regarding her anguished face with none of his earlier sternness. 'At least we reported her missing. There will be an alert out for her now.'

'Graham, there's something you need to know.' Hesitantly, she told him of her conversation with Sinead the previous night and how her daughter had admitted having overheard the pilots speaking of Dervla's resemblance to him. 'It was when you were on the floor dancing together, and they were quite graphic about us too,' she shot him a troubled look. 'Oh Graham, if only I had been there to protect her it wouldn't have happened. I should never have allowed the children to go on their own to the wedding.'

'Nonsense! You did your best,' Graham spoke brusquely, appalled at the thought of his fellow pilots' lewd discussion within earshot of the impressionable young girl. 'You can't hope to protect your children from every threat, Kitty, you know that.'

'If only I could have told her the truth myself,' Kay said wretchedly. 'But given the brutal manner in which she found out how can she ever forget or forgive?'

'Whatever way she learned it she'll always see it from her father's viewpoint.'

'I suppose so. At least it makes it easier to understand the way she has been acting ever since the wedding.' Without thinking, she went on to tell him about Sinead's destructive behavior.

Graham's expression darkened and he exclaimed in disbelief, 'Are you saying she broke her sister's locket and her own too!' His mouth twisted in distaste as he thought of the gentle-faced girl who had shyly confided her love of plants and danced so happily at the wedding. It was incredible and disturbing to think of her acting with such spite. 'Naturally, I very much regret that she had to go through such trauma so soon after her father's death but such behavior is totally unacceptable.'

Kay could see that he was no longer in sympathy with the troubled child, and bitterly regretted telling him. She knew that Graham was not without compassion but his own flesh and blood would always come first. It was as simple and basic as that. Aware of all that was passing through his mind - for Dervla was part of her too - she could not fault the fierce possessive love he had for the child, could only wish the incident might have never happened. It seemed so unfair that Sinead who had always been a model child, unselfish and uncomplaining, indeed almost too protective of her little sister, should now have to suffer this double loss – first of her own father and then the one who in time might have taken his place.

'Please don't think too harshly of her,' she pleaded, her heart torn. 'She has suffered such a lot and this last has been almost too much for her to bear. She feels betrayed, I know she does. We must do all we can to try and help her.'

'Of course, we will, you may be sure of that, for your sake, if nothing else...' He broke off with a frown. 'But Dervla must not be subjected to any more of this malicious bullying. I will not have her made unhappy, not for anything. She's such a sunny little girl and doesn't understand anyone being actively unkind.'

'I know!' The tears started to Kay's eyes. 'It breaks my heart to see it too.'

Graham stood up. 'I don't like leaving you and still no word of Sinead but I should be going. It's getting late and if I'm here much longer your neighbors will begin talking. You have your reputation to consider.'

Kay thought he was joking, but he was quite serious. She walked with him to the door and once there, he stared down at her indecisively. Well, if he wasn't going to kiss her, she thought frustrated, he might as well leave and not be tormenting her like this. But when she reached up to open the door, he stopped her.

'Just a moment,' he said, making her wonder what could be making him look so serious. Then surprisingly he said, 'Look, Kitty, maybe now is not the time to speak of this but well, I have given the matter a lot of thought and I would very much like to legally adopt Dervla. What do you say?'

Kay was astonished, even affronted. She stared at him, feeling somehow terribly let down. It was as though after all their talk of Sinead, the troublesome daughter, he could not wait to rescue his own child and distance himself from the pair of them.

'No, it's certainly not the moment to bring it up,' her voice quivered with anger. 'I think it's time you went,' but before she could jerk open the door the telephone suddenly shrilled. She hurried to answer it, fearing the sound would waken Dervla, and found her sister-in-law on the other end.

'Sinead is with Mammy,' Breda told her. 'She's all right and sleeping now.'

'Oh, thank goodness!' Kay cried in relief. 'I'll go over and get her.'

'No, Kay, don't do that. Let her sleep. I've already told Ma you'll pick her up in the morning. You'll only upset her if you go now. Okay?'

Kay nodded dumbly, then finding her voice muttered. 'Thanks for letting me know, Breda.' She turned towards the door but Graham had gone, the tail-lights of his car disappearing down the road. He hadn't even bothered to wait, Kay thought wounded. Closing over the door, she went slowly up to bed.

***

Graham's own thoughts were troubled as he drove home. He found Kay's outrage impossible to understand. For God's sake, why wouldn't she want him to adopt Dervla? He would have thought she would be pleased. Moody and distracted, he entered the house and went to sit in the conservatory, his brow furrowed in thought.

Nicholas wondered at the old man's moodiness and then remembering how his father had rushed out of the gym in response to the distress call, he reckoned he was merely hungry. 'Like me to rustle up some bacon and eggs,' he offered, but Graham impatiently batted away the suggestion.

'Not hungry.'

Something was definitely amiss here. 'So how did you leave Kay? She must have been relieved to know Sinead was safe.'

'I imagine she was,' Graham grunted.

'So did you learn what happened at the wedding?'

Graham looked at his son coldly. 'Enough with the questions, Nicholas. I'm going to pour myself a whisky. Do you want one?'

'Sure…why not?' Nicholas agreed good-humouredly, determined not to be fobbed off. 'Do us good, a nightcap after the rigors of the day.'

His father shot him a suspicious glance and stood with the decanter poised. 'You're not flying tomorrow I presume?'

Nicholas laughed. 'You presume right,' he said with a tinge of asperity. 'I think I know better than to infringe the rules.'

'I should hope so!' Graham carried his glass back to his seat, he seemed to have forgotten his son's existence.

Nicholas sighed. 'This is jolly. Having a companionable drink in companionable silence. What more could a man want after a tiring day!'

Graham glanced at him. 'Sorry, Nicky. I'm acting boorishly. I'm afraid I've been letting my worries get on top of me.'

'Want to talk about it?'

'Not sure I do.'

'Something to do with Kay, is that it?'

Graham sighed. Perhaps Nicky could shed some light on the female point of view. God knows he had knocked about with enough of them. 'I'm afraid Kay took offence at something I said,' he shrugged. 'I have absolutely no idea why.'

'Well, she's under a lot of strain at present,' Nicholas pointed out. 'Her recent bereavement, plus the upset over Sinead…enough to unhinge anyone!'

'Yes, yes, I know all that. But she over-reacted to a proposal I happened to put to her, one she should have welcomed.' He met his son's quizzical glance. 'Well, all right! My timing mightn't have been the best,' he admitted. 'Nevertheless, there was no reason to behave as she did.'

'What kind of proposal?' Nicholas raised his brows suggestively 'Dad! For goodness sake! You never...'

'Certainly not!' Graham snapped. 'I merely told her that I would like to adopt Dervla and have her name legally changed to mine. What was so bad about that?' He was genuinely bewildered.

Nicholas was horrified. 'Have you thought how it would look if you were to do that?'

'Of course I have,' Graham growled. 'Naturally, I had no intention of doing it right away... not for a long time, damn it. Not until the circumstances were just right and Kay happy about it.'

'I suppose you did explain all that to her?' If not, Nicholas understood why she had objected. Whew! what a time for the old man to exercise his parental rights.

***

Kay picked up Sinead next day at her grandmother's house and found her daughter subdued and tearful. She wondered if Sinead realised all the worry and stress she had caused them, but when she began to scold her Eileen put an arm about her protectively.

'She didn't mean to worry you. It's all forgotten now, isn't it, Mammy?' appealing directly to Kay. 'Sure why wouldn't she go to her Gran's? No harm done.'

'Of course,' Kay agreed reluctantly, 'Just so long as you're all right, darling,' vastly relieved when Sinead did not shrink when embraced, tearfully hugging her back.

Kay realised what a child Sinead still was beneath the aggressive attitude of the past weeks; she saw it now for the protective skin it was, enabling her to deal with the shocking revelation about her mother and the man she had hero-worshipped.

Eileen watched the reconciliation approvingly. 'It's not easy for you bringing up two children on your own, Kay,' she told her. 'Poor David would be proud of you, seeing you coping so well.'

Kay felt both surprised and grateful for her understanding. She had never thought to hear Eileen speaking so well of her, in the past they had had their moments which she preferred to forget. On reflection, to be fair to her mother-in-law she had always liked her independence and, to Kay's knowledge, never expressed a wish to live with them. Indeed, she probably never would have sold her house if Dave had not pressurised her like he had, for his own selfish reasons.

Kay felt quite emotional as they said goodbye, remembering the good things about Eileen rather than the bad, and undeniably whatever Eileen had said to her granddaughter it had gone a long way to comforting and reassuring Sinead. Maybe all she had needed was a bit of TLC from her grandmother, Kay thought, relieved to see the sisters friends once more, chattering together in much their old amicable way as they sped home. Remembering Eileen's confused reading of the situation, Kay couldn't help smiling,

'This boy Graham she's so upset about,' Eileen had murmured. 'Seems there was some little tiff between them but, as I told her, a pretty girl like her will have lots of boyfriends when the time comes.'

Over the following days, Kay was disappointed that despite the fact Sinead was more like her old self, she was still a bit aloof where she was concerned. Clearly, it was going to take a lot more time and patience to win her confidence. In the meantime, Kay felt lonely in her exile, still wounded and confused by Graham's talk of adopting Dervla, angry too, for it made her feel that he cared more for his child than he did for her. She felt sad and worn out from all the emotion, and badly missed Sinead's former unstinting affection, the chats they used to share. She wished there was some way she could get their relationship back on its old footing. And then matters improved when Florrie, learning of the rift, suggested that it might do Sinead good to come over and spend a night with Jocelyn and herself at her apartment. They would watch a video, Florrie said, and maybe get her talking about what had happened at the wedding. Kay readily agreed, she was willing to try anything that might help the situation and was relieved when Sinead brightened at the proposed treat. It seemed that Danny would be visiting and Florrie had Sinead's favourite meal of burgers and chips laid on, followed by a luscious chocolate cake. Later, Florrie told her she was planning to show the video of *Little Women* she had rented from the video shop near her, by which time Danny would be gone and it would be an all-girls-night. Kay waved them off, praying that good things would come of the sleepover and that she and Sinead might soon be friends again. If anyone could achieve this, it was Florrie, she told herself, her friend had always been close to Sinead.

Nicholas was also affected by the falling out between his father and Kay. He loved his little half-sister dearly and did not want anything to spoil their relationship. Should this happen he feared his family would be the losers. It was this last that spurred Nicholas to call to Kay's office one afternoon and try and put matters right.

As he peered at the names on the doors, the dark good-looking pilot was unaware of the interested glances he drew from passing hostesses. He was just about to knock on Kay's door when all of a sudden it opened abruptly and a pilot in CA uniform, like himself, came hurrying out, almost bumping into him.

'Oh it's you, Pender. Coming on or off duty?' Captain Canavan inquired pleasantly, and Nicholas replied, 'On my way to Liverpool, Chris. How about you?' hardly listening for his reply, thinking: Good God! Is he after Kay too!

Nicholas found Kay sitting at her desk with a pile of files out in front of her and immediately made himself agreeable, telling her how worried he had been about Sinead and how much he hoped that she was over her upset. At once Kay responded and they got talking. It was much as Nicholas had suspected, it was his father's failure to adequately explain his intentions to Kay, before dropping his bombshell that had aroused her anger.

'Your father should have discussed it with me first, Nicky,' she said stiffly. 'Not just come out with it like he did.'

'I agree it was badly done but, believe me, the very last thing he meant to do was give offence,' Nicholas hastened to reassure her. 'He just wanted to show you how much he cares for Dervla. I honestly don't think it crossed his mind that he might be taking things too much for granted.' But despite his best efforts, Kay was not convinced of Graham's selflessness or his sincerity.

'I'm afraid it didn't seem that way to me,' she said. 'He made it very clear what *he* wanted, regardless of my feelings in the matter.'

'You're right. He handled it badly and his timing couldn't have been worse,' Nicholas readily agreed. 'But he was most upset once I pointed that out to him.'

'Well, if he's all *that* upset why didn't he come see me himself instead of sending you? I don't think too much of that!'

'Oh dear,' Nicholas sighed comically. 'I'm afraid like father like son. I don't seem to be doing a better job of explaining than my old man.. You see, he doesn't *know* I'm here, Kay. Failed to mention that, did I?' he said winningly. 'No, well he's so cursedly proud he would almost certainly have stopped me.'

'Not that any of it matters a jot, of course!' Nicholas hurried on. 'The main thing is to try and fix it now, and not only for Dad's sake either. We're all going to suffer if it isn't resolved, for you must know how very fond we are of Sinead. We have come to look upon her every bit as much a part of our family as Dervla.'

Here it seemed Nicholas had said the right thing for Kay was immediately mollified at the kindly inclusion of Sinead into the concerns and affections of the Pender family. Undoubtedly, it went a long way towards bringing her around to viewing his father more kindly and she thanked Nicholas for his concern, even saying he was an exceptional young man, which pleased him greatly.

Going aboard his flight, Nicholas was suddenly reminded of seeing Captain Canavan coming out of Kay's office earlier, and was of the opinion this tidbit was something that should be passed on to his father. Nothing like a bit of competition to get things back on track.

That evening Nicholas waited until after their meal, before breaking it to his father how he had spoken to Kay in her office that day, steeling himself against the expected reaction.

'You did what?' Captain Pender thundered. 'How dare you go and see her behind my back. You had no business interfering like that.'

Nicholas rode out the storm until his father had finally calmed down and was in better mood to hear what had passed between them.

'So what did she say?' Graham demanded, adding more quietly, 'Is there a chance she might hear me out if I went to see her?'

Nicholas nodded. 'I do. Most definitely!' taking a breath before going on to mention the fact that earlier he had seen Captain Canavan emerging from Kay's office.

'Whom did you say?' Graham was startled. 'You mean that chap who was with BA before joining Celtic Airways?'

'That's the one!'

'Did you know that Canavan applied to MacDoolAer first, but he was over qualified for the position we had to offer. Very able guy,' Graham opined. 'Could be he'll succeed Ben Higgins as Chief Pilot. So why was Canavan there?'

Nicholas shrugged. 'Now what do *you* think!' he asked, and got the satisfying explosion he was after.

***

After giving it much thought, Graham decided to pay Kay a visit that Sunday morning and put an end to the unfortunate misunderstanding between them. From his son he knew that she was due back from London around midday. Nicholas admitted that he was actually flying on the UK flight with her, adding by a coincidence their captain was none other than Chris Canavan, 'Your rival, Dad.'

Not that Graham took his son's claim too seriously, but what he could not ignore was the unmistakable compatibility in their ages. Graham reckoned that Chris had to be in his late thirties, remembering how he had been much the same age on first laying eyes on Kay himself, and this made him all the more determined to settle their differences quickly. On arriving at Kay's house shortly before one o'clock the door was opened to him by Sinead. It was their first time meeting since her upset at Judy's wedding. To his relief she seemed friendly, and even smiled at him. Much of this was due to Florrie's frank talk with Sinead when she had greatly helped the teenager to a better understanding of her mother's relationship with Captain Pender, once she made it clear to her that Kay had known Graham long before ever marrying her father. 'So you see,' Florrie had pointed out, 'They were sweethearts way back when she was still single,' considering any other information inappropriate at that time and none of Sinead's business anyway.

Graham followed Sinead into the kitchen where Dervla was reading a story book, propped against the sugar bowl, and munching on cornflakes. 'Graham!' she shrieked, 'Mummy never said you were coming.'

'Surprise visit, Dervla,' he smiled. 'Thought the pair of you might like to go for a drive this afternoon.'

'Oh, yes. We would, wouldn't we, Sinead?' Dervla said excitedly, and Sinead nodded, not averse to the suggestion.

Graham beamed. 'Capital! Well, this is the thing. I promised your Mummy that I would help get you over your nervousness about flying, Derry, Today's weather looks pretty settled, so how about it? Would you like to visit the flying club and go up for a short spin?'

Dervla went very quiet. 'I don't know,' she said at last.

Graham was aware he had sprung it on her. 'Look, you don't have to fly today if you don't want to. No pressure. But we could have something to eat at the club. Maybe sample some of Christy's special burgers and chips, what do you say?'

Dervla brightened. 'Cool…so long as you're not cross with me.'

'Not a bit,' Graham assured her. 'Of course, we'll have to see what your Mummy says. She might have made other plans.' He glanced at Sinead, seeing her doubtful expression. 'You'll come too, won't you, Sinead?'

'Sure, I'd like that… but if Derry cries or anything you must bring her back.'

'No problem,' Graham agreed, pleased at this concern for her sister.

'I won't cry,' Dervla said. 'Not if Uncle Graham is with me… and…and I just might fly after all,' she said bravely. 'If *he* wants me to.'

Graham patted her head affectionately. 'Only if *you* want to, Derry. 'He glanced at his watch and was surprised to see it was half past one. 'Your Mummy is late. I was sure she would be here by now.'

'Oh, Mummy rang to say she's having lunch with a friend,' Sinead informed him. 'She said she'll get us takeaways when she comes.'

Graham was struck by the unpalatable notion that Nicky might have been right after all about Captain Canavan. From what he had seen of the pilot he was not the man to waste an opportunity when it was handed to him. With that, he came to a decision.

'Oh, I think we can do better than takeaways,' Graham told them cheerfully. 'Let's be on our way, we'll eat when we get there. Better wear sweaters, the pair of you. Oh, and bring anoraks. It can be cold out on the airfield.'

As the girls ran to get ready, Graham went to the window and stared out at the neglected garden. Takeaways, he thought disgustedly. No way to feed growing children. He knew he was being unreasonable but the thought of Kay lunching with Captain Canavan irked him unbearably. Almost as much as Nicholas's, 'I told you so.'

It was after three by the time Kay let herself into the house. She was surprised not to see the girls come running to meet her, half-expecting them to be on lookout by then. Since the day Captain Canavan had called to her office to sympathize with her on her husband's death, they had shared a couple of flights; today on landing he had asked her to have lunch with him in the canteen. Kay had been happy to go along and soon forgot the time for he was an agreeable companion. Besides, it was nice to relax in adult company for a change, even nicer having a man looking at her again with interest, her self-esteem badly bruised on learning of Dave's long-term infidelity.

Perhaps the girls were in their bedrooms. She went upstairs calling to them but it was soon apparent they were not in the house. No panic! Dervla was sure to be up the street playing with Gemma and she would know where Sinead had gone. But when Kay hurried up the street and questioned Gemma, the little girl shook her head.

'Dervla isn't here.'

'But where can she be?' Kay was dismayed.

'I saw her getting into a car with Sinead,' the child shrilled. 'I wanted to go with them but the man wouldn't let me.'

'What man?' Kay was instantly alarmed.

'Dervla's uncle.'

Gemma's mother peered around the door. 'I didn't realize it was you, Kay. Anything the matter?'

'I thought Dervla might be with Gemma but she says their uncle took them for a drive. I expect they must have gone for takeaways.'

Even as she spoke, Kay felt her anger rising. What on earth was Graham thinking, to be taking them anywhere without her permission?

Gemma said excitedly, 'They weren't going for takeaways. I heard him saying it was a good day for flying. Dervla's really lucky.'

Kay stared, unable to believe what she was hearing. He had taken them flying! Both of them, Sinead too! Panic filled her, and she began to tremble.

'Kay, are you all right?' Pam looked at her curiously, but Kay hardly heard her as she rushed back home, her mind filled with terrible visions. First the train crash in which her husband had died, then the light aircraft getting into difficulties, like that time with Nicky. She could see it crashing down out of the sky, another disaster, this time wiping her whole family out in one go. She began to shake so much she could hardly get into her car to drive across the city to the Penders' house.

Nicholas was changing out of uniform when he heard the persistent pealing of the front door bell. He was still buttoning his shirt as he ran down stairs and saw the outline of a woman through the frosted glass. Too tall for Carol, he was thinking, as he flung wide the door and saw Kay on the step.

'Nicky, Nicky, I must talk to you. Can I come in?'

'Of course! Is something the matter?' wanting to bite his tongue the minute he said it, it was obvious.

'Oh Nicky, I'm so worried,' she gasped. 'When I got home there was no sign of the girls. My neighbor told me your father has taken them flying. I can't *believe* he'd do such a thing without telling me.' She caught hold of his arm. 'Oh Nicky, Nicky if anything happens to them I'll go out of my mind,' and to his horror, she began to cry.

What on earth was the old man thinking, Nicholas asked himself for the second time that week, as he poured her brandy and rang the club. According to Christy who answered his call, his father had fuelled up the Cessna and taken off with Sinead and Dervla on board fifteen minutes earlier. Such a time to go joy riding without Kay's permission, thought Nicholas in dismay. If his father was setting out to deliberately kibosh their relationship, he could not have gone about it better.

Graham arrived at the airfield and brought the girls into the bar for lemonade while he enquired which planes were ready to go and checked the meteorological report. There was a new engineer since Liam and he was a pleasant, capable young man who made himself agreeable to Captain Pender and he soon had one of the Cessna's checked out and refueled. Graham was conscious of Dervla's slight hesitancy when he suggested they might go for a spin but he managed to reassure her and she soon regained her confidence and climbed aboard willingly enough. Once they took off he made a few more circuits of the airfield, pleased to see her showing no fear, indeed she was enjoying every minute of the ride; Sinead too, chatty and smiling. It seemed a pity not to go a bit further afield, he was thinking, give them a bit longer in the air. It was then that he had got the notion of calling in at Baldonnel to have a chat with Jeremy. He had a reason for this, lately he had noticed letters arriving from Sri Lanka for Ranjan, and he was concerned that his adopted son might be planning to return to his homeland, not something he could approve. Maybe Jeremy might know something, Graham mused, at any rate it would be good to sound him out on the subject. Besides, the detour would make the trip all the more interesting for the girls, and it might be a while before he could take Dervla up again. His suggestion was greeted with delight. Graham was pleased, confirmed in the soundness of his judgment.

On putting down at Casement Aerodrome he and the girls received a warm welcome from Commdt. Pender who brought them into the Pilots mess to meet his friends, there was much laughter and praise from the young officers for Dervla's artistic skill when she began at once drawing for them pictures of what she was calling her 'Cadet Cats'. Watching her, Graham was proud to think that she had inherited this gift from his mother. One day he hoped to show the little girl her grandmother's paintings and sketches, but when he did, he told himself, he wanted the child to be aware of the family relationship between herself and the artist who had produced such striking work.

While the girls spent a happy half hour climbing in and out of the Air Corps training jets, Graham chatted to Jeremy about Ranjan, and was not too surprised by his lack of enthusiasm; his eldest son had always been critical of the Indian boy, never growing close to him like Nicky.

'Well, all I can say if Ranjan has any sense he'll stay in Ireland now that he has his engineering degree,' Jeremy drawled, not caring either way. 'But I expect he wants to trace his family so why not let him go!'

'Why not indeed!' Graham clapped Jeremy's shoulder tolerantly. Of course, Ranjan must be free to make his own way, but part of him had always fervently hoped his adopted son would settle in Ireland, or at least somewhere closer than Sri Lanka.

Graham knew that he should have left a note for Kay and was beginning to feel a bit guilty about it, but decided he would give her a ring from the club before bringing them back home. The truth of it was, he heartily disapproved of her neglecting her children to have lunch with a friend, one who was almost certainly Captain Canavan, and felt the situation needed drawing attention to. In the circumstances, he told himself, it was just as well he had taken them out for a treat, for all he knew she was not back yet from the airport.

Calling to the girls it was time to go, Graham walked them back to the Cessna. Helping them aboard, he instructed them on fastening their seatbelts, before strapping himself in and running his pre-take-off checks. Hearing his daughter shouting, 'Blast off!' he chuckled, knowing he had been right to make her face her fears. Next time it would be easier for her, but really she had done very well.

Before long they were coming in low over the M & K Aeroclub and as Graham circled the airfield before landing, his eye was caught by two familiar figures standing on the grass verge outside the clubhouse. By their grim expressions he deduced this was no welcome party and concentrated on putting down safely on the runway.

Kay felt overwhelming relief at the sight of the small plane coming in to land. Thank God, they were back! She almost sagged in relief. And then at the thought of the terrible anxiety she had been forced to endure these past two hours, unnecessarily so, her relief turned to rage against the man responsible. Frowning, she watched him climbing out of the Cessna and come strolling nonchalantly towards her, with his arms about her daughters, smiling and unrepentant for the anguish he had caused her.

'Would you please get the girls something to drink,' she told Nicholas in a trembling voice. 'I would like to speak to your father alone.'

'Sure, Kay.' Nicholas waited uneasily for them to draw level. 'Hey Dad, why don't I bring the girls into the bar,' and Graham nodded, beginning to frown himself.

Grimly, Kay led the way into the clubhouse and, choosing a room at random, she barely waited until the door was closed, before turning on him furiously. 'Just what do you think you're doing taking my children out of the house without even a word or a note to say where you'd gone? I've been out of my mind with worry these few hours.'

'Sorry about that, Kay. Somehow, it never occurred to me I needed your permission to bring them on a treat,' and now Graham's voice had an edge to it.

'Just how do you think I felt at finding the house empty?' Kay demanded. 'I had no way of knowing where they were until I spoke to my neighbor, and then to learn you had taken them flying, without ever even thinking to ask my permission. It was too bad of you, Graham.'

Captain Pender's jaw tightened at the criticism and he cleared his throat, seeing he needed to do a better job of explaining, 'Well yes, I should have left you a note but when the children told me that you had stopped to have lunch, my first thought was to get some food into them.'

'They wouldn't have starved,' Kay snapped. 'Anyway, no one asked *you* to feed them. Sinead is well able to cook up something for herself and Dervla. She's used to doing it when I'm flying. I can't always be sure what time I'll get home.'

'Oh, for goodness sake, Kay!' Graham threw up his hands in exasperation, 'I just thought they would enjoy a treat and if you decide to stay out all afternoon clearly someone needs to see they are properly fed.'

Kay choked. 'Despite your low opinion of me, I assure you I'm quite capable of looking after my children myself and I don't need *you* to tell me.'

'That's *not* what I was implying …'

'No matter,' she grated. 'None of this excuses your high-handed behavior.' Her voice broke, the strain beginning to tell on her but she refused to give into it.

'I have already agreed it was inconsiderate of me. Perhaps you would like me to abase myself further?' Again there was that sarcastic note.

She glared at him, suddenly distracted by how attractive he looked in the bulky fleece-lined jacket. It must be new, she decided, she had not seen it on him before.

With an effort, she returned to the attack. 'And how dare you force Dervla to fly. Only I wouldn't have dreamed of putting her through such an ordeal I would have insisted she fly to Cork that time. Such niceties don't bother you, of course. '

'There was absolutely no question of forcing her to fly,' Graham protested. 'I've already explained,' He took an agitated turn about the room, before saying incredulously. 'You surely don't want Dervla afraid of flying for the rest of her life?'

"Of course not! I'm just not happy about my children going up in rickety old planes. Supposing...just supposing.' She swallowed and rushed on, 'Even if you've forgotten, I haven't... the difficulties Nicholas got into that time, the dreadful fright we all had.' In her upset she was almost shouting. 'If anything had happened, I would have lost *both* my children. Do you realize that? My entire family wiped out in one go.'

'Don't be utterly ridiculous,' Graham blazed, 'There was absolutely no danger of that. I think at this stage I am qualified to fly well-maintenanced light aircraft without crashing.' He controlled himself with an effort. 'However, I realize how upset you are and make allowances on that account. Just don't talk such melodramatic rubbish.' His words, cutting and true, were like a blow.

Sanity returning, Kay drew in a shaky breath, shocked at having let her anger and resentment betray her into criticizing his flying skill. 'I'm sorry,' she said haltingly. 'I didn't mean that.' She sighed, worn out with wrangling but unable to stop. 'Just don't dare criticize how I bring up my children. It's none of your business.'

Graham's expression which had softened at her stumbling apology grew stern again. 'I have every right to be concerned about what happens to *my* child.'

'Well, regardless of how you see it she is *not* your concern,' Kay rapped back. 'Anyway, I've had enough of this. I'm going home now. It has been a terrible day although not all of it I'm glad to say,' filled with the mean desire to shake his composure. 'At least the earlier part was enjoyable, before *you* succeeded in turning the rest into a nightmare.'

'I suppose you are referring to your luncheon date with Captain Canavan,' Graham said coldly, and Kay flushed and tossed her head.

'And if I am that's something else that's *not* your concern.' Picking up her bag, she marched towards the door.

'Kitty, don't go. Please come back,' Graham said in an altered voice, and Kay hesitated a moment then resolutely kept on going. She tore open the door and stopped short at the sight of Dervla and Sinead huddled fearfully outside.

At the sight of her, they threw themselves at her crying, 'Mummy, Mummy, we want to go home.' Emerging into the corridor, Graham was in time to hear Dervla stammering. 'I...d...don't like it here, Mummy,' and then seeing him she said forlornly. 'Why were you sh... shouting like that at my Mummy?'

For Graham this was the unkindest cut of all and throwing up his hands in frustration, he growled one word, 'Women!' before striding off down the corridor and vanishing into the night.

Nicholas was dismayed at the unfortunate turn of events as he drove Kay and the girls back to town. Turning in the wide gates of the family residence, he noted the absence of his father's car and told himself it was the first sensible thing the old man had done in a long time. Certainly Kay didn't need any more hassle after all she had already endured. But it was for the children that Nicholas felt the most pity, touched by the way Dervla earnestly clutched her mother's arm, whimpering, 'We're sorry, Mummy. We didn't mean to worry you.' Poor kids, he thought.

Kay got into her own car looking exhausted. 'Thanks for driving us there and back, Nicky.'

'Only too glad. We aircrew must stick together,' making oblique reference to the flight they had shared earlier in the day,.

Kay nodded, as though even the effort of returning his smile was beyond her, and tiredly drove away with her children.

It was late by the time Graham returned home. Hearing his key in the lock, Nicholas had immediately put out his beside lamp, not wanting any postmortems on the day. Later, Ranjan crept past his guardian's study, equally anxious to avoid attracting attention. Like everyone at the club he had heard the raging row going on behind the closed door. When they had finally emerged he had made sure to be out of sight.

Graham eventually turned out his study light and went up to bed, where he lay tense and wakeful into the small hours, pondering on how he could have got things so horribly wrong and once again managed to grievously offend the one person in his life he most wanted to please.

Across the city, Kay had no better success in getting to sleep. Like Graham she had found herself endlessly mulling over the events of what she now thought of as 'Black Sunday' and their irrevocable falling out. She realized she had become a little unhinged by her anxiety over the children to have reacted in the way she had. But on recalling Graham's remark about her lack of trust she knew that never again could she take her children's safety for granted, nor trust them to anyone else. The sudden violent manner of Dave's death had robbed her of what she had always before taken for granted. And yet, paradoxically, the one person that she always felt most safe with was Graham Pender. Indeed, she had never been in any doubt that he could protect her. Why this was so, she didn't quite understand. Suffice to say she knew that with him she would always *be* safe as opposed to *feeling* safe. No question about it!

In the days that followed, Kay found herself going back over it all again, and feeling every bit as troubled, not only because of her row with Graham but the arrival of the official report on the Charleville rail crash, and with it the grim reminder of Dave's tragic death. On reading it, Kay was deeply upset to learn that a combination of circumstances had led to the train's derailment. The main factors which caused the crash were first of all the excessive speed the train was moving, much faster than the maximum permitted speed of 75 m.p.h. on the Dublin/Cork line, as well as the existence of a length of badly cracked rail in the vicinity of the railway track some miles beyond Charleville station. It was further discovered that the driver had been self-medicating for a painful shoulder injury, the tablets causing drowsiness and affecting his judgment, so that he had failed to recognize the dangerous speed at which he was travelling. There was reference to the Buttevant rail crash two years earlier when 17 people had been killed and others injured, following which it was required by law that the existing timber bodied mainline coaches with poor damage-resistant qualities should be replaced by all-steel coaches mounted on heavy underframes with buck-eye-type automatic couplings and Pullman-type gangways. The report confirmed that this work had been satisfactorily carried out in accordance with regulations and all coaches in service on the day of the Charleville crash were found to be the required all-steel variety, which undoubtedly saved lives.

But not my poor husband's life, thought Kay sorrowfully, he was not as fortunate. All that stressful day, she found herself dwelling on what she had read and knew that ahead of her lay another night of wakefulness, and so it turned out to be. When not thinking of her husband's tragic end and the dead driver's part in his death and the deaths of all those others, Kay's thoughts dwelled obsessively on this second falling out with Graham Pender. She told herself that she had had every right to be angry over his practically kidnapping her children and taking them flying without her permission, but agonized over her temerity in accusing him, a senior captain with an excellent flying record, of having endangered her children's lives. Why, she might as well have implied that Captain Pender was a grave danger to the general public every time he took off with a planeload of passengers. No way would he ever forget or forgive the insult. Mortified, she wondered how she could have acted so stupidly.

But, of course, Kay knew it was not stupidity but jealousy that was at the root of it, unable to rid her mind of the image of Graham with his arms clasped affectionately about her daughters, all three happy and smiling, and in no need of her at all. When added to the memory of how rejected she had felt on the night Graham had spoken of his desire to adopt Dervla, there seemed to be no end to her misery.

***

Kay arrived into work to learn that the Super was back from her honeymoon. By all accounts, Judy looked marvellous, deeply tanned and elegantly attired in a white designer dress and jacket, so the reserves had it, envious and critical by turn. Skin like leather, some of the meaner ones said, but the same deep tan glimpsed on Taylor when entering the building with his bride merely succeeded in arousing their admiration. So it was a clear case of sour grapes, Kay decided, getting on with her paper work when the door suddenly opened and her boss looked in all smiles.

Immediately, Kay jumped up and positioned her only visitor's chair for Judy to sit on. She supposed she should consider herself highly privileged at the visit but her mood was still very low, and before long Judy broke off her description of scuba-diving in the Caribbean to say, 'Kay, my dear, forgive me but you look rather tired and drawn. I had hoped things might have eased.'

'Oh, they have, quite a bit,' Kay assured her, trying to smile, but it was an effort. 'The girls are quite good really but still not over the shock of their father's death,' her voice faltered, 'It will take a little longer I'm afraid.'

'Of course! It's still very recent. I was hoping you might allow them to visit us soon. In another week we will be having a few friends in for drinks to show the wedding video. You must come too. I'll let you know when we fix a date.'

Before Kay could speak a sudden knock at her door recalled Judy to the time.

'My goodness, I must be getting back. Such a lot to catch up on, the downside of being away so long.'

'Sorry for the intrusion, ladies.' Captain Canavan popped in his head. 'No, please don't stir,' as Judy stood up. 'Why don't I come back, Kay, when you're not so busy,' and he vanished.

'What nice manners.' Judy glanced at Kay thoughtfully. 'I fear I scared him away. Nothing important I hope.'

'Not at all,' Kay lied. 'I can't imagine what he wanted.'

As soon as Judy was gone, she glanced in her compact mirror and was vexed to see how flushed she had become. Resolutely, she settled down again to work but Judy's account of honeymooning in the Barbados had produced in her a restless longing. She sat daydreaming of balmy nights and guinea moons when there was another knock, and this time the appearance of another captain.

'Graham!' she said self-consciously, remembering their angry parting on Sunday evening.

'I'm glad to find you on your own.' He shut the door and took the seat so recently vacated by Judy. 'You weren't joking, were you?' His dark eyes were amused. 'You said your office was small but I would think that must be the understatement of the year.'

Kay banished unpleasant memories and smiled tentatively. 'I call it my cubby-hole but until Judy okays something bigger I'm stuck with it,' catching sight of his expression she thought: Why, he's actually nervous.

'Please listen, Kay,' Graham said urgently, 'I came here to apologise. I should never have taken the girls flying without your say-so on Sunday and, believe me, I never meant to offend you when I spoke of my desire to adopt Dervla. I shouldn't have sprung it on you like I did.' He spread his hand ruefully, 'I do seem to keep putting my foot in it, don't I?' meeting her eyes unhappily. 'Please say you forgive me?'

'Of course!' she managed to say, and heard his sigh of relief.

'Thank heavens for that. I am very conscious of how quickly Dervla is growing up. I suppose I don't want to waste any more precious time in getting to know her.' He glanced at Kay. 'How was she? Her first flight after the accident?'

'She has been fine,' Kay assured him.

'Well, that's a relief. I did think she was happy in the air, not a bother on her, But afterwards she was clearly upset overhearing our disagreement.' He met her eyes and admitted ruefully, 'It has been worrying me ever since.'

Although Kay could see that Graham sincerely regretted their row all this talk of Dervla only reinforced her belief that he cared more for his child than her. It made her slow to respond. Until he spoke the right words, Kay told herself stubbornly, she could take no pleasure in any of it, no matter how flattering or seductive his behaviour. To be honest what Kay most wanted to hear was Graham admitting that to be a part of *her* life, not just his daughter's, was the most important thing to him. She felt an irrational anger that he could not see this for himself, and wondered if Dervla actually could be more important to him, at once sheering away from this unpalatable thought.

Turning to him, she said diffidently, 'I appreciate your coming here like this, Graham. I was very upset myself on Sunday, I hardly knew what I was saying.'

Graham looked relieved but she knew by his slightly puzzled air that it was not quite what he had been hoping to hear. But how could it be when what he was saying fell so far short of what she herself *needed* to hear. She looked at him helplessly, struck as always by the beautiful shape of his head, his dark expressive eyes which betimes were full of humour or melting concern, and never more satisfying than when she was the one inspiring the emotion. So what, if he loved his child more than her, she told herself desperately, she would have whatever affection was left over, wouldn't she? Surely, that should be enough for her?

Consumed by the desire to get their relationship back on track, she blurted,

'Graham, I do so hate wrangling with you. Couldn't we...' but what she was about to say was lost, interrupted by another annoying knock, and turning her head she saw it was Captain Canavan back once more trying his luck.

'Oh, dear!' Chris said comically. 'Not my morning, is it? Perhaps I should pick a number and get in line.'

Kay flushed, not knowing how to respond to this, but Captain Pender was already on his feet. 'I was just going. You must have my seat,' he said, 'I'm afraid Kay's cubby-hole doesn't run to more than one visitor at a time.'

'That's very decent of you but please don't let me drive you away,' Chris said politely, clearly unsure whom he might be.

'Oh, I almost forgot,' Graham took an envelope from his inside pocket. 'I want you to have this, Kitty. When you get a moment you might put it somewhere safe.'

Somewhat distractedly, Kay held the envelope until he had gone, wondering what on earth it could be until a discreet cough reminded her of her visitor.

'Sorry!' she told Chris. 'I'm afraid I've got a lot on my mind just now,' filled with the impatient desire for him to go. 'I'm afraid I still haven't risen to that coffee machine I promised you last time you dropped by.'

'Not to worry, Kay. I expect I'll be getting any amount of coffee on board. Look, I'll just say what I came for and run. I was rather hoping to persuade you to have dinner with me Saturday night?'

'Thanks Chris. It's nice of you to ask me but I'm afraid it's still way too early for me,' Kay firmly turned him down, and as soon as the disappointed pilot had hurried away she ripped open the envelope in her hand.

On looking inside she found two share certificates and reading their value she was amazed to see that each one was to the value of five hundred shares in Cement Roadstone. They were made out in the names of her children and she was bowled over by the fact that Graham had given Sinead the same amount as his own child. Sitting down slowly behind her desk absentmindedly tucking them back into the envelope, she was struck by how handsomely he was attempting to make amends for the falling out between them. She reached across the desk, her first impulse to ring and thank him, and found to her relief that he was back in his office and answering the phone himself.

'I really don't know what to say,' Kay began, 'Your gift to the girls is most generous. I'm not sure that I can accept it.'

Graham chuckled. 'Oh, come now, Kay. Of course you can.'

'Well, whatever about Dervla... but for you to include Sinead too. It's really too much.' The enormity of it began to hit her, and along with it a sense of obligation not perceived before.

'I wouldn't dream of doing anything less. Both girls should benefit and Sinead's father not there to take care of her. I like to think my gift might be what he would have done if he had had the chance.'

413

'Well, it's good of you to put it like that,' Kay said awkwardly. 'I never expected anything of this nature.'

'Why not? Don't you want me to look out for your children? I'm very fond of them, you must know that. Which reminds me, how would you feel if I were to take Dervla to the flying club again fairly soon? Of course, if you are at all unhappy about it you must say so,' he said hastily. 'But if the improvement in her is to continue it would be wise to follow up the first desensitising session as soon as possible.'

Kay went very quiet, but not as Graham believed from reluctance to expose her youngest child to the perils of flying so soon. The truth of it was she was assailed once more by all her former doubts and insecurities regarding Graham's motives in becoming actively involved in Dervla's life. Could this gift merely be another devious means of binding her gratitude and ensuring her compliance? Her spirits dipped and she found it difficult not to sound her disillusion.

'You're probably right,' she told him at last. 'But if you don't mind I'd prefer to wait a while before letting her go again. There's no rush, is there?'

'Not at all. It's only the child I'm thinking of,' he said evenly, plunging her emotions still further. Kay replaced the receiver reading new meanings into every remark he had uttered, and then came another knock on her door. Oh dear! What now!

'Nicky!' she breathed in relief. 'Come in. Nothing but visitors this morning and hardly space to turn around in. Any suggestions on how to cater for the hordes?'

He grinned back, pretending to take her seriously. 'How about slinging a couple of hammocks. Might even become the fashion.'

They were talking nonsense, of course but she welcomed it after all the recent tension. 'So Nicky, any reason for your visit?' adding hurriedly. 'Not of course that you need one.'

'Well, that's good to hear. I just dropped by to see if you and your daughters would like to come to a barbecue at the house this weekend? With this hot spell all set to continue we're ordering in loads of steaks and burgers and a ton of wine.'

414

Kay wondered that Graham had not mentioned it. 'Thanks, Nicky, we'd love to come. Anything we can bring?'

'Just yourselves. Oh, by the way I'll pick you up, Kay. It will save you driving.' And when she protested, 'Believe me, it's no trouble. It's going to be a long day and lots of wine flowing,' as if she had no choice but to become as blotto as the rest. 'Expect me around three. Barring disasters, we'll be eating by five.'

One down and one to go! Jubilantly Nicholas hurried off, planning to break the news to his father that evening. With regard to the old man, it was all on a need-to-know basis these days. It worked best that way.

The weather held fine and Saturday was another blistering day. Although Sinead did not go into raptures like Dervla about the barbecue, Kay could see she was pleased all the same. It was the chance to attend something enjoyable and promised to be good fun. Glancing over her wardrobe, she decided on summery slacks and a flame-coloured Italian off-the-shoulder knit she had picked up in a boutique sale recently. Maybe a lacy wrap for when the sun went down? The girls could wear their new jeans and matching candy-striped tops. Kay seldom dressed them alike but it was their wish to 'twin' it, as Dervla engagingly put it, and she could only rejoice to see them so fond again. At least there was no more name-calling, crying jags or jewellery-throwing, thank goodness. She felt cheered when they told her they would be wearing their mended lockets, clearly another' twin it' decision.

Nicholas was delighted when the day dawned so fine but then he had predicted it the previous evening, describing it poetically to his father as 'strands of Titian hair fanning the western heavens,' adding with a grin. 'So long as those rosy tresses are not there again at dawn we can share in the wise old shepherd's delight.'

'Seems promising enough,' Graham said, raising his eyes from his book. Although stormy weather is predicted later. Let's hope it holds off until we serve the food.'

He was pleased the girls were coming. 'Just what they need. Brighten them up after all the gloom of the past months. And that little imp, Dervla,' he chuckled. 'She'll be in her element. We don't see enough of her, Nicky. She'll be sure to keep the party lively.' All of it sounding just what Nicholas was hoping for, an end to the unfortunate misunderstandings that existed with Kay.

Before he left to collect them Nicholas set up the tables and sun umbrellas and seen to it the charcoal fires would be lit in good time. He found Kay and the girls in great form and looking forward to the barbecue. On arriving back to the house with them, his father's glowing good humour was evident too, he was evidently on the lookout and came out at once to greet them.

With his arm about her, Graham ushered Kay on to the patio where he made the introductions to his MacDoolAer pilots, before circulating with her amongst the other guests. Kay had flown with Captain Brennan a few times but she had not met his wife Mona, and as they chatted they were soon joined by Ben and Linda Higgins. It was a merry gathering and Nicholas had never seen Kay looking so well. He guessed that she had no idea of how striking she looked, her shapely figure set off to advantage in the well-cut slacks and pretty Italian knit. He was conscious of the younger pilots in his father's airline eyeing her with interest and asking, 'Who *is* that! What do I have to do to get an intro?' and smiled at the thought of what their Chief of Ops would think of that!

Nicholas gazed about him, glad to see everyone pitching in, even Jeremy was cheerfully manning the drinks trolley and Ranjan turning steaks on the glowing coals, while Carol tackled the salads and amused them all with her zany flying jokes. Altogether there was a great atmosphere with everyone enjoying the balmy weather and the booze flowing. He turned about in satisfaction to check the barbecue when all at once his blood ran cold. For there, coming around the side of the house, with a bottle of wine stuck under each arm and wearing a big grin, was Captain Canavan.

Immediately, Nicholas sprang into action, urgently enlisting Jeremy's help and Carol's too, in an attempt to decoy the smitten pilot. But Chris somehow managed to shake them all off sticking close to Kay's side, until Jeremy began noisily thumping a metal tray and calling, 'Come and get it!'

By this Captain Pender was becoming increasingly irritated by Chris Canavan's attentions and Nicholas furiously blaming himself for being so lavish with his invites.

Without being rude, Kay found it impossible to shake off Captain Canavan, he shadowed her everywhere and she brightened in relief at Jeremy's rallying cry. Maybe now she would be rid of him. But Chris eyeing the crowd congregating about the buffet table kindly offered to fill a plate for her. 'Save you getting trampled in the rush, Kay.'

'Sure...thanks, Chris,' she agreed weakly.

As soon as he moved away Graham came to join her. He too offered to save her queuing, and she found herself helplessly nodding again.

'Shall I bring the girls over to the table with me?' Graham suggested. 'I imagine it won't be hard to guess what they'll go for,' he chuckled, his good humour restored now that his rival had moved away.

'No prizes for guessing,' she smiled up at him in conspiratorial fashion, and he stared back at her with a certain look in his eyes that caused her heart to double trip. When he put his arm about her she forgot all about Chris, until with a beaming smile the pest came hurrying back, balancing a loaded plate on each hand.

'Got you a bit of everything on offer, Kay,' he announced cheerfully. 'Hope I didn't overdo it. Here, take these, will you, while I go back and get us some wine.'

Helplessly, she accepted the plates, aware of the mounting tension in the man beside her. 'I didn't *ask* him,' she told Graham helplessly. But now there was only fury in the dark eyes that had so stirred her moments before, and he stamped off.

Kay could have wept. Was there never to be an end to these stupid misunderstandings? Stuck with Captain Canavan, she knew that she had no one to blame but herself. Worse was to come, with the wine gone to his head he began tweaking her sweater and further exposing flesh, becoming far too familiar, unaware he was giving offence.

'Do you mind!' Kay pulled away, trying not to sound like an outraged prude and injecting just enough frost in her tone to get through his inebriated skin.

'Sorry!' Canavan was unrepentant, too drunk to care. 'I say, let's go explore the garden, Kay. Pity not to take advantage of it,' his hand fondling her knee.

'Where's Mummy? I can't see her anywhere,' Dervla's plaintive wail carried to Graham's ears and he looked around at once with a frown..

'What is it, Derry? Something wrong?'

Nicholas had just returned from stowing Ranjan's backpack in the boot of his car, the only one to know that Ranjan was leaving that afternoon on the mail boat to Holyhead, the first stage of his journey back to Sri Lanka. Against his will, Nicholas had reluctantly promised not to say anything to Captain Pender and to drive Ranjan to the boat. But he regretted his promise the minute he made it, knowing had been wrong to agree and feeling horribly guilty about deceiving his father. Hearing Dervla, he intervened quickly,

'Your Mum is down there just taking a stroll about the garden,' immediately sorry for drawing attention to Kay when his father got to his feet and glared angrily down at the tipsy pilot lurching unsteadily about the lower terrace.

Some of the other guests had begun to notice too, and Ben Higgins stood up frowning and shading his eyes the better to see.

'Bit familiar, isn't he?' he said in a low voice.

'This is intolerable, Nicholas,' Graham growled, the pilot's cheeky garment-tweaking incident earlier had not escaped him. 'Who the hell invited that man I'd like to know?'

Playing for time, Nicholas bid Dervla, 'Run and fetch your sister,' before telling his father, 'Look, Dad, once word of a party gets around the pilots mess there's always gate crashers, you know that! Canavan's not really a bad fellow,' he felt constrained to say. 'I've flown with him a few times and he's always been most pleasant. I think he's just a bit smitten, sir, and a bit drunk.'

But Captain Pender was in no mood to regard lovesick pilots with any leniency.

'Damn cheek!' he growled. 'I saw him acting most inappropriately earlier. I'm sorry now I didn't go over and throw the fellow out.' He turned his brooding gaze to the far end of his property and seeing that the couple were still in view, he relaxed somewhat. 'Damn it! Someone should put manners on the fellow,' but Nicholas was already heading down the steps in the pilot's direction.

Kay was never so glad of anything when she saw Nicholas approaching with her children. She hurried at once to meet them, leaving a much chastened Captain Canavan slumped on one of the many rustic benches that featured throughout the Penders' garden, her sharp set-down still ringing in his ears.

'Mummy! I couldn't see you,' Dervla ran to her and Kay hugged her close. 'I was here, darling,' she told her, putting her arm about Sinead too. 'Why don't we go back now and join the others. We'll have to be going home soon, you know.'

'Oh, please not yet,' Dervla pleaded. 'We're having such fun, Mummy. We haven't played croquet and Nicky promised we would,' forcing Kay to agree.

'Very well, we won't go just yet, Derry. Okay?' And the little girl brightened.

'Can we play boules too, Nicky?' Sinead was saying. 'I like them best,' but Nicholas did not say anything, conscious of Kay's reproachful glance.

'Sorry about that, Kay,' he murmured, with an apologetic grimace. 'I think he drank not wisely but too well. Whatever you said seems to have got through though.'

Kay ghosted a smile. 'You might say that!'

'Yeah. Looks a bit deflated, poor chap.'

Actually, Kay had held herself back from saying to Captain Canavan what she really wanted to say, cutting things like how he had spoiled for her what had started out as such a lovely party and how she hoped never to set eyes on him again. But mindful of how drunk

419

the man was she had reined in her temper, telling herself that he would be mortified at his behaviour when he sobered up – that's if he actually remembered any of it, which was doubtful.

Leaving Nicholas to speed Captain Canavan's departure, she took hold of her children's hands and climbed the steps to the patio with flushed cheeks, feeling everyone must be looking at her. The last thing she had wanted was to draw attention.

Nicholas dealt with the inebriated pilot as tactfully as he could, before ordering a taxi for him, and then he did what he should have done all along, he went to inform his father of Ranjan's imminent departure, it was time the old man became aware of it. As he had expected, Captain Pender was justifiably angry, and wounded too. When Carol found out that Ranjan had intended slipping off without saying goodbye, the couple had a blazing row. Between Canavan and Ranjan the barbecue was turning out to be a disaster, Nicholas told himself in dismay.

Kay emerged from the house where she had gone to recover herself and renew her lipstick, she found the party beginning to break up. Even as she looked about her a man rounded the corner of the house wanting to know if anyone had ordered a taxi, and within seconds Captain Canavan went unsteadily past, followed by an inebriated, tearful Carol calling determinedly, 'Hey, wait up, Chris, I'm coming with you,' not waiting around until Ranjan departed for the boat.

Kay stared after them, not sorry to see Chris go. Seeing Nicholas approaching with the girls, she went to meet him and heard him say apologetically, 'Sorry, Kay, I should never have invited him. Look, if you like these two can come with me for the ride. I promised to drop Ranjan to Dun Laoghaire to catch the mail boat.'

'Oh, please Mummy,' Dervla begged. 'I love looking at all those little boats in the harbour,' and Sinead added her pleas.

Still Kay hesitated, not wanting to be left on her own.

'They'll be quite safe with me,' Nicholas assured her. 'By the way you'll find Dad at the far end of the garden. He's a bit cut up over Ranjan leaving, he had no idea he was going back to Sri Lanka so soon. Ranjan should have given him some warning.'

Kay could imagine how Graham must be feeling.

'Maybe you could go and cheer the old man up,' Nicholas dropped his voice, 'Ranjan isn't the only one he's upset over. He's flaming mad at the way the afternoon turned out. He wanted to throw Canavan out or knock him down, or both!'

What he was saying was sweet to Kay's ears. She felt a sudden rush of gladness at this confirmation of Graham's jealousy, not to mention his fierce disappointment so akin to her own. She found him lashing tennis balls against the back wall and warily approached, keeping an eye out for backswing.

'Oh, it's you,' was his offhand greeting. 'I thought you had gone with Canavan.'

'Can we please talk, Graham?' Kay begged, as he continued belting balls. 'I'm really sorry about Ranjan. I can imagine how disappointed you are.'

Graham impatiently lobbed aside his racquet and turned to face her. 'If you had wanted so much to spend time with Canavan,' he said furiously. 'You didn't have to meet him here in *my* house, you could have gone elsewhere with him.'

'W...what?' Kay was taken aback. 'So that's what you think?' And then anger flaring she returned the attack. 'If I *needed* to do that, this would be the very last place I would dream of coming.'

'Well, what do you expect me to think?' he scowled at her. 'Letting that chap monopolize you all afternoon. I had looked forward to you and the girls being with me and my family, and to everyone getting to know you better.'

Kay suddenly felt extremely sorry she had acted so spinelessly, she should have chilled Canavan off. 'Graham, please believe me, the last thing I wanted was to spend this afternoon with Chris Canavan. Somehow I got stuck with him and didn't want to be rude.' She shrugged helplessly. 'I would have much preferred to be with you and the children, you must know that.'

He gazed back at her his dark eyes sombre, shadowed by unfathomable sadness, wanting to believe her but not convinced. 'Kay, you don't have to pretend,' he told her heavily. 'He's much nearer to your own age and I can see how you might possibly find him attractive.' He shrugged and reached for his sweater. 'If that's the way you feel that's fine with me.'

Kay caught hold of his hand. 'Is it really fine with you?' she looked up at him beseechingly. 'Because I have to tell you it isn't fine with me.' Her voice trembled. 'Surely you know that?'

'I don't know anything anymore,' Graham admitted flatly, taking back his hand and pulling his sweater over his head. 'I thought I knew Ranjan too, but it seems I was wrong.' He sighed as though his heart was broken, and she felt sudden terror that this latest misunderstanding would not be so easily settled, if at all. 'It's growing cool,' he said. 'Shall we go back to the house?'

In silence they climbed the steps, walking far apart. Kay's own heart felt like it was breaking. If only she had seen the danger in time, she though anguished, if only she had not let Canavan cheat her out of the wonderful day that had rightfully been hers.

In all their long association she was aware that she and Graham had been given a generous amount of second, even third chances. Only so many were afforded in a lifetime and already too many had been squandered.

In her extreme misery, Kay believed they had been given their last.

Nicholas was miserable too. On arriving at the point of embarkation, he felt a constriction about his heart as he clasped Ranjan's hand, and then dropping all pretence that this was merely a temporary parting and might actually be their very last time together, the pair clasped each other close.

His voice husky, Ranjan bid him, 'Courage, my brother. We will surely meet again, if not in this life then in the next.' With this final farewell, he shouldered his backpack and joined the passengers moving steadily up the gangway, turning once to wave before moving on out of sight.

Dejectedly, Nicholas watched him go. The attitude he had maintained over the weeks that Ranjan had to be a fool to want to return to his ravaged homeland and should he go he deserved all that he got, dropped cleanly away from him, with the stark reality of Ranjan's departure. All Nicholas could feel now was an acute sense of loss.

Beside him the girls were silent, their instincts telling them not to comment on the powerful emotion working Nicholas's face muscles. Like he was trying not to cry, Sinead thought, feeling afraid. And Dervla, with instinctive empathy, squeezed comfort into her brother's hand. Suddenly she tripped on the lace of her runners and at once Nicholas dropped down onto one knee, making a big thing of tying a double knot and taking his time about it.

Struggling to control his emotions, he became aware of his little sister's hand on his bent head, gently stroking his hair. At the touch, he was engulfed by such sorrow that he was hard put not give way to his grief and break down altogether.

Ranjan leaned his arms on the ship's rail and gazed out to sea tormented by the memory of his agonising leave-taking from his adoptive father. Fresh shame flooded him at being caught sneaking out of the house like a criminal. He never regretted anything so much in his life as that ill-judged decision not to say goodbye, and all to save the pain and anguish of parting from the man he loved and revered above all others. The memory of Nicky's expression as they parted was an added sorrow tearing at Ranjan's heart, and his spirit grew heavier still at the confirmation he had seen mirrored in his brother's eyes that once he went back to his homeland, he would never return to Ireland.

***

That evening Graham's heart was heavy too, not only for his acrimonious parting from Ranjan, the bitter words he had regretted uttering when he saw the stricken expression in his adopted son's eyes, but for the crushing awareness of his withered hopes of ever winning Kay. For so long had he held fast to his belief that they were destined for each other and no matter how daunting the obstacles they had encountered in those grim years since the Colombo plane crash, his faith in their shared future had remained doggedly unshaken. But now Graham's spirit was at its lowest and he no longer felt sure of anything anymore, least of all Kay's expressed indifference to Captain Canavan. As he had pointed out, they were nearer in age. It would not be all that surprising.

When the last of the guests had gone Graham went down to his beloved garden and sat on his favourite seat amongst the softly illuminated trees and shrubs. There in that peaceful setting he found himself looking back over his long and complex relationship with Kay. For the first time in all these years he realised that he had been like someone flying high above the clouds in holding pattern, only awaiting permission to come in to land, convinced if he could just maintain his course and remain patient he would one day succeed in winning her. It was this unwavering belief that had delayed his walk to the altar with Judy, causing her to eventually lose hope of him ever committing to her, and she had looked instead to Taylor Duval for her happiness. Alas, it had all been for nothing, Graham told himself dispiritedly, the years of waiting and hoping beyond every setback to win her, and now it was he whose hopes were dashed at the end of this long day embarked upon with such high expectations.

As always when his heart was unbearably heavy and there seemed no further reason for hope Graham was reminded of the shabby, dog-eared book of psalms he had left behind him in his cell in the jungle camp containing the stirring words of the 139th psalm, words of spiritual comfort that had become for him a reality in those dark days of his captivity. He had lived them a thousand times since his rescue and was ever mindful of the Lord's providence every time he sat at the controls of a jet and took the wings of the dawn. Into his dark eyes now crept a faraway look and in his desolation he sought and found comfort in them once more.

That night, Dervla crept into bed beside Sinead and the sisters huddled close together, saying little, but both experiencing a crushing sense of anti-climax. On returning with Nicky from Dun Laoghaire there had been no sign of Graham and when Nicky had come out of his gloom to remark on this, their mother had merely shrugged and indicated she would like to go home. Clearly, Ranjan's departure had cast a cloud on the Pender family, the girls understood that much, but not why it should send their mother into such low spirits.

In her own room, lying tense and wakeful, Kay painfully reviewed the events of the day and came to much the same conclusion as her daughters, that Ranjan's going had cast a pall on the Pender household. Earlier, Graham had put her sitting with Jeremy and his friends, poured drinks for them all and gone into the house with the excuse of bad migraine. There had been no mention of taking Dervla flying again or of meeting up with Kay or his daughter in the coming weeks. Kay had no way of knowing whether this was because of Graham's sadness over Ranjan's departure or her own unfortunate dalliance with Captain Canavan. Going out front, she had waited dispiritedly by the gate for Nicholas and the girls to return. As soon as she had sighted the car she had rung for a taxi. On the drive home the sultry weather had given way to the promised storm and heavy drops spattered the windscreen, putting pay to any possibility of Dervla flying on the morrow with her father, even if arrangements had been made, and of course they had not.

Seeking a cool spot on her pillow, Kay felt the need to put distance between herself and her troubles. Recalling, with a pang, Graham's birthday gift to Dervla chosen for his little daughter and her family at a happier time, she resolved to take the girls to Florida and visit Disneyland just as soon as she could get leave from work. It would be a much needed treat and long overdue. With the decision, Kay told herself that once and for all she was finished with men; in future she would seek fulfilment in her work, her happiness in her children.

***

That Monday morning when Kay tapped on the Super's door hoping she would be granted leave at such short notice, there was the delicious aroma of Jamaican coffee in the air. While Judy hospitably poured her a cup, Kay made her request for a fortnight's leave and drank the delicious brew quickly, not wishing to impose.

'So when would you like to go?' Judy was sorry to see the dark circles back under Kay's eyes, she had seemed much happier of late.

'I was thinking of the last week in August and first in September. Not a lot of notice but...' Kay hesitated. 'Well I... *we* feel the need to get away for a bit.'

Judy detected a certain desperation in Kay's manner and instinctively sensed it was not caused by grief over her dead husband but rather someone who had once caused her own self quite a bit of hassle. She was reminded of the look Graham Pender had given her as she had walked the aisle on her wedding day. Oh, drat the man! Judy sighed, still not entirely immune to him herself.

'Just let me check.' Unerringly, she picked out her appointments book from the jumble of correspondence on her desk, and flicked over the pages. 'Yes, the first group of air hostesses are not due to start training until end of September. That's fine. You'll be well back by then.'

Kay was relieved. She could not bear it if she had to postpone this holiday that had suddenly become vital for her sanity and balance.

'Anywhere special in mind?' Judy asked with interest. 'Teneriffe would be fairly hot at this time, even Malaga, if you don't want to go as far as the Canaries.'

'Actually, we are going to Florida. Graham arranged the trip way back in May for Dervla's birthday. Dave and I would have taken the girls but...Well, anyway, I'm planning to bring them to Disneyland and they are very excited about it.'

Well, they would be when they knew, Kay thought, having held off telling them until sure of getting her leave. No point in getting their hopes raised.

'What a good idea,' Judy was enthusiastic. 'Oh, how I would love to see Dervla's face when you bring her to sea world. Those dolphins are amazing. How they manage to get them to do all those clever things, I'll never know.'

Kay nodded, although actually knowing very little of what was on offer only that everyone said it was magical for children, and even adults. She supposed it was why Graham had generously arranged the treat for them. At this reminder of how things used to be between them, her face shadowed.

'Kay dear, is anything the matter?' Judy's eyes never left the anguished face, noting the way the young woman looked up defensively, as if to deny this. 'You can tell me, you know. I assure you it won't go any further.'

Moved by Judy's sympathy and the need to confide in someone – these days Florrie was so taken up with Danny she hardly ever saw her – Kay relayed how Nicholas had dropped by her office the previous week to ask herself and the girls to a barbecue at his house, even insisting on picking them up to save her driving.

Judy nodded. 'He was always a considerate young man.'

'Yes, he's very kind. Dervla adores him. We were having a lovely time until one of the newer pilots turned up... you may remember him,' Kay glanced at Judy embarrassed, 'Captain Canavan. He dropped by one day when you were in my office.'

'Ah yes, nice manners,' Judy approved.

'Unfortunately, he drank a bit too much and things got out of hand. I was just being polite but Graham seemed to think I was encouraging him.' Kay choked with upset, remembering his accusation.

'I see... what a pity.' Judy frowned. 'So what happened?'

'I'm afraid Chris became far too familiar. It must have been evident to everyone there. It quite spoiled the day. '

'I can imagine,' Judy threw up her hands. 'My dear, the poor chap is obviously smitten. I saw the way he looked at you. What was Nicholas thinking to invite him?'

'I don't think he actually did,' Kay said unhappily, 'But you know how it is in the pilots mess once word of a party gets out. What made it worse Graham discovered that Ranjan was leaving that day to go back to Sri Lanka. He had not known and it came as a shock,' she sighed wretchedly. 'I don't know why but lately nothing seems to go right.'

'Give it time, Kay,' Judy patted her arm. 'It will all sort itself out, you'll see. And don't forget you and the girls are coming to the house on Saturday to see the wedding video. I promised Dervla, and it's only natural she'll want to see herself.'

'Yes, of course,' Kay agreed without emotion.

When she had gone back to her own office, Judy continued to muse on the young woman's problem. Her own happiness with Taylor made her want others to be similarly blessed and she was aware that the path of true love had never run smooth for Graham and Kay. She wished there was some way she could help them.

When Ben dropped in for a chat it occurred to Judy that maybe he could be prevailed upon to do something to help the star-crossed lovers, if only to remove Graham's rival from the scene. When she put it to him, Captain Higgins clearly felt Judy was taking too much on herself but good-naturedly agreed to think about it. Soon after leaving Judy's office he bumped into Captain Canavan in the corridor. Not that Ben immediately recognised the man for he was almost obscured by the largest bouquet of flowers that Captain Higgins had seen since his own courting days!

'Ah, so Birnham Wood has come to Dunsinane, 'he reflected to himself sardonically, as the floral hedge came to a stop outside Kay's office, and the bearer edged awkwardly inside. It would seem Canavan was all set to continue his determined pursuit of the young widow, Ben reckoned wryly, and wondered how many other smitten pilots would follow suit.

For the first time Captain Higgins saw what a grave error it had been allowing flight operations to be housed in the same building as the hostess section. Judy was right, he frowned, discipline amongst his pilots needed tightening up and the sooner the better!

***

Nicholas began to worry when his father was still in the dumps a week after the barbecue. The rift between Kay and himself showed no signs of healing and even when Ranjan rang from Colombo one evening, there was no discernible lightening of his parent's mood; if anything, it was even blacker.

'So Ranjan landed okay?'

428

'He did!'

'What exactly did he say?' Nicholas felt it was important to know if Ranjan had expressed any contrition over his manner of leaving.

'Enough, Nicholas,' his father growled. 'Ranjan made his decision and as far as I'm concerned the subject is closed. I don't want to hear mention of it again.'

Not exactly the most forgiving of attitudes, but Nicholas knew better than to question further. He guessed that his father was as incapable of making his peace with Ranjan as he was in sorting out his differences with Kay. Another relationship in a sorry state, Nicholas judged, and found even more to sigh about when his father finally came out of his gloomy reverie to announce his intention of withdrawing his suit and leaving the way open to Captain Canavan.

'What!' Nicholas exploded. If his father had announced his intention of giving Kay away in marriage to his rival Nicholas could not have been more taken aback at what he considered his old man's spineless attitude. What happened to all's fair in love and war, he thought indignantly, what about the eternal challenge existing between red-blooded, competing males, pilots in particular?

'You're surely not giving up,' he said disgustedly.

'Let it be, Nicky,' Graham bade him heavily. 'Believe me, it's better this way. Canavan is a young man going places and Kay and the children deserve the best.'

Nicholas decided to find out if Kay shared this apathetic view, but when he stopped by her office next day he felt as though he had somehow strayed into a florist shop by mistake, so many hothouse blooms on her desk she was hardly visible.

'Nicky please, just ignore them and sit down,' Kay begged.

'But how can you breathe? Aren't you overpowered by them?' Nicholas protested, and she agreed, 'Suffocated, but it seems a shame to just dump them.'

'From Captain Canavan, I presume?'

She nodded unhappily.

'Would you like me to bring them over to the airport chapel,' Nicholas suggested helpfully. 'I'm sure the chaplain would be only too delighted to have them.'

'Oh, would you?' Kay looked at him gratefully. 'You are such a good friend, Nicky,' and she began to cry.

Nicholas felt a bit awkward but took it in his stride. Carol had been weepy ever since Ranjan's departure and he had learned to let it run its course. 'Don't give it a thought,' he said gallantly. 'This has been a most upsetting time for you.'

'I don't know what came over me,' she tried to smile. 'It's just that the girls can't understand why Graham wasn't there the other night to say goodbye to them. Dervla keeps begging me to bring her over to your house so she can ask your father what went wrong. I haven't the heart to tell her.' Kay bit her lip, tears starting to her eyes again. 'He has made it very clear he doesn't want anything more to do with us.'

There was no way that Nicholas could honestly deny this. 'Sorry, Kay, I'm afraid he has let what happened at the barbecue get out of all proportion.' Meeting her eyes, he said ruefully. 'And now he has some bee in his bonnet about *you* being better off with Chris Canavan or, at least, someone nearer your own age. Crazy! '

'Maybe he's right,' Kay shrugged. 'Anyway, I've applied for leave and got it. The girls are looking forward to the holiday and I've no doubt it will do us all good.'

'You're going away?' Nicholas was dismayed.

'Yes. We're going to Florida, Nicky. You may remember it was your father's birthday present to Dervla,' she smiled wanly. 'We have a trip to Disneyland all lined up so we'll be all right. Please don't worry about us, okay?'

***

For the next week Captain Pender did his best to take his mind off his personal life and to put all his efforts into his work, staying later at his desk and drawing up new, tighter schedules for the younger pilots. Ben Higgins was not the only one worried about the slackening of discipline in his airline; Captain Pender felt that MacDoolAer could do with an overhaul too. At a meeting of pilots he laid out a program for more random flight checks and the introduction of aviation quizzes at different levels to test the knowledge and aptitude of his senior pilots, throwing in twice monthly pep talks for the First Officers, before pulling out files to study and reassure himself as to the opportunities afforded the female pilots for advancement. Graham was nothing, if not fair-minded, and believed all his pilots, regardless of gender, should be given equal opportunities for promotion. Besides, there was nothing like a bit of healthy competition between pilots to keep them on top of their form, he decided, not seeing such thinking at variance with his own decision to opt out of the arena lately. How his son would have given a cynical smile having seen the exact opposite in practice.

But for all Graham's exhausting routine none of it helped improve his mood which was blacker than ever, and when mid-week he received a summons from Judy to present himself at her office without delay, he was unable to think of any reason why he should obey so peremptory a command. 'This better be important, Judy,' he growled hovering in her doorway. 'I have an airline to run and no time for chat.'

'Who has?' Judy remarked coolly. 'Do come in and relax, Graham.'

Captain Pender dropped into the nearest chair and folded his arms. 'Well?' he demanded, looking anything but relaxed. 'Get to the point!'

'No need to be disagreeable,' Judy scolded. 'Believe me, what I have to say is of vital concern to you *and* your enchanting little daughter.' There! She had put it into words at last, what she had long believed.

Graham looked stunned at this bold assumption. Speechless for once, Judy was pleased to see. 'Now, Graham, if you have any love for little Dervla you'll listen carefully to what I have to say, and naturally it also concerns Kay, not to mention a certain bedazzled pilot.'

'I take it you are referring to Captain Canavan,' Graham said coldly. 'I know all about that!'

'And do you also know that Kay is going away with the children to Florida and there is the very real possibility he may be accompanying her?'

Graham stared, such a thing would never have occurred to him. To be honest it had not occurred to Captain Canavan either, but Judy was pulling out all the stops.

'Good God! The man has the hell of a nerve. Do you mean to say Kay would welcome that?' His voice shook slightly but Judy did not let that deter her.

'Now, Graham, don't jump the gun. I never suggested any such thing. But it seems Chris Canavan is greatly taken with her girls, especially Dervla. I mean who could blame him. She's such a little pet,' Judy gave a besotted smile. 'Actually, he considers the child to be absolutely adorable, his very own words and from all I hear he's reputed to be very good with children.' Judy gazed thoughtfully at the ceiling. 'I'm not sure but possibly he has a couple by his first marriage.'

'He was married before?' Graham exploded, and Judy could almost feel sorry for the man but kept on skilfully mixing fact with fiction.

'Damn his eyes!' Captain Pender sat bolt upright and banged his fist on Judy's desk, with such force a heap of files slid to the ground. 'That bastard had better not lay a finger on my child. If he does,' he raged. 'He'll have me to reckon with and be damned lucky if he manages to secure a job in the Isle of Man bunji jumping.'

'Of course, you know there may not be any truth in the Florida rumour,' Judy neatly back-stepped, aware this little fairytale might not even be required, Ben having already agreed to do his best to sign up Chris for a spell of winter duty in Karachi. But she pressed on. 'And to think of Kay's late husband planning such a wonderful Disneyland treat for Dervla's birthday and then dying before he could take them. So very tragic!'

The mention of Disneyland was enough to bring Graham to his senses, Judy was pleased to note, watching with interest the range of outraged emotions brought about by this mention of the magical holiday that *he* and not Kay's husband had planned for his daughter's tenth birthday. Good to see him getting a bit of fire back in his veins, she thought, and now that he was fighting mad she casually threw out the invitation she had in mind all along to give him.

'Oh by the way, Graham we are having a few friends in for drinks on Saturday. Around 6.30? Do come. We'll be showing the wedding video,' seductively dropping more bait. 'Some gorgeous shots of our little flower girl. Just wait till you see.'

***

Sinead and Dervla were bubbling over with excitement at the prospect of visiting the Duval mansion, even Kay came out of her sad reverie over Graham to give her opinion on whether Dervla should bring any other drawings, apart from the one of the two honeymooning cats she had done as a gift for the newlyweds.

'What about the drawings you did the day we went flying with Graham?' Sinead put in, and Dervla agreed sunnily, 'Oh yes, Sinead. Thank you for reminding me about the Cadet Cats. Should I bring those with me, Mummy?'

'Why not bring your portfolio, darling? That's the best selection of your work.' The amount of drawings she had done was impressive, for once Dervla had produced a drawing for anyone she later repeated it, all the time improving on the original. She was growing remarkably proficient and Kay marvelled at the way her pencil seemed to effortlessly slide around the shapes she put on paper, capturing all the little details right down to the elongated cat claws, the graceful individual whisk of their tails.

On Saturday, Kay dropped the girls off early at the Duvals' house, Judy having indicated that she would enjoy some time with Dervla and Sinead before the other guests arrived. Kay was just as glad to have time to herself to shop for the holidays. She was pleased to snap up some end of season bargains in swimwear and was relaxing in the store cafe with a mug of coffee when she heard her name called. Glancing around in surprise she saw the young woman from the barbecue, Ranjan's girlfriend, Carol. Her hair was damply slicked down as though she had been swimming.

'Mind if I join you?'

'Not at all. Please do,' Kay smiled, and Carol carried over her coffee.

'Look Kay, I really feel that I owe you an explanation.'

'I can't imagine why.' Kay sipped her own coffee and waited.

'It's to do with Chris Canavan. I don't know what you must have thought of me going off with him after the barbecue. I'm afraid I had a bit too much to drink or I never would...what with all the upset of breaking up with Ranjan.' She gave Kay a shame-faced glance. 'I couldn't bear the thought of being alone.'

'Listen, Carol, you don't have to go beating yourself up on my account.'

'Well, I just hope that I didn't spoil things for you.'

'Not at all!'

'Well, if it's any consolation he never stopped talking about you all the way into town. He has got it bad, Kay. I suppose you know that?'

'Carol, I've told you it doesn't matter. Actually, I'm heading off to Florida with the girls,' wanting off the subject. 'I've been shopping for something to wear.'

Carol looked interested. 'You know I wouldn't half mind joining you,' she said half-joking. 'Anything to take my mind off Ranji.'

Kay shrugged, 'Well, why don't you come with us then?'

'Are you serious, Kay? You don't have to be polite, you know.'

'No, I'd really like some company,' finding that she actually did. It would be nice having another woman along.

'Brilliant!' Carol beamed. 'First thing Monday I'll put in for some leave and cross my fingers.' Walking with Kay to her car, she said, 'If you really don't want the dashing Canavan I might just try him out.'

'Do. I look forward to hearing all about it,' Kay drove off smiling. But her smile soon faded and she felt an anxious fluttering in her chest for it had occurred to her that Graham would be at the party, he was sure to be invited.

Judy was on the lookout for Kay and pounced on her immediately she set foot in the house, putting pay to any deluded hope she might have entertained about slipping in and out undetected.

Putting a glass of wine in Kay's hand Judy said, 'Come along and join the others,' guiding her through the chattering throng of glamorously gowned women and across the hall into another room, where Dervla and her drawings were exciting great interest. Sinead was flushed and smiling and having a good time too. It seemed that Taylor, greatly impressed by Dervla's portfolio, had arranged an impromptu exhibition, even gone to the trouble of mounting the drawings on cardboard sheets, wherever he got them from, and propping them about the room.

Gosh! Displayed like this, Kay could not get over the impact of those drawings. She went closer to look at them and was struck by their maturity of line and execution, not at all like the work of a child, she thought, feeling both proud and tearful by turn.

'It's just like a proper exhibition, isn't it, Mummy?' Dervla dragged her excitedly around the room.

Kay's heart jolted at the sight of Graham and wondered what he felt about this poaching of what should have been *his* role of proudly introducing his child's work *en masse* for the first time. She hardly dared to hope they were friends again as he kissed her cheek and catching the familiar scent of his aftershave, she felt the familiar weakness in her knees.

'So what do you think of Dervla's exhibition?'

'Awesome!' Kay shivered exaggeratedly. 'Can't take my eyes off her for a blessed minute,' pretending not very convincingly to be cross. And, of course, he saw through it at once.

'Like myself, I suppose, bursting with pride. Quite an accomplishment isn't it, for one so young! My goodness!' he grinned. 'She must have close on one hundred drawings in her portfolio. Can you credit it?'

'I know, I know,' was all Kay could say, moved by the pride in his eyes, and not even the teeniest bit jealous. It was how she felt herself.

'You know she could probably win a scholarship to art school on this collection alone. I'm only ashamed it had to take Duval to realise the potential and to set it up in the course of one afternoon.'

'Did I hear my name?' Taylor joked. 'Let me tell you I intend to be even busier on the behalf of this talented little girl,' and they looked at him wonderingly.

'What are you planning, Duval?' Captain Pender asked, with an amused glance at Kay. 'An exhibition in the RDS next, I suppose,' but Duval was quite serious.

'Better than that, Pender. I have a friend in the publishing business and I believe he might be interested in putting these drawings together in a collection.'

Graham and Kay were digesting this when Judy began calling them all to come and view the wedding video in the adjoining room. It seemed quite natural for them to sit down together before the screen that Taylor had hooked up on the far wall, and for the girls to come running and plonk down at either side of them. Kay found herself very much aware of Graham. She wondered uneasily if he still blamed her for encouraging Chris Canavan but took a certain comfort from his friendly manner. Then as the lights dimmed and images began flashing on the screen, she forgot all about such troubling issues and gave herself over to the wonder and glamour of the scene. Most people present had attended the wedding, but for Kay it was all new. She was soon lost to everything else, captivated by those first moments as the bride entered the church porch. Kay thought she had never seen anything so regal as Judy's walk up the aisle, followed by her bridesmaids and the little flower girl so carefully carrying her floral basket. Even though she had dressed Dervla herself on that particular morning and carefully tied the apricot sash, it was as if she was seeing her for the first time. How lovely she looked, how touchingly innocent, with the circlet of yellow rosebuds resting on her dark head. Kay was hard put not to cry, and knew Graham was affected too by the way his hand suddenly found and held hers a moment in the darkness.

Placing his mouth close to her ear, he whispered, 'How in the world did we ever make anything so beautiful, Kitty?' and she would not have cared if his words had been magnified one thousand times and been heard by everyone in the room, and beyond.

***

It was late when they got home from the party. Kay shooed the girls ahead of her up the stairs, urging them to get straight into bed. Folding Dervla's clothes, she reminded her absently, 'Don't forget to clean your teeth, darling,' so deep in her thoughts she was not aware of Sinead coming into the room, or the way she and Dervla exchanged conspiratorial glances and began whispering together.

Kay was oblivious of everything but the memory of herself and Graham holding hands briefly in the dark, the pair of them at that stage beautifully in accord. It was only later when the party was on the point of breaking up that something Judy said to Graham about Florida had sent him rushing off in fury. Kay remembered how he had swung her around to face him, his fingers painfully gripping her arms, demanding,

'What's all this, Kay? You never told me you were taking the girls to Florida?'

'It was a spur of the moment thing,' she admitted startled. 'I just decided it after the barbecue. After all, we already have the air tickets,' she reminded him, and his expression darkened.

'Well, I hope you will *all* have a wonderful time,' he grated. 'You and whoever else is going with you,' adding sarcastically. 'Doubtless some lucky pilot!' With that he had headed out the door, not saying goodbye to Judy or Taylor, and Kay thought in bewilderment: For heaven's sake! Surely he can't be jealous of Carol!

Judy had hurried up in dismay. 'Don't tell me Graham has left already?'

'I'm afraid so!' Kay struggled with her hurt. 'I don't know what got into him but he seemed to be under the impression we are going to Florida with someone from the airport. As it turns out one of the MacDoolAer pilots may be coming with us but Carol only decided this afternoon. He can't possibly know about it.'

'Oh, dear! I'm afraid it's my fault,' Judy confessed. 'I gave him to understand Chris Canavan might be going along.'

'What...but why?' Kay cried, and Judy muttered something bizarre about the path of true love and she had only been trying to smooth the way.

'But I hardly *know* the man,' Kay yelped.

'Sorry, Kay,' Judy had been so obviously sincere Kay could have wept.

'Mummy, would you please listen,' Dervla was tugging fretfully at her arm. 'You're not hearing us, Mummy, I know you're not,' Kay's mind having once more drifted unhappily backwards.

On hearing the mention of Graham's name, Kay suddenly snapped to attention. 'What's that about Graham?' she asked urgently. 'What's that you said, Dervla?'

'I only said we want him to come with us to Disneyland,' Dervla glanced at her sister for support. 'Don't we, Sinead?'

Sinead gave a non-committal shrug.

'You said you did... you *know* you did,' Dervla cried. 'Please Mummy, won't you ask him? We love Graham and, after all, he was the one to plan the brilliant holiday for us.'

Sinead said firmly, 'Not love, like, Derry,' and Dervla made a dismissive sound and rushed on. 'Well, I love him. So please, please ask him, Mummy.'

Seeing the pair of them regarding her, Kay nodded helplessly. 'Okay,' she sighed. 'I'll tell him you want him to come. Satisfied?' and saw Dervla's face brighten. But what if he doesn't *want* to come, Kay thought, what then?

***

First thing Monday morning, even before checking into Flight Operations, Carol headed over to Captain Pender's office to make her request for a fortnight's leave. Morning time, she knew, was always the best time for asking favours, before the Chief got bogged down by other airline business.

'So, Carol, what brings you here so early?' he asked pleasantly, and she thought what an attractive man he was and how much Nicky resembled him.

'I was wondering if there might be any chance of taking two weeks leave beginning next Saturday,' she said in a rush, and saw an immediate frown. Oh dear, she was going to be shot down. But it appeared it was merely a frown of concentration as he checked his schedule.

'Looks okay,' he said at last. 'No refresher courses or pilot briefings you can't afford to miss. So you may take it you can go, Carol.' He gave her a friendly grin. 'Off somewhere hot?'

'Well...' she hesitated. 'I was thinking of going to Florida, Captain Pender.'

'Indeed!' The grin became a scowl. 'Popular spot these days!'

Carol wondered at his change of mood. 'Actually, I'm going with Kay and the girls. I'm sure you know they are off to Orlando at the end of the week.' When he said nothing, she hurried on. 'It will help take my mind off Ranji,' swallowing at the pain of saying his name. 'Believe it or not, I've never been to Disneyland but you know what they say about it being pure magic for kids...' she grinned. 'Even quite big kids... between nine and ninety!'

Captain Pender laughed delightedly. 'Despite being at the further end of the scale myself, Carol, I understand what you mean and I'm sure you'll have a great time.'

Now he surprised her by positively beaming, she would never have put him down to be so moody. 'So you and Kay and the children are heading off to the sun. When was all this decided?'

'Just this weekend,' Carol admitted. 'I'm afraid I rather sprang it on Kay when we bumped into each other. Oh my gosh!' she recalled the time in horror. 'I'm due out to Cardiff and I haven't even checked in yet. Captain Bellamy will crucify me.'

'No doubt about it!' Graham was familiar with Bellamy's misogynist views. 'Well?' he said sternly. 'Hadn't you better be on your way then?'

Before long, Captain Pender had another visitor, only this time when his secretary glanced up from her typewriter she was struck by the beauty and grace of the slim dark-haired woman entering her office. Hannah approved her quiet reserved manner as she stood politely waiting to be noticed, unlike the brash young woman who had come dashing in earlier.

'Is Captain Pender in his office?'

Before Hannah could answer, Graham appeared in the doorway. 'Kay! to what do I owe this unexpected pleasure?'

As the door closed behind them, Hannah heard the woman say with a smile in her voice, 'I have a proposition to put to you, Graham,' and strained her ears. But to her regret she failed to hear his reply.

'Intriguing,' Graham was murmuring as he angled his chair closer. 'So tell me. What's your proposition?'

'Well, it's not so much mine as Dervla's ...Oh, and Sinead's too.'

Graham's dark eyebrows shot up. 'I see...and what kind of proposition would that be?' leaning over to press the intercom and instruct his secretary to bring them coffee and biscuits.

Kay had rehearsed what she would say on the way over to the MacDoolAer building, anxious it should not appear to Graham as though it was *she* and not the children who desperately wanted him to accompany them to Florida. She was conscious of this as he turned back to give her his full attention.

'So, do tell me, Kitty. I can't wait to hear.'

He seemed in unusually good form, she noticed, with relief. He had left Judy's house so abruptly the previous evening that she had been prepared for him to be cool with her, and here he was smiling all over his face, seeming pleased to see her.

'Well, it's like this,' she attributed the wish to Dervla, for naturally he would pay more heed to anything she might desire, she was his daughter after all. 'When you planned the Disneyland holiday for Dervla's birthday she was thrilled - I think you could see that for yourself - and, of course, at the time, she believed it would be her father...well, Dave that is,' Kay amended, 'who would be going with us. But it seems that ever since he died she has been entertaining the possibility of *you* taking his place...I mean on the holiday, of course,' Kay added hurriedly, put off her stroke by the alert way he was regarding her.

Oh damn! Conscious of the innuendo, she desperately tried again. 'What I mean to say is she seems to feel you *might* like to go on holidays with us. I don't suppose you do, of course,' she hurried on. 'I mean you would probably find it an awful bore. Not that Derry would understand *that*, of course,' Kay excused her daughter. 'Well, the thing is she told Sinead how she felt and Sinead ...'

But what Sinead said had to be put on hold as the stern-looking secretary came in with a tray. Kay bit back what she was about to say, something about Sinead also very much wanting Graham to come, and waited for the woman to leave. But Hannah took an inordinate time fussing over the coffee pot, until Graham said rather sharply, 'You may leave it, Hannah. We'll help ourselves.'

Only when the door closed behind her did Kay continue with what she had been trying to convey, but her voice soon tailed off. After all, it was not as if it had anything to do with her own wishes, she reminded herself, quickly finishing up, 'Anyway, I promised them I'd put it to you, and now that I have discharged my duty I can tell them it's no go!'

'Duty? Is that how you see it?'

'No, of course not,' she contradicted herself. 'I was just trying to be funny.'

Graham smiled. 'But why are you assuming I wouldn't want to go?'

'Well, Disneyland is very popular with children, of course, but I can't imagine *you* finding it at all enjoyable.'

'You would be wrong, you know,' he said seriously. 'Think what a kick we would get out of watching the girls' delight in the Disney characters, not to mention the rides and side shows.'

Kay blushed, she had not missed the way he had said 'we' but did not allow herself to dwell on it. 'Whatever about all that, I imagine you must be very busy at this time of year with training and stuff,' she hazarded, having only a vague idea when his presence was crucial. 'Certainly far too busy to take off at a moment's notice.'

Graham considered this. 'Well, busy and demanding as my job undoubtedly is I do occasionally manage to tear myself away from my duties,' he told her straight-faced, 'I'm not exactly chained to my desk, you know.'

'Of course, I know it's not much notice... I mean we're leaving in a few days and the flight may be full.' She was playing the devil's advocate, Kay realized, and quickly changed tack. 'Of course, to be honest I'm quite looking forward to Disneyland myself,' she admitted. 'I've always wanted to go, you know. And as you said, it will be fun watching the girls' reaction to all the wonders in store for them.' She dropped her disinterested attitude, and said eagerly. 'I believe there's even Tom Sawyer's island. Sinead adored the book.'

'Me too!' Graham said enthusiastically. 'Yes, it's going to be a lot of fun.'

'You want to come?' She stared amazed.

'Maybe.' He took her hand and stroked it. 'Do *you* want me to come?'

'Well, of course,' Kay took refuge in the plural. 'We all want you to come.'

'Yes, I know that,' Graham said patiently. 'That's why you are here this morning. To tell me that both Dervla and Sinead have entrusted you with the message that *they* want me to come with them on this holiday.'

Kay blushed, knowing he had seen right through her subterfuge but kept her cool. 'Quite right,' she agreed. 'So what am I to tell them?'

'You may tell them if their mother really wants me to come along then I will be delighted to go. But not otherwise.' He cocked an eyebrow at her and waited.

'So which is it to be?' he asked gently, as the silence lengthened.

Kay looked into his teasing dark eyes. 'Yes, Graham, I do really want you to come,' she told him crossly.

'Well, in that case, my dear Kitty, I accept. In fact nothing on earth could keep me from coming. Believe it or not, I have always wanted to go too.' He drew her to her feet and brushed his lips dangerously close to her mouth. 'It will be a first for us both and I have to say I'm looking forward to it already.'

Me too, thought Kay, trying not to look too thrilled.

'So you can go ahead and tell *that* to the girls.'

'Great!' She dazzled him with her smile, 'I'll tell them this evening.'

***

On checking her calendar, Judy saw that Kay's fortnight in Florida was almost up and she and the girls were due back at the weekend. She made a note to speak to Taylor about some kind of welcome home party. There was an added reason to celebrate with the latest news on Dervla's cat book, and the publisher's proposal to bring it out in good time for Christmas. Judy smiled, aware that this would cause quite a stir. How excited they would all be, especially Dervla. Her expression softened. What a talented little girl she was!

Propping her chin on her hand, she thought of Kay and Graham and hoped they had made the most of their time away, maybe even managed to straighten out their relationship. At least for Dervla's sake, if the child was ever to know her father in the way he deserved. Ben dropped by a little later and it was obvious the holidaymakers were on his mind too, 'Heard anything from them, Judy?'

'Nooo,' Judy admitted. 'But they are due back in a few days. No doubt, we'll know soon enough how things stand...so long as they are still speaking to each other!'

'You're not serious!' Ben exploded in frustration. 'If I've sacrificed one of my best pilots for nothing...'

'Oh, cheer up, Ben,' Judy laughed. 'I'm still confident of winning our bet. But you know what they say about stress running highest during Christmas and vacations.'

'What stress?' Ben demanded in disgust. 'Lying in the sun and knocking back the booze. If Pender can't bring it off in a fortnight then he's beyond redemption, and as far as I'm concerned Canavan *deserves* to have her!'

After two wonderful weeks in the Florida sunshine there was no doubt the couple in question had made the most of every minute of their time together, starting with Graham's gift of first class flight tickets for all six of them to Orlando, Nicholas having been persuaded to join the party. On arriving at the five star hotel Kay and Carol found they were booked into a luxury suite with the girls, overlooking the Magic Kingdom. It boasted a Jacuzzi and steam shower making them feel like film stars, as well as all kinds of extras from a well stocked mini-bar to a 40 inch color television, and access to hundreds of channels; all of it with the compliments of Captain Pender. The second week Graham had surprised Kay with a romantic two-day cruise and they had flown down to Fort Lauderdale. where they were met by a stretch limousine to drive them to Port Everglades. There they had boarded the cruise ship 'Queen of the Caribbean' while back in Orlando Nicholas and Carol took good care of Sinead and Dervla, at the same time even managing to indulge in a light flirtation once Carol admitted to being over Ranjan and allowed herself to relax and enjoy the holiday.

During that magical fortnight Kay had spent much of her holiday tussling with the problem of how long she should remain in mourning for Dave. Aboard the cruise, Graham had spoken of his love for her, telling her that his greatest desire was to make her his wife. While thrilled and overjoyed, Kay worried that three months was a little soon to come out of mourning, besides there were Eileen's and Breda's feelings to consider. Kay had seen how older women could be very critical of young widows who too quickly resumed normal life after their husband's death. Wryly, she thought how Eileen would have much in common with those who supported the old Indian custom of Suttee, with wives perishing on the burning pyres along with their dead husbands. Probably, be the one to light the fire! But she knew she was being unfair, the real censure she dreaded was not from her mother-in-law but her teenage daughter, who had doted on her father and still deeply grieved for him. Sinead may have supported Dervla in the idea of Graham coming on holidays with them but Kay did not make the mistake of thinking she was ready to accept him in place of her beloved father. There was too, her own chronic insecurity regarding Graham's feelings for Dervla, the troubling question of which of them came first in his affections still needing to be addressed. It was all going too fast for her, she was not sure if she were ready to move to the next stage of the relationship, with all the attendant problems of her grieving daughter's shocked reaction and public opinion to contend with. But by the end of that wonderful holiday Kay was no longer in any doubt of Graham's enduring love for her or which of them came the closest to his heart. This was finally brought home to her following the near tragic incident in Daytona Beach when vandals, having torn down the warning red flag, she and Dervla, all unknowing of the danger, swam out from the shore and got caught in a riptide. Distraught, seeing her mother and sister being swept further away, Sinead had gone running for help. Fortunately, she remembered Graham saying that he needed a haircut and quickly located him in a barber shop, not far along the esplanade. She had gasped out the danger her mother and sister were in, maybe even at that very moment, she blurted, they were being swept out to sea, and she begged him to come at once. Only delaying long enough to alert Nicky and Carol having coffee not far off, Graham had led the way at a run back to the beach. When almost there Nicky had torn on ahead and gone plunging into the sea with Graham close behind him, and Sinead and Carol had stood on the shore, fearfully shouting encouragement. Graham had left it to his son to save his daughter and struck out to where Kay was desperately resisting the current that threatened to pull her under. Some distance away, Dervla was floundering as she tried to obey Kay's exhausted exhortations to keep paddling, calling to her plaintively, 'Help me, Mummy, help me. I'm so tired.'

445

'Don't give up, darling, Please don't give up.' Desperately, Kay called back, just managing to keep her eyes open long enough to see Nicky reaching Dervla, conscious of surprise that the one to rescue her had not been Graham. And then, all her strength and motivation gone, she could no longer keep battling to stay afloat and was disappearing under the waves when Graham swam the last few powerful strokes and caught hold of her. 'You're safe, you're safe. I have you safe,' he told her hoarsely.

Half in-and-out of consciousness, Kay tried to follow his shouted instructions, lifting her aching arms over her head; first the right one then the left, with barely enough strength to clear the surface of the water. With his voice constantly urging her on, she forced her exhausted body to adopt the life-saving motion and to keep backstroking against the current in the direction of the shore. Without him, she could not have kept going but he wouldn't let her give up, relentlessly forcing her on, until what seemed like endless ages later, she collapsed in the shallows thoroughly spent.

Lifting her in his arms, Graham staggered with her further up the beach and laid her down. Gradually, Kay regained her strength and for a bit she relived her terror, telling Graham how the waves had roughly parted her from Dervla and she had been forced to let go of her hand, seen her swept further and further away. Looking about her now for Dervla, she trembled at the thought of how very differently it might have all turned out, but she soon relaxed when Graham pointed the little girl out, sitting with Nicky and the others further up the beach, wrapped in a towel, seemingly no worse for her ordeal. Although it was not the time to speak of it, Kay had recognised in those soul-searing moments how close she had come to death. With the terrifying experience her own priorities had changed and she acknowledged to herself that too many chances had already been squandered, and now she must waste no more time in seizing her happiness with Graham, to do anything else would be tempting the fates.

As they all came together on the beach there was great hugging and heartfelt rejoicing. Dervla ran to her mother and hugged her fiercely, and then Nicholas firmly took hold of her hand and they all began the slow trek back to the beach house. Not for a second did Dervla let go of Nicky's hand, intent on sticking as close to her rescuer as she could. At her sister's side, Sinead walked tiredly along, saying little but with a contented expression, remembering all the praise meted out for her quick action in finding and alerting the others. Carol held her hand in a comforting clasp and Graham kept a watchful eye on Kay, his arm tucked supportively about her in case she took weak and stumbled. On reaching the beach house, he immediately set about cheerfully directing operations, insisting on hot showers to be taken at once by the rescuers and the rescued, followed by hot drinks laced with whisky for everyone.

'Even those water babies who weren't in the water with us,' he joked, and Kay was pleased to see Dervla's slightly doomed expression lifting in a smile.

'You'll make topers out of us yet,' Nicholas told his father, but they were all glad of the hot toddy to get the chill out of their bones. Soon Carol was lining up the mugs a second time and busily measuring out more whisky. Admittedly, the mix for the young ones was light enough but it helped soften the impact of what had happened and she was aware that Captain Pender was deliberately turning the occasion into a treat.

That night Kay sat with the children until at last they fell asleep and no longer needed her, and then she and Graham came passionately together, their lovemaking containing a wildly driven urgency about it. The beach house, their sleeping children, everything was forgotten in their overriding need to possess each other as completely as they were able, the feeling between them like a bushfire gathering momentum until it was raging and beyond control. In those deeply intimate, deeply felt moments even thought was obliterated and Kay was aware only of the heavy beat of Graham's heart against her, the knowledge that he was so deep in her they were no longer separate, his breath her breath, his blood the same that flowed in her veins, their pulses strongly beating as one. Afterwards they had talked seriously of the future, and Kay had known she would never again entertain such foolish notions that he cared more for their child than for herself, never again would she doubt his love for her.

'I only know that I'll marry you whenever, wherever you want!' she told him softly, not caring any more what anyone else might think or say. 'That's if you can forget all the stupid stuff I've been giving such importance to for so long and if,' her voice trembled. 'you still *want* to!'

'If I want to!' Graham's own voice was unsteady. 'You bet I do!' And turning her face up to his, he kissed her hard on her trembling lips. 'Oh, my darling Kitty, my dearest love,' there was a wealth of feeling in the softly expressed endearments. 'What in the world do you think I've been trying to tell you all this time?'

In the following days, Kay had never felt so happy and at peace. All the past uncertainties put to rest, to love and be loved, nothing else mattered. If it had not been for her worries about how Sinead would react to their news there would have been nothing to mar her contentment. Back home again, she and Graham agreed to waste no time in telling their children they planned to be wed in December, with barely three months to call the Banns there was not a lot of time.

'My dear Kitty,' Graham said, when they met mid-morning for a quick coffee. 'If you had never held out the promise of a Christmas wedding I would have been content to wait until spring. But now it has to be December, not a second later.'

Kay nodded, her own feelings spilling over in the look she gave him. 'No later,' she agreed, once she had contacted her parish priest they would tell the children, but even December seemed too long to wait. Too many years had already been wasted. Graham's sons took it in their stride and toasted their father's happiness in the champagne Nicholas had been optimistically keeping chilled. Much as Kay expected, Dervla was overjoyed at the news that she and Graham were to be married, but Sinead saw it as a betrayal of her beloved father and ran stricken from the room.

December was only three short months away, Kay fretted, would she ever be reconciled to it by then? She prayed that by some miracle she would and went to ring Florrie and tell her the good news.

'And what would that be?'

'Can't you guess?'

'Now let me see....' But Florrie relented at once, she had her own escalating relationship with Danny McCarthy to tell her about, but there was no rush. 'Oh Kay, I'm so terribly happy for you. Are you over the moon?'

Choked silence and then, 'Flo, will you be my maid of honour?'

'Of course I will. Don't you *know* I will. Have you set a date?' Later, Kay was to ask if Danny would give her away, and Florrie remembered the awful brother-in-law who had made such heavy weather of it when she had married Dave. At least this time she would have a man worthy to walk her up the aisle.

Kay was not looking forward to telling Breda but when she did, she found her sister-in-law sympathetic, even offering to break it to Eileen. 'Don't be surprised if Ma can't take it in,' she warned her. 'She has become very forgetful lately,' which proved to be a blessing in a way.

Kay felt her own relatives could wait, apart from a letter from her cousin Winifred at the time of Dave's death they had not been in touch in years. With Molly's death all obligations on either side had ceased.

Soon there was the excitement of Judy's welcome home party and her heavy hints about some announcement regarding Dervla, swearing Kay to secrecy. 'I won't breathe a word,' Kay assured her, not difficult for she had no notion what Judy was talking about. Getting into the car with the girls that Sunday to drive to the Penders' house for drinks, after which they would all go on to the Duval's party, Kay was conscious of how well the children looked after their holiday, healthy glowing faces and tanned arms bore witness to this. As she drove, she was thinking of her engagement ring, the sensational solitaire that she and Graham had chosen together that week and which he would surely produce very soon and do the traditional thing. She thought if only Sinead looked happier, there would have been nothing to mar the day. Graham had promised to have a word with her daughter before the party, and Kay hoped he might be able to impress upon her the great happiness that lay ahead once they were married and all of them living together.

As Graham waited at the front window for Kay and the girls to arrive he was speaking to Nicholas on this very subject. 'You know the poor kid is still very troubled over losing her father,' he was saying. 'She has had a lot to contend with. I only hope she will come around to viewing it more happily by the time we get married. Anyway I promised Kay I would speak to Sinead this afternoon, to try and get her to see it in a more positive way. My one reservation is that I might end up doing more harm than good '

Nicholas said tentatively, 'Dad, I have a suggestion to make. Why don't you let *me* have a word with Sinead? I think I understand better than anyone what she's going through.'

Graham turned in surprise. 'You do!' he exclaimed.

'Well, I remember how betrayed I felt when Mum decided to marry again after you were believed killed in the plane crash.' Even after all the years his voice shook. 'I wasn't much older than Sinead at the time and Tom Conway was hanging around all the time. It was like she couldn't wait to forget you and marry him. It hurt damnably.'

Graham gripped his son's shoulder in sympathy, the spectre of the past casting a cold eye on his present happiness. 'Very well, Nicky,' he agreed soberly. 'You take Sinead down to the summer house where you won't be interrupted. We'll keep Dervla occupied.'

So it was arranged. When Kay and the girls arrived soon afterwards Sinead was surprised when Nicholas suggested that she take a walk with him in the garden, not including Dervla in the invitation. On glancing back, she saw her little sister happily working herself higher on the swing and her mother and Captain Pender sitting close together on the patio. All of them so contented, so wrapped up in themselves, Sinead thought with a pang. It made her feel lonelier than ever.

'Let's go sit down,' Nicholas drew her into the summerhouse. At first he spoke of the holiday they had just shared, what fun it had been and how he had always wanted a sister. 'You know when your Mum marries my Dad I'm going to have not just one sister but two! How lucky I am,' chuckling. 'You'll have to promise not to gang up on me.' And despite herself, Sinead grinned.

'There's something else...did you know when I was much the same age as you, Sinead, I learned my father had died in a plane crash. Not long afterwards my mother married again and Jerry and I had to go and live with our new stepfather. He had children and we hated each other on sight.'

'Really, Nicky?' she looked at him startled. 'But what did you do?'

'Well, there wasn't a lot we *could* do. They were always telling tales on us and trying to get us in trouble. But, you know, on looking back, they were probably just as miserable as we were. I mean their parents had broken up and their father remarried.'

Nicholas stuck his hands in his pants pockets, and gazed out at the garden. 'My brother and my stepfather were so chummy I felt really out of it. Most of all I resented my mother for so quickly forgetting my father.'

'I feel a bit like that,' Sinead admitted in a low voice. 'I can't stop thinking how hurt Daddy would feel if...if he knew Mummy was marrying again.'

'And you feel it's your job not to let anyone forget him,' Nicholas said understandingly. 'I remember thinking it was up to me to keep my Dad's memory alive when no one else seemed to care, all of them happily getting on with their lives.'

Sinead sighed. 'Yes, that's exactly how I do feel, Nicky. My grandmother is the only one I can talk to about Daddy. I feel we are the only ones who really miss him.'

Nicholas put his arm about her. 'It's a lonely feeling, isn't it? But believe me, my Dad is not trying to take your father's place, Sinead. He knows that he can *never* do that. He just wants to be *like* a father, looking out for you, helping you make the right choices in your life. Do you believe that?' Sinead nodded, trying to overcome her tears, ashamed for him to see her crying. She took the handkerchief he gave her and rubbed at her eyes, blew her nose.

'Will you give him that chance?' Nicholas asked earnestly. 'It's what *your* father would want, you know.'

Sinead did not doubt he was speaking the truth. It came to her that Captain Pender had never shown her anything but kindness and it was a blessed relief to acknowledge it at last. 'Yes, Nicky, I will,' she blurted. 'I really want to. I never meant...' but whatever it was she let it go.

'That's good,' Nicholas was relieved. 'Your Mum will be glad. She has had a hard time of it and deserves some happiness now.'

Sinead nodded, still overcome with emotion brought on by all this talk of her father. 'Yes, she does,' she managed to say at last, and was glad of the brotherly hand he gave her as they walked back up the steps to the house. Nicky is really nice, she thought, stealing a glance at his profile, wishing now she had told him in turn how she had always wanted a brother, for it was true.

Later at the Duval's party, she felt reassured by all the affectionate assurances Nicholas had given her, especially when the exciting news of Dervla's 'Crazy Cats' book was announced and everyone was making such a fuss of her little sister. And then there were more kisses and congratulations when it became known that her mother was going to marry Captain Pender. Sinead would have felt out of it only for Nicholas, who immediately slipped his arm about her, whispering encouragingly,

'Hi Sis, if Dad keeps this up we'll soon be family,' and she felt her heart lifting with the joy of belonging at last, and the future took on for her in that moment a rosy glow entirely absent before.

On the way home from the Duval's house Graham suggested that Dervla might stay overnight with them so Kay decided to take Sinead with her when she visited Dave's grave next day. Stopping off at a flower shop she was remembering how Sinead had spoken of her father's fondness for white flowers and impulsively she selected a bunch of chrysanthemums. Apparently, it had something to do with the cherry trees being in bloom when he had asked her to marry him. Listening, Kay had felt sad, there were so many things she had failed to pick up on where Dave was concerned. From what Graham had told her she knew that he was planning on telling Dervla of their relationship that morning, and about her grandmother too, from whom she had got her name and her artistic gift. Naturally,

Kay had felt a little apprehensive at the thought of Dervla's reaction but trusted Graham to break it to her gently, and at the same time, knowing how the little girl loved Graham, Kay honestly believed she would welcome the truth.

Now driving on up the mountain road Kay was thinking of all the excitement of the night before and Judy's thrilling announcement that 'Crazy Cats' by Dervla Mason would be out in time for the Christmas market. As the clapping broke out Graham had whispered to her how much it would mean to him if the name on the dust jacket could be Derry Pender. 'How would you feel about it, Kitty? It would mean a lot to me,' and she had told him softly, 'Of course, it's a wonderful idea. I'm looking forward to taking that name for my own very soon, darling, so you go ahead and talk to the publisher.'

Sitting in the car, beside her mother, Sinead was very quiet. She was thinking how soon she would be standing at her father's grave and how she would tell him how much she loved and missed him. Even now the words were forming,

'Mummy marrying Graham won't make any difference, Daddy. You must know I'll always love you the best.' Her sister would be known as Dervla Pender but she would still be Sinead Mason, and proud to be!

When they got out of the car Sinead ran off into the adjoining field to pick wildflowers to put on her father's grave, and Kay walked on up the hill until she found the plot where Dave was buried. She had visited his grave only once since his funeral and as graveyards went it was a pleasant enough place to be, airy and relatively new, set high on the mountainside. Kay recalled how early in their marriage Dave had told her as a boy scout he used go camping in the vicinity, describing the pleasure he got from hiking with other scouts, their company all the more appreciated since he had no brothers himself. At the time of his death she had remembered what he had said and been relieved there was no problem about buying a grave there at such short notice.

Standing motionless beside the narrow plot, she gazed down at the smooth white marble pebbles covering the surface and the headstone showing his name and the date of his birth and his death. Of the relatively brief lifetime in between there was no record and she was struck by how impersonal his memorial appeared, compared to nearby graves heaped with photos and keepsakes of departed loved ones. But then Dave would not have wanted such sentimental clutter, she excused the barrenness of his grave, as she positioned the freshly cut chrysanthemums against the marble base.

Kay was not conscious of saying any prayers or of uttering expressions of regret, only that she was saying a goodbye of sorts. And when she turned away at last she knew that she would not be coming back, her allegiance was now to Graham and his clan. The realisation brought a sudden wrenching sadness that took her by surprise, all the more deeply felt as the memory of her first year of marriage struck her with fresh poignancy. Happy and light-hearted, Kay acknowledged, if sadly short-lived.

Looking up, she noticed Sinead coming towards her, carrying her posy of wildflowers and trailing ivy. As Kay smiled back at the fair-haired, grey-eyed girl, so like her father in so many ways, it came to her on a wave of consolation that so long as she had Sinead she would always have Dave, and felt further consoled.

While Kay and Sinead were visiting the cemetery, Graham was preparing to carry out the delicate task on which his heart was set. He told himself that once Dervla knew the truth she would experience a similar emotion to the joy flooding his own heart. She was very young, of course, there was a certain risk in forcing the confidence too early but he felt he knew his daughter by this and, besides, it was the right thing to do now that he and Kay were about to marry.

That morning he had put his own plans on hold, taking time to help Dervla make a welcome banner for her mother, and together they had hung it in the hallway where she would see it when she and Sinead arrived for lunch. And then he had gone into the garden with the little girl and patiently played croquet with her not, however, letting her win. Captain Pender didn't believe in pandering to his children, he was in the habit of telling them when earned their laurels would be all the sweeter.

'Okay, we are going back now,' he said eventually, kindly but firmly refusing her the opportunity of 'beating the socks off him' and merely chuckling at her vehement, 'But we have to, Graham. I *know*I'm going to win!'

'Another time. I have something I want to show you. Come along now!' he said more sternly, wanting to have their talk over and done with while there was no danger of interruption. 'Put away the mallets now, Derry. Chop! Chop!'

Startled, she obeyed and ran back to take his hand submissively, exerting all her efforts to charm him. The little minx, he thought, hiding a grin, she instinctively knew when to soft peddle and now she was all penitent charm, dancing along beside him and encouraging him to laugh at her antics.

Back at the house, he instructed Rita to take any phone messages and brought Dervla into the conservatory, where in readiness he had already laid her grandmother's portfolio. Untying the tapes, he began taking out the drawings and laying them on the low, wrought-iron table where, beneath the apex of the roof, the natural light was strongest and would best show them off.

'What are you doing, Graham?' Dervla wandered over, curious to see, and he told her to lift some of the drawings off the table and help him prop them against the low surrounding walls.

'Oh, I see! You're displaying these drawings just like Taylor displayed mine.' Dervla hung over his shoulder. 'I like that one,' she said, pointing to a drawing of a heron standing gracefully on one leg, with a fish trapped in its beak.

Graham followed her finger, and nodded pleased. 'Yes, that's one of my favourites too. Good, isn't it?'

'Oh yes, I wish I could draw like that.'

'Have you ever tried drawing birds?' Graham asked, and she shook her head. 'Maybe we might drive down some weekend to visit the Wexford sloblands and you could bring your sketch pad. All manner of birds fly in and some most unusual species can be seen pecking about the flats. Actually, there's an observation hut where you can spy on the birds, without alarming them. Would you like that?'

'Yeah, that would be cool.' Dervla laid her head against his arm and he looked down at her with a smile. 'Not missing your Mummy too much? She'll be along soon.'

'No, I like being here with you.' She went over to the portfolio and began looking through it. He was glad to see how carefully she handled the drawings, it showed respect for other people's work and the thought gave him an additional surge of love and pride in this child of his, who as yet had no idea that he was her father.

'Who did all these drawings?' Dervla was asking. 'There are loads more here. I think they are good,' she looked up at him uncertainly. 'They are good, aren't they?'

Graham nodded. 'Yes, they are very good, Derry. Did you know that my mother was an artist? Well, she was and a fine one too. All these drawings and paintings you are looking at now were done by her. There are a lot more in the attic,' he went on, observing her surprise. 'Bigger paintings in oils, and quite a few watercolours. If you want I'll show them to you some day.'

'I'd like that,' Dervla nodded solemnly. 'Is it difficult painting in oils?'

'Not when you get lessons. We might arrange for them when you're a bit older.' Graham put out his hand. 'Come and sit down. I want to talk to you.'

Dervla went with him and they sat together on the wicker settee. The little girl relaxed with her head back and stared up at the glass roof.

'Did you know when you were born you were called after your grandmother,' Graham began. 'Her name was Dervla too.'

'Yes! Mummy told me ages ago.'

'Did you know *my* mother was called Dervla and it was actually after her that your mother called you?'

'Really?' Dervla sat up interested. 'But why? Did she know her or something?"

'No, she did it because she knew it would please me.'

456

'That's nice,' Dervla was not really taking any of it in. Then she said puzzled. 'But I thought I was called after my other grandmother. Mummy's mother.'

'Not quite.' Graham was going very slowly now, wanting her to work it out eventually for herself. 'Your grandmother on your mother's side was called Evelyn.'

Dervla wrinkled her forehead. 'Yes...I remember now. But why did Mummy call me after your Mummy and not her own?'

'Well, there was a special reason, Dervla. You see *my* mother was actually your grandmother and you are called Dervla after her because you are *her* granddaughter.'

Dervla turned to look at him. 'You mean the Dervla who drew all those pictures, the lovely heron and...and all the others?'

'Yes. She was an artist and she was your grandmother,' Graham said again.

'But I thought my Daddy's mother was my grandmother,' Dervla was confused, her dark eyes pondering on what he was telling her, trying to understand.

'Yes in a way…you see your Mummy's mother is your grandmother on your Mummy's side of the family, and she is Sinead's Grandma too. But on your father's side *your* grandmother was Dervla Pender.'

There! It was out. Graham decided to leave it sink in, before saying any more.

'But my name is Mason,' Dervla protested. 'Not Pender and my granny is called Eileen so how can *your* mother be my grandmother?'

'Well, she could if I was your father, Derry,' Graham said gently. 'In which case she would be your grandmother, do you understand?'

'My father?' Dervla said, her eyes very big, her mouth wobbling, looking a bit lost and frightened.

Graham felt a pang and wondered had it been a mistake to tell her. She was very young. Damn! he thought in dismay. I've been selfish. But he had wanted so much for her to know her true parentage, to have the joy of claiming her as his own.

He took a deep breath and said, 'Yes Derry. I'm your father.' He smiled at her and visibly relaxing, she smiled back. 'As I said you got your gift for drawing from the Pender side, from your grandmother, and some day I hope you will do paintings every bit as fine as those done by her. She was very talented.'

'Would she be pleased about my cat book?' Dervla tucked her hand into his arm and he saw that she had accepted what he had told her and, having naturally and easily absorbed such a tremendous truth, was moving on past it.

Graham sighed, his heart beating very fast as he covered her small hand with his. 'Oh, yes, pet, she would,' he told her, emotion breaking through at the wonder of the trusting little face gazing up at him. 'She would be so *very* proud of you, Dervla. Just as I am, my dear.' And they sat like that until Rita came in with coffee for Graham and a slice of chocolate cake for Dervla, who was already a favourite with her.

'What time will you be wanting lunch, Captain Pender?' Rita asked. 'I can set it out in the dining-room if you like.'

'Please don't go to any bother,' Graham told her. 'We are in no hurry for the moment, not until Kay and Sinead arrive. They should be here around about twelve...or thereabouts.'

'Very good. I'll put it on the trolley and you can help yourselves.'

Dervla bit into the chocolate cake. 'Scrumptious!' she sighed, 'Rita is a good cook, isn't she.'

Graham laughed. 'Greedy gut!' he said fondly. 'Finish that up now and we'll go out front and watch for your mother.'

Dervla finished stuffing her mouth, before grabbing his hand and pulling him to his feet. As they stood on lookout by the gate, Graham wondered when she might begin calling him Daddy. Probably not until after he and Kay were married, he mused, preferring it should come naturally. Well okay, with just a *little* prompting from himself, he relented smiling, no point in leaving *too* much to chance.

***

458

That Monday morning, feeling the effects of too many generous top-ups of Taylor's fine Merlot, Ben settled his bet with Judy. Now that Graham and Kay were engaged to be married and Chris Canavan no longer a threat, Captain Higgins was even less reconciled to losing one of his best pilots. Not even for the few short months Chris would be away in Karachi, but it was too late now for second thoughts.

Judy, on the other hand, could not have been better pleased, too familiar with the saying, 'Many a slip between the cup and the lip' to ever take anything so fiercely competitive as romance for granted. Just then Judy had more important matters on her mind than lovelorn pilots, and she spent the rest of that morning closeted with her successor, whom by a coincidence also happened to be related to her.

The news that Judy Mathews had resigned from CA took the airport by surprise and the grapevine, irked at being caught on the hop, quickly produced the information that her niece, Laura Mathews, was to succeed her, along with the usual predictable accusation of nepotism. But Judy was not too bothered by such bias, more concerned about getting the right person for the job. At this stage she was confident that her niece, if only tolerably stylish, possessed a good brain and admirable management skills, and should do very well. About Laura little was known, even Judy was as ignorant as the rest beyond the fact she was unmarried, commuted from Balbriggan each day, and had risen so swiftly in the ranks as to be most eligible to succeed her as head of the hostess body. By the time Laura stood up to go, Judy was satisfied her well run hostess unit would not come to a standstill once she was no longer in control. For the first time in years she felt as though a load had been lifted from her and she began to experience a heady foretaste of the fancy-free state soon to be hers. Not that Judy intended to rusticate in her retirement from CA, quite the opposite as the airport would soon learn.

By afternoon the resignation of the Chief Executive was announced; some thought he was being lured away by Virgo Airways, others by Delta. Not until later that week did it become known that the couple's plan was to set up a consultancy specialising in the training of aircrew. It was a new and novel concept fast taking hold in the United States where Taylor had first studied it in action, and proving to be both lucrative and competitive. The Duvals had done their research most thoroughly and discovered that in Britain there was only a handful of consultants and few, as yet, registered in Ireland, and therefore ample opening in the market for two such highly qualified, highly trained airline executives as themselves. Once back from their world tour they intended going ahead with it, and having it up and running by the autumn.

In the meantime there was a constant stream of well-wishers dropping by Judy's office and the one person she had been fully expecting and, indeed, for once desirous of seeing, rapped on her door.

'Judith, I have come to congratulate you on your good sense,' Beattie announced, surprising Judy by her choice of words, although on reflection she supposed her early retirement *could* be regarded in this light.

'I wish to inform you that you are not the only one who has a new life mapped out for herself,' Beattie told her with coy inflection. 'You are looking at she.'

Judy was moved to murmur, 'At *her*, Beattie!' thinking this was at variance to her own plans but, hopefully, still negotiable.

'*Ja*, at her,' Beattie smiled in tolerant acknowledgement

'Was there something you wished to speak to me about?'

At once Beattie drew an envelope from her bag and placed it on Judy's desk. 'My own passport, Judith, to the fulfilment of my dream.'

'Why, Beattie!' Judy exclaimed. 'Don't tell me you are resigning?' She was astonished and strangely discomfited in view of the proposal she had fully intended making Beattie, with regard to the new company she and Taylor were forming.

'*Yawohl*!' Beattie prepared to voice the immortal words of Goethe, her mentor and source of all inspiration. '*Whatever you can do or think you can, begin it!*' she staunchly quoted. '*Boldness has genius, power and magic in it!*'

'Indeed!' Judy said faintly, wondering what she was talking about.

'The truth of this I have always had the suspicion,' Beattie was confessing. 'But never sought to put into action until today. You, Judith, have been *my* inspiration. I want you to know I am going to put from me all fear and emulate Herr Goethe by plunging boldly into the thick of life!'

'I see!' But Judy did not see at all, convinced that Beattie was making an enormous mistake to so lightly abandon a pensionable career with CA to boldly go, nor did she agree with Herr Goethe's nonsense about it being a person's mistakes that make him (or her) endearing. If she had her way, she thought crossly, she would have banned him *and* his sayings.

With that, Beattie did an about turn and marched right out of Judy's office, off no doubt to embrace whatever new challenges awaited her in the ether of her imaginings. The dole queue most likely, Judy thought dourly, not about to give up without a struggle, one of their brand new company's key trainers of flight attendants, and all because of some eccentric whim of the misguided Burgenhoffer.

***

With his arm about her, Graham ushered Kay into the house while Sinead and Dervla excitedly ran on ahead. What a lovely warm welcome, Kay thought, appreciating the heavenly scented blooms in the hall, the striking banner executed in bold colours draped over the mirror, bearing the words. 'Congratulations to Mummy and Graham and lots of happiness for us all,' obviously the work of their child.

As Kay bent to hug Dervla, tears misted her eyes. Somehow the well-chosen words made it all so real, even more than the sparkling engagement ring on her finger, for it reminded her they would all soon be sharing a future together, here in this house, a whole new beginning, a whole new life.

In the conservatory the champagne was on ice, the delicate crystal flutes placed in readiness on the silver tray; and only the work of a moment for Graham to pop the cork and pour the rose Krug in a foaming stream.

461

'Champagne! Oh, goody!' Dervla's tongue was hanging out.

'And who said *you* were getting any, Missy?' Graham teased.

Sinead stayed shyly beside her mother, looking pleased when Graham said, 'Well, as this is a very special occasion I think maybe Sinead and Dervla might be allowed a drop too. What do you think, Kitty?'

'Oh, yes, can we please, Kitty?' Dervla chimed, and Kay had to smile.

'All right,' she agreed. 'Just this once!'

Graham called in Rita and handed her a glass. 'We would like you to join us in a toast, Rita,' he smiled at her and she smiled back saying, 'What lovely champagne, Captain Pender. May I wish you both every happiness.'

'Indeed you can,' Graham put his arm about Kay and she smiled her thanks at the housekeeper, and they all touched glasses. Giggling, Sinead and Dervla buried their noses deep in the bubbles gasping, 'Ooh, it tickles.'

Rita glanced at Kay and said, 'I believe there's congrats due to Dervla too. I heard about her book. Isn't she a clever little girl! You must be very proud of her.'

'Yes, we are,' Kay glanced up at Graham and he smiled down into her eyes and murmured, 'Clever and talented, just like her mother.'

'I'm sure that's true,' Rita said warmly. Conscious of the lunch she was preparing, she quickly finished her champagne and returned to the kitchen.

Kay was relieved, wanting to be alone with Graham. He obviously felt the same for he turned to Sinead and said, 'Why don't you take Derry down the garden and show her that surprise we talked about last evening.' He had ordered in some young trees to be named after them and planted in their honour.

'Okay!' Sinead put down her glass and held out her hand to her sister. 'Come on, Derry, and I'll show you,' rolling her eyes, heightening the mystery, so that Dervla began clamouring, 'What surprise? Tell me! Do you know, Mummy?'

'No, darling. I don't. Go with Sinead, she'll show you, whatever it is.' And Graham smiled and said, 'Away with the pair of you.'

What a good father he was going to make, she thought, seeing how much he enjoyed giving them treats, genuinely got a kick out of it.

The girls joined hands and scampered into the garden, where they were soon lost to sight, although Dervla's high-pitched chatter could still be heard.

'They are very good together,' Graham remarked, watching them go with a faint smile. 'It's lovely to see it. You have done a good job there, Kitty.'

Kay flushed at his approval. Taking hold of his hand, she pulled him down beside her. 'I'm longing to know. Did you speak to Dervla? I mean did you...'

'Tell her that I'm her father? Yes, I did.'

Kay waited, anxious to know how the child had reacted, and putting his arm about her, Graham told her, 'Well, all things considered she took it well. But to be honest I'm not sure if she really understood what I was telling her.'

'That's not surprising,' Kay stroked his hand. 'It's a big thing for anyone at any age to absorb. But she wasn't upset or anything?' she asked anxiously.

'No, not at all. She seemed to grasp what I was saying. She wanted to know more about her grandmother ... *my* mother. She was understandably mixed up about Eileen, having always believed *her* to be her granny.'

'Sounds like it went well. I couldn't help worrying a bit,' she admitted.

Graham laughed. 'I did my own share too, believe me. But the great thing was the artistic link between Dervla and her grandmother. I concentrated on that and showed her my mother's paintings and drawings. After that the rest came naturally and her grandmother ceased to be a shadowy figure. As a matter of fact, I couldn't help but notice Dervla's own good judgement in picking out some of the best sketches in my mother's portfolio.'

He said it with such simple pride and awe that Kay turned to look at him. 'You know, she has a natural talent, an instinctive eye for line and form, Kitty, which is really quite astonishing in one so young.'

Kay's own voice betrayed her feelings as she told him unsteadily. 'But then she's an unusual little girl, and in that she takes right after her father, I believe.'

Graham's dark eyes lit with fun. 'Do you really? Well now, I would have said in that she takes after her unusual mother,' brushing his lips lingeringly against hers.

'Oh, you would, would you!' Kay pulled him close, turning it into something more passionate.

'Hey, much more of this and I'll have to take you upstairs,' he joked, lifting his head at last. 'Okay by me!' Kay muttered, which had the effect of making him draw her back into his arms, and begin kissing her all over again.

Down by the summerhouse, the girls were gathering late daisies and threading them together when all at once Dervla dropped hers and clutched her sister.

'Sinead! Wait till you hear! Graham isn't our uncle after all,' she announced in portentous tones. 'He's our Daddy!'

Sinead shook her head. 'No, Derry, not my Daddy...*your* Daddy.'

'How do you know that?' she looked puzzled.

'Because I do.' Sinead threaded another daisy, before saying, 'My Daddy was called Dave.'

'I thought *he* was mine too,' Dervla confessed in a small voice.

Sinead flung her daisy chain up in the air and caught it around her wrist as it fell. 'Well, he was too, in a way.' She frowned. 'But Graham is your real Daddy. He's so nice and kind, you're very lucky. And you know what, Derry, you're a bit like him.'

'Am I?' Dervla brightened at this. 'I love that and I love him. He told me all about his mother and showed me her drawings. He says that's why I can draw so well 'cos I take after her. I'd *love* to draw like her,' Dervla said longingly. 'She draws lovely birds and animals and things. I can't do any of that stuff, not for anything.'

'But you draw great cats, Derry,' Sinead praised. 'You know you're lucky that your Daddy is alive,' she looked forlornly down at the bedraggled daisies hanging limply on her wrist. 'I wish mine was alive...I really do.'

Dervla looked at her sister and her mouth wobbled. 'Don't cry, Sinead,' she whispered. 'I'll share mine with you.'

Sinead looked up with a reluctant smile. 'Don't be silly, Derry. You can't share him just like that.'

'Yes I can and I will,' Dervla said fiercely. 'We share Mummy, don't we?'

Sinead considered this, and nodded. 'Yes, but that's different.'

'No, it's not! Adding generously, 'We can share Nicky too, if you like.'

Sinead jumped to her feet, looking more cheerful. 'Okay!' she agreed. 'C'mon, let's go look at our trees again. Graham says we can measure them and see how fast they grow. Bet my cherry tree grows faster than yours.' She ran around the paths until she got to where the white cherry and the Acer leaned against the summerhouse.

Dervla ran after her. 'No, it won't. I bet mine will be the biggest. It will grow right up to the sky,' she boasted. 'And have so many flowers and leaves on it that when they drop off it they will cover the house and the entire garden.'

At this Sinead said, 'Oh, Derry, you are silly! Just look at it. It's only a very little tree,' and she burst into peals of spontaneous laughter and Dervla began to giggle too, and they joined hands and wildly tug-danced each other around and around in an ever-widening circle, until giddy and breathless they dropped down on the grass.

The sound of their laughter carried to the two adults sitting in the conservatory with the doors and windows open in the autumn sunshine, and they turned to look at each other and smile indulgently, aware it was the first carefree laughter they had heard from the eldest child in a very long time. Kay sighed.

'It's a start, darling,' Graham told her. 'The main thing is we're getting there,' he smiled lovingly into her eyes. 'By December, think how much closer we'll all be.'

'What a lovely thought,' Kay squeezed his hand. 'I can hardly wait.'

***

EPILOGUE

(December, 1982)

Beyond the mullioned windows of the church the first flakes of snow began to fall, causing the wedding guests to smile and murmur amongst themselves about the chances of a having a white Christmas. And then the soulful strains of Handel's Largo signalled the entrance of the bride, and all got to their feet and looked around expectantly. At the sight of the bride they began to murmur appreciatively.

Florrie felt a rush of emotion as she prepared to follow her dearest and best friend up the aisle on Danny McCarthy's arm. How beautiful, how radiant Kay looked, she thought, her face partly concealed behind the wisp of white netting attached to the elegant little white pillbox hat *a la* Jackie Kennedy. Her shapely figure showed to perfection in the long stylishly cut white jacket, the white fur at the throat, the long slim skirt and white suede boots straight out of Vogue.

Stunning and strangely innocent, thought Florrie, not at all like a widow but more like a young, first time bride going to wed her lover.

As the organ swelled into the traditional wedding march and the procession moved forward over the red carpet, Florrie touched the scrap of lace to her brimming eyes and felt unbearably stirred by the music and the beauty of her surroundings. As she walked with Sinead and Dervla at either side of her she was thinking how lovely the church looked, the festive red candles flickering in the narrow arched windows and everywhere the bunches of red berried holly, tied with red ribbons. Struggling not to give way to her emotion at this most poignant of moments, she glanced ahead to where the handsome mature Captain Pender stood, and he by contrast in the autumn of his years, looking lean and fit, his erect bearing denoting him every inch the military man he had once been. As the pilot looked around him and his dark eyes wonderingly beheld the vision of his bride, his expression became at once entranced and adoring and the look he bestowed on Kay caused the breath to catch painfully, not only in Florrie's throat but in the throats of many in the congregation.

Oh, my God, Florrie thought shaken. Oh, my God, he's crazy about her, and trying to regain control of her see-sawing emotions, she thought fiercely: You better be good to her or else you'll have me to deal with,' and then her tears turned into a gulping giggle at the thought of her own puny efforts to sort out the tall, assured pilot.

'You all right, Flo?' Danny looked concerned as he passed her on his way to his seat. 'Are you sure?' when she nodded at him fiercely.

'Of course I am,' she growled at last, torn between amusement and sorrow, moving forward to lift back the white netting from the bride's face. 'Ah Kay, my dearest Kay,' she silently begged. 'Be happy, that's all I ask!'

Down the church another person was sending forth similar goodwill vibes to the couple on the altar, but Nicholas had no need of a handkerchief to mop his eyes, nor was he in any doubt that his father and Kay would be anything but happy. He glanced fondly to where Dervla and Sinead sat along the bench from him in all their finery, their expressions spellbound under the circlets of early spring flowers resting on their shining tresses; the one so dark and the other so fair, bringing to mind two little princesses at the court of King Arthur.

Nicholas was remembering the events of the past weeks, the press of the crowd attending the book launch of little Derry Pender's 'Crazy Cats' held at the Airline Pilots club beside the airport, and felt a twinge of amusement recalling the young newshound who interviewed the budding artist cum author.

'This has to be a very exciting time for you, Derry,' she gushed. 'I'm told that very soon you and your sister are going to be bridesmaids at your mother's wedding. So how do you feel about having a new Daddy?' putting the question coyly, as she gazed admiringly at the smiling dark-eyed pilot talking to the child's publisher, thinking him a dish despite the prematurely white hair.

'He's not my *new* Daddy,' Dervla corrected her, about to scamper away. 'He's my old Daddy,' and the young woman looked taken aback.

'Old? Oh no,' she protested. 'Not old at all,' mortified as she became aware of another good-looking, dark-eyed pilot, listening with amusement to their conversation, obviously the son of the prospective bridegroom.

Nicholas felt the day would have been perfect if only Ranjan had come back for their father's wedding. But there had been no word from him since the phone call he had made soon after landing in Colombo some months before. It was disappointing, even disillusioning, Nicholas thought, to have forgotten them all so quickly, and he owing so much to their father. Nicholas was not the only one who felt wounded by his absence. Despite all Carol had said in Florida, Nicholas guessed that she still wasn't over Ranjan for she had declined Captain Pender's invitation to attend.

Feeling a poke in his ribs, he came back to the present, aware the rings were about to be exchanged, and saw the best man rummaging desperately in his pockets. And then there was a gasp of dismay from the congregation as Captain Higgins let one fall, and it went rolling away out of sight under the seat. But Dervla had spotted it with her sharp eyes and, jumping up, she quickly retrieved it from where it had come to a stop, just out of reach, beneath the kneeler.

'Here, Ben,' she said in a kindly voice. 'You won't drop it again, will you?'

'No, Dervla, I'll try not to,' he said, his face alight with laughter and soon everyone in the benches was laughing too.

Without a doubt she was a character. Leaning over, Nicholas whispered in her ear, 'Right old butterfingers that Ben Higgins,' and heard her appreciative giggle.

Exiting from the church with Taylor in close attendance, Judy approached Graham and Kay where they stood surrounded, and quickly seized her moment to embrace the bride. 'Every happiness, my dear Kay. You look stunning enough to make the cover of 'Bride' magazine. I mean it, darling, although it goes against the grain to say so having recently walked the aisle myself *and* with all the attendant glamour.'

Kay kissed her back, laughing at this extravagance before accepting Taylor's embrace and his lavish compliments, whereupon Judy moved in to congratulate Graham on his good fortune, exercising great restraint and merely kissing his cheek.

'My dear, how like you to keep the best wine until last,' she murmured, the oblique reference not lost on the groom. 'I'm so happy for you, Graham, but then no one deserves happiness more than you do!'

Later, after the meal, listening to him joyfully paying tribute to his beautiful bride on this their wedding day, Judy mused on what might have been but only in passing, like one remembering a long ago summer romance in winter time and warming oneself on the memory. Having let go the past, she chuckled with those around her as Graham, with predictable repetitious references to 'My wife' in every other sentence, concluded humorously,

'Once upon a time in the days we crewed together in Celtic Airways, I was Kitty's commanding officer,' deepening his voice to a growl, 'and *she* had to answer to me. But today the roles are reversed,' casting a long suffering glance upwards. 'Now I'm the one must answer to *her*, God help me!' dodging the playful blow she dealt him with her rolled up napkin.

When the appreciative laughter had died down it was Nicholas who solemnly proposed a toast to, 'My little sisters,' and Jeremy, having put away an amount of champagne, joked about them being, 'Blessed among women' but in Graham's opinion it was Dervla who stole the show.

Emulating her favourite brother, she said earnestly, 'I want to propose a toast to my Mummy and my Daddy. Please stand up and raise your glasses.'

To her proud father there was no nicer, more satisfying words in any language than that 'my Daddy' coming so freely and naturally from the lips of his little girl, as she innocently claimed him for her own. Moved beyond words, Graham raised his hand in acknowledgement, all the time marvelling that she had said it of her own volition, without prompting of any kind and, to his mind, all the sweeter for that.

THE END